BOMBAY
MONSOON

ALSO BY JAMES W. ZISKIN

The Ellie Stone Novels
Styx & Stone
No Stone Unturned
Stone Cold Dead
Heart of Stone
Cast the First Stone
A Stone's Throw
Turn to Stone

BOMBAY MONSOON

JAMES W. ZISKIN

OCEANVIEW PUBLISHING

SARASOTA, FLORIDA

ISBN 978-1-60809-584-1

Published in the United States of America by Oceanview Publishing

Sarasota, Florida

www.oceanviewpub.com

10 9 8 7 6 5 4 3 2

To Bill, whom I miss every day.
So proud of you, brother.

ACKNOWLEDGMENTS

This book would not have been possible without the advice and encouragement of a lot of dear people. I must thank friends and family for their generous assistance. From vetting the language—Hindi and Marathi—to confirming everyday details about Bombay in the 1970s, to reading and critiquing my story and characters, these wonderful folks have earned my heartfelt gratitude.

For helping me navigate the India of 1975—and today—thank you to Dr. Kunda, Vidhya Kannan, Vinu Syriac, Raik Sabeel, Anand Sethi, and Deepa Raghavan Sethi.

To my writer friends who offered their advice and expertise, I'm grateful to Robert Rotstein, Keenan Powell, Keith Raffel, Diana Chambers, Claire Thompson, and Kim Hays.

To Lani Stone and Fred Glienna, I appreciate your friendship and willingness to read an unfinished product.

To Bill Reiss, Ann Hawkins, Moses Cardona, and Warren Frazier of John Hawkins and Associates, thank you for your honest critiques and all you've done for me.

Thank you to the team at Oceanview Publishing: Bob and Pat Gussin, Lee Randall, Faith Matson, and Christian Storm.

Warmest appreciation to my brilliant, tireless agent and champion, Kimberley Cameron.

To my siblings, Bill Ziskin, Jennifer Ziskin, Lynnette Ziskin, Mary Ziskin, Susie Mudge, and Joe Ziskin, thank you for your support and opinions.

And, of course, my greatest gratitude—as always—is reserved for Lakshmi.

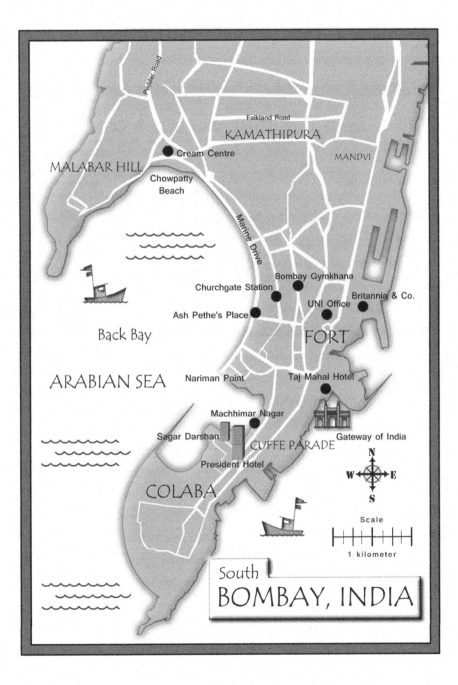

Peddar Road

Falkland Road

KAMATHIPURA

MANDVI

MALABAR HILL

Cream Centre

Chowpatty
Beach

Marine Drive

Bombay Gymkhana

Churchgate Station

UNI Office

Britannia & Co.

Ash Pethe's Place

Back Bay

FORT

ARABIAN SEA

Nariman Point

Taj Mahal Hotel

Machhimar Nagar

Sagar Darshan

CUFFE PARADE

Gateway of India

President Hotel

N

W   E

S

COLABA

Scale

1 kilometer

South
BOMBAY, INDIA

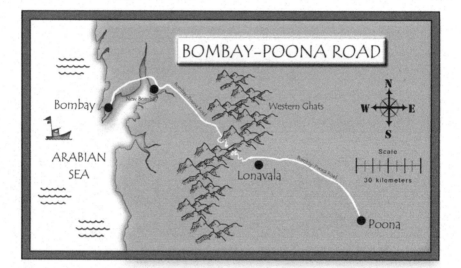

PART ONE

THE EMERGENCY

CHAPTER ONE

"Tell me. Why did you plant the bomb?"

The guy squinted at me in the low light of the hut. I stared back at him. We sat cross-legged on the dirt floor. What little concrete there was had crumbled long ago and been swept into the corners.

"To kill him," he said.

His eyes twinkled. I couldn't tell if he was smiling beneath the scarf he'd tied over his face, but I thought so.

"Well, good job, then," I said, shifting in my uncomfortable seat.

The hut was tucked away deep inside the dense labyrinth of Dharavi, Bombay's—and the world's—largest slum. Acre after acre of shacks packed together as far as you could see. Some—the nicer ones—were built partially of brick, semi-permanent if lopsided. Most, however, were corrugated tin with burlap sacks for doors and tarpaulins on the roof to keep out the rain. Rat's nests of wires, strung along crooked poles, carried stolen electricity to the shanties. And there was even the odd TV antenna, aimed cockeyed at the sky.

I asked him why he'd wanted to kill a sub-inspector of the CID— the Criminal Investigation Department—in the first place.

"Revolution," was all he said.

I found that obvious and trite.

"What do I call you in my story?"

"Bikas."

I noted it in my pad. "Can I take a photo?"

He seemed to be debating with himself. It was risky, even with the scarf over his face. Risky but bold, he must have decided. In the end, he wagged his head in that way Indians do. His ego had won out. He simply couldn't resist the attention.

•   •   •

TUESDAY, JUNE 24, 1975, 8:43 P.M.

The first time I met Willy Smets, he told me I could think of Indians either as the obstacles to my happiness or the means to achieve it. Having materialized from the smoke and chatter behind me, he spoke directly into my ear and scared the hell out of me. I reeled around to see who belonged to the voice with an accent I couldn't quite place. A European man of about forty-five or fifty.

"My name is Willy Smets," he said. His thin lips stretched into a smile, baring a line of long teeth. "This is my place. And you, young man, have only recently arrived in Bombay."

I blushed. "Is it so obvious?"

"It is." He sipped his cordial. "But no worries, my boy. You're the new tenant in the flat on the twelfth floor, isn't it? What's your name again?"

"Daniel Jacobs," I said, the words sticking in my throat. "Dan. Danny."

He put an arm around my shoulder to give me a friendly squeeze. No handshake, just a half-hug. "I shall call you Danny Boy."

I offered one of those numb smiles in return. The kind that betrays your discomfort despite your best efforts to hide it.

No, I'd never seen Willy Smets before, but I'd heard about him. The expatriate community in Bombay tended to stick together.

Socialize and play together. It didn't matter if you were an American or a Brit, German or French, you ran in the same circles, and everyone knew everyone else. Except for me. I'd arrived six weeks earlier and was still finding my way. But I knew about Willy Smets, by name and reputation at least.

A couple of weeks before, an Irish stringer from the office—Flaherty—had asked me where I was living. You didn't so much go by street addresses in India, but sectors and building names. I'd told him I had a two-bedroom flat in a building called Sagar Darshan, Cuffe Parade, in South Bombay. Small by American standards, but of recent construction and comfortable, except for the lack of air conditioning.

"Sagar Darshan? Right, you're in Eric's old flat," he said, referring to my predecessor. "It's Willy Smets's building. Have you been to one of his parties?"

I hadn't. And even though he'd never been invited to one himself, Flaherty said they were the best gatherings for foreigners in Bombay, with beautiful women and free-flowing liquor—a scarce and expensive commodity in India. Eric Nielsen—the guy who'd occupied my flat before me—had been obsessed with the parties, according to Flaherty. He'd talked about this Willy Smets constantly.

And then one day, I received a handwritten note inviting me for cocktails in the penthouse flat. I'd made the grade. Now I stood beside the celebrated Willy Smets, still thinking about his first words to me.

"What was that you said before?" I asked him. "Something about Indians and happiness?"

"Some friendly advice for a boy who looks lost in a strange land. India is an enchanting place, but it can be overwhelming to foreigners."

That hardly cleared up my confusion. He took note and explained that he was advising me to take the second path. Let Indians be the means to achieving my happiness.

Smets signaled to a young servant across the room. Domestic help was ubiquitous in India. Middle-class households—even lower-middle-class—always had one or more servants. The rich had several. I didn't like the word, *servant*, when I first heard it. An outdated and condescending way to refer to people. But that's what they were called in India.

Willy Smets's guy was outfitted in wrinkled white livery a few sizes too large for his frame. He glided over to us on bare feet. Smets called him Sandip.

"Yes, *sahib?*" he said. When he opened his mouth, I saw his teeth were stained red from *paan*, a betel leaf preparation that some folks chewed like tobacco.

"A drink for my guest," said Smets. Then he turned to me. "What will you have, Danny Boy?"

I didn't drink a lot, but I enjoyed the occasional scotch. My dad always said, "One to whet your appetite and one to rinse down dessert."

"Whisky, please," I said. "I mean, if you have any."

"Of course we do."

He relayed the order to Sandip, then waved him away. "*Jaldi, jaldi.*"

"You don't want the local spirits," said Smets. "The beer and rum are okay, but not the whisky. If you find yourself running dry, I can help you."

I thanked him, feeling like a charity case. He asked if I was satisfied with my servant.

There was that word again.

"He only started this morning," I said. "I'll have to let you know."

"You've been without help all this time? I wish we'd met sooner; I could have arranged something for you."

"My office is handling it, thanks," I said. "I'm still getting used to the idea. I never thought I'd have someone taking care of me."

"A very American attitude. Canadians are even worse. It's as if they feel they don't deserve to be comfortable. But that's a habit you must break here. Servants are one of the pluses we enjoy in India, even if they're always underfoot." He sipped his drink then winked at me. "Provided they don't slit your throat in the night."

A pretty German woman, Marthe, interrupted us to speak with Smets. I assumed he was German since he spoke the language as effortlessly as he did English. Only later did I find out he was Belgian. Flemish, but he also spoke French perfectly.

I studied him as he entertained the lady with what sounded like a humorous story. Bony and toothy, he was, by any objective standard, a homely man. Of average height and weight, he managed nevertheless to project a wiry magnetism that was mismatched to his unremarkable frame. His baritone voice, seasoned by what I was sure were decades of wine and brandy and black-tobacco cigarettes, bore witness to a lifestyle well enjoyed, if not healthy. Yet, despite his want of physical gifts, Willy Smets had confidence and natural social facility in spades. An unexpected charisma.

Sandip returned with my drink, which was sloshing about in a crystal tumbler on a salver. He balanced two glass bottles on the tray as well. They were identical in every detail except for the crown caps. One was red, the other yellow.

"Do you take soda, or would you like some ice?" Smets asked.

"Soda, please," I said.

Ice never lasted long in that heat, of course, and you were never sure how safe it might be. Soda was the wiser choice. My host must have read my mind. He assured me that all the water was boiled in the kitchen and the ice was perfectly pure.

"Soda's fine," I said.

Smets smiled to indulge me, then told Sandip to add some soda to my whisky. The kid reached for the bottle with the yellow cap.

"No, Sandip," said my host. "That's tonic water. Never serve tonic with whisky."

Sandip said nothing. He poured from the red-capped bottle instead, then slipped away.

"He's new," said Smets as he raised his glass to mine. "Welcome to Bombay." We sipped our drinks. "Is it true you're a reporter for United News?"

"Yes. But how did you know I was with UNI?"

"The fellow who occupied the flat before you. He was also UNI."

"Eric Nielsen? Did he come to your parties?"

"Only once," he said with a frown. "He behaved badly. Didn't understand that Indian girls are not as liberal-minded as Americans. I didn't invite him back."

Smets gazed around, taking inventory of his guests and their needs. I returned to what he'd said in my ear a few minutes earlier. Had he meant that the locals—the Indians—were beneath him? Beneath me? Should I be afraid of them? He'd mentioned slit throats, after all.

I wondered if Smets might not be some kind of latter-day colonialist, pining for the old days of the Raj. Or was he merely looking out for a newcomer in an exotic and challenging place? A spoiled American, used to clean water running from the tap and bottles marked clearly to distinguish soda from tonic. I tried to convince myself that he was only telling me how things stood for a *gora,* that's what they called white people in India. Yet, the taste left in my mouth was the same either way. Like whisky and tonic. Undrinkable.

What happened next, however, gave me cause to consider him in a totally different light. The inspiration for my change of heart was the arrival of a bright-eyed young woman as beautiful as Smets was not.

Her name was Sushmita. Easily half Smets's age, she was a couple of years younger than I was, too. An extremely attractive girl, she was sexy, but hardly perfect. There was that one slightly crooked incisor, for example, and a small scar at the side of her right eye, caused perhaps by a childhood fall. And those matrimonial classifieds in Indian newspapers might have described her complexion as *dusky*. Shameful, I thought. She wasn't quite as fair-skinned as the Hindi film starlets, but so what? I found her enchanting. I entertained a brief fantasy, wondering what chances I might have with such a woman. Then it became painfully clear that, not only was she uninterested in me, she was unavailable.

Draped in a shimmering green sari, which revealed her fetching midriff for all—for me—to see, Sushmita leaned her left hip against Smets in a casual, intimate gesture and regarded me with what I could only describe as sociable indifference. Even if she hadn't been attached to my newfound friend and neighbor, I'd never have had a shot with her.

"You're quite tall," she said, extending her right hand to me. Her voice was smooth and easy, like her confidence.

Fully aware that my American imperialist attitudes were at play, I found her accent exotic and bewitching. I'm sure she thought mine was unsophisticated and dull.

As I took gentle hold of her fingers, four diamond-encrusted bangles slid down her wrist and clattered to a stop at the heel of her thumb. She squeezed my hand, enough to make me wonder about her intentions. That was stupid. Wishful thinking.

The social niceties completed, she smiled, withdrew her hand, and cocked her head to one side as she sized me up. I couldn't tear my gaze away from the *bindi* on her forehead. Not the red dot I'd seen on some women, but a small crescent-shaped moon with the horns pointing upward.

"It's impolite to stare, Mr. Jacobs," she said. "Would you like me to remove it?"

"I ... I'm sorry. Of course not. I was ... admiring it."

"Don't mind her games," said Smets, interrupting my stammering. "Mita is a playful girl."

He even had a pet name for her.

"It's called a *chandrakor bindi*," she said. "Typically Maharashtrian."

"It looks like a crescent moon. What does *chandrakor* mean?"

"It means crescent moon," she said.

"Oh," was the wittiest riposte I could manage.

I suspected she was laughing at me. At my awkward attempt at sophistication. And each smile, every spark glinting off a tooth, and the curl of her lips only made my discomfort more difficult to hide. I took a sip of my whisky, which dribbled down my chin.

"What are you doing in Bombay, Mr. Jacobs?" she asked, shifting her weight from her left foot to her right, opening a narrow space between her hip and Smets.

My eyes betrayed me again. Without realizing it, I glanced at the bare skin of her waist, where the fabric of her sari wrapped around her middle. She uttered a soft cough. Trying to act as if I hadn't been ogling her, I told her I was a reporter for UNI.

"How interesting," she said, those brilliant eyes fixed on mine, a mischievous smile on her lips. "Can you tell me about that without spilling your drink?"

But, in that moment, I could think of nothing remotely interesting to share with her. Instead, trying to calm my nerves, I tapped the roll of film in my pocket, the one that I'd been carrying around for days. The one with the bomber I'd interviewed. The one I was so afraid to lose that I kept it with me always. I put that thought aside and told Sushmita I worked at the UNI bureau in Fort, on Phirozshah Mehta Road.

"Of course, I know the place. Have you tried the *pani puri* from the *chaatwallah* outside?"

"You mean the . . . that guy who sells food in the street?" I asked. "With all the flies?"

"That's the one. And don't worry about the flies. You're going to get Delhi belly sooner or later. You might as well be done with it."

"That's enough for now, Mita," said Smets. A man in a white safari jacket approached us. "Danny Boy, I must introduce you to Ashok Pethe. Ash to his friends."

Ash, an engineer for GE, was in his forties, with longish black hair and a friendly smile. He was single and knew every corner of the city. He'd lived in South Bombay his whole life, in fact, and tooled around town in a large Chevrolet. Where he'd found it, I couldn't guess. The only cars I'd seen on the road were round-bodied Ambassadors, black-and-yellow taxis, and tiny Fiats. And, of course, the two-wheelers—bikes, scooters, and motorcycles.

Ash seemed like a nice guy. He invited me to a dinner party he was hosting the following week at his place on Marine Drive. Fancy area, also known as the Queen's Necklace. The buildings along the seawall offered great views of the Arabian Sea. I knew that because I ran there every morning.

"You should go, Danny Boy," said Smets. "Ash always invites pretty girls."

"Are you two going?" I asked, referring to him and Sushmita.

"We'll be out of station next week."

I shrugged and, embarrassed by the pity everyone was taking on me, said I'd love to go.

Ash waved to someone across the room and, taking my business card, excused himself with a promise to send me details for the dinner party.

"And now Mita and I must attend to our other guests," said Smets. "We're off to Poona tomorrow for a couple of days, but don't hesitate to let me know if you need anything when we return. A gas cylinder, a driver, or liquor. Anything."

"Goodbye, Mr. Jacobs," said Sushmita, fixing me again with those sparkling eyes. "I enjoyed our conversation. And I was joking, of course. Please don't eat anything from the *chaatwallah* in the street."

"Thank you," I said. "I'll remember that."

Smets led her away. I watched them go. More specifically, I watched her go. And—just my luck—she threw a glance over her shoulder in time to catch me contemplating the swaying backside of her sari.

CHAPTER TWO

I was adrift in a warm cloud, swirling into the gentle eddy of stupor. A seductive snare—a silk scarf or a length of green sari—tightened around me and drew me toward sleep's embrace. My consciousness dissolved.

What the hell is that pounding?

Nothing more than a pulsing at first. Then it swelled into a warped, surreal thumping, like a mallet beating on a kettle drum. Finally, it surged into focus, and my dream burst.

Where am I?

The rain was streaming down the window. The onset of the monsoon had fallen a week earlier. Now I lay in the dark, sticking to the sheet as the clicking ceiling fan twirled overhead. It barely managed to move the wet air from one fold of the bedding to another, with no appreciable relief that I could detect.

The banging resumed with loud, rough voices bellowing on the other side of the front door. I shook the fog from my head, tumbled out of bed, and flicked on the light. Where the hell was Ramu and why wasn't he answering the door? Hadn't he assured me just hours earlier not to worry about a thing? That he would take care of everything? Cooking, washing, ironing, cleaning. Everything. Except answering the door in the dead of night.

"Who's there?" I shouted.

A gruff voice answered in Marathi or Hindi—I couldn't tell which. But I recognized one word. "Police."

"Open the door," called one of them in a fierce, strangled, high-pitched voice.

Bleary and sweating, I pulled on a T-shirt. Then I obliged, turning the dead bolt and unlatching the chain. A stocky cop in a khaki uniform and cap stepped through the doorway. He glared at me, sizing me up, then flicked his bristly mustache with his right forefinger. Unsettled by the menacing squint, I stepped back to give him wide berth.

His four stout adjutants, each carrying a *lathi*—a long stick used to beat back protesters—remained outside the door, dripping rain on the terrazzo floor. The cop in charge was dry; surely he'd arrived in the back of a police car driven by an underling. He issued some orders to his men before striding past me for the veranda. I had no idea what he was after, but he seemed to know where it was.

He removed his cap and, bent at the waist, stuck his head out the sliding window. He craned his neck upward to see as the rain pelted his head and shoulders, soaking his hair and epaulettes. Then a powerful beacon flooded the window with light, nearly blinding me. The beam hovered for a moment on the cop, framing him in the window, then twitched to the left and back again before climbing skyward against the building.

The cop barked at someone above. He rattled off an angry string of orders, punctuated by sharp whacks of his right hand against the windowsill. Clearly he was yelling at whoever was there. But who could be outside the window in such a downpour in the middle of the night? There was nothing but a narrow ledge and twelve stories of air.

Finally, after nearly a minute, the cop pulled his dripping head back inside and, mopping his face with his cap, waddled back into the flat. He summoned one of his men, who handed him a cloth. Once he'd rubbed himself dry, he gave the junior officer some instructions. Then he snapped his fingers at the other men. They hustled inside and over to the window just as a sandaled foot, then a white cotton pajama leg, descended into view. The searchlight from below followed and illuminated the room again like a Friday night football game. A slight, waterlogged man shimmied the rest of the way down the external drainpipe and dropped into the veranda, his wet clothes dripping water everywhere.

Jesus Christ, it was Ramu.

Before I could even ask him what he'd been doing out there, the cop in charge approached him and cuffed him hard on the back of the head. Ramu flinched, but didn't try to protect himself. The cop hit him again, all the while spitting questions and abuse at the poor guy. Ramu answered with a rapid-fire explanation in Hindi. Then the cop did something strange. He wrapped an arm around Ramu's neck—wetting his shirtsleeve as he did—and shook him, I could have sworn, almost affectionately.

The police officers searched the prisoner. He had nothing on him.

"What's going on?" I asked.

The cop looked back at me as if he'd only just noticed I was there. Then he motioned to his men to take the prisoner away. Ramu offered me a sheepish smile and a "sorry, sir," as they hustled him out the door.

The cop stood before me, glaring with the same menacing squint as before. "Who are you?" he asked. "What are you doing in India?"

I explained that I was a journalist and showed him my press card. He gave it a cursory glance, hardly enough time to read the name printed on it, then shoved it back to me.

"What's your name?" he asked.

"Jacobs. Daniel Jacobs. I'm with UNI, United News International," I said, wondering if he was going to cuff me the way he had Ramu. "Why was my servant climbing up the side of the building?"

The man brushed his mustache again, then turned to consider the rest of my flat. There was no wall between the drawing room—the estate agent's term, not mine—and the dining area, which consisted of a small Formica-top table and four wooden chairs. A few steps away, in front of the veranda, two small faux-leather couches faced a coffee table in the center of the room. A bulky black-and-white television sat against the wall. I'd tried watching the news once or twice, but the reception was spotty, and India's sole channel, Doordarshan, only broadcast in the evening.

The cop strolled over to my bedroom door and peeked inside. Shit. I'd left the roll of film in plain view. Had he noticed it? Okay, I was being paranoid. Why would he care about a roll of film? Still, I knew I had to find a better hiding place for it until I was ready to present my story.

"How long have you been in Bombay?" he asked once he'd rejoined me near the dining table.

"About six weeks."

"Are you working here?"

"Yes," I said, annoyed at having to repeat myself. "I work at UNI, United News International."

He asked to see my passport and visa. I showed him my documents.

"Can't you tell me what Ramu was doing out there?" I said as he flipped through my passport. "We're on the twelfth floor. He could have fallen and killed himself."

The cop grunted. "He was climbing up to the fifteenth floor," he said, still examining my passport. "You travel a lot, Mr. Jacobs. Vietnam, Italy, Chile . . ."

"It's my job. I'm a—"

"Yes, a journalist, I know." He continued to read my entry stamps. "You haven't been to Pakistan?"

"No. Why?"

He ignored my question, closed the booklet, and looked up at me. "You don't know what your servant was doing?"

I shook my head. "Today was his first day on the job. I didn't even know his name until a few hours ago. The office manager arranged everything."

"You have to watch these fellows," he lectured, as if it were somehow my fault Ramu had climbed the drainpipe. "One of the sweepers downstairs called the police. Said there was a *bhoot*—a ghost— climbing up the drainpipe. Then he recognized him as your new man."

"But why would he climb the drainpipe?"

"He claimed he was going to the roof. Said he loves to climb. But I think he wanted to rob the flat on the top floor. Maybe peep through the window."

"Peep through the window?"

"A pretty lady stays there."

I was addled and still reeling from my rude awakening, so it never even occurred to me to ask whose flat it was on the fifteenth floor. The cop cleared that up.

"A pretty lady," he repeated, frowning this time. "But a shameless *randi*. Living with a foreigner. And not married. From a good Maharashtrian Brahmin family."

I gathered *randi* meant slut or some such thing, but wasn't about to ask for confirmation.

He glared at me. Again, I felt he was blaming me for the transgression of another, this time Willy Smets. I was a foreigner, after all. Surely we all had the same intentions: tarnish the honor of good Indian women, Brahmin or otherwise, wherever we encountered them. I wasn't about to volunteer anything in defense of Smets's relationship with Sushmita. What did I know about him? Or her, for that matter?

The cop might well have been reading my mind as he tapped my passport against the palm of his hand. Then he tossed it aside onto the dining table.

"How do you know all that?" I asked. "About her family, I mean."

"How do I know it? I'm a police inspector," he barked. "You don't think I know what goes on in my district? I can tell you everyone who stays on this floor." He began counting on his fingers as he named them. "Malhotra, Sharma, and Advani the Sindhi across the landing . . ." Now he was scowling. "So, of course I know about that Deshpande *mulgi* and her *fireng* up in the penthouse."

"Is that her surname?" I asked. "Deshpande?"

Again, no answer. He stared me down. I was sweating under the scrutiny, and not because of the moist heat. I changed the subject and inquired about Ramu instead.

"What will happen to my servant?"

"We'll have to decide how to deal with the *bhoot*," he said at length. "But you, Mr. Jacobs, will require a new servant."

Since he'd opened the door to names, I asked him his. No evil glares this time. He simply said in his high-pitched voice that he was Inspector Lokhande.

"You will come to the Cuffe Parade police station tomorrow to give a statement," he said, yanking his hat back onto his head as he made for the door.

CHAPTER THREE

Returning from my morning run, I collected the loaf of bread and the pint of milk at the door, and let myself inside. Even when it rained, I made sure to get my five miles in. The weather had, in fact, forced me to buy two extra pairs of sneakers at the Bata store in Colaba Causeway, since it took two days for the shoes to dry out after a run in the rain. But that wasn't an excuse to sleep in. Neither was a night's rest disturbed by a visit from the police.

After my bath, I managed to boil water and make my own instant coffee without the *bhoot,* Ramu. I'd been doing it myself for the six weeks before he'd shown up for his one-day tenure with me. I really didn't see the need for a *servant.* Especially one who climbed drainpipes in the middle of the night.

The Times of India arrived and I sat at the dining table with my breakfast of buttered toast and coffee to read the headlines. An Eastern Airlines flight had crashed on approach to JFK, killing 113. I closed the paper.

A messenger rang the bell a few minutes later and handed me an envelope. My telephone still hadn't been installed, so this was the only option for off-hours communication from the office. I tipped the man two rupees and returned to the table to read the message. It was a telex from my boss in New York, Kate Erving.

06/25/75
ATTN: MR. D. JACOBS

REQUEST FOLLOW-UP AT EARLIEST ON 06/24/75
SUPREME COURT RULING. ADVISE ON MRS. GANDHI'S
STATUS AS PM. IN JEOPARDY? SUGGEST YOU FLY TO
DELHI IMMED. RUMORED PROTESTS PLANNED
OUTSIDE PM'S RESIDENCE.

KE

The day before, I'd filed a story on the Supreme Court's conditional stay of Indira Gandhi's guilty verdict, handed down earlier in the month by the Allahabad High Court. That first decision had voided the prime minister's 1971 election victory and barred her from holding office for six years. The stay granted by the Supreme Court gave Mrs. Gandhi twenty days to prepare an appeal and allowed her to remain in office and perform the duties of the PM, but stripped her of the right to vote in parliament until the case had been heard. It was a dramatic development. Demonstrations were in the works across the nation to demand her resignation.

I needed to make travel arrangements. Inspector Lokhande could wait.

.   .   .

On first approach, Bombay assaults you, blinds and confuses you. The smoky air and muddy roads, rumbling taxis; the baking heat and the stinking garbage; the squawking crows; the visual pollution of billboards and signs covering buildings and blocking the sky. There's rubble wherever you look, swept into piles alongside the footpaths, which, by the way, pedestrians never used. The road was so much more inviting.

Later, you begin to discover the city's subtleties. Surprising urban scenes that charm and challenge your assumptions. A green parakeet, unfazed by the noise of the metropolis, perched in a tree; the flower seller, plucking marigold blooms from a basket and sewing them into a long garland; the horse-drawn carts competing gamely with automobiles; and even the white cow outside the local temple, chomping on bundles of grass, offerings from the supplicants.

Of course, none of those tableaux was on display in the pouring rain. Outside, I climbed into a black-and-yellow taxi and headed to the office.

· · ·

WEDNESDAY, JUNE 25, 1975, 12:51 P.M.

Frank Muller summoned me to his cabin as soon as I arrived. That's what they called personal offices in India: cabins. He was a good guy. Sometimes. Understanding and friendly one minute, screaming himself hoarse the next.

"So I'm off to Delhi?" I asked.

He squinted at me through the smoke irritating his eyes. Maybe if he gave the cigarettes a rest, he might be able to see. But he loved chain-smoking his Chesterfields, and a minor inconvenience like dry, red eyes wasn't going to discourage him.

"I just got off the horn with New York. Chuck's going to take the lead on this story."

"Chuck? Chuck who?"

"Kohlner. He's a stringer, based in Bangkok. But he happens to be in Delhi now."

"What does he do in Bangkok?"

"Besides sampling the local hookers, bargirls, and hash? He writes the occasional piece on Vietnam and the war."

"The war's over. And now he's in Delhi?"

Frank shrugged. "Maybe he's in Delhi to get a cure for a dose of the clap. Or maybe he's there for the chicken tikka masala. The point is, as long as he's already in place, he's going to cover this."

"Jesus, Frank, does Kate know?"

He stubbed out his cigarette and shifted some papers on his desk. He was steamed but trying to keep the lid on. "Kate's the one I spoke to."

Kate Erving was Frank's boss. And she'd been my boss too back in New York. Like so many other young lions, I was eager and impatient to make a name for myself. I'd risked my neck in Chile, reporting on the *Desaparecidos* in '73 and '74, until I got roughed up by the police and expelled from the country. From there, I'd flown straight to Vietnam on Kate's orders, where I stayed until April 29, 1975. I made it out of the country on a military transport, a day before the last helicopter left the roof of the U.S. Embassy in Saigon.

I returned to New York, but only for a month. I wanted another opportunity to prove my worth. Kate encouraged me. And when Eric Nielsen abruptly quit his position in Bombay, I begged her for a chance. She arranged everything.

"Look, you're a good kid, Dan," said Frank. "But don't play that game with me. Kate's not going to protect you here. Budgets and speed count. Chuck's already there."

"Sorry, Frank. I never meant it that way. It's just that I want a chance."

"You'll get it. But not today. We're a growing wire service. We simply don't have the time or resources right now to send you to Delhi for a story that'll probably turn out to be nothing."

I nodded in resignation, all the while fuming that a hash-smoking hack with the clap had stolen my story.

· · ·

As I licked my wounds, I thought of the tattered reporter's pad in the bottom drawer of my desk. The notebook Eric Nielsen had left behind. I'd never met him, but, judging by his journal entries, he was an odd one. He took notes on people, places, and events, and scribbled addresses and dates in a disorganized manner. As if writing in a diary, he documented in telegraphic language his social life, too. Failed attempts to bed girls he'd met in restaurants, shops, and hotels. "Frigid bitch," "has a boyfriend," "probably a dyke," "not that pretty anyway," and "cockteaser" were some of his comments.

It was one of his other entries that had led me to my meeting with the mysterious bomber in Dharavi a couple of weeks earlier. I'd tracked Bikas down by following Eric's references to debates at the Marxist Union, a student organization at the University of Bombay. My predecessor had a fascination for left-wing politics, which, according to Flaherty, had earned him the nickname "Eric the Red."

The secretary of the Marxist Union—a guy named Gopal—remembered Eric well. A smart fellow, but a little too interested in scoring with the female comrades. He made them uncomfortable. That jibed with what Willy Smets had told me about him. I asked if there was anyone named Bikas in the Union. Gopal said there had been, but he left their merry band of revolutionaries at about the same time Eric Nielsen abruptly disappeared.

I handed Gopal my card and asked if he knew where to find Bikas. He regarded me warily, maybe because I was American and, therefore, the natural adversary to his ideology. But he said he'd try to locate him. A few days later, I received a call in the office. It was Bikas. We set up the interview in Dharavi, and I took the pictures of him.

The thing about Bikas was that he wasn't too smart. Couldn't resist bragging. He talked way too much and showed none of the discretion an admitted revolutionary/terrorist on the lam should.

"No one will recognize me with my face covered," he'd told me that day in Dharavi.

True enough. For the pictures I took when he was wearing the scarf. But it slipped off his face for a brief moment as I was packing up to leave, and—yes—I got off one shot of him in profile. He didn't notice.

That frame could get me killed if he ever knew it existed.

Now, I retrieved the notebook from the drawer. Flipping through the pages near the end, I noticed Bikas's name again, this time with a location, "Oval Maidan." The Maidan was the parade ground near the High Court and the university. I wondered what that was about. But just as soon, I forgot it. There, at the bottom of the same page, after some notes about cricket, was Willy Smets's name.

"What's that you're reading?" asked Janice, Frank's secretary. She was standing above me.

I closed the notebook and placed it facedown on the desk.

"Some old dispatches," I said. "Trying to catch up."

A shapely, middle-aged divorcée who'd come to Bombay five years before to start a new life away from her ex, Janice had told me she'd always been fascinated with India. And when the opportunity arose at UNI, she'd jumped at it. We enjoyed our morning and afternoon tea breaks together on most days.

"What can you tell me about Nielsen?" I asked.

"Eric the Red? Smart enough. But secretive and paranoid about his assignments and features."

"What about personally?"

"He had a roving eye. And hands, too, if you know what I mean."

"Why did he leave so suddenly?"

She shrugged. "Just came in one day and said he was through. Didn't like it here. He left the next day for Seattle."

"What about his stories? What kind of stuff interested him? Politics? Terrorism?"

"You should ask Mr. Muller. I didn't talk to him much after he *accidentally* brushed against me one too many times."

Once Janice had decamped, I took up the notebook again. Eric Nielsen had been obsessed with getting an invitation to Willy Smets's parties. He'd lived in the same building as Willy, in my flat, in fact. I was curious to see what he'd written about my neighbor.

There was a date—Wednesday, March 5—with "cocktails" underlined after it. Three exclamation points, too. About a third of the way down the next page, he'd provided his recap of the evening. "Sushmita. No dice. Bitch."

I stashed Eric's notes deep in the drawer and turned back to my story on the Supreme Court decision. I'd run into a newspaper guy, Jithender, who covered legal matters and, though politics weren't normally his bailiwick, he was well connected and informed. Seemed nice enough, so I called him and asked if he'd meet me. On my way out the door, Kishore the "office boy" handed me an envelope. *Office boy* sounded even worse than *servant*, but everyone said that was his title. I hated referring to him that way and made a point of always calling him by his name. Inside the envelope was Ashok Pethe's business card along with a brief note about the dinner party the following Wednesday. He'd scribbled his home phone number on the back of the card.

. . .

Jithender G. met me at Cream Centre, across the road from Chowpatty Beach. He was already deep into an oily *chana bhatura* when I arrived. I ordered a coffee and sat down opposite him.

"Not eating?" he asked, tearing off a hunk of the fried bread and digging into the chickpeas.

"I had lunch."

He grunted, his mouth full. "Me too. What's so urgent?"

"Listen, Jithender, I'm covering this Mrs. Gandhi story, and I was hoping you'd give me your take on it. I'm new here and don't know much about the legal system."

"Call me Jeetu."

"Sure thing. So what do you think about her?"

"Mrs. Gandhi? Well, the court ruled her election invalid two weeks ago. It's hard to be PM when you're not even an MP."

"Then she's out? You think they'll remove her from office?"

"If she loses the appeal in twenty days' time."

I sipped my milky coffee. "You don't think she'll lose?"

Jeetu sniffed, wiped his lips with a paper napkin, and considered the question. He took another bite of his second lunch, then gave me his opinion.

"What makes you think Mrs. Gandhi has any intentions of giving up power now? For charges no more serious than a traffic offense? This is minor stuff. She'll manage."

"Bribery?"

"Too big to throw out of office. She'll win the appeal. Or the Supreme Court will hand down a new ruling that allows her to stay. She's Nehru's daughter, after all. She and her father have ruled this country for twenty-six of the past twenty-eight years."

"So from a legal point of view, you think she'll survive this?"

He chuckled. "Not from a *legal* point of view. But from a political one? Yes."

He finished off his *chana bhatura* and excused himself to wash his hands in the little sink against the wall. When he returned to the table, he said he had an idea.

"You should talk to JP Narayan. That would be a feather in your cap."

"The opposition leader? I've read about him."

"*Lok Nayak*, the People's Leader. My cousin is a protégé of his. JP's in Delhi now, planning a large rally for tomorrow. If you can get there, I think I can arrange an interview."

"We barely know each other," I said, eyeing him with suspicion. "Why would you do that for me?"

"Maybe because you'll thank me with a bottle of Vat-69."

. . .

I accompanied Jeetu to his flat behind nearby Wilson College. My newfound friend and protector, Willy Smets, was in Poona, so I thought of Ash Pethe instead. He might be able to help. I retrieved his business card from my wallet and called him from Jeetu's phone.

"I need a bottle of scotch," I said, prevailing on our brief acquaintance for a favor. "I'll pay, of course. The local shops only have the domestic stuff. I'm looking for Vat-69."

Ash let loose a big laugh and said, "Sure. I can help you."

He told me to stop by his place, where his servant would "do the needful." Jeetu would have his bottle of Vat-69, which was going to set me back the larcenous sum of 170 rupees. About twenty-one dollars. For Vat-69.

Next, Jeetu made a trunk call to his cousin in Delhi. We had to wait about twenty minutes for the call to go through, but the meeting was set. By 5:30 that afternoon, I was holding a ticket to Delhi on the next morning's first flight. It had cost me 330 rupees each way, but I'd get my story. And JP Narayan would have some welcome international publicity for his mission to see Mrs. Gandhi thrown out.

Of course, I'd have to convince Frank Muller that an exclusive with JP Narayan was an opportunity too good to waste. His man in Delhi—Chuck Kohlner—could go back to Pattaya or Bangkok or Phuket. For all I cared, he could go to hell. I was flying to Delhi to interview the *Lok Nayak* and earn my stripes.

· · ·

WEDNESDAY, JUNE 25, 1975, 6:27 P.M.

Frank Muller's head nearly exploded when I told him what I'd done. He couldn't very well deny it was the right decision. But he was seething behind the veil of smoke. I worried he might fire off a telex to Kate to demand she take me back. He stubbed out his cigarette and promised me he'd fire me and send me packing if I ever pulled a stunt like that again.

He cooled down, but not before he'd kicked me out of his office. A half hour later, he appeared above me and dropped a packet of fresh and not-so-fresh ten-rupee notes on my desk.

"Reimbursement for the ticket," he said in a calm voice. "And here's your hotel reservation." He handed me a teletype confirmation from the travel agent. "One night. Make the most of it."

CHAPTER FOUR

I waited in the lobby of Sagar Darshan for the car our office manager, Girish, had arranged to take me to Santa Cruz Airport for my flight. As the minutes ticked by with no sign of the driver, I worried something had gone wrong. Or was about to. I had no way to contact him, no access to a telephone. And even if I'd had, I didn't know his number.

The liftman watched from his seat in the elevator as I fretted. A *durwan*—doorman—and a sweeper lay on the stone floor in the dim fluorescent light, sleeping as soundly as if on a bed of goose feathers. No use asking them where the driver was. How would they know, even if I could make myself understood? I decided to rouse one of the black-and-yellow taxi drivers who parked at the President Hotel across the road.

I grabbed my overnight bag and briefcase and stepped through the folding security gate into the night. The rain had stopped for the moment. Gone was the pungent odor of dusty smoke I'd smelled when I arrived at the International airport six weeks before. Now the air was heavy and wet.

I hurried toward the *marg*, the main drag at the end of our narrow cul-de-sac. Across the road, barely a hundred yards from my door, the President Hotel was asleep. But I knew there would be taxis.

A policeman appeared, *lathi* at the ready, and barked something at me in Marathi. He motioned to Sagar Darshan with his left hand, as if ordering me to go back inside. I made a proper fool of myself, repeating "Santa Cruz" over and over to communicate where I needed to go. But his insistence grew stronger, and he approached me in a menacing manner. With no other choice, I retreated into the lobby.

I was an experienced traveler who knew how to get by in less-than-ideal conditions. I'd reported from Africa, Vietnam, and Chile, after all. But this was different. Besides the language barrier, there was also the time of day working against me. The city was asleep. No one to ask for help. At least no one who spoke English. Then there was my flight. I was sure to miss it, and my huge story, if I didn't get into a taxi soon.

I tried asking the liftman what was going on. Why had the policeman sent me back inside? Of course I knew he didn't speak English, but I took a stab at it anyway. Next, I woke the sweeper and the *durwan*. Same language barrier. I made a dialing gesture, and the *durwan* caught on. Somewhat reluctantly, he opened the small cabin at the rear of the dim lobby. There was a radio, a cluttered desk with schedules, rubber stamps, papers, and a telephone.

A baksheesh was in order. I slipped the man a couple of rupees and lifted the receiver, intending to dial the number on my ticket. But the phone and my sorry luck had other ideas. No dial tone. What the hell was happening?

Peering out through the security gate, I caught sight of the policeman who'd chased me back inside. He was prowling around a tree on the other side of the lane. Then he clamped his *lathi* under one arm and began to undo his fly. I put the phone down and scooped up my bag. There was a side entrance to the lobby for the servants' use, and I dashed through it into the compound with the building between me and the cop. Sticking close to the trees along the wall, I emerged into the lane out of his line of sight. Two minutes later, I strode up to the entrance of the President Hotel, confident I could still make my flight.

The door was locked. No *durwan*. That was strange. At the finer hotels, there was always a mustachioed doorman in a turban, ready to salute you. Even odder, there were no taxis waiting outside. Not one. Through the glass, I could see staff at the reception desk. I tapped on the door, and a smart-looking young man in a maroon blazer came to open up. He unlocked and stepped aside to let me in. His name tag read "Akshay."

"Sir, please come in," he said. "It's not safe."

"I need a taxi. I'm going to miss my flight."

"No, sir. Flights are canceled. No taxis are plying."

"What? Why? What's happened?"

"The government has declared an emergency," he said. "That's all we know. Please go back to your room."

The staff at deluxe hotels in India always assumed that any foreigner walking through the door was a guest. I was sure they didn't extend the same respect to Indians.

"I'm staying across the road," I said. "In the Sagar Darshan building."

"It's all right, sir," he said. "Come sit in the lobby or the coffee shop. It's not safe to be out."

I resigned myself to missing my plane and my scoop. What did an "emergency" mean, anyway? Had another war broken out with Pakistan? Akshay didn't know much.

"We received a tip from Delhi about five hours ago," he said. "Before the phones and electricity were cut. We're running on generators now."

I wandered across the darkened lobby to the coffee shop. In Indian hotels, coffee shops were the in-house restaurants, usually open twenty-four hours. It was a misnomer, at least for Americans, as they in no way resembled what we would call a coffee shop back home. The restaurant was empty at 5:10 in the morning except for an American businessman, dressed for the day in a dark suit and narrow tie. He sat at a table near one of the walls, reviewing some papers through his horn-rimmed glasses. We made eye contact, and the connection was instant. We had to talk to each other and right away.

"Do you know what's going on?" he asked, offering me the seat across from him with a tilt of his head. I joined him.

"Not much," I said. "Everything was fine when I turned in last night. I was supposed to catch a flight to Delhi at six. But no car, no taxis. I had to sneak out of my building and avoid a cop to get here. How about you? Any idea what's happened?"

He neatened his papers then leaned forward to speak. His accent was Southern. Maybe lower Midwestern, and his hair was cropped close to his scalp on the sides. Mine was wavy and longish. We must have looked as mismatched as Mutt and Jeff.

"Mrs. Gandhi has taken over," he said in a low voice. "Might as well be a coup. Mark my words, no court is going to throw her out of office. That conviction of hers will disappear faster than shit goes through a goose. World's largest democracy, my ass. This country's no better than a tinpot dictatorship."

I considered his words. He might well have been right. One thing was for sure, though. He was an asshole. The ugly American. I wished I hadn't sat down, but I wanted information, and he seemed to have some.

"Name's Harlan," he said, extending a firm hand for me to shake. Then he slipped me his business card. "Russell Harlan, Jr. I've written the hotel's number on the back. In case you want to reach me."

"Dan Jacobs," I replied, wondering why the hell I'd ever want to reach him.

"Where you from, Dan?"

"New Haven. New York, actually. I'm a reporter. I was supposed to interview one of the opposition leaders in Delhi later this morning. Christ, if we're locked down here, I wonder what'll happen to him."

Harlan raised his brows and drew a sigh. "You know, they don't have a long democratic tradition in this country. India is still a backward frontier of modern civilized governance."

I didn't agree, but now wasn't the time to debate the point.

"What about you?" I asked. "You look ready for a day in the office."

"I'm an agricultural consultant. Corn. These people couldn't grow a beard if you didn't show them how."

I frowned.

"I was going to fly to Bhopal this morning when they told me no way," he continued. "I managed to call my office in St. Louis, and they gave me the news. Pretty sketchy, but they said the president declared some kind of domestic emergency at midnight. In the dark of night. And the president? Give me a break. Mrs. Gandhi surely dictated the thing and told him where to sign."

"You found a working phone?" I asked. "Any chance I could make a call?"

"Not anymore. They cut the phones around one in the morning."

A waiter appeared and presented us with a menu. One menu for the two of us. I asked if he might be able to scare up a second one, and he set off in search of it. He returned a moment later with three. I ordered some coffee and the breakfast buffet, which was being assembled across the dining room. Harlan wanted eggs over medium with toast and bacon.

"Not a fan of buffets," he said to me once the waiter had assiduously repeated our order and retreated. "Never sure how clean they are."

"So what's going to happen next?" I asked.

"I expect things'll get quiet real fast. The unrest, the strikes, and demonstrations are history. Might be a good thing in the long run." He paused. "Unless you're on Mrs. Gandhi's bad side."

. . .

By seven, I'd made two decisions: one, get away from Russell Harlan, Jr. This guy was precisely the kind I tried to avoid back home. And I wasn't going to change my spots simply because I was trapped in a deluxe hotel in the middle of an "emergency." The second decision had to do with the hotel. The President's comfort beckoned to me. The air-conditioned rooms, restaurant, telephones, and telegraph services. I knew I couldn't stay long, but one night was doable.

The stack of tens—more than 600 rupees—Frank Muller had dropped on my desk the night before, would cover the cost, so after my breakfast with Harlan, I approached Akshay at the reception desk and asked for a room. Once I'd shared my passport with him, he handed me a key. Ten minutes later, I was showering in room 915. This wasn't the bucket bath I was becoming used to in my Sagar Darshan place, but a real shower. Hot water.

By seven thirty, the phones and electricity were working again. I tried calling Frank Muller at his flat, but the connection didn't go through. Hardly unusual in Bombay on any average day. From the window, I could see people and cars on the *marg* below, the one that intersected with Cuffe Parade Road. The television was broadcasting nothing but the test signal. That was no surprise, of course. Programming aired only in the evening. And there was just the one channel, Doordarshan, which was run by the state.

I tried the radio instead. Jackpot. At 8:00 a.m., Mrs. Gandhi herself came on All-India Radio to address the nation. She gave a brief statement, in Hindi, then in English, intended to reassure the populace.

"There is nothing to panic about," she said, then justified the Emergency—capital E now, I figured—as necessary to protect the country from threats to its stability. She concluded her address with a plea for cooperation and trust in the days ahead.

And that was it. Everything was going to be fine. For Mother India and, I assumed, for Mrs. Gandhi.

I dressed and ventured down to the street where I found a black-and-yellow taxi to take me to work. It was after nine, and the office was humming. Our reporters were all present. The stringer—Flaherty—who'd first told me about Willy Smets's parties was chatting with Yusuf "Joey" Rahman, an Indian-Canadian who'd returned to the old country to find a wife and never left. He was still single, by the way, living with his grandparents in Mandvi. Herbie Reichel was a veteran American journalist who'd earned his stripes writing for—coincidentally enough—*Stars and Stripes* during World War II. He'd served in the CBI Theater during the war, met an Anglo-Indian girl, and got married. He'd been in Bombay ever since. He was planning on retiring soon.

The telex rattled as messages arrived in bursts every thirty seconds or so. Frank was pacing in his cabin, reading a newspaper and puffing on yet another Chesterfield. Where did he find those in India, anyway?

I tapped on his door. When he saw me, he nearly swallowed his cigarette and threw the special edition of *The Indian Herald* he was reading to the floor.

"What are you doing here?" he bellowed. "Why the fuck aren't you in Delhi covering this?"

"Take it easy," I said, stepping inside. "There were no flights this morning. No car came to get me. No taxis either. Believe me, I wanted to be on that plane."

He ran a hand through his thinning hair then snatched up the newspaper he'd tossed a moment before. He held it out for me to see.

"You don't usually read the *Indian Herald*. Nothing else available?"

"This is the only one we could find. They're saying the government shut off the electricity to the papers to prevent this news from getting out."

I read the headline.

EMERGENCY DECLARED
JP, Morarji, Advani, Asoka Mehta & Vajpayee Arrested

"JP is Narayan," I said. "The guy I was going to interview."

Frank sank into his chair behind the desk. "You don't think I know that? I was hoping you were there in Delhi, standing by his side, when they slapped the cuffs on him. Good job, Jacobs."

He'd dispensed with "Dan," meaning I was on the outs. Next he'd be handing the plum assignments to Joey Rahman instead of me. I didn't have to worry about Herbie. He was running on empty, energy-wise. Joey, on the other hand, was eager and resourceful. Too bad he couldn't write.

"Come on, Frank," I said. "There were no flights this morning."

He stewed despite my reasoning. "On top of everything else, we're out your airfare. Maybe Janice can get a refund. If not, it's coming out of your salary."

Great. Not only had I already spent it on my room at the President, I'd have to spend it again to pay him back if he didn't cool down.

I spent the next several hours digesting what news I could piece together and writing an article on the evolving situation. I ran it by Frank then filed it by telex to New York.

Around six, he called me to his office again. The rain was streaming down the windows outside, and it was hot. He called to Janice to get some coffee. She informed him that Vikram—Vikky—the *chaiwallah*, had left for the day.

"Goddamn it!" he said. "Get me some coffee."

"Take it easy, Frank. It's not her fault."

He took a deep breath, lit a cigarette, and asked me what I thought our next move should be.

"I called the Press Club," I said. "Looking for some guidance. They told me the government was preparing rules for the domestic and international press organizations."

"Censorship?"

"Most likely. The guy said to call again in the morning, maybe he'd have more information by then."

"Okay," he said, taking a deep drag and blowing out the smoke. "How are we going to get the news out if they censor us?"

"Could be risky."

"Nevertheless, we've got to prepare. Any ideas if they put us in a headlock?"

I thought for a moment. "I was in Chile when Pinochet took over two years ago. I got around the censors by shooting pictures of my typed stories. Then I went to the airport and begged passengers traveling to New York to take the film back with them. Our people met them at JFK."

Frank nodded. "Not a bad idea. Yours?"

Actually, it was. But I didn't want to come across as cocky, so I told him it had been Kate Erving's idea.

"Should've figured," he said. "Still, we'll keep that one in our back pocket."

Janice knocked on the glass and waited for permission to enter. Frank had come out of his furious fog and waved her in with a smile. Panicky, inconsiderate bastard, I thought. She placed two cups of instant coffee she'd begged from the CPA firm next door.

"Thanks, darling," said Frank, and she withdrew.

CHAPTER FIVE

I'd paid for a night in the President Hotel and I was going to make the most of it. It was a little after nine when I jumped into the shower to hose off the grime of the day. Clean again and wrapped in a robe, I checked for news on the television. They were showing a Marathi-language serial.

I was too wound up to go to bed, plus I hadn't eaten since lunch. So I dressed—open-collar shirt and bell-bottoms—and made my way down to the lobby. My friend Akshay namaste'd me from behind his desk. I returned the greeting.

The coffee shop was doing a brisk business, but the hostess found me a free table near the buffet. A waiter materialized before I'd even parked myself in the chair. He took the folded linen napkin from the table and, once he'd shaken it out, draped it over my lap with great ceremony.

I ate alone, keeping myself entertained by watching the other diners. The foreigners tended to order à la carte. The Indians went for the buffet, which featured a wide variety of local and Western options, including beef Stroganoff. Made with buffalo meat, of course. I wasn't touching that with Bill Cody's lasso.

While the hotel's clientele was mostly businessmen—foreign and Indian—there were some tourists and even a newlywed couple. They sat together nearby on a bench seat in a booth. They seemed happy.

The bride was decked out in a beautiful sari, her hands stained with henna in intricate, lacy patterns. The groom wore a Western shirt and slacks. They ate with their fingers, as was customary. I'd once asked an Indian friend in the States about this, and he gave me an education.

"Do you really trust that the restaurant's dishwasher is cleaning your flatware properly?" he'd asked with a sly smile. "We wash our hands before we sit down at the table, so we know they're clean."

He had a point.

By ten, I'd finished my modest *thali*: some *dal*, rice, *palak*, and *sabzi*. Vegetables. I signed the bill to my room and headed up to the nineteenth floor where there was a bar, what the Indians called a "permit room." After the day I'd had, I felt a drink was the least I could do for myself.

A pleasant surprise. They had Dewar's White Label, my dad's brand. A black-vested waiter took my order and dutifully repeated it to me, before returning a few minutes later with my scotch and soda. He asked how many ice cubes I wanted, then doled out the exact number into my glass with a pair of silver tongs. The floor show aside, I wanted my drink. This guy was taking his time. But when I caught sight of the little carafe with my peg of whisky, I did a double take. The tiniest puddle of amber liquid sat at the bottom.

"Excuse me," I said. "May I get a double?"

"A large whisky, sir?" he asked.

"Maybe a triple."

At length, I had my scotch. I didn't even add the soda for fear of drowning what little whisky was in my glass. The triple amounted to a short single back home. Resigned to paying the exorbitant price for my night at the President, I ordered a second drink a few minutes later. Not exactly "one to whet your appetite and one to rinse down dessert," but the addition still came to two.

"Pretty miserly with the imported liquor, aren't they?"

I turned to see who had spoken. It was Russell Harlan, the American I'd met early that same morning in the coffee shop.

"They serve it with an eye dropper," he continued, referring to the liquor. "Mind if I join you?"

"Be my guest," I said, wishing he'd push off instead.

He took the seat opposite me. "Does that mean you're buying?"

I must have blanched, because he assured me he was kidding. In fact, he offered to stand me another drink.

"What'll you have?"

"Dewar's," I said. "My dad's scotch. They don't give you very much, I'm afraid."

"The thing you have to realize," he said, "is that you're going to spend a fortune on alcohol in this country. Might as well accept the fact. I'd rather blow forty bucks on a few healthy-sized drinks than three on the fumes they serve here."

When the waiter arrived, Harlan ordered a double large for each of us. I made an exception to my dad's rule. If I had to listen to this guy, I wanted some anesthesia. And double large sounded worse than it was; four pegs at the President amounted to a modest double back home.

"Cheers," he said, offering his glass for a clink. "You know what's great about international travel, Dan? Meeting folks from back home. Folks you'd never give a second thought to if you ran into them stateside."

"I suppose you're right."

"Take us, for example. If we weren't in this toilet of a country, we'd never be friends. I'm a Nixon Republican, and I'll bet you voted for McGovern."

"That's true, Russ. But I'd rather you didn't refer to India as a toilet."

He laughed out loud. "See what I mean? I should've known you'd say that. It's to your credit, Dan. I respect a man who's not afraid to scold a guy who's just bought him a quadruple whisky."

I offered to pay for my own drink. His, too.

"Now you've gone and got offended," he said. "I was only making a little fun. I like you, Dan. I promise not to disparage our hosts."

"Okay," I said. "And, yes, I did vote for McGovern. Campaigned for him, as a matter of fact. Canvassed the rich suburbs in Connecticut and phoned about a million voters."

"And I paid several hundred bucks to eat rubber chicken at more than one Nixon fundraiser."

Starting to feel the effects of the scotch, I leaned in and smiled at my new acquaintance. "Tell me the truth, Russ. You gotta admit he was a crook, right?"

"Whether or not he was a crook doesn't matter. For me, Nixon was everything McGovern was not. And that's what's important. We take the bad with the good, because we think it's a lot better than the alternative."

"I wouldn't go that far," I said.

"Really? Would you vote for Teddy Kennedy? After Chappaquiddick?"

"Over Nixon? Yes."

"You prove my point, Dan." He raised his glass again. "It ain't what he did wrong that matters. It's what he did right."

"Fair enough," I said. "But I'm not that cynical yet. And, of course, the tragedy for you guys is that Watergate was unnecessary. Nixon was going to beat McGovern like a rug no matter what. And he did. If they'd been smarter, Tricky Dick would still be in the White House."

"Doesn't bother me," he said. "Ford'll do. Provided he can get himself reelected next year."

I pointed out that Ford had never actually been *elected* president.
"Touché."

Our conversation turned to less-contentious topics.

"You see that woman over there?" he asked me in a low voice. "At the table by herself. The blonde with the brushed-out hair? Like Farrah Fawcett."

"The one in the green-flowered dress? She's the only blonde in here."

Harlan aimed a long gaze at her. It was as if he was trying to decide whether to answer me or send her a drink.

"It pains me to tell you she was giving you—not me—the eye. The sad thing about being a tight-assed Republican in a dark suit and wingtips is that hot numbers like that blonde don't give us a second look. What say I ask her to join us?"

"Why would she want to do that?" I said. But before I knew what was happening, Harlan had pushed himself out of his seat and marched over to her table.

She frowned at him. And why not? A middle-aged man with a brush cut and a narrow black tie interrupts your privacy to propose God knows what? I watched. He stood there, bending slightly forward to speak to her as she squinted in a bemused manner, a cigarette smoldering in her hand.

Then—Jesus Christ—Harlan turned and pointed to me. What the hell was he saying? The woman leaned in her chair to see around his broad hips and focused her gaze on me. I looked away. Too late. This was humiliating. Even worse, the next moment, Harlan was waving me over to join them.

I pretended not to see. I could always say I was nearsighted. But if the mountain will not come to Muhammad . . . Harlan and the pretty blonde appeared before me.

"*Taken Sie a seat, Fräulein,*" he said in God-awful German, offering the chair next to me. I rose to my feet until she'd sat. Then he turned to me. "What's wrong with you, Dan? Didn't you see me waving?"

"Sorry. I'm nearsighted."

Harlan took the chair on the other side of the young lady and signaled to the waiter. Another round of drinks was soon on its way. The blonde was drinking Lillet Blanc.

"Dan, this is . . . Sorry, what did you say your name was?" he asked her.

She rolled her eyes. "Birgit Fuchs."

"Fuchs? That's a funny name."

Another frown from our guest. "It's not a funny name. It means fox."

Harlan slapped the table, causing my glass to jump. "It suits you perfectly," he said in a booming voice. "You're a foxy lady." He chuckled at his wit.

"I think I'll talk to your friend," she said.

The waiter returned, performed his act with the drinks, and withdrew. Now that we were all friends, Harlan flashed his brightest smile at her.

"What's a foxy chick like you doing in Bombay?"

Her full lips were painted pink, her eyelashes coated with heavy mascara. She wore a narrow emerald-green choker around her neck and a green headband in her shag-cut to match her short dress.

"Right now?" she answered, her accent clipped and precise. "I'm wishing to be elsewhere."

I laughed and raised my glass to her. She smiled at me, pretty blue eyes twinkling in the low light.

Over the next hour, we chatted about my job and hers. She was a stewardess for Lufthansa. Harlan offered the tired old standby, "Coffee, tea, or me?" She didn't get it. We didn't discuss Harlan's work. He insisted the details of corn cultivation would only "bring us down." His words. Birgit needed no convincing. I found her to be sharp and well informed about world events. She was twenty-seven, spoke German, English, and French, skills that surely came in handy for a stewardess. Especially in the first-class cabin of the long-haul routes that she worked.

"Don't airline crews usually stay near the airport?" I asked.

"Yes, but they canceled our flight this morning. This Emergency. I'm here for three days more. And since there's nothing to do near the airport, I came here."

"All the better for us," offered Harlan.

"What do you do for fun in Bombay?" she asked me, ignoring him.

"Mostly, I go to the office and come home."

"That's sad," she said. "You should explore the city. Have you seen the temple caves at Elephanta? Maybe we could visit them on Saturday?"

I blushed. "The Emergency is big news right now. I won't have time to take the whole day for that."

"Maybe a party, then? Do you go to parties?"

I thought of Willy Smets. And Sushmita. Much more interesting to think of her. But they were in Poona. I wasn't sure when they'd be back in Bombay or if they were planning any parties. Unlikely. There was Ashok Pethe's dinner the next week, of course, but Birgit would be long gone by then.

Harlan offered to take her to see the elephants.

"*Elephanta*," said Birgit. "It's an island."

"Fine. Or we could have a party in my room."

"Can you call it a party if you're the only person there?"

I laughed so hard, some of my drink came out my nose. I coughed for the next five minutes. Harlan took her joke pretty well, considering how devastating it was.

The waiter appeared above us to say the permit room was closing. He presented the bill. Harlan wanted to know whatever had happened to last call. He was pretty drunk by then, but signed the charge to his room without even checking the total.

Harlan was on the eleventh floor. My room was on the ninth, Birgit's on the fifth. When the lift stopped on the eleventh, he stumbled out, waving to us over his head without turning to look back. The doors closed and the next stop was nine. I glanced at my watch. It was a little after midnight. The doors rolled open, and I told her this was my stop. She leaned in and gave me a kiss on the cheek.

"*Gute Nacht, Dan,*" she said, an adorable smile on her pink lips.

The doors closed and the lift was gone. Was that flirting?

The first girl I'd ever slept with had told me I was so dense I needed a ton of bricks to fall on my head to get the message. Then she'd pulled her sweater over her head and wrapped me in a sloppy kiss.

CHAPTER SIX

On my morning run to Marine Drive and back, I'd seen people heading to work. At least the ones who hadn't been arrested. The buses and trains were running again. But life in the city was tense.

New York was happy with the job we'd done in the difficult circumstances the day before. They weren't at all concerned about the lost airfare. It was a good call to try for the JP interview. That made Frank Muller happy, which was good for me.

I was working the phones, prevailing on the few reporters and politicians I'd met in my six weeks in India, asking for information. I talked to two Congress Party MLAs, state assemblymen. They had nothing to say except that Mrs. Gandhi had taken the correct action to prevent further "internal disturbances" harmful to the security of the nation. Both used the same words.

"I'm patching a call through to you," said Padma, our receptionist.

"It's Jeetu," came the voice from the other end. "Don't say my name. I'm phoning to tell you to keep our meeting a secret. You don't even know me if anyone asks."

"What? Why?"

"*Yaar*, do I have to paint a picture for you? They've arrested JP Narayan and my cousin. If they connect them to me through you, they'll come for both of us."

"Okay," I said. "Got it."

"Get rid of my number. And if you noted our meeting in your appointment book, tear out the page."

He rang off without saying goodbye. I replaced the receiver and went straight to my appointment book. I tore up the page in question, then went back through my notes and carbon copies, looking for any mention of Jeetu, Jithender, or Cream Centre.

Jeetu's call spooked me. Triggered my paranoia about other things besides our meeting. I remembered my roll of film. The one with Bikas the bomber on it. I still hadn't found an acceptable hiding place for it. There was the safe in the office, but I hadn't even told Frank about the story yet. He'd only chew me out for yet another bad decision, so I decided to sit on the film a little longer. The Emergency was the only news New York was interested in anyway.

I'd stashed the roll in a drawer in my flat. Not good enough. That film was dynamite, what with the dangerous photograph of Bikas's uncovered face. I finished sending a couple of urgent responses to New York, then grabbed my umbrella. I wanted to get to that film and find a place for safekeeping, but a commotion across the newsroom caught my attention. A couple of men and three police officers were on the receiving end of Frank's ire. I approached and asked Janice what was up.

"They're from the government," she said, as we watched the tug-of-war before us. "The one in the white outfit is the censor. We can't send out any news stories without his approval."

I studied the censor. His long white *kurta*—under a beige vest—reached halfway down the thigh of his cotton pants. A Gandhi *topee* sat atop his head. A *Mahatma* Gandhi cap. No relation to the PM.

"Who's the other man?" I asked.

"An undersecretary from the Information and Broadcasting Ministry. Censorship falls under their purview."

"I figured there'd be some trouble, but this is fast."

Janice regarded me with concern. "Mr. Jacobs, I don't think that *babu* even speaks English. How can he censor our dispatches?"

"*Babu*? What's that?"

"It used to be a respectable title for clerks. But it's become a pejorative term for lazy, corrupt, entitled civil servants."

"How do you know all that?"

"I've been here for a while. I've picked up a few words. Quite a few, actually."

"And? There must be more to it than that."

She allowed herself a little smile and leaned in to whisper to me. "My gentleman friend is an excellent teacher."

I grinned. "*Gentleman friend*? You've been keeping secrets from us, Janice. Come on. Spill it."

"Don't make a big deal out of it, Mr. Jacobs," she said. "I have a life outside of work, you know."

"Wait. Your gentleman friend knows Hindi?"

Her cheeks flushed red. "Mr. Jacobs, I'd prefer to keep my personal life private."

"Sorry, Janice. Question withdrawn."

"It's all right," she said at length. "He's an accountant."

"An American accountant over here?"

She drew a sigh. "No, Mr. Jacobs. You might not approve, but he's Indian."

"Jesus, no," I said, feeling like a heel. "Don't think that. Tell me, what's his name?"

"Shirish. He's a widower. And as I said, he's an accountant. Has his own firm that does very well."

"How did this romance start?"

"I don't know that I'd call it a romance. I met him four years ago. We have an . . . understanding."

"I'm happy for you."

"Please don't mention it to Mr. Muller," she said. "Or to anyone else. Who knows how they'd react?"

I assured her that her secret was safe. Janice watched the censor, the undersecretary, and Frank for a long moment before turning back to me.

"I'd like to keep an eye on the *babu*," she said. "My Hindi's good, and my Marathi's even better. He'll never suspect I understand. Will you talk to Mr. Muller for me? Maybe move my desk closer to his?"

"You're full of surprises today. I'll talk to Frank."

• • •

Once the police and the undersecretary of Information and Broadcasting had decamped, Frank called me into his office. The *babu* had been installed at a desk near the telex terminal and was giving his tea preferences to Vikky, the *chaiwallah,* who was collecting stray cups for cleaning.

"That son of a bitch is going to be in our hair from now on," Frank said, glaring at him through the glass window of his cabin. "What the hell are we going to do about him?"

"First, we're going to move Janice's desk next to his," I said. "She'll tell us how good his English is. With any luck, he doesn't speak a lick."

"Where does Janice fit in?"

"She speaks Hindi and Marathi. Didn't you know that?"

Frank shook his head.

"Well, she does. Let's have her eavesdrop on his calls and conversations. She'll tell us what we have to worry about."

Frank rocked in his chair, weighing my advice. He lit a cigarette. "How the hell did Janice learn Hindi and Marathi?" he asked.

"She's been here five years. Maybe she takes classes."

. . .

My flat wasn't nearly as welcoming as the President Hotel. No one to open the door for me. No one to smile and greet me by name. No one to make me feel special, even if it was only a mirage. Something I was paying for.

Under the door, I found a note from Inspector Lokhande. An order to drop by the station again the next day, Saturday, at eleven. I crumpled the paper and tossed it into the dustbin. If he wanted my statement, he could come to me.

The first thing I did was take care of my film. I hid it in the battery compartment of one of the two radios I'd found in the flat when I arrived. The thing took D batteries, which were about the size of the roll. The radio wouldn't work, of course, but there was the other one if I needed it, and I felt the film was reasonably secure in its hiding spot.

Then, with little to eat or drink in the house, I made do with toast and tea. I settled in to watch a Marathi-language serial on the crappy TV set, wondering what the hell the family in the show was getting so dramatic about. They looked healthy and well off. But the grown daughter and the mother were constantly crying. And the severe father looked like a stroke was in his future.

The doorbell rang. I glanced at my watch: 9:12. Peering through the eyehole, I saw a slight young man with a skinny mustache. He looked familiar. Then I placed him. It was Sandip, Willy Smets's manservant. Was that a better word for it? I couldn't tell anymore. He was bearing a large plastic tray with three heavy bowls and a bag of something lying flat.

"Good evening, sir," he said. "From Willy *sahib*."

"Come in, Sandip. Put the tray down on the table."

He did as I asked, but not before slipping out of his sandals, which he left on the landing. Once he'd placed the gifts on the table and rubbed some blood back into his arms, he produced a small envelope from his pocket.

"From Willy *sahib*," he repeated.

After a cursory namaste, he left, pausing only to step back into his sandals. I bolted the door and sliced open the envelope. The note was from Willy, but written in a woman's hand. I smelled sandalwood on the paper, and wondered if Sushmita was wearing it or if they'd been burning incense up in the penthouse.

Danny Boy,

We are back from Poona, and I am worried about you. You've no help. The durwan told us your servant was arrested, and you're at work all day. I'm sure you've nothing to eat in the flat, so I'm sending you some dinner. And a little drink to enjoy with it.

Since you have no servant, please join us tomorrow evening at nine for cocktails. Bring a guest if you like. We will be eleven or twelve at dinner, which will be served at ten thirty.

Cheers, Willy

Inside the bag was a liter of Chivas Regal scotch. Damn good stuff. And, given the difficulty in finding foreign spirits in Bombay, I didn't want to waste it washing down a spicy Indian meal, no matter how delicious. And it smelled great. No, whisky would not do justice to a hungry man's dinner. I'd save it for another time.

I unwrapped the plates with care. Taped to the edge of each bowl was a label—again in a woman's hand—to identify the dishes by name. Without the cheat sheets I'd never have known what I was eating. I spooned out an aromatic *pulao*, some *baingan bharta*—smoky eggplant—a Maharashtrian *varan*, and *rajma masala*, a rich kidney bean dish in gravy. Pure veg, as the restaurants advertised.

The meal was exactly what I needed after a tense day in the office. As if the job weren't tough enough on its own, invading police, government undersecretaries, and censors interfered with my concentration. And Frank Muller reacted to the smallest inconveniences—like no more coffee—as if the Hindenburg had just exploded.

But now, a satisfying dinner under my belt, I felt all was right with the world. Except, of course, it wasn't. Not in India, at least. I thought about Indira Gandhi, a woman I had greatly admired. She'd always shown tremendous strength, determination, and intelligence, and had been hailed as the goddess Durga after India's victory over Pakistan in the 1971 war. But what was I to think of her now that she'd used her position as prime minister to subvert democracy with the excuse of a domestic Emergency? Article 352 of the Indian Constitution allowed for broad powers and suspension of civil liberties when the nation was in peril. It also gave Mrs. Gandhi permission to throw her political opponents in jail and to head off any attempts to remove her from office. My admiration for her was at an end.

But the Emergency could wait till morning. I tasked myself with composing the perfect thank-you note instead. I sat on one of the matching sofas, imagining I was writing to Sushmita even as I addressed my words to Willy. And, since I hadn't seen them since the night Ramu supposedly tried to break into their flat, I apologized for that, as well.

CHAPTER SEVEN

Birgit Fuchs slipped into the seat opposite me in the permit room on the nineteenth floor of the President Hotel. I'd arranged to meet her there to enjoy a drink before heading over to Willy Smets's place. She was looking fine in a low-cut, white peasant dress. And I couldn't help but notice she was wearing no bra underneath. Very European, I thought. And rather risqué for India, even the relatively cosmopolitan denizens of South Bombay.

Gone was the brushed-out look she'd worn Thursday night. Now her hair was natural, somewhere between wavy and curly with long bangs, giving her a bohemian sophistication. The sexy hippie with blue eyes, a couple of freckles, and golden tan all over. I was sure she'd brought the color with her from Germany, since it had done nothing but rain for the past week in Bombay.

"What is it, Dan?" she asked. "Is something wrong with my face?"

"Forgive me," I stammered. "You look lovely, is all."

She beamed an adorable smile at me, prompting thoughts of how bold I might be this night if she offered me another *gute Nacht* kiss.

"Are you flirting with me, Dan?" she asked.

"Just a little."

She giggled, rocking gently back and forth in her seat, and I caught a glimpse of her right breast down her dress.

• • •

Sandip answered the door and, once he'd recovered his composure, which he'd lost in reaction to Birgit's outfit, he stepped aside to let us in. I couldn't prove it, since I never looked back, but I sensed his eyes continued to follow her as Willy Smets greeted us, me with a warm handshake and Birgit with an even warmer kiss on both cheeks.

"Danny Boy," he said, "you didn't mention your guest was such a beautiful treasure. Shame on you."

Then, turning to my date—if I could describe her as such—he introduced himself, and she did the same. Recognizing her accent, and judging by her name, he launched into a long conversation with her in German, effectively shutting me out. I scanned the room— easily two times the size of my entire place—searching for Sushmita. She was near the window, dispensing instructions to a second servant. Wrapped in another beautiful sari—gold and violet this time—she looked as if she'd stepped out of a Raja Ravi Varma painting. Classic and beautiful. But also sexy.

"Danny Boy. Didn't you hear me?" It was Willy. "I asked if you would like a drink."

"Sorry," I said. "Maybe later. I had one at the hotel."

Willy squired Birgit around like he was an enamored suitor at a sock hop. More than once, I looked to Sushmita to gauge her annoyance but, by all appearances, she was indifferent. Oblivious, even. Either she didn't care or she trusted him. Or maybe they had an understanding.

I took advantage of my freedom to work my way across the room toward her. But I got shanghaied by a Norwegian married couple and a Soviet merchant marine captain whose broken English was beyond repair. I extricated myself from their conversation as soon as I dared, and finally reached the divan where Sushmita sat in splendor.

She wore a different *bindi* this night. A small gold teardrop. It took great concentration and resistance on my part, but I managed to tear my gaze away from her forehead before she noticed. She'd brushed some brownish-red color onto her lips, but that was the sum total of her makeup. The rest of her beauty was what nature had provided.

She patted the cushion beside her, an invitation to sit. "Hello, Daniel," she said. "I'm so glad you came. I've been hoping you might try to explain again what's interesting about your work. But without spilling your drink this time. Oh my. You have nothing to drink. Willy has been neglecting you."

"No, it's all right. I begged off."

"Nonsense."

She signaled to the second servant, Jagdish, who was hovering nearby. Speaking in Hindi—I could tell by the word *hain,* which came up three or four times—she gave him instructions for my drink. The young man wagged his head then set off to fulfill the errand. I felt flattered she was taking care of me.

"Now," she said, "there's so much happening in the news. Tell me."

"The political situation is dicey. We're trying to do our jobs and report as honestly and fairly as we can."

"But?"

"But there's a censor now. A chubby *babu* who sits in our office, reviewing every word we write."

"Really?" she asked, unable to suppress a grin. "A *babu?*"

I blushed. I'd wanted to impress her, trying to pass off the word as my own.

"Yes," I said, stumbling over my response. "You know . . . a functionary. Lazy. Entitled."

Jagdish returned with a large glass of whisky and a couple of ice cubes. "I know what a *babu* is, Danny."

I took the drink and sipped it as if licking a wound. Jesus, she thought I was an idiot. And I was. But then I realized she'd called me Danny. For the first time.

"Nothing for you?" I asked.

"I don't drink alcohol," she said.

Then she did something I almost wish she hadn't. At least not at that moment with so many people around. She reached out and touched my wrist with her fine fingers. Regarding me with her sparkling eyes, she told me she was sorry. Willy had asked her not to tease me. Or laugh at me. If I'd been alone with her, I'd have shown her I wasn't an idiot to be pitied, but a smoldering, romantic, take-charge kind of guy who would teach her a thing or two about love.

Okay, even I had to laugh at myself for that. Relax, I thought. You're making conversation with her. Not trying to get her into bed.

"What's so funny?" she asked. Apparently, I was grinning.

"Nothing," I said, finally relaxing. "Let me tell you about my job instead. It's actually quite interesting."

. . .

Dinner was served at 10:35. Willy—or was it Sushmita?—had decided to make it casual. *Chaat*, samosas, *bhel*, *pani puri*, and other Indian snacks. The guests sat where they wanted and with whom they wanted. The Norwegian couple made feeble attempts to disguise their displeasure. They moved the food around on their plates, but never really ate much. The Russian captain was shoveling it in like a fireman feeding a hungry steam engine. He was particularly partial to the samosas, which were filled with potato and peas, but he sampled everything with gusto. There were three middle-aged German businessmen who, gulping their beer, chatted amiably with the other guests.

Then there was Birgit, who was being monopolized by our host. She truly was a pretty thing, with her blue eyes, blonde curls, and tanned arms and legs. Terrifically sexy. And yet I couldn't stop throwing sideward glances at Sushmita, who was kind enough to keep me close while she held the three Germans enthralled with her wit. Had she not, I'd have been sitting alone in a corner, blending into the wallpaper pattern, had there been any wallpaper to blend into.

I drank more than I wanted to. So much liquor. Where did Willy get it? Some guys at the office said there were smugglers around South Bombay who could always deliver a bottle of whatever you needed. But at a price. There were the wine shops, where the selection was pathetic, poorly stored, and you needed an alcohol permit card to buy anything anyway. And I doubted you could find anything besides the local spirits. No Red Label or Dewar's in those places.

The first guests to go were the Norwegians. That was around 10:55, right after Sandip relieved them of their plates. The Germans drifted away one by one, but not before yucking it up with their compatriot, Birgit. I caught all three of them staring at her breasts. As if they had a chance with a beauty like her. The Russian captain seemed to have no intention of pushing off. I don't know how he communicated with anyone, including Willy, who spoke more languages than the rest of us. Yet Arkady, as I later determined his name was, kept smiling and drinking. The guy could pack it away, I'll say that for him. And the only sign that alcohol affected him was a slight reddening of his cheeks. Other than that, and perhaps the odor of liquor on his breath, you'd have thought he was drinking apple juice.

I had the next day off. Frank had set up a revolving duty schedule that gave everyone a free day each week. But despite having the luxury of sleeping late in the morning, I felt it was time to go. I didn't want to wear out my welcome with Willy and Sushmita. Their get-togethers

were the only entertainment I had. And more than that, I couldn't
get enough of her, of her warm skin that once or twice that evening
had brushed up against mine. So I announced that maybe I would
say goodnight and escort Birgit back to her hotel.

"What nonsense is this?" asked Willy, feigning offense. "It's only
one o'clock. Why would you leave us so early?"

I retook my seat, and Jagdish handed me another drink.

Arkady finally tired himself out, presumably by smiling, eating,
and drinking nonstop for four hours. One minute he was there, and
the next he was gone. There was a curfew of sorts, but it had been
relaxed. And Westerners were usually given a pass where Indians
might have been rounded up. Or at least stopped and questioned.
I figured Birgit and I would have to make a quick dash across the
road to the President Hotel. Willy said it wouldn't be a problem.
Relax.

She didn't seem ready to leave anyway. Engrossed in a long conversation with Willy, she might have been interviewing him for a television program. She hadn't exchanged more than three words with
me since we'd arrived. If I'd been the jealous type, Willy would have
had a fat lip by then. Of course he might have felt the same way about
me and my attentions to Sushmita.

It was just the four of us now, Willy, Birgit, Sushmita, and me.
There were the two servants and a cook in the kitchen, but in India
they didn't really count. I was struggling to understand such attitudes
toward other human beings. I wasn't so idealistic to think that the
help had to be treated like guests. Or friends. But they were people.
And they were there. How could you ignore them? Yet they might as
well have been part of the décor. Until you needed them to fetch you
something.

"Now you're sad," said Sushmita in my ear so as not to disturb her
lover and my stewardess in their tête-à-tête. Her breath whispered

warm on my neck, provoking an intensely intimate shiver that ran down my spine.

I turned to face her, probably blushing. Practically nose to nose, we sat there in silence for a brief moment before I found an acceptable excuse to feed her.

"I was thinking about work."

"Liar," she said.

"No, really," I lied again. "You see, there's this man I interviewed about a bombing. The one that killed that CID policeman last year. I met him."

"Are you a spy, Danny?" asked Birgit. Everyone laughed.

"No, seriously," I answered, probably slurring my words a bit. "He's some kind of revolutionary. Claimed he planted the bomb that killed that poor cop."

"So why are you thinking about that now?" asked Sushmita. "In the middle of a pleasant evening?"

"Because I've had too much to drink. And because the story worries me. I took pictures of him."

Willy remarked that it all sounded quite dangerous.

"He was wearing a mask," I said. "To protect his identity."

"Then you never saw him?" asked Birgit.

I frowned. "Well, about that . . . I was putting away my camera, and the guy stood up. The scarf dropped, and . . ."

"You snapped a pic," said Sushmita. "Danny!"

"He never realized."

Willy, Sushmita, and Birgit all scolded me, urging me to use better judgment in the future. This story sounded dangerous.

"Where's the film now?" asked Sushmita.

"It's safe," I said. "No one knows about it."

Willy announced I deserved a drink to raise my spirits. I tried to say no, but Jagdish handed me yet another glass of scotch. Then Sushmita suggested we change the subject.

"When were you born?" she asked. "I want to do your horoscope."

"Oh, I don't believe in that kind of thing."

"Come on. It's fun."

I shook my head. "What if it's bad news?"

"I'm not a real astrologer. But if you and I ever want to get married, Danny, you'll have to submit to a complete astrological investigation."

Willy and Birgit laughed. Besides being a little drunk, I was more than a little titillated. Willy interrupted.

"Danny Boy, do you know that Birgit and I think you're a very handsome young man?"

"And quite tall," said Birgit.

Sushmita concurred and added that I was rather shy and polite, but that was endearing.

Everyone laughed again, and Sushmita placed her hand on my forearm. Everyone laughed except me.

. . .

It was after three when I weaved my way toward the door, an arm around Birgit for support. Willy looked fresh despite the heat and humidity, his white bush coat still crisp and dry. How did he manage that? I was rumpled and sweating. Sushmita was as alluring as ever. Her sari slipped off her shoulder for a moment, exposing the blouse underneath. I didn't know why, but somehow I'd thought she was wearing nothing but the six yards of silk. Our hosts said we must do this again soon. Birgit reminded him that she was leaving Monday.

"When you come back, then," said Willy.

He leaned in and kissed her on both cheeks, as he had when we'd arrived. I didn't dare do the same with Sushmita. But she settled the matter herself, first kissing Birgit then me on the cheek.

"You're a Gemini," she whispered in my ear. "I can tell."

CHAPTER EIGHT

Sheltering under an umbrella, Birgit and I crossed the *marg*. We made it to the President without running into the police. She didn't invite me to her room, possibly because she knew I was ready to drop. Or maybe she liked me as a friend. That was fine with me. As attractive as she was, my head was filled with the memory of Sushmita's touch of my arm and her breath on my neck. And her last words to me at the door.

Yes, I was, indeed, a Gemini, even if I put no stock in astrology. She'd had a one-in-twelve chance of guessing correctly. Not short odds, but not impossible either. Still, she'd been thinking of me, of my birthdate, my sign. I wished Birgit goodnight.

"Are you all right to get home alone?" she asked.

"Don't worry about me," I said trying to act suave, even as my eyes crossed.

"I'll be in touch when I come back to Bombay."

One chaste kiss on the cheek later, I was tramping through the rain back to Sagar Darshan.

.   .   .

MONDAY, JUNE 30, 1975, 5:01 P.M.

"Frank, you see this?" I asked, dropping a copy of the *Times of India* on his desk. "It's a couple of days old, but worth reading."

He considered the death notices I'd circled in pencil.

"What the hell?" he asked, puffing on his cigarette. "'*D. E. M. O'Cracy, beloved husband of T. Ruth, father of L. I. Bertie, brother of Faith, Hope, and Justice, expired on 26 June.*' I can't believe someone actually got this into the paper."

"That's how we get around the censor," I said. "Whoever wrote that was brilliant. Guts and imagination."

"And in Delhi, the *Indian Herald* published a blank editorial on Friday. Would've loved to see that."

"We can do the same. Not a blank editorial, of course. But we can work around the censor."

Frank chewed on that for a while then said no. "Sure, we get our stories out and then what? The ministry figures out what we did and they shut us down. Or worse."

I considered his argument. We didn't have to circumvent the censor every day, I explained. Just when a story merited it. And we could always have the byline read New York or London. How could the censors blame us for what was published abroad?

"There's a lot to lose," he said. "They're arresting more people every day. And I don't want to end up in some hellhole of an Indian prison."

Once Frank had left for the day, I sent a telex to a pal of mine in the New York office. I wanted to know if he could find some information—any information at all—on a Belgian named Willy Smets, for a story I was working on. It was a lie, of course, but I wanted to know who he was and how he'd managed to reel in a girl like Sushmita.

· · ·

I'd already filed two stories Tuesday morning. Plus, I'd managed a five-and-a-half-mile run before work. Feeling self-satisfied, I enjoyed a cup of Vikki's tea, then visited the loo. Returning to my desk, I glanced out the window at the rain, which was coming down in buckets. Four floors below in the street, a black police car pulled to a stop. A stocky officer got out. I watched and waited until the man had scurried into the building, disappearing from view, before I slipped out the office door and down the stairs.

Finding a taxi in South Bombay during the monsoons should have been an Olympic sport. Even if you managed to flag down a black-and-yellow, the drivers often balked if the destination wasn't far enough. And, with foreigners, they didn't want to turn on the meter. Such was the case that day. I had to agree to the driver's insistence on a flat fee of five rupees to take me to Cuffe Parade. Highway robbery. Literally. But I gave in.

I folded myself inside the tiny cab and shut the door.

"*Jaldi*," I told the driver, and we were off.

·   ·   ·

Yes, I was avoiding Lokhande. I didn't feel like facing him just then. So I went home to sit for twenty minutes. I washed out some clothes, hung them to dry, and had a glass of chilled water from the fridge. Figuring the police might well be on their way to find me at my flat, I headed back to the office again. Janice met me at the door.

"Where have you been? A policeman was asking for you."

"I know. I saw him as I was leaving."

"Mr. Muller was not happy. But the inspector said you weren't in any trouble. He wanted to speak to you about something that happened at your building last week."

I didn't like the way Lokhande had squinted at me. And the way he'd cuffed Ramu before wrapping a paternal arm around him. I'd have to speak to him eventually, but I didn't mind putting it off as long as possible. He'd probably headed over to my flat when he didn't find me at work. I expected to find a note under my door when I got home that evening. What I didn't expect was Sushmita.

CHAPTER NINE

Dressed in saffron bell-bottom jeans and a black T-shirt, she was squatting on the floor against the wall beside my door. Her hair was free, hanging long, past her collarbone.

"Where's Willy?" I asked.

She seemed distracted. Maybe high. "In Poona, and I'm bored, Danny. Take me to dinner."

"Dinner? It's almost ten and I've got to work tomorrow."

"How dull. I thought you were fun." She reconsidered. "No, interesting. I thought you were interesting. But you're as dull as Willy."

"Come on inside," I said. "I've got some whisky."

She scoffed. "I know. I sent it to you. But you thanked Willy. And I don't drink, remember?"

I didn't quite know what to say. The note had been signed "Willy," even if I'd recognized a woman's handwriting. I wanted to apologize but wasn't sure that was the right strategy.

"Everything okay?" I asked instead.

"Are you going to Ash Pethe's dinner party tomorrow?"

"I was planning on it. Why?"

She gazed up at me. "Take me?"

I uttered a nervous laugh. What was going on here? "Of course," I said. "Come on. Come in and keep me company."

"No," she said, rising to her feet. "I'm going to bed. And you can't come, you dull man. Call for me at eight tomorrow. Good night."

• • •

There was indeed a note from Lokhande waiting for me under the door. Right to the point, he'd written that I couldn't hide forever. But he didn't summon me to the station or threaten me in any way. I was determined to avoid him as long as possible.

There was nothing to eat besides tea biscuits, ketchup, *chakli*, and *shankarpala*—Indian snacks that Ramu had squirreled away in his cubbyhole. The *chakli* were a new experience, crunchy orange rounds of I don't know what, but they were my dinner. The *shankarpala* was sweet. That was my dessert.

At midnight, I bedded down in the wet heat. I fell asleep and dreamt a lewd dream of Sushmita. Not as wet as the night air, but it was close.

• • •

WEDNESDAY, JULY 2, 1975, 10:12 A.M.

A telex from my friend Gary in the New York office was waiting for me when I arrived at my desk. He'd checked news archives for the name Willy Smets, and called in a favor with a contact in the State Department and another at the CIA. Both dead ends. Then he did some nosing around in Belgian phone directories on microfiche in the library. Nothing.

"This guy's a ghost," he wrote. "Must be using an alias."

I twirled my pencil back and forth between my fingers, debating whether I should get my roll of film developed. At a random photo-processing shop? I couldn't risk it. The story was too dangerous. The film would have to stay in the radio for now.

That reminded me of Bikas and Eric Nielsen's notebook. I'd only read a fraction of it. I returned to the pages I'd been reviewing a couple of days before when Janice had interrupted me.

This Eric the Red was an asshole, if his opinions of Indian women were any indication. More descriptions of being shot down in flames by university students. That seemed to be his hunting ground, the university. Maybe because the students were single, and older women were not? Or maybe because he thought younger women were an easier target. Who knew? But he came across as a loser in his own words.

Janice appeared above me. I dropped the notebook on my desk, thinking I'd take it home that night to study at my leisure. She invited me to lunch at Britannia, a Parsee eatery in nearby Ballard Estates.

Janice knew the ropes. Ordered the berry *pulao*, since she was keeping vegetarian in India, and the chicken *dhansak* for me, even though I, too, was trying to avoid meat. It was delicious nevertheless, and I had a nice chat with the proprietor, who asked me to tell Richard Nixon that he was a naughty boy. I wasn't sure if he thought Tricky Dick was still president, or if he meant it as a general observation. Smiling and doing my best to show my appreciation, I complimented him on the food and fine service.

Once he'd moved on to chat with other customers, I found myself asking Janice about English in India. Exactly how many Indians spoke it well?

"Impossible to say. Some estimate one or two percent speak it as a first language. Maybe ten percent as a second language."

"That means ninety percent don't speak English at all?"

"Or barely. In the big cities and the South, you'll find more people who know some English."

"That's not much."

"Yes, but if you speak it well, you enjoy tremendous advantages, both social and professional."

"How so?"

"You get to run in the fancier circles if you have a good English accent. And employers think you're smart and educated and cultured. They give you jobs you're not even qualified for. It may not be fair, but that's how people are prejudged here. That and by the color of their skin."

It was true. Indians obsessed over fairness. The privilege that light skin afforded was at least as advantageous as good English skills. It didn't seem right. I suggested a change of subject.

"What does your gentleman friend say about all this?" I asked as I sipped my fresh lime soda through a straw. "The Emergency, I mean."

"Please, Mr. Jacobs," she said in a whisper. "We're in public. Be careful what you say."

"Sorry. And call me Danny. We're old friends, aren't we?"

She weighed my request. "I'm only a secretary. You're a reporter. I know my place."

"I'll make a deal with you. You call me Mr. Jacobs in the office, and I'll call you Miss Spenser. But I'm Danny and you're Janice when we're not."

"All right, Danny," she said, her eyes crinkling just so.

"What does he say about all this, your accountant?" I repeated in a low voice.

"Shirish is a Congress man," she said. "He has mixed feelings. It's hard to denounce the party and family that led the fight for independence. He's struggling with that."

I nodded, all the while uncomfortable with half measures and excuses when it came to right and wrong.

"I'd love to meet him sometime," I said. "Your gentleman friend."

• • •

Ours was a small office—eighteen people including the *chaiwallah*— which probably explained why the ministry had sent us our censor, Onkar. There were larger operations to monitor, and sharper blue pencils were assigned to those outlets.

Frank's idea was to fly under the radar for a while. We played it safe in the days following the declaration. Our stories ran straight down the middle of the road. Nothing controversial. Nothing that might alarm the censor or incur the wrath of the government. As I considered my vanilla reportage, I had to admit that nothing I'd sent to New York qualified as true journalism. Like the Indian papers, we were simply repeating what the government told us, virtually verbatim. But I knew we were biding our time, waiting for the opportunity to slip a scoop past the censor.

A ten-year-old company, UNI was trying to gain a foothold against the big boys in the wire service business. Frank Muller, a career newspaperman from Philly, was top dog in our office, which oversaw all of Southeast Asia. He'd been in India for a year and a half. Then there were three full-time reporters; the stringer, Flaherty; two photographers; accountants; the receptionist; and a couple of guards. We had contacts in Delhi, Bangalore, Madras, and Calcutta who filled in when necessary. Ultimately, though, it felt like a mom-and-pop operation, if Pop was a balding ass who hated bad news, even when it was the only news. And, of course, there was no Mom, unless you counted Janice. I admit that I couldn't picture a long future working for a guy who'd rather shoot the messenger than reward him.

•   •   •

WEDNESDAY, JULY 2, 1975, 7:52 P.M.

I wanted to have a bath before picking up Sushmita for Ash's dinner party. And while she was my friend Willy's girl—one who'd never take a romantic interest in me—I still permitted myself a stray fantasy or two where she was concerned. Maybe Willy wasn't serious about her. Maybe they had an open relationship.

What the hell was I thinking? Willy had taken care of me, invited me to his home, offered his help. Was I really considering seducing his girlfriend? And what chance would I stand if I actually made a pass at her? Sushmita would shoot me down like a clay pigeon. What was it Eric the Red had written about her? *"No dice. Bitch."*

No, she wasn't a bitch. Eric was an asshole.

I intended to be the perfect gentleman that night. I'd escort her to Ash Pethe's party, keep my eyes peeled for pretty girls suitable for possible future dates, and take her safely back home at the end of the evening. Friends.

After my bath, I splashed some Aqua Velva on my freshly shaven face. I'd understood it was to be a casual dinner. Still, I wanted to look my best, not for Ash Pethe, but for Sushmita. I wasn't thinking beyond the dinner and drinks, but I figured you couldn't score if you weren't in the game.

Jesus, I had to make up my mind. Was I trying to get laid or not?

· · ·

"It's tonight?" asked Sushmita once Sandip had ushered me into the drawing room. He switched on the ceiling fan and was gone.

She was dressed in cotton pajama bottoms, white T-shirt, and *chappals*—sandals. Her jet-black hair was mussed, as if she'd just risen from a nap. Taking a seat quite close to me on the sofa, she scratched her head, then rested it on my shoulder. It was a hot, wet evening and the intimate gesture set me to sweating like a horse.

I wiped my brow, worried she'd be turned off by my perspiration. She didn't seem to notice. I didn't dare budge, for one thing, because I didn't want her to move away from me, and for another, because I was scared. Scared of her, of what I might foolishly try to do, of what Sandip would think if he came back into the room.

"Do we have to go?" she asked in a feigned whine. "Let's stay here and have drinks and dinner and to hell with Ash Pethe and his party."

"Come on," I said, wanting to call her "Sush" but not daring. If she was "Mita" to Willy, she could be "Sush" to me. "It would be impolite to stand him up after I accepted the invitation."

We sat in silence for a minute after that, until she finally raised her head and pouted at me. Then she smiled and laughed.

"Okay, I'll go. But you owe me, Danny. And you smell nice. What's that aftershave you're wearing?"

I must have blushed scarlet. Aqua Velva, for God's sake . . .

She disappeared down the corridor to her room to get ready. We were going to be quite late for Ash's dinner, but I wasn't about to barge in on her bath to tell her to make it quick.

Sandip brought me a fresh lime soda with salt. I hadn't asked for it, but he pointed down the hall and said, "From *Didi*, Danny *sahib*."

I had to smile. *Didi* was a term of respect for an older woman. Like sister. Familiar yet respectful. And this skinny kid had found his name for me. I was "Danny *sahib*." He must have got it from *Didi*, from Sush, and that gave me the warmest of feelings a red-blooded young man can have.

The lime soda was refreshing. Its tang and salt helped me regain my cool. *Stop thinking of this as a date.* Sushmita was fond of me, nothing more. A friend.

Emerging from the darkened corridor, she appeared like a vision, dressed in a sparkling deep blue-and-black sari. She was twisting the screw of an earring into place.

"Danny, be an angel and fasten me up?" she asked, presenting her back to me.

I leapt to my feet and obliged, buttoning the top three hooks of her blouse. I confess I took my time, pretending to fumble with the last one as I savored the closeness. Eventually, she fidgeted. Asked if I was finished. I closed the last hook and pronounced her beautiful.

"Finally," she said, turning to face me as she draped the sari over her shoulder. "Poor Danny. No experience with blouses or brassieres, I see."

. . .

We didn't make it to Ash's until 9:45. Sushmita drove us in Willy's white Mercedes, a 280SE. One or two years old, but just about the nicest car I'd seen in Bombay. She parked it in the compound of Ash's place, where a security guard and two loiterers eyed the big car with interest.

"Here," she said to me, pulling the gearshift right out of its cradle and handing it to me. "Keep it in your pocket if it's not too big."

I chuckled. "But why?"

"To prevent theft. Willy's idea. I always take the shift handle with me when I park the car."

I apologized to our host, taking the blame for our tardiness. He brushed off my concerns and said we were among the early birds. Sushmita informed Ash in an indulgent tone of voice that I was new to Bombay and didn't understand that a nine o'clock invitation meant ten. Or ten thirty.

Ash might have been exaggerating a bit about the early birds. There were seven other guests present when we were shown into the parlor, a large room with a bank of ten windows looking out on Marine Drive and the Arabian Sea. I suddenly felt my little place in Sagar Darshan wouldn't do if I were to stay in Bombay for more than a year.

"Listen, Ash. I wanted to thank you again for your help with the scotch," I said. "I have the money I owe you."

"Rubbish," he said. "Buy me a drink at the Taj sometime. By the way, how did it go?"

"Go?"

"Your big scoop. Did you get it?"

I frowned. "Actually, no. My flight was canceled the next morning. That was the day they declared the Emergency."

He nodded and sipped his drink. "What'll you have, Dan?" he asked. "Vat-69?"

I blushed.

"Just kidding," he said. "How about Red Label?"

"This is a great place you've got," I said once we were provisioned. "What does a workingman like me need to do to find digs like this?"

He chuckled. "Be born rich."

I sighed to myself, thinking I was lucky to have a rent-free place to stay in.

"Say, Dan, do you play golf?"

"A little," I said.

"I'm a member of the Willingdon Club and I need a partner tomorrow. Are you free?"

"Sorry, no. Work."

"Too bad. Another time, then."

To change the subject, I asked him how many guests he was expecting for dinner.

"Two more. Here they are now."

I turned to see who'd arrived. It was Russ Harlan. And Birgit Fuchs stood beside him in the doorway in an orange miniskirt and white go-go boots.

CHAPTER TEN

"I thought you'd gone back to Germany," I said to her once Ash had taken Birgit's drink request and escorted Harlan to the bar.

"My flight was rescheduled again," she said. "The Emergency."

"Too bad. But it's nice to see you again. Not so nice to see Harlan."

"I was bored. He was coming to this dinner. So I thought, why not?"

"I'm around if you ever need something to do that doesn't involve Harlan. Not flirting," I said. "I get bored sometimes, too. And I'm a gentleman."

"I know that, Danny. You're the most well-behaved boy I've ever met."

Sushmita appeared, gave Birgit a kiss, and pronounced herself happy to see the two lovers reunited. I choked.

"We're not lovers," I said, a touch too insistently. "We're friends, that's all."

"You don't want to be my lover, Danny?" asked Birgit, and the two women had a laugh at my expense.

After a show of suitable good humor at her joke, I excused myself and ended up prey to Harlan. He found me sitting alone by one of the large windows, nursing my whisky and staring out at the choppy Arabian Sea.

"You're some kind of playboy," he said, taking the seat beside me. "Squiring Birgit around the other night and now that beauty over there." He gave a bob of his head in Sushmita's direction.

"She's the girlfriend of a friend of mine. I'm making sure she has an escort."

He stared long and hard at her as she chatted with Birgit across the room. "If my tastes ran to dark meat, I'd give her a try. But we all have our types, don't we?"

"Enjoy your drink, asshole," I said and left him there.

. . .

Dinner was served, buffet style, a little before eleven. A mix of Western and Indian fare, the food was good but never rose to the quality of the *chaat* we'd enjoyed at Willy's place the week before. I studiously avoided Russ Harlan, sticking to my girls, Sush and Birgit, instead.

At half past midnight, the guests began to filter out. Sushmita gave me a short blink and nod that said she wanted to go. As we headed for the door, Birgit asked if we could drop her at the hotel. Harlan wasn't about to be left out either, despite what I'd called him earlier, and offered himself as a passenger in our car.

In the compound, I went to open the door to climb in. Sushmita laughed at me.

"Are you planning to drive, Danny?"

Out of habit, I'd opened the right-side door, confusing the driver's side for the passenger's. I lied that I was holding it open for her. She climbed inside, and I handed her the gearshift.

"Nice car you've got here," Harlan said from the back seat, as she turned onto Marine Drive. "Is it yours?"

"Yes," she answered.

"Where'd you get it?"

"I'm sorry?"

"The car. Where did you get it?"

"West Germany. Where else?"

"Wasn't Ash's place nice?" I asked, running interference. Sushmita threw an appreciative glance at me in the rearview mirror. I'd let Birgit sit in front, away from Harlan. "Beautiful view he has," I added.

"But this car," said Harlan. "I mean, how does a young gal like you afford it? The import duties alone."

Sushmita was fed up. No longer worried about being polite, she told him she was rich.

"But—"

"Russ," I interrupted. "Weren't you taught it's impolite to talk about money?"

He apologized. "Sorry about that, miss. I was only trying to make conversation. However you got this car is fine with me."

We dropped Birgit and the charmer at the President, then crossed the road to our lane. The night guard opened the gate and delivered a half-hearted salute. Sushmita parked in the garage beneath the building. Once she'd switched off the engine, she blew out a long sigh.

"Thank you, Danny, for shutting him up," she said, fixing me with those sparkling eyes.

"Don't mention it. He's an idiot with no manners."

"And I'm sorry Birgit and I teased you. She'd be lucky to have you for her lover."

•   •   •

THURSDAY, JULY 3, 1975, 6:01 A.M.

The crows woke me. Each morning they started quietly enough, a murmur before first light. But as the breeze carrying the smell of fish and brine rolled in from the Back Bay, the chorus swelled in a long, droning crescendo, like cicadas, before erupting into a full-throated, rasping, demonic call to greet the rising sun. Even on days when it rained—which was the case for what seemed like half the year—the crows' wake-up call was the only alarm I ever needed.

The last thing I wanted to do was get out of bed and take a long run, followed by a cold bucket bath. I lay under the sheet for a few minutes recalling the night before. God, I'd almost found the courage to kiss Sushmita in the garage. She'd seemed sad. She was often sad. I should have listened to her the night before and ditched Ash Pethe's dinner.

I groaned, rose, and dressed. Moments later, I was running—past the Machhimar Nagar fishing village—pushing myself to ever-faster speeds. I ignored the curious stares from the pedestrians, commuters, and even the men in *lungis* brushing their teeth and taking bucket baths on the side of the road. People surely wondered why this crazy *gora* tortured himself so every morning in the heat and rain.

• • •

I wrote a long piece, outlining the current situation in the country including updates on the opposition. Onkar, the censor, cut it to shreds. Maybe his English was better than we thought.

The other news of the day came from our own Chuck Kohlner, stringer extraordinaire, in Delhi. Mrs. Gandhi had declared that democracy was alive in India. A whole lot of folks disagreed. Thousands of her opponents were under arrest, with the number growing each day. There was more. She charged that the opposition had taken advantage of India's democracy to weaken the nation.

As if on cue, at two in the afternoon, Onkar informed us, somewhat apologetically, that we were not to file any more stories that day. Frank tried and failed to maintain his cool. He lost it and started cursing loudly to himself, all the while pulling at his hair and pacing back and forth in his office. When Onkar went to the loo, I dashed off a quick telex to New York, telling them not to expect anything from us today.

I closed with, "Do not reply. Big brother is watching," then tore up the printed copy of my message.

•   •   •

THURSDAY, JULY 3, 1975, 9:21 P.M.

Everyday life in Bombay seemed to have returned to normal. Delhi might have been a different story. But in Bombay, the buses were running—not that I wanted to squeeze myself into one of those smoke-belching behemoths any time soon—and the trains were packed as always with the armies of workers commuting to and from the suburbs. Still, I sensed a wariness about me. People were vigilant and distrustful. Of each other, of the police, of me.

After work, I dropped by Dadabhoy's in Colaba and picked up some rice and *dal*. The vegetable stands had long since shuttered and disappeared for the night, so rice it was. In a low voice, I asked the proprietor if he knew where I might find some whisky. A thank-you bottle for Ash Pethe. He said nothing and gave me my change.

I wished him good night, and ceded the right of way at the door to another customer who was leaving.

"Sir," called the proprietor, waving me back. "Come, sir."

He told me to wait, and he disappeared into the back of the shop. A minute passed before he returned with a parcel rolled up in newspaper. He unwrapped it to reveal three bottles, two scotches—a Black and White and a Haig Dimple—and one red wine. The wine had no label. I examined the Dimple and, fairly confident the cap hadn't been tampered with, I asked him how much.

He wrote "Rs. 280" on a scrap of paper. Christ, that was more than thirty dollars. "No duty, sir. Good price."

That was steep. I asked him where he'd got it, still not entirely sure it was the first time around for this particular bottle.

"Air India pilot," he said. "No issues. *Bohut acchha*."

He seemed sure it was good. And I knew he wasn't going anywhere if the bottle turned out to be filled with something other than scotch. So I decided to trust him and fished out the bills. It was a lot to part with, but I figured when in Rome . . . I wondered how I was going to eat for the next week.

Back home, I couldn't bring myself to make rice and lentils at that hour, so I nibbled on some more of Ramu's orphaned snacks and listened to the radio. Hindi film music.

By eleven, I was flagging. I'd been out late the night before. And that reminded me of Sushmita three floors above. I wondered if I would have the guts to climb up the drainpipe to reach her. Like some latter-day Romeo. Unlikely. I was ridiculously afraid of heights. Seriously terrified. They turned my stomach over and paralyzed me. So with a yawn, I dropped onto the bed. Lying on my back, I reached over for the radio and checked to make sure my film was safe. It was.

• • •

FRIDAY, JULY 4, 1975, 10:06 A.M.

I made a short detour on my way to work to drop off the bottle of Dimple and a thank-you note for Ash Pethe. I'd totally forgotten it was the Fourth. A hundred ninety-nine years of American independence. Janice had hung some bunting around the office. That was what jogged my memory. She told me that Onkar had pitched in, too. Got right into the spirit and helped distribute the miniature American flags she'd brought out of storage.

"What are we doing to celebrate, boss?" I asked Frank.

"Celebrate? Are you kidding? We're working today. You can have August fifteenth off for Indian Independence."

What a jerk.

Yes, it was the 199th birthday of the United States. Despite our warts—and there were many—the U.S. still held free elections, didn't throw political opponents in jail, and enjoyed freedom of the press. India, on the other hand, was approaching her twenty-eighth birthday on August 15, in fact—thank you, Frank—and she'd just kicked democracy in the teeth.

"Mr. Jacobs, you have a visitor."

Janice stood behind me. I swiveled in my chair to see who it was, and swore under my breath.

"Inspector Lokhande," I said.

He aimed his squint at me as he rocked from heel to toe. "You've been avoiding me."

"Shall we talk in the conference room?" I asked. "It's private."

He grabbed a chair from the desk next to mine and sat down. "I have no need for privacy."

He smiled. Not a friendly smile. Vikky materialized to offer the cop tea.

"I'm happy to make a statement," I said. "Would you like me to type it out and sign it?"

Vikky handed him the tea, and Lokhande waved a hand at me. "I don't care about your statement."

"What about Ramu? What's going to happen to him?"

"Your servant is fine. A capable fellow, in fact. He's been very useful at the station."

"You mean he's working for you now?"

"Not for me. For the station. He's a good cook. Reliable messenger boy, too. Did you know he's also a fine barber? Cut my hair yesterday

and trimmed my mustache. You don't know what you had, Jacobs-*ji*."
His eyes twinkled at me as he said that last bit.

So, my servant had been arrested for scaling the side of the building
and trying to break into the penthouse apartment, and all he got for
his trouble was a new job waiting on the police?

"We'll keep him a little longer," continued Lokhande. "This tea is
very good, by the way."

Great. Next he'd arrest Vikky and have him serving tea at the
station.

"Excuse me, Inspector," I said. "But if you don't care about my
statement, why are you here?"

The smile vanished, replaced by his scowl and squint. He really
needed to see an ophthalmologist.

"It's about your friend Bikas," he said.

I choked on my reply. "I don't know what you mean."

"Is that so? Didn't you meet him?"

"I . . . um, yes, I did," I said. How the hell did he know that?

"Tell me about this Bikas fellow. Where is he?"

"I don't know. I only spoke to him that one time."

He drained the last of his cup and repeated how good it was. "Do
you think your man might give me a repeat of my tea?" he asked.

I signaled to Vikky, who returned and did the *needful*.

"Just the one time?" asked the cop, returning to the subject of Bikas.
"Yes."

"Where was that?"

"Dharavi. He arranged a meeting there."

"Then you can describe him to me."

"No, I can't. He was wearing a motorcycle helmet. Then a mask
when I interviewed him."

Lokhande squinted at me. "A motorcycle helmet? Nobody wears
motorcycle helmets."

"This guy did. To cover his face."

He nodded as he gave my story some thought. Then he asked if I could show him where we'd met in the slum.

I shook my head. "Sorry. He made me wear goggles. Motorcycle goggles. He'd taped over the inside of the lenses so I couldn't see anything. Then he put me on the back of his bike and took me somewhere inside. I have no idea where."

Lokhande stared me down for a long moment.

"Goggles? Sounds fishy to me. You're not lying, are you?"

I'd told him the truth. Okay, maybe I'd withheld a key detail. The photographs. I wasn't a photographer, so I doubted he suspected there were pictures. I'd used a borrowed camera for the interview.

I figured he'd want to see what I'd written about the meeting. Or my notes of what Bikas had said. But he surprised me. He already knew.

"So, this Bikas fellow told you he killed a CID officer?"

CID was a branch of the state police, the Criminal Investigation Department. And that was exactly what Bikas had told me.

"Yes," said Lokhande, "we know he planted the bomb that killed that officer last year. These anti-government revolutionaries . . . Cowards. Sub-inspector Gokhale was a bright young man. A fine policeman."

I risked a question about jurisdiction, even as I feared it might rile him. "Isn't this a matter for the CID? Not the Bombay Police?"

He finished his second cup of tea and placed it on the corner of my desk. Then he moved his chair closer to me.

"I've made this case my business, Jacobs-*ji*, because I am Bala Gokhale's *mama*. His uncle. He wasn't just a fine officer. He was my sister's only son."

"I'm sorry for your loss, Inspector."

He wagged his head then rose from the chair. I stood. He looked up at me, again rocking on his feet.

"Your name also turned up in the agenda of a young associate of JP Narayan," he said. "You have all the wrong friends, Jacobs-*ji*."

I feared he might wrap his arm around my neck and shake me the way he'd done to Ramu the night he arrested him. But I was too tall. And maybe the *gora* thing. He turned on his heel to leave instead, then stopped just as soon, glaring at Onkar. Lokhande lit into him in Marathi. I can't say for sure what he was steamed about, but he dressed him down in his high-pitched voice. Onkar, for his part, nodded in the Indian fashion, his head wobbling from side to side, as the cop screamed at him.

Once he'd said his piece, Lokhande turned to address me one last time. "For your story on Bikas . . . Pity you didn't think to take a photographer with you."

And then he was gone.

"That was scary," whispered Janice in my ear. "You were great, Jacobs-*ji*."

I drew a deep breath. "Pathetic is more like it. What was he yelling at Onkar about anyway?"

"He wasn't happy about the American flag on his desk. Wanted to know where his Indian flag was."

Poor Onkar. I liked the guy. But after the encounter with the fire hydrant of a police inspector, he was changed. Less friendly, more inclined to distrust us. That day, without even reading what we'd written, he rejected everything we submitted to him.

· · ·

Unable to find a taxi in the rain, I made my way home on foot. My umbrella gave up the ghost when a particularly strong gust of wind broke its ribs. I lost hold of it, watched it pirouette away, and forged on, pelted mercilessly by the rain.

Passing the Machhimar Nagar village, I covered my nose to block the smell of fish. Depending on the wind, the air near Cuffe Parade was either tolerable or you needed a gas mask. I asked myself what the hell I was doing in India, drenched and unable to do my job thanks to the censor and my asshole of a boss. I was wasting my time.

Then there was Sushmita. I'd known her about a week, had pined after her, lusted after her, and gotten nowhere. She belonged to another man, anyway. A man much more interesting than I would ever be. And he was rich. Willy Smets could give her the best imported goods, diamond bangles, beautiful saris, a penthouse flat, and even a Mercedes 280SE.

And the cherry on top was that Inspector Lokhande might arrest me at any time.

When I finally turned onto the *marg*, I was waterlogged and feeling quite sorry for myself. Then I could have sworn I saw him. Ramu. He was hurrying along the other side of the road in the opposite direction. Like me, he had no umbrella. Lokhande had told me he was free to run errands for the cops at the station, but it was after nine. Where could he be rushing to?

I watched him from the shelter of the overhang of the Mafco stall, a tiny little shop that sold milk and eggs and bread on the corner opposite the President. He turned into the drive of the hotel, where I lost sight of him. There was no way he went inside, I thought. They would have given him the boot before he reached the door. That's how it was in India. A guy dressed like Ramu, with the hungry look in his eyes, would never be allowed in a high-end business hotel. Unless it was through the staff entrance. And maybe not even there.

As I gazed out from beneath the overhang, trying to decide whether the rain had let up any—it hadn't—I noticed a man on the opposite side of Cuffe Parade Road. He seemed to be dawdling. My radar was up. I thought he resembled a guy I'd seen when leaving the office a few minutes before. But, in fairness, he was dressed like any of a couple of million men in Bombay. Dark trousers, shirt a mite too large for his size, and *chappals* on his feet. Still, to be safe, I didn't want to lead him back to my place if he was following me.

I crossed the road and, pretending to head into the hotel, I slipped into a black-and-yellow taxi instead. Five minutes later, the driver dropped me at the Taj Mahal Hotel at Apollo Bunder. The majestic Gateway to India loomed large on the other side of the road, but the rain dampened my appetite for sightseeing. The doorman saluted me and remarked that I was soaking wet, as if perhaps I hadn't noticed.

A historic hotel, one of the finest in all of Asia, the Taj was built in 1903 by Jamshedji Tata, some say because he wasn't allowed in the Europeans-only hotels of Bombay. It was home to chic restaurants—the Apollo Room and Rendez Vous—as well as a shopping arcade offering jewelry, high-end clothing, rugs, and art to foreign tourists. There was also a swimming pool.

I took advantage of none of those amenities, choosing instead to sit in the lobby for ten minutes before heading back outside for another taxi. I told the driver to take me to Cuffe Parade. As we neared the President Hotel, I could see no man lurking in the shadows this time. The taxi turned into the Sagar Darshan compound and dropped me at the door.

. . .

The night liftman namaste'd me with all the enthusiasm of a slug. I returned the greeting and maintained silence during our ascent to the twelfth floor. Once home, I bathed and changed into my Indian cotton pajamas. I switched on the radio, which was playing Hindi film music, and lay down on the sofa. I was growing to like some of the songs. Kishore Kumar came on, singing one I'd heard several times. *"Pal Pal Dil Ke Pass Tum Rheti Ho"* was a gentle love song. I later asked Padma in the office—a Hindi film fanatic—what the title meant.

"It means you stay near my heart every moment," she told me. "From the film *Blackmail.*" She swooned over the film's star, Dharmendra. "The most handsome man in the world."

But in that moment, flat on my back, I closed my eyes and listened to his sweet voice. I thought of Sushmita. Maybe I could learn the words and sing it to her.

Stupid idea. I began to plan my next career move instead. Insurance? Teaching? Maybe write a book? None of it inspired me to get off my duff.

Then the bell rang.

I glanced at my watch, 9:47, and went to look through the hole to see who was calling so late. I opened up.

"Harlan?"

"Happy Fourth of July to you, Dan."

"How did you know where to find me?"

"Birgit said you were living over here."

"She did?" I asked. "Why would she do that?"

"Funny. How's about you invite me in and offer me a beverage? I treated you, after all."

I stood aside and let him in. "What's up, Russ?" I asked once I'd poured him a glass of the Chivas Willy—scratch that—Sushmita had sent me.

"You're not drinking?" he asked.

"Not tonight."

We sat opposite each other in front of the dormant television.

"Don't tell me there's no white meat on the menu over at the President," I said.

"Now, Dan, don't hold that against me. My generation is different from yours. We were brought up that way. I don't have anything against other races. But I'm new to this kind of thing."

"I don't feel comfortable with that kind of talk. And I don't want to hear it."

"Understood. We won't let a little thing like this ruin our friendship."

It wasn't a little thing to me. He tipped his glass in my direction to toast.

"This is good. Chivas? Where did you find this here?"

"It was a gift."

"From that girl? Sushmata?"

"Sushmita."

He savored another taste of scotch and glanced around the room. I wondered what he was thinking. I'd been mildly surprised—not to say disappointed—that a flat in a recent development was so ordinary by our spoiled American standards. I was growing used to my surroundings, however, and no longer minded—too much—the cold bucket baths and lack of air-conditioning. But if I'd reacted to the place that way, what must Russ Harlan have been thinking?

"How much are you paying for this apartment, anyway?" he asked.

"I don't know. The company takes care of it." That was a lie. Yes, the office was paying my rent, but I knew very well how much it cost.

"I suppose it's comfortable," he said. "What I don't get is how these places are so pricey. And how does that girl of yours afford a Mercedes? I'm sure they don't sell them for less over here than they do back home."

This guy had gone far past annoying. I was only putting up with it because he'd said I owed him. I didn't know how Sushmita afforded a Mercedes. Or did I? Was I as big a jerk as Harlan? I had to admit to myself that I'd assumed the car was Willy's, not hers. And the flat, too. He'd probably paid for the beautiful saris and the servants. Everything. Maybe I shouldn't judge Harlan as harshly as I did. The only difference between us two *gore* was that I wanted to sleep with her, and he didn't.

But actually, I wanted more than that from her. With her. She was clever, sexy, and . . . complicated. I'd always had a thing for complicated girls. Easy had never interested me.

"She's rich," I said. "She said so last night."

"Sure. But how did she get rich? If you ask me, she's got a sugar daddy bankrolling her."

"Russ, I have no fucking idea. She said she was rich. I thought you didn't like the dark ones anyway."

"Take it easy, friend. Forget I asked. Tell me how your work is going instead."

"Look, Russ," I said, faking a yawn. "I've got an early start tomorrow. Would you mind if we continued this another time?"

"You're working on a Saturday? That's downright un-American. But, come on, Dan. One more."

With his exit nowhere in sight, I decided to turn the tables and ask him some questions.

"So, Russ, are you from St. Louis originally?"

"Fayetteville, Arkansas," he said. "Home of the Razorbacks."

"What's that? A mascot?"

"University of Arkansas Razorbacks. Don't you follow college football?"

I told him no, even though I did. Hell, I'd played football at Yale. But I wasn't about to admit that. He'd talk my ear off for hours if he thought I was a fan.

"You look like maybe you played sports."

"Sorry," I said.

"Well, a handsome, athletic boy like you should sow some wild oats. Go find yourself a girl."

"Yeah, the ladies aren't exactly breaking down the door to have their way with me."

"Maybe that's for the best. You don't want any little Dannys running around out there." He sipped his drink. "Leastwise not any brown ones."

He apologized at least ten times on his way to the door after I told him to get the fuck out of my flat. Then he got all quiet and contrite.

"Truly, I'm sorry," he said. "I shouldn't have said that. I'll go, Dan, but let's not leave it on an ugly note."

"Russ . . . If you could stop being an asshole for ten minutes, maybe we could be friendly. But, frankly, I doubt it."

"Fair enough. I rub people the wrong way. Folks tell me I make a good first impression and a horrible second."

I would have argued his first impression wasn't all that great either. But, upon consideration, I had to admit it had been stellar compared with what I'd witnessed since. Succumbing to his seemingly sincere pleas, I agreed to give him a fourth chance. At the door he wished me good night, shaking my hand as if priming a pump. He called the lift and, as he waited, he turned to ask me one last question.

"That pretty girl," he said. "Sushmilla. She's your girlfriend? Good for you. She's a keeper."

I sighed. "Sushmita. And I told you already she's not my girlfriend."

He looked surprised. "Sorry. So she has a boyfriend?"

I closed my door and bolted the lock. What an asshole.

CHAPTER ELEVEN

SATURDAY, JULY 5, 1975, 5:14 A.M.

Something about Harlan's stubborn desire to insult, aggravate, and pry got my goat. He'd ingratiate himself through apologies and humility, only to outdo himself with his next bigoted salvo or intrusive question. I hated the guy. What I couldn't shake was the suspicion he was doing it on purpose.

I ran five miles, stewing about Harlan the whole time. If nothing else, I was working my way into top shape. Back at Sagar Darshan, I took my cold bucket bath and got ready for the office. Nothing to eat in the flat, so I was looking forward to one or two of Vikky's sweet, milky teas. I was a twenty-six-year-old man who couldn't seem to feed himself. That had to change or I'd starve. I needed to find a new servant and soon.

"Indians can either be the obstacles to your happiness or the means to achieve it."

· · ·

SATURDAY, JULY 5, 1975, 10:47 A.M.

The office was mostly empty; it was just Vikky, Onkar, Janice, the guard, and me. By noon, I'd finished a couple of stories that Onkar sliced up like Zorro on a rampage. He offered a sheepish look of apology. I filed the censored stories with New York anyway, thinking there goes my Pulitzer. Maybe I should have started on something new, but I wasn't feeling it. And Onkar would have blocked it anyway. It was Saturday afternoon. For me, almost Sunday—my day off—and I would have killed to get an early start.

I hadn't seen or heard from Sushmita since early Thursday morning after Ash Pethe's dinner party. Was she free? And where was Willy? If he was back from Poona, that was the end of that. Me alone in my flat, with no food in the house. There was always the President Hotel across the road. Plenty to eat and drink there. But also Russ Harlan.

I wandered over to Janice's desk. "Hello, Miss Spenser. What are you doing here on a Saturday? I thought you mirrored Frank's hours."

She frowned. "Normally, yes, Mr. Jacobs. But he asked me to come in to straighten out his expenses. Five months' worth. I'm working with a jigsaw puzzle here." She indicated the scattered receipts on her desk.

"Sorry," I said. "Can I help?"

She flashed one of those skeptical glances my way. "Nothing you can do. And you didn't mean it besides."

She sorted a few more receipts then let out a little gasp. "Oh, my . . . ointment." She leaned toward me to speak in a conspiratorial whisper. "Mr. Muller says the air here irritates his skin, so he claims this cream as a business expense. But I happen to know it's some snake oil cure for baldness."

"It's not working," I said.

I returned to my desk and flipped through my predecessor's Rolodex, weeding out old contacts. Then I perused his notebook, searching for references to Bikas. I could find no other mentions of him. As Onkar settled in to enjoy his tiffin lunch, I sent a brief note to my friend Gary in the New York office. Could he find Eric Nielsen and ask for any information he might have about Bikas?

Janice appeared above me at the telex.

"Okay, I know you're new here and probably don't have much of a social life yet. Don't make me regret this. Would you like to join me and my gentleman friend for dinner at Bombay Gym tonight?"

. . .

SATURDAY, JULY 5, 1975, 7:01 P.M.

Sometimes life smiles on you. Or at least that's the conclusion we draw when a wish comes true. Never mind if it's for the best. But I was feeling lucky when Sandip rang my bell and delivered an answer to the note I'd sent up to Sushmita, inviting her—if Willy was still out of station—to join me for dinner at Bombay Gymkhana.

"Really? Bombay Gym?" she wrote. "With those snobs? The food won't win any awards, but all right. Only because it's you who's asking."

I took a bucket bath—seated on the little wooden stool—then I shaved and cooled myself under the ceiling fan until I was actually dry. There would be no repeat of the sweat fest of Wednesday evening, when she'd laid her head on my shoulder, only to have her cheek stick to my shirt when she tried to lift it again.

Relaxing under the fan in the drawing room, I sipped ice water as I waited for the appointed hour. I thought back to the rest of her note. She'd written that I'd saved her life by asking her to dinner. Willy was God knows where, in Poona or Chandigarh or Kathmandu, and she was about to slit her wrists when my invitation arrived. I was happy to be her savior, even if it meant treading on Willy's territory without first asking permission. Surely he wouldn't object to my taking care of his precious Mita in his absence. I could be trusted, after all, couldn't I?

Sure. As long as Sushmita said no.

Look, I told myself, I had no intention of betraying my friend with his girl. But then, how well did I know him? And even if I allowed myself wild fantasies of what might happen with Sushmita, I certainly didn't have the guts to act on my baser instincts. It was a game. Get as close as I dared to crossing the very desirable point of no return, then step back with honor intact. The only problem was determining where the point of no return began and where honor ended.

· · ·

Sushmita greeted me in a form-fitting white bell-bottomed jumpsuit that wiped out any illusions I may have entertained that I was worthy of Willy's trust. My will and my flesh were weak, and the only thing standing between my resolve and betrayal was a crook of Sushmita's finger.

"What's wrong?" she asked. "Don't you like it?"

I wanted to tell her no. But, God, she was gorgeous.

"You look nice," I answered instead.

"*Nice*? Clearly, I overestimated my charms. I was hoping you'd swallow your tongue. Never mind, you dull man. Let's go. *Chalo*."

· · ·

Bombay Gymkhana recalled the grandeur of the Raj. Once a restricted haven for the British, it was now an exclusive sporting club for well-heeled Indians who'd appropriated its elitism and snobbery for themselves after Independence in 1947. The waiting list for membership was said to be decades long. A beautiful property near the Azad Maidan, Bombay Gym offered cricket and rugby pitches, badminton and tennis courts, game rooms and dining halls. Once inside, you entered a world that, though faded, provided glimpses of a glorious and enduring history.

A long veranda, bordering the playing fields, led members and guests to the different dining halls, lounges, and changing rooms. Small tables and chairs lined the way, as well as the occasional Bombay *fornicator*, a low-slung seat so named for the extendable armrests that provided support for one's legs while one . . . well . . . reclined.

The host at the entrance nearly choked at Sushmita's outfit. He informed us there was a dress code. Sushmita refused to hear it, and when I mentioned we were guests of Shirish's, he reluctantly acquiesced and let us in. I noted the turned heads and the raised eyebrows as we made our way past Bombay's elite. I figured their disapproval was one part foreigner-with-an-Indian-girl, one part Sushmita's tight Western outfit. We weren't in New York or London, after all.

I spotted Janice at a table about twenty yards ahead. She was looking like a proper *memsahib* in an elegant light-blue sari. At her side sat a silver-haired gentleman in a white-collared shirt and tan slacks. He was holding an English cigarette in one hand and a tumbler of something delicious in the other. He rose as Sushmita and I approached.

Janice beamed at me. Had I not known better, I would have sworn she was a matron of high society, not a harassed, underappreciated secretary. She was lovely.

She extended a hand from her seated position and greeted Sushmita warmly. Then she turned to me. "I thought you were lying about this young lady, Dan. Bravo to you."

A stocky man of sixty or sixty-five, Shirish was charming and strikingly handsome, with a full head of silver hair slicked back with a sweet-smelling pomade.

We enjoyed our drinks as the rain poured down onto the grass not ten feet from our table. Well-dressed folks strolled by and greeted

Shirish and Janice and—it seemed to me—turned up their noses at Sushmita. We chatted about the weather, the traffic, and the best Hindi films of the year. Janice said *Deewaar—The Wall*—was her favorite so far.

"I'm in love with Amitabh Bachchan," cooed Sushmita. "I've got a secret fantasy that I'll marry him one day."

"He's already married," said Janice. "What will you do about Jaya?"

I assumed Jaya was Bachchan's wife. Sushmita said she'd give it some thought. Janice wanted to know more, and the two huddled for a few minutes in discussion. Shirish agreed *Deewaar* was an important film. I had nothing to add to the conversation and sipped my Red Label instead. The bottle had come from Shirish's private stash, stored in a locker in the bar where he kept his preferred brands.

Sushmita and Shirish were soon engaged in intense consultation over some tax issue or other. I knew not to broach the topic of the Emergency. Not with someone I'd just met. Not in public. Perhaps noticing how quiet I'd been, Janice took pity on me, scooting her chair closer to mine and leaning in to speak.

"She's lovely, Danny. Why didn't you tell me you had a girl?"

"She's not my girl," I said. "She's . . . with a friend of mine."

"All's fair . . ."

I brushed off her suggestion. What I didn't say was that I was thinking the same thing.

We ate in the main dining room on the ground floor. The fare was eclectic, certainly not haute cuisine, but I'd been subsisting on crumbs for a couple of days, so I dug in. First there was chili cheese toast, a kind of spicy toasted-cheese sandwich. That was good. Next came some soupy lasagna that tasted nothing like any lasagna I'd ever eaten. But it wasn't bad. Then I had some Indian veg dishes that, though a little bland, filled me up. I topped it off with vanilla ice cream for dessert.

Janice was right at home in India. She knew her way around, spoke a good deal of the language, and had found herself a well-connected gentleman friend. Plus she was conversant about Hindi films and local politics. I, on the other hand, was the ugly American, expecting everyone to adapt to my needs. Well, not exactly, but I hadn't really made an effort to embrace the Indians yet. If you didn't count Sushmita. And maybe a Hindi film song or two on the radio.

An hour and a half later, we kissed Janice goodbye and thanked our host, Shirish, who'd signed the meal and drinks to his account. Janice squeezed my hand and whispered that I should make sure to win that wonderful girl. In the foyer, I borrowed an umbrella and told Sushmita I'd get the car while she waited inside, safe from the rain. I slipped the detached gearshift back into place and started the car. I had no intention of driving her Mercedes back to Cuffe Parade, even if it wasn't far, but I could handle the right-hand drive long enough to fetch her at the door of Bombay Gym.

I pulled the car around and jumped out, umbrella at the ready, and scanned the porch for her. Where was she? I dashed through the rain, into the foyer, but still didn't see her. The disapproving doorman directed me back inside the club. He seemed eager to see Sushmita and her jumpsuit leave the premises. There, about thirty feet away, I saw her. She was engaged in conversation with none other than Russ Harlan. What the hell? Was this guy following me?

"What did he want?" I asked as she shifted into gear and drove off.

"Who?"

I could barely conceal my annoyance. "Russ Harlan."

"That bore? He tapped me on the shoulder while I was waiting for you."

"What did he say?"

"Just that since he and I were friends now, maybe we should get together with Willy sometime."

"He mentioned Willy? By name?"

She glanced at me as she drove. "No. He called him my boyfriend. I didn't get the impression he was referring to you, my darling. But maybe he was."

I coughed. "You should steer clear of him."

We pulled to a stop at Flora Fountain and waited for the light to change. "No issues," she said. "I told him I was going out of station."

Had she actually called me *darling*?

"I'm not tired," she told me as she set the parking break and removed the gearshift. "Take me to the permit room at the President."

I consulted my watch. It was after midnight. "It's closed by now." I paused, then figured why not. I called her "Sush."

She didn't seem to notice. Instead, she informed me I wasn't going to abandon her so early when she had no other options.

"I have some *chakli* upstairs," I said.

"*Chakli*? Oh my. However do the girls resist you?"

CHAPTER TWELVE

"Do you have some music?" she asked hopefully. I shook my head. "Never mind. Any juice?"

"Afraid not." I made a mental note to get some the next day.

"How about AC? Can we at least be cool?"

I felt like a pauper. I could offer nothing that she wanted.

"I'm sorry," I said. "Maybe you'll want to call it a night."

"What rubbish. It's early, Danny darling. Come on. I've got food, wine, whisky, and AC upstairs."

I wasn't sure how wise it was to take the lift up to the penthouse. The staff probably loved to gossip about the residents, especially the Indian woman living with a *gora*. And I was a *gora*, too. Just not hers. But Sushmita was indifferent to the risks. In fact, she didn't even acknowledge the liftman. As if he didn't exist.

On the fifteenth floor, she dug into her bag and retrieved the latchkey. But before she could insert it into the lock, the door swung open.

"Danny Boy!" Jesus Christ, it was Willy. He was dressed in his Indian pajama. "I was hoping I'd be awake when you returned. Sandip said you went to Bombay Gym. I thought you hated that place, Mita."

"I do," she answered, kissing him on the cheek. "But Danny was lonely, so I accepted his pitiful invitation."

She was a cool one. Me? I was sweating under a crumbling façade of smiles. I tried to bid them good night and retreat to my flat before Willy could decide he suspected something.

"Going to bed?" he asked. "Nonsense. Come in, Danny Boy, and have a drink with me. I've been on the road, driving in this infernal rain for six hours. I need some company."

"Come, Danny," said Sushmita. "I told you Willy would want a drink with you. Don't disappoint him."

"Six hours in the car?" I asked, once we were seated in the drawing room. Sushmita had disappeared down the corridor. "Where were you coming from?"

"Poona," he said, reaching for the decanter of whisky to his right. He poured us each a healthy two fingers and handed me my glass. "Normally it's four or five hours, but there were accidents and heavy rain."

"What were you doing in Poona?"

"I have business there."

"You know, I've never asked you what you do."

"Import-export. Dull stuff. The roads from Poona, on the other hand, are quite exciting indeed. One risks one's life at least twenty times on the journey. It's a terrifying experience if you don't train your driver to take care. The roads in the flats are filled with holes and clogged with traffic. But those are minor annoyances. It's when you climb the *ghats*."

"*Ghats?*"

"The mountains that rise up from the plains to the plateau. Like steps. The road switches back and forth, and there are only two lanes. Very tight. That doesn't stop the lorries from overtaking with little or no room. And the margin for error is small. I've seen cars and buses tumble over the edge to their doom."

"That sounds terrifying."

He smiled and nodded, baring his long teeth. Then he raised his glass to cheer me. "A good driver will turn back into his lane at the last second."

"And you drive yourself?"

"Of course not. I can't get used to driving on the left side. Better to have an Indian driver in any case, especially if you have an accident. A Westerner will be taken for everything he's got on him."

Sushmita returned, appearing above us in a sheer pajama. It was hot, of course, but did I really need to contemplate her curves and skin in such proximity? With Willy standing by to witness and dissect every one of my reactions?

"What may I pour for you, my darling?" he asked Sushmita. "Fresh lime soda?"

Sushmita plopped down next to me on the sofa and fanned herself with her hand. She was a mere twelve inches away. I couldn't help but breathe in her scent.

"I'd like some . . . absinthe," she said at length.

Willy laughed. "Not permitted, my love. And we haven't any besides."

She pouted.

"How was your evening with Mita?" Willy asked me. "Not too much trouble?"

"Trouble? Not at all," I said. "We met a colleague of mine and her friend at the gymkhana."

"She didn't bore you?"

"I beg your pardon. Who?"

"Mita," he said, as if it weren't obvious.

"Just the opposite. She was charming as always. Made a wonderful impression on my colleague."

"Good. Drink up, Danny Boy," he said. "It's still early."

I thanked him, but said it was past my bedtime. Of course I wanted to stay, but Sushmita's nearness was driving me mad.

"I'm sorry you must go," said Willy. "We should see each other more often. Perhaps next Saturday. I'm leaving again tomorrow, but I'll be back Thursday or Friday."

I stood and smoothed my pants and shirt. "That sounds great. Thank you for the drink."

Willy yawned, then wandered off into the flat. Sushmita saw me to the door. Her eyes were more intense than I'd ever seen them. Clearly, I hadn't misunderstood what had been in the offing when I accepted her invitation to come up to the penthouse.

"We must be more careful," she whispered.

"When will I see you again?"

"Danny, darling. Go to bed."

She looked over her shoulder, perhaps for Willy or Sandip. Then, sure of our safety, she put her right palm on my heart and pushed me gently away. "Go to bed, Danny," she repeated. "He's leaving tomorrow."

CHAPTER THIRTEEN

After a grueling, hot five miles, I bathed and lay down in my bed, wondering if Willy had left yet. My stomach was rumbling, but there was nothing to eat in the flat, so I resigned myself to wait for Sushmita to reach out to me. Finally, around five, after checking the door for messages, I let myself out and crossed the road to the President. The roast chicken was tasty.

"Hello, friend." It was Harlan. He took a seat opposite me. "All alone? Where's your girl, Sassmulla?"

"Leave me alone," I said, unwilling to play his games.

"Sorry," he said, making himself at home. "But you mustn't fret about her. You're a young man. There'll be others."

"What the hell are you talking about?"

"She's taken, isn't she? Move on. Plenty of other fish in the sea."

"Russ, please. I'm fine. Just hungry."

Harlan got all serious and leaned in closer to talk. He folded his hands and drew a breath. "I worry about you, Dan."

"Worry about me? Why?"

"Is that girl worth it?"

I glared at him, and he held up his hands in defense.

"I get it, she's real pretty. But that's not everything. Take Barb, my wife. Not a beauty. No one ever accused her of that. But she's a good gal. I met her at a church social when I was seventeen. You should look for a girl like that."

"Russ, now is not the time to convert me."

He reached across the table, patted me on the shoulder, and said he understood. For the next two minutes he held his tongue.

"Can I ask you something?" he said finally. He didn't wait for my answer. "If she's not your girl, why do you torture yourself so by hanging around her? I mean, she's got a boyfriend, doesn't she?"

"You wouldn't understand. You fell in love with Barb at a church social. I've never been to church. To temple a few times."

He made a sour face, probably wondering which was worse, the fact that I was a heathen or a Jew. He swallowed the foul taste my words had caused him, and I was happy with my small victory.

He tacked in another direction. "You know, you and I come from different worlds, Dan. But where it counts, we're the same."

"Really? You voted for Nixon—twice, no three times—and I voted for McGovern. My parents voted for Humphrey, Johnson, Kennedy, Stevenson—twice—Truman, and Roosevelt before that. I'd say we're quite different."

Harlan chuckled. "My folks threw a party when Roosevelt died. So don't you think it's remarkable that we're sitting here together in this back-of-beyond, godforsaken country, visiting so amiably?"

Surely he couldn't fail to notice the disbelief on my face. He lit a cigarette.

"That's why I worry about you, Dan. That German girl, Birgit. Now there's a filly worth your wild oats."

"Birgit? She's not even in the country. And we're just friends."

"Well, if I were a young man and hadn't met Barb, that cute German girl—Christian, too, mind you—she'd be on my radar."

I sighed. "The Christian thing isn't necessarily a plus in her column for me."

He thought it over for a bit. Then he suggested I might want to reconsider that, as well.

"So if Sushmita were a Christian," I said, "you wouldn't object? They have those here, you know. Indian Christians."

He shook his head. "I'm afraid I couldn't condone it. Nothing against her kind. There's six hundred million of them, after all. But I believe God intended for the races to remain separate."

"Russ," I said, blinking as slowly as I could manage. "You've somehow worn me down. Yesterday, I would've thrown my plate in your face and stormed off. I hate everything you say. But right now, I just want to pick at this food."

He smiled, then asked if Sushmita wasn't Christian, what about her boyfriend? Was he a Hindu or a Muslim?

· · ·

I dashed back across the *marg* around seven, skipping over the puddles and through the rain. Once again, I marveled that the road didn't have a name. At least not that anyone knew. I'd asked plenty of times. It was often that way in India, at least for smaller streets. People navigated using landmarks instead of addresses.

I figured I'd read a book or listen to the radio until Sushmita contacted me. But my exciting plans for the evening were ruined when I found Inspector Lokhande waiting for me at Sagar Darshan. Sitting in the chair usually occupied by the liftman, he was frowning straight ahead at the wall.

He rose to meet me. "I've been waiting for you, Dan," he called, his strangled, high-pitched voice sounding all the more menacing due to his use of my first name. He'd never called me that before.

I approached, glancing to the corners and the side entrance, look-ing for other policemen. He was alone. And he seemed different that night. Friendly.

"Hello, Inspector," I said. "How can I help you?"

He fixed me with his stare for a brief moment, then smiled, baring the white teeth behind his bristly mustache. "I think you might want to offer me a tipple," he said.

"A *tipple*? Really?" I'd never heard that word actually spoken. "Sure. Why don't you come up and have a . . . tipple . . . with me?"

· · ·

Lokhande shuffled into my flat and helped himself to a seat before the television. I broke out the Chivas Sushmita had sent and asked him if whisky was all right. He nodded and told me he took it neat.

"Fine stuff," he said once he'd taken a sip.

We sat there in silence for a minute or so. He appeared perfectly at ease as he swirled the whisky in his glass and examined the color and legs like a connoisseur.

"Why do you add ice to your drink?" he asked, gazing at his scotch. "You'll ruin it."

"Isn't it too strong neat?"

He frowned. "The sting tells you you're alive. Do you drink like a woman?"

Lokhande took a swig and grinned his self-satisfied smile. He held the power in our relationship, after all, whether I was serving the booze or not. He might just as easily have commandeered my stash for himself and arrested me for smuggling. Still, I felt we were nearing some kind of equilibrium. I could stand my ground with him.

"I don't have anything to offer you to eat," I said. "Nothing but some *chakli*."

"*Chakli*? I love *chakli*."

I went to the kitchen, dumped what was left in the bag into a bowl, and served it up to the cop. He broke off a piece of one of the rounds with his right hand and chomped away, orange crumbs collecting in his mustache as he did.

"A little stale," he said. "I'll tell you where to get the best *chakli* in Colaba Causeway."

Then he waggled his glass to indicate he was ready for a refill.

"How can I help you, Inspector?" I asked once I'd poured him another.

"You don't think I might make a social call? You and I are getting to be old friends, Dan."

"You must want something besides a drink and Ramu's stale *chakli*."

"*Kya*? This is Ramu's *chakli*?"

I nodded.

"You serve me your servant's food? Are you mad?"

He would have spat out the snack if he hadn't already chewed and swallowed it. Instead, he went to the kitchen and rinsed his mouth out with water. Once he'd returned, he lectured me on serving guests the food servants ate. It wasn't hygienic, he said. After several minutes and a couple of swigs of whisky to kill the germs, he regained his calm.

"Speaking of Ramu," I said, "I could have sworn I saw him the other night. Near the President Hotel."

"Could be. He comes and goes."

"So when can he come back to work for me?"

"*Araamse*," he said, then translated. "Not so fast. He's still of use to us. Remarkable fellow, that Ramu. Smart, nice-looking, and fair. You don't see that often in a servant."

"But you still won't eat his food."

He softened a bit. "You're new here, Dan. You don't understand how things work. The servants have their place for a reason. And we don't mix things up by sharing food and friendly chats with them."

I let his comment slide, then noted that I could offer him more than stale snacks if I had Ramu back. He scowled and said he'd see.

"Where did you get this whisky?" he asked, changing course. "I don't see any tax strip on the bottle. You're not buying from smugglers, are you?"

"Me? Smugglers? I wouldn't know where to find them. This was a gift from a friend."

He finished the last of his drink, wiped his mouth and mustache with his fingers, and stood to leave. "Thanks for the whisky, Dan. I'll send the *bhoot* back to you tomorrow. If you're feeling grateful, a bottle of that imported booze would be nice."

I saw him to the door, where he paused and asked me if I'd managed to recall anything else about Bikas the bomber. I offered a helpless shrug as an answer. Then I asked him how he'd found out about my meeting with Bikas in the first place.

"I had a nice talk with a fellow named Gopal at the university," he said. "He was very helpful."

He pulled his cap on, then opened the door to leave. Sushmita was just exiting the lift. Shit.

CHAPTER FOURTEEN

"Why do you have policemen visiting you?" asked Sushmita once we were safely alone inside my flat.

"He's been harassing me about that bomber story. This cop wants to find him. But now he's taken to making social calls."

"You're a man of mystery, Danny," she said.

"Has he . . . Has Willy left?"

"Yes, several hours ago."

"He's going back to Poona, then?"

"I have no idea. He doesn't tell me about his business."

"If he left hours ago, why didn't you come see me earlier?"

She snorted a short laugh. "What rubbish, Danny. Don't you think I have things to do?"

"Of course. But I thought after last night . . ."

"You thought what?"

"Nothing."

I tried to let it go, but I was mixed up. It seemed she'd been inviting me up to the penthouse for something more than a drink on the sofa. But she'd reacted so coolly to Willy's surprise return. Maybe I was seeing interest where there was none.

She wanted to sit, so we watched the rain through the veranda windows. A terrific storm was rolling in, with great booming claps of thunder and bolts of lightning overhead. The glass shook and the lights dimmed a few times before Sushmita suggested we switch them off altogether.

"It's more dramatic this way," she said, hooking her right arm around my elbow and drawing me closer. "I've always loved the rain. Thunderstorms, especially. They're terribly romantic."

She couldn't possibly see my expression in the dark, unless she happened to glance my way as a streak of lightning flashed across the sky. But I must have looked like Hamlet, hesitant and indecisive. Would she find that endearing, sexy, or lame? I was overthinking everything. She was clutching me tight, pressing herself against me, talking of romance and rainstorms.

I closed my eyes and breathed in her scent. Sandalwood. So close and enticing in the darkness. I needed to do something. Take charge of the situation. Kiss her. Lift her in my arms and carry her to the bedroom, where I'd lay her gently on the sheets and ...

Jesus, listen to me. I wasn't Hamlet or Casanova. I was Walter Mitty.

"Look," she said, interrupting my fantasies of seduction. She released my arm, pushed off the sofa, and stepped onto the veranda. "The Parsees across the way. Their grandson is finally walking."

Beyond our compound, the neighboring building presented fifteen floors of viewing pleasure when there was nothing to watch on television. I joined Sushmita—and my missed chance—at the window. She pointed to a flat a floor or two below mine. I could see an elderly man in white pajamas hovering over a toddler, ready to catch him if he stumbled. The child took palsied steps toward an old woman a few feet away. Sushmita cheered him on as he neared his grandmother's outstretched arms. Then he fell into her warm hug. They looked so happy, the three of them. Sushmita, too, was overjoyed. Me? I was pissed off. Stymied by a baby and his grandparents a hundred feet away.

"Isn't he adorable?" she asked. "Wouldn't you love to have one of those?"

"Of course," I lied. The last thing I wanted at twenty-six was a little crumb-cruncher.

Another bolt of lightning flashed, illuminating the thick clouds and loosing a window-rattling boom. Sushmita practically leapt into my arms, grabbing me around the waist. This time I was determined not to miss my chance.

"Let's go into the other room," I whispered in her ear.

She continued to hold me tight and seemed to give a curt nod. Was that her way of saying yes? Maybe I hadn't been clear enough. What the hell did I mean by "the other room"?

She released me from her embrace and stared into my eyes. "No, Danny. Let's go up to the penthouse instead."

More lightning lit up the night and the side of her face. My patience wouldn't last long enough to climb three flights of stairs, and forget about waiting for the lift. That sometimes took three or four minutes to arrive.

"We don't need to go to Willy's flat. We can stay here," I said.

She pinched her lips together and drew a sharp breath through her nose. "Why do you say *Willy's* flat?"

I didn't understand. "It's his place, isn't it?"

"Don't you think it might belong to both of us? Or to me?"

"I'm sorry," I said. "Is . . . is it yours?"

She stepped away from the window and me. "*Now* you think to ask? A moment ago, you were happy to assume the worst about me."

"No, really. I apologize. Please, don't be angry."

"It's none of your business anyway," she said, heading for the door.

"Sush, wait. Where are you going?"

"To *Willy's* flat!"

. . .

I wondered how I'd managed it. How had I blown a sure thing? I thought about going after her, begging her to calm down and listen to my apology, but I sensed that would make matters worse. Sometimes you have to accept you've screwed up and leave it. Better to let the anger cool and try again another day.

I dragged myself into the "other room," the bedroom, and tore off my clothes. Lying flat on my back, I gazed up at the clicking ceiling fan and cursed out loud. It wasn't only that I hadn't gotten laid. My frustration ran much deeper than that. I couldn't stop thinking of her. I was fucking crazy about her.

. . .

MONDAY, JULY 7, 1975, 10:57 A.M.

With Vikky's tea for my breakfast, I perused the news coming off the wire. In Pakistan, more than fifty people had been killed when their bus tumbled down a ravine. I couldn't imagine the terror, given my acrophobia.

I thought I might propose a story on bus safety to Frank. Willy had told me trucks and buses sometimes took the hairpin turns in the Western *Ghats* too quickly and ended up plunging down the mountain. Maybe Frank would spring for the cost of a government tourist vehicle to take me there.

Thinking of Willy reminded me of Sushmita and the crappy end to our evening. Served me right, I supposed, for trying to steal a friend's girl. And yet I wondered if I was in love with her. Obsessed, for sure. Love was too soon, wasn't it? Hell, no. I'd fallen in love faster than that plenty of times.

She was wittier and more beguiling than any woman I'd ever met. Our ages were well suited and, while I was aware of the race difference, it didn't matter to me. Nothing prevented us from falling in love and making a go of things. Nothing at all. If you didn't count Willy Smets. And I was counting him.

My fear of heights convinced me to chuck the idea about bus safety, and I went to work on the latest Emergency news. Not sure it would pass the censor, I nevertheless wrote an article profiling the most prominent figures who'd been arrested, including JP Narayan, Morarji Desai, and Raj Narain, the guy who'd lit the fuse leading to the Emergency in the first place. He'd opposed Mrs. Gandhi for her seat in parliament in '71 and lost by a mile. But he'd sued over her election victory, charging irregularities and abuses—minor though they were—of governmental power. When he won the case, it forced the PM's hand. And now Raj Narain and the opposition were in the shit, along with Indian democracy.

After he'd waved a reproachful finger at me, Onkar tore up my story and deposited it in the dustbin.

Janice joined me for our afternoon tea. She said I'd received a strange phone call when I was out to lunch. Someone named Bikas wanted to talk to me urgently.

"Did he say what about?" I asked.

"No. Just that he'd call again."

•   •   •

MONDAY, JULY 7, 1975, 8:25 P.M.

It took a couple of beats before I realized the smell of food cooking was coming not through the open window, but from my own flat. I noticed a pair of *chappals* against the wall in the entryway, and went to investigate. Ramu was in the kitchen, preparing dinner in his bare feet. He'd also had the foresight to pour me a glass of whisky, which he'd covered with a small saucer to keep dust and flying bugs away. He shooed me back into the drawing room.

"Come, sir. *Aapka* drink. *Khana* soon."

"But how?" I asked. "How did you get in here?"

"Inspector, sir. Take your drink," he repeated.

Khana, I assumed, was dinner. It smelled delicious, and I was starving. Somehow, Lokhande had opened my door and let Ramu in. He must have given him money to buy food, too, as I doubted Ramu had two *paise* to rub together.

I settled on the sofa and watched as Ramu placed my whisky before me. He mimed a question to ask how much ice I wanted. I held up two fingers, and he fulfilled the request.

"Now sit," he said. "Take rest. *Khana, bis minnit*," and he showed ten fingers twice. Twenty minutes.

I resolved to put myself in his capable hands and enjoy the drink he'd poured me. If I'd been able to listen to some Oscar Peterson— maybe with some air-conditioning—the tableau would have been perfect. I tried to avoid thinking of Sushmita, three floors above, probably still stewing at me for my remarks about her flat. What a jerk I'd been. And yet, I can't deny, I still wondered whose place it was. She hadn't exactly cleared up the mystery. And the residents' board in the lobby listed Willy Smets, not Sushmita Deshpande, as the owner.

Twenty minutes later, more or less, Ramu delivered on his promise of *khana*. He brought out the dishes one after the other and placed them on the Formica dining table. There was *pulao*—rice and peas— *dal*, *chole*, and *bhindi*—okra—and a salad of onion, tomato, and cucumber. He laid out a variety of *pickle*, a sort of spicy relish. As I dug in, the *bhoot* reappeared with, of all things, a bottle of wine. Who knew if it was any good, given the heat and the wretched storage conditions? I gave it a try and was not disappointed. Not the best thing that had ever passed my lips, but it tasted like wine.

"Tell me, Ramu," I said, as he cleared the dishes onto a platter. "Where did you get all this food and wine?"

He didn't seem to understand, claiming—I believe—that it had come from the kitchen. He'd cooked it.

"No, I mean the money. *Paise*. Where did you get the money to buy everything? Surely I owe you."

"Money?" he asked. "Sir has gave. No issues."

Sir was Lokhande, I figured, and let it drop. I'd pay back the cop the next time I saw him. He'd named his price, after all. A bottle of Chivas Regal.

I tried to relax on one of the sofas. But, feeling no small measure of discomfort, I realized the scene reminded me of the first words Willy Smets had said to me. *Indians could be the means to my happiness or the obstacle to it.* Despite the inconvenience this memory caused me, I had to admit he was right. It was powerfully tempting to let someone take care of you, even when it stank of exploitation. At the same time, I felt like a shit. There I was, enjoying the fruits of low-cost labor, all the while indifferent to the challenges Ramu might have been facing. Far from his family and friends, he was from some forsaken corner in the North of India, earning a pittance from a *gora* who barely appreciated him. Surely he was sending his entire salary back to his family. I was ashamed to think I'd been seduced. I was a convert. A believer in what Willy had told me. That the hardships of the Indian lower classes, to me, amounted to little more than a convenience. A means to achieve my own happiness.

CHAPTER FIFTEEN

Ramu tapped on my bedroom door and swept inside. I'd already done my run and had my bath. He opened the curtains and placed a tray with tea and biscuits on the table beside my bed.

"Newspapers, sir?" he asked.

I flipped through the *Times of India* as I sipped my tea, a *masala* I could only assume was Ramu's own concoction. It was damn good. Not as sweet as Vikky's at the office. Just right. Fragrant and fulfilling, without the risk of diabetes.

. . .

A telex from New York was waiting for me in the office. "Unable to locate Nielsen. No trace of him in Seattle. Maybe he went elsewhere. Gary."

I thumbed through the latest news coming over the wire. For Christ's sake, Ruffian had to be destroyed after breaking down in her match race with Foolish Pleasure. What a tragedy. A waste of a beautiful animal.

Ford announced he was going to run in '76. No surprises there. But who would the Democrats put up against him? Probably Birch Bayh or Mo Udall, I figured. In India, the news was drying up. I was struggling to find an angle to pursue or a lead that needed a follow-up.

Frank told me I'd better get on my horse or he'd send me back home. Joey Rahman had plenty of good ideas, he said.

I decided to write a piece on the film industry under the Emergency. That would keep me busy, and I might get to meet some beautiful actresses. Despite my obsession with Sushmita, I had to admit it didn't seem to have a future. I sketched out a plan of action and showed it to Frank. He liked the idea. That would give me at least another week before he'd threaten to send me home again.

•   •   •

TUESDAY, JULY 8, 1975, 6:43 P.M.

Armed with some film magazines I'd bought at the newsstand outside the office, I headed home early to relax and do some research. Ramu greeted me at the door again, shoeless as was his custom, practically bumping into me with my scotch on a salver. I thanked him, but said I'd like to have a bath and change my clothes before anything else.

I emerged twenty minutes later, refreshed and comfortable in the white pajamas I'd bought when I'd first arrived. I felt like one of the Beatles in my Indian clothes. Or maybe like the Parsee grandfather across the way. I pushed that thought out of my mind as quickly as I could. It only reminded me of the Sushmita disaster.

Settled on the sofa, I opened up the first magazine, *Cine Blitz*. There, on the cover, was Amitabh Bachchan, the actor Sushmita had gushed about the night at Bombay Gym. He was good-looking, and that made me jealous. I read up on him and his upcoming film, *Sholay*, due out in August, mostly because I wanted to impress Sushmita if I ever got the chance to speak to her again. That's when I noticed that Dharmendra, the handsome actor Padma had told me about, was also in the film.

Ramu appeared above me with the whisky and ice. He needed no coaching this time, dispensing the desired number of ice cubes and amount of scotch. I thanked him, and he smiled brightly at me.

"What is it?" I asked.

"Amitabh Bachchan, sir," he said, pointing to the magazine cover and wagging his head.

I raised my glass to him, smiled, and took a sip. He gave a little bow and turned for the kitchen.

"Ramu, *eik minnit.*" He came back. "What is this whisky?" I asked. "It's not Chivas."

"No, sir. Devars."

I rose from my seat. "Devars? What's that?" Then I caught on. "Dewar's? We don't have any Dewar's."

"*Prejent*, sir."

"Present? From who? Not Lokhande."

"No, sir."

"From a lady?"

"No, sir. Mr. *Aarlann.*"

"Aarlann? Who's that?"

He made a hand gesture that I understood to mean "wait." He ran to the kitchen and returned a moment later with the box the bottle had come in. Taped to the top, a handwritten note said, "No hard feelings, I hope. You said your dad drinks Dewar's. Enjoy. Russ."

"Harlan," I said aloud, the mystery solved.

"*Do* bottle," said Ramu, holding up two fingers. "*Eik Devars aur eik Chivas.*"

"Two bottles?" One Dewar's and one Chivas. That fixed my Lokhande problem. I would send Ramu back to the police station in the morning with a *prejent* for the inspector. I'd be square, thanks to Harlan. Did this mean I *owed* him again?

I flipped through the second magazine, *Filmfare*. A sublime beauty named Shabana Azmi graced the cover. She was a stunner, with big eyes, bright full lips, and glowing skin.

Waiting for *khana*, I sank into a reflective mood and listened to the rain hissing through the thick air outside the window. I wondered if the Parsees were playing with their grandson. No reason to check. I didn't really care. Not unless I could watch Sushmita's face light up at the spectacle.

"Sir, *khana tayar hain*," announced Ramu. Dinner was ready.

Feeling grateful, I decided he deserved a raise, after barely three days on the job. Lokhande had been right. This guy was a useful fellow. No wonder the police had given him such a long leash and generous privileges.

. . .

FRIDAY, JULY 11, 1975, 1:11 P.M.

I'd spent the better part of three days building up contacts with a few film stars and producers. At first, their reps seemed skeptical. But in the end, they caught on that international publicity might be a good thing. Especially since I wanted to do a positive piece, not a hatchet job to make Hindi films look backward and silly. Some Western outlets had done exactly that in the past.

I was waiting for confirmation of appointments with Shabana Azmi—she of *Filmfare* cover fame—and another big actress named simply Rekha, a smoldering gorgeous woman. Actors Shashi Kapoor and Jeetendra had already accepted my request for interviews, though they weren't available until the following week. And only for fifteen minutes each.

"You're kidding me," said Janice when I told her over afternoon tea what I'd scheduled. "Those are huge stars. How did you manage it?"

I shrugged. "My boyish charm."

She smirked, and I admitted it was more dogged persistence and a little luck that got me past the gatekeepers.

"I have something for your lovely girlfriend," she said.

I frowned. "She's not my girlfriend."

"Sorry. For Sushmita. It's an autographed photo of Amitabh Bachchan."

I'd been hearing a little too much about that guy, and it was getting on my nerves. He didn't strike me as all that special. Just another tall, good-looking actor. And I'd seen many men who were more handsome. Dharmendra, for one. But Amitabh Bachchan was the one Sushmita had dreamt of marrying. He was on magazine covers and movie billboards all over town. Even my servant was an admirer.

I must have made a face without realizing it.

"Never mind, Mr. Jacobs," she said. "If it's too much trouble, I'll deliver it myself."

"No, no. Of course I'll take it over to her."

Janice handed me an envelope. She'd scrawled something across the front in Hindi. I asked what it said, and she told me it was "Sushmita."

I spent my lunch break learning how to write it.

●　●　●

FRIDAY, JULY 11, 1975, 4:16 P.M.

I was on the phone to a producer named Ravi Om Gopal. He'd made a couple of successful Hindi-language films—the typical melodrama they churned out: boy meets girl, three fight scenes, and six songs. I'd read in my film magazine that he was considered to be a man on the rise. He wasn't thrilled about the idea of talking to a journalist about the Emergency. He made a big show of supporting Mrs. Gandhi and her efforts to defend the nation from "internal disturbances." I told him I wasn't interested in his politics, but only in the challenges or advantages the Emergency had created in the film business. I promised him anonymity, if he wanted, but he wasn't biting. He finally asked me to leave him out of my story.

I hung up and rubbed my eyes. Next on the list was an up-and-coming actor a director had referred me to. I was about to pick up the receiver when Janice interrupted me.

"That man called again," she said. "While you were on the phone."

"Which man?"

She pulled up a chair next to me and spoke in a low voice. "Bikas. Danny, I'm worried for you."

"Why? What did he say?"

"He said he's changed his mind. He wants the film back. What film?"

"There's no film. I don't know what he's talking about."

"Danny," she said, fixing me with a dead-serious gaze. "He said he left a note at your place with instructions to deliver the film tonight. If you don't do it, he says he'll kill you."

PART TWO

FLIGHT

CHAPTER SIXTEEN

Panting for breath, soaked from the rain and my sweat, I arrived to find my door open. I called for Ramu, but got no response. Everything seemed quiet, so I slipped inside. His *chappals* were not in the entry-way. He wasn't there.

"Bikas?" I asked, dreading an answer. Still nothing.

I grabbed the only object handy—a letter opener—and made my way into the corridor. To my right, I could see that my bedroom had been ransacked. To my left, the kitchen, as well. Both rooms were empty of burglars. I quickly checked the second bedroom and bath-room down the hall. They'd been turned upside down as well. I drew a breath. There was no one in the house but me. Where the hell was Ramu?

He was, in fact, standing right behind me.

"Sir, *kya hua*?" he asked. I'd learned this phrase. It meant, "What happened?"

I told him I didn't know, and returned to my bedroom. The cup-board against the wall had been opened, and my clothes were strewn on the floor. The bed had been torn apart, sheets pulled back, and the pillow removed from its case. I surveyed the room for the radio. Where was it? Not on the bedside table where I'd left it that morning. Christ, if it was gone, so was my story. Or worse.

Stooping to look under the bed, I found it. The radio had been knocked off the table and fallen to the floor. I still needed to check for the roll of film inside before I could relax.

Oblivious to Ramu, who'd followed me from the second bedroom, I pried open the radio's battery compartment. The film was there. But not for long. I grabbed it and stuffed it into my pants' front pocket.

"Sir?" he asked again. "*Kya hua?*"

"Burglar," I answered. "Thief. *Chor.*"

He tried to explain something to me, but wasn't up to the task in English.

"*Eik minnit*, sir," he said and ran out the front door.

Who knew where he was headed, but I couldn't worry about that. I wandered back into the dining room. There, I noticed a small folded sheet of paper on the table. Had it been there when I'd come in? I couldn't say.

I picked it up and read:

"Sassoon Docks, 14 number. Ten o'clock. Bring film. Come alone. B."

Bikas. He must have phoned the office right after he'd searched my flat. I slid the note into the same pocket as the film and turned back to my bedroom. I picked a few shirts, slacks, and some underwear off the floor and folded them into a small suitcase. Two pairs of dry sneakers, too. I closed it just as I heard Ramu return. He wasn't alone.

"Sushmita," I said, but that was the only word I could get out before she threw herself against me.

Her arms around my neck, she squeezed me and wept apologies into my ear. I found the courage to lift my arms and place them gently on her back. Yes, Ramu was standing there watching it all, but I didn't care. I tightened my hold.

At length, she pulled away and asked if I could forgive her. I didn't know what to say. I simply smiled as I rejoiced at the change in my luck. She gave me a kiss on the cheek, then laughed and wiped the tears from her eyes.

"Are you all right, Danny?" she asked. "Your servant told me someone broke in here. When he was out to deliver a bottle to that policeman, he said."

"I'm fine. But I've got to get out of this place for a while."

"What? Why?"

"I got a threat today in the office," I said. "Then this." I indicated the mess on the floor.

"Who threatened you?"

"Our friendly neighborhood bomber. It's not safe for me to stay here."

"And you were going to leave without telling me?"

"Of course not. I was coming up to see you after I'd packed."

She looked skeptical. "Where will you go?"

"Maybe to a hotel. Someplace in the suburbs."

"Mad or what?" she said. "I know a place where you'll be safe."

She took charge, instructed Ramu to make some sandwiches and fill two bottles with drinking water. Then she rushed up to the penthouse to get some things, as I inspected the damage in the flat and tried to determine what was missing. Everything appeared to be accounted for.

Barely five minutes later, she returned and announced we were leaving. I pulled ten rupees from my wallet and handed them to Ramu.

"For your meals while I'm away," I said.

"*Jaldi*, Danny. *Chalo*," said Sushmita. "We want to make it to the top of the *ghats* before dark."

"Where are you taking me?" I asked as she drove through the Sagar Darshan gate and into the lane.

"We're going to my house in Poona. I wrote out a telegram just now and told Sandip to send it to Willy right away to let him know we're coming."

I knew it wasn't the moment to wonder about such things, but I'd distinctly heard her say the house in Poona was hers. Did she mean that legally? Or simply in a practical sense?

"Do you think it was the bomber who broke into your flat?" she asked me as we turned onto Cuffe Parade Road. "Looking for the film you shot of him?"

"Yes. I found a note on the table. It was Bikas."

"Just be glad you weren't there. And you're safe now."

But I wasn't glad. The thought gave me chills. This was a guy who'd murdered a CID officer and bragged about it.

• • •

We made good time leaving Bombay on the Eastern Express Highway. Sushmita was a fine driver, and I was glad to be in a comfortable car. I'd ridden in the back of enough black-and-yellow taxis to know I was too tall to sit inside without banging my head on the roof every time we hit a bump. Which was about every seven feet. So the air-conditioned Mercedes felt like we were traveling in a cloud, despite the pitiful condition of the roads. Still, even with the roar of the driving rain, I could hear the constant car horns tooting at other motorists and the pedestrians about, neither of whom would pay any attention, I was sure. The aim of the nonstop honking in India was more therapeutic—a way to work out frustrations—than an effective means of moving traffic. Sushmita played the game, too, making liberal use of the horn, with no result.

We figured to beat sunset to the top of the *ghats*, and from there the roads would present only the usual dangers of bad drivers, potholes, and buses that switched off all their lights at night when they stopped to drop off passengers. Echoing Willy's accounts of the *ghats*, Sushmita explained that they offered spectacularly terrifying views and countless opportunities to plunge over the side of the road to certain death. No guardrails, mostly. And many that had once been there had been knocked down. Twisted witnesses to what had surely been a fatal crash.

I consulted my watch and did some math in my head. Yes, we should make it up the zigzagging road to the top before dark. But when we crossed Thane Creek, traffic became snarled by an ugly accident involving a bus and an auto rickshaw in New Bombay, the massive development project being built on the other side of Vashi Bridge. That delayed us twenty minutes. Then, once we'd moved on, we came upon an overturned truck that blocked the entire road in Panvel. Another thirty minutes gone.

"I don't want to alarm you, Danny," Sushmita told me as she switched on the headlights. "But we're not going to make it to the top before sunset."

I was alarmed. Not outwardly, of course, but in the gathering dusk of the day, my guts were churning at the prospect. Imagined terrors are usually more frightening than those you've seen. There's the element of the unknown added to the certainty that whatever it is will scare the daylights out of you. And it was precisely daylight that I was longing for. Glancing at the phosphorescent dial of my watch, I saw that it was 7:19 p.m., exactly one minute before sunset. A journalist has to know these things.

.   .   .

FRIDAY, JULY 11, 1975, 7:19 P.M.

"Are you okay?" I asked Sushmita as she navigated the twisting road, climbing slowly, steadily up the *ghats*.

She squinted into the glaring headlights of a truck descending the curves in the opposite direction. A horn blared before us—the truck—as it swerved out of our path back into its own lane with, perhaps, eighteen inches to spare.

"Jesus, that was close," I said.

"Normal. You'll get used to it."

She was trying to act cool, but I caught her chewing her lip and strangling the steering wheel with an iron grip. The weather was a complicating factor. At times roaring down like a blinding waterfall on the windscreen, then lightening up for a few minutes before resuming its assault, the rain only served to remind me that we were doomed.

It's no exaggeration to describe the two hours of scaling the *ghats* that night as the most terrifying of my life. And I'd been in Vietnam. The cars and trucks paid no mind to the dangers of the road, the conditions, or the sharpness of the turns. It might have been the Hindu belief in reincarnation that prompted such insouciance in the minds of the drivers who, one after the other, tempted fate and death by passing vehicles in no more space than you'd need to park a car. And I do not exaggerate. Those drivers were indifferently crazy, as if their lives and the lives of those coming in the opposite direction didn't matter at all.

"Do you want to pull over and wait for the rain to ease?" I asked.

"The turnoffs can be as dangerous as the road," she said as an oncoming Ambassador ducked out of our path like a matador avoiding the bull. "Drivers misjudge the turns and bash into the cars parked off to the side. I've even heard of motorists sleeping in their cars pushed over the edge and down the mountain. Awful."

"Maybe keep driving," I said. "You're doing great."

I must have worn out the invisible brake, pumping it as I did for the better part of two hours. My leg was cramping from the constant stress, so when we finally breached the crest of the *ghats* and leveled out, I let out a cheer.

"Wow," I said, relieved the road had finally straightened. "You are an amazing driver, Sushmita."

"Very sweet of you, Danny," she said, staring straight down the road. "But there's still a long way to go. Probably two hours or more with this rain. I'm going to stop ahead for a rest. It's safe enough here."

She pulled over at a petrol station with a nearby *dhaba*, a roadside eatery. We filled the tank and found a place to park, not too close, but not too isolated from the other vehicles.

As the rain drummed on the roof of the car, we ate the green chutney sandwiches Ramu had packed in Bombay and washed them down with the water from the bottles he'd filled.

"You're not ready to eat from the *dhaba*, Danny," she said. "Trust me."

"It's still quite far to Poona, isn't it?" I asked. "Do you want me to drive?"

She laughed. "Oh, Danny. You're even less prepared to drive in India than you are for *dhaba* food. We'll sit for a while and see if the rain lets up. If not, there's a place I know in Lonavala where we can stop for the night."

· · ·

It was nine thirty, and the rain had let up some. It seemed now or never to set out again. I asked Sushmita how she knew the way, given the lack of road signs. She said there weren't many turns to go wrong along the route. Plus, she'd driven it many times before, albeit in better conditions.

"But never after dark," she added.

We pushed on in silence for a couple of miles, and I only needed to avert my eyes from oncoming traffic a few times. At length, Sushmita said she needed to pull over before she fell asleep at the wheel. She found a turnoff and parked the car. Then she popped open the door and stepped out.

She leaned back and spread her arms, as if to welcome the rain. It drenched her face and her top, and she began laughing hysterically. She shook her black hair from side to side, then rubbed her face vigorously with both hands. Splashing through the puddles, she called for me to join her. I didn't need a second invitation.

Atop the *ghats*, the temperature had dropped considerably, and the rain only served to cool things down even more. Soaked to the skin, we chased each other through the muddy gravel, laughing till we were out of breath. I caught Sushmita around the waist near the edge of the turnoff, and we almost fell as one into the wet grass, but she resisted.

"Not in the grass!" she yelled through her laughter. "Do you know what drivers stop here for?"

Point taken. Instead, I steered her to the hood of the car, what they call the bonnet in India. I rolled on top of her, trapping her beneath my body. Her face, shimmering wet, was the most beautiful thing I'd ever seen. My mouth was mere inches from hers, and I was resolute. There was no turning back now. I was going to kiss those full, warm lips. But as I turned my head and closed my eyes, preparing to grab the brass ring, she poked my sides with her hands, producing an intensely ticklish reaction in me. I slid off her, and she wriggled away, laughing so hard she was crying. She was a slippery one, figuratively and now literally.

A half hour later, we were shivering in the rain. Our breath puffed light billows of mist into the air. It was past ten thirty, and I knew there was no chance we'd make Poona that night.

"Okay, I think we can go now," she said. "But we have to change into something dry."

She didn't want to soil the inside of the car, so she instructed me to turn my back and block the view of any cars passing at that late hour. Then she stripped out of her jeans and *kurta*.

"Keep your eyes on the road, Danny, I'm warning you," she said with a tinkly laugh.

I didn't move. But I caught a remarkably clear reflection of her half-naked body in the car's glass as she stepped into a new pair of jeans. I bit my lip so hard it nearly drew blood.

When it was my turn to change, she assumed the lookout position. She was less of a gentleman than I had been. I'd accidentally caught her in the window's reflection. She, on the other hand, cranked her head around and took a long, healthy look at me as I tried to hop into a dry pair of pants.

"Don't put that belt on," she said once I was clothed again. "It's soaked. Throw it in the boot."

Back inside the car, we wiped our faces with a cloth. The euphoria of our romp in the rain was melting away, as we warmed up and regained a measure of our dignity and decorum.

"You've cut your lip," she said. "How did you do that?"

I'd drawn blood after all. "Must have been the wrestling. I'll be fine."

"No, let me see." She found a dry corner of the cloth and brushed the little red mark my teeth had left on my lower lip. "Oh, it's nothing, you big baby," she said, tossing the cloth into the back seat. Then she turned the ignition, shifted into first, and we were off.

• • •

Sushmita drove us to Lonavala, a hill station about 2,000 feet above sea level and forty miles from Poona. She said she had a bungalow not far from the INS Shivaji, the Naval College of Engineering.

"My father was a scientist," she said. "He taught at the college. But don't ask me anything else, because I won't answer. Not tonight."

I wondered why they would build a naval training facility sixty miles from the coast. On the Deccan Plateau?

She parked the car behind the house, out of sight of the road, and switched off the ignition. Grabbing the loose gearshift, she handed it to me and said we'd arrived.

The bungalow was a large three-bedroom house, probably built in the late eighteen hundreds by the British as a holiday residence. An escape from the heat and bustle of Bombay. The doors were padlocked and the windows shuttered. Sushmita pulled a key ring from her overnight bag and let us inside. There was no light. I couldn't tell if that was by design, because the place was rarely occupied, or if the electricity had been cut. Power failures—what they called *bunds*—happened daily throughout India, so it wouldn't have surprised me.

"No current tonight," she told me, confirming my suspicions, as she sparked up a flashlight left at the door for precisely such a common occurrence. "There are more torches in the drawing room and bedrooms."

The narrow throw of the flashlight jittered before us as she led the way. The drawing room was the first we crossed. Expansive, with stone floors, covered by Oriental rugs of different sizes, patterns, and colors. Sushmita told me later that they were mostly Kashmiri and Turkish carpets that had belonged to her grandfather. No questions about him, either. More rugs still hung from the walls, alongside Indian and Western paintings in heavy frames made of wood and antique glass, some bearing a crack or two.

The furniture was colonial era—as in the Raj—probably all from the nineteenth century by the looks of them. There were divans, a daybed, a hanging chair, and mahogany tables. Against the wall to my left was a large sideboard, bedecked with peacock miniature paintings in the door panels. Three beveled-glass cabinets dominated the center, flanked by drawers and nooks on the sides. A small shrine to Ganesh and Lakshmi was on display, with a blackened brass *diya* ready for the next *puja*.

We moved slowly through the dark, heading into a corridor with doors on either side. She stopped at the first one and inserted a key into the lock.

"This is my bedroom," she said, and pushed opened the door.

"It's locked?" I asked.

"Of course. We always lock our rooms in India. You can't trust the servants."

"What servants?"

"Be still, Danny, and come in."

Sushmita placed her bag on a chest against the wall then lit a long tapered candle on either side of the bed. She regarded me quizzically in the low light.

"Well?" she said. "Aren't you going to put down your bag?"

CHAPTER SEVENTEEN

The morning came too early. I knew we had to get back into the Mercedes and drive the rest of the way to Poona, but lying next to Sushmita was a bliss I didn't want to end. I certainly had no intention of getting up for a run. The wee hours of the previous night had put an end to all the hesitation and missed opportunities. And never mind the betrayal of my friend and benefactor, Willy Smets. That was the furthest thing from my mind. All I could think of was her. I wanted to take her away from him, take her back to Bombay or to New York, wherever we could spend more nights like the one we'd just shared. Together. Alone.

I was subject to falling in love at the drop of a skirt, but this was a whole new experience. The intimacy jacked up my emotions. Something about sex turned me inside out. The bond became much more than physical. I know that sounds sappy and pathetic, but I considered myself a romantic. Not an idiot for once.

Sushmita was the only thing I could see. I didn't care about my position at UNI, or whether Frank Muller might send me home for being AWOL, for shacking up with an Indian beauty in a bungalow sixty miles or so from my office on Phirozshah Mehta Road in Fort. It didn't matter. Nothing mattered that morning. I only wished the sun had never risen.

She stirred, snuggled into my chest, and buried her eyes to block the light streaming through the window. I stroked her temple and hair, willing her to continue sleeping. We couldn't leave if she was asleep.

But eventually, her eyes blinked open, and she stretched, pushing up against me. She held my hand in hers, saying nothing for several minutes, before wrapping her arms around me. Finally, she lifted her head and propped herself up on the pillow to sit straight.

"What time is it?" she asked.

"Four thirty," I said. "Go back to sleep."

"Liar. The sun is up. Come, Danny," she said, rising from the bed.

I couldn't take my eyes off her as she pulled on a pair of pajama bottoms, then dared me to catch her. I leapt to my feet, intending to do exactly that. But I tripped over my pants, which I'd pulled off the night before—turning them inside out in my haste—and thrown on the floor. She made good her escape.

. . .

For once it wasn't raining. Sushmita locked up the bungalow as I loaded the car. I was sorry our tryst had ended. I could have stayed in that picturesque house for another week without coming up for air. Maybe we'd have a chance to stop there again, perhaps on our return trip to Bombay, provided Willy wasn't sitting between us in the car.

She'd finished securing the padlocks now and was heading toward me, totally unaware of her own beauty and the power she held over me. I prayed for the car battery to be dead. Why hadn't I thought to sneak out in the night and turn on the headlights? Or maybe simply lose the gearshift?

"What are we going to tell Willy?" she asked me after a few miles.

"What . . . what do you mean? You think we should tell him? About us?"

"Mad or what?" she said, taking her eyes off the road long enough to throw an alarmed glare my way. "I meant what will we tell him about why we stopped overnight."

"Tell him we were delayed by the traffic and rain, and got too tired to continue."

"We're not telling him that. In fact, I know exactly what we'll say."

She pulled over at the next petrol bunk, where, reaching for something in the glove compartment, she asked if I knew how to change a tire. We climbed out of the car. I examined the four tires and pointed out that they were all fine, properly inflated, and didn't need changing.

She crouched next to the driver's-side rear tire and plunged a screwdriver into the tread. "What about this one?" she asked.

"Why would you give yourself a flat tire on purpose?"

"Because it will confirm the story of why our clothes are wet and dirty. We had a puncture and had to change the tire in the driving rain. By the time you'd figured out how to work the jack, I was too annoyed to continue driving. We decided to spend the night in the car."

"In the car?" I asked. "Why not say we went to the bungalow?"

"Willy doesn't know anything about the bungalow. And he's not going to know. Understood, Danny?"

I unbolted the tire and switched it with the spare in the trunk. It only took me ten minutes. My first car had been an old Chevy Nova with bald tires, which, for some reason, blew out one by one in the weeks after I'd bought it. I became an expert grease monkey thanks to that crappy car and its tires.

"Rub your trousers and shirt from last night on the punctured tire," she said. "And mine too."

"Why?"

"If we changed the tire last night, our clothes would surely have grease stains. You're really useless sometimes."

Sushmita had some soap, and using the water and the cloth from the night before, I scrubbed my hands mostly clean. She said a little black under my fingernails would make our story more believable.

The thoroughness of her lie impressed and troubled me at the same time. Why, for example, didn't Willy know she owned a bungalow in Lonavala? It sat only a couple of miles from the Bombay-Poona Road, which he drove regularly. Surely he might occasionally need to stop for the night on his trips. Why not there?

Another question nagging me was whether her deviousness was a skill she'd developed over time or a spontaneous stroke of inspiration. Either way, she was damn good at it.

We rehearsed our story and vetted it for holes. Then it was time to get moving again. I fastened my lap belt and encouraged her to wear hers. But she declined.

"Why wouldn't you use it?" I asked. "It's there for your safety."

"Because if I'm strapped down, I can't do this." She leaned over and planted her warm mouth on mine for a long kiss. "Any more questions?"

. . .

SATURDAY, JULY 12, 1975, 12:07 P.M.

We rolled into Poona about an hour later. We still had to cross most of the city before we reached Koregaon Park, where Sushmita's house was located. That was the rather hip part of town, with gorgeous bungalows, cafés, and restaurants. The rain had stopped, and there were lots of people about. I noticed several Westerners in robes and sandals perusing the roadside stands for souvenirs.

"Who are those *gore* in the maroon robes?" I asked as we cruised east along North Main Road.

"Followers of Rajneesh," she said.

"Is that the ashram I've heard about? The free love?"

"Of course a naughty boy like you knows about the Poona Ashram."

"I try to be well informed. You don't approve of the meditation center? Super-consciousness?"

"That place makes us look like randy heathens, dropping our robes at the first invitation to fornicate with foreigners."

"I'd pegged you for more progressive than that," I teased, well aware that I was a foreigner who'd fornicated with her. I willed myself not to think of Willy, also a foreigner who'd . . .

"I'm a Hindu," she said. "Perhaps not a good one. But I don't believe orgies are some kind of spiritual tourism."

She turned right into one of the lanes off North Main and continued past several ancient banyan trees, whose characteristic prop roots grew down to the ground from above. Through the window, I watched the sleepy city pass by: grand old homes, surrounded by stone walls.

Then, without any warning, Sushmita pulled up to the gate of a large bungalow, sitting on green grass behind a high stone wall. She sounded the horn.

"This is it," she said. "Stay calm and remember what a poor excuse for a tire man you are."

"Sush, wait," I said. She looked over at me as a man in a brown uniform and cap rushed toward us from within the compound. He saluted smartly, then wrestled open the gate.

"Yes, Danny?"

"Never mind," I said, afraid to tell her how I felt about her.

She must have understood my turmoil, because she reached for my hand, well out of sight from the guard. He held one half of the open gate as he waited for us to enter. She gave me a little squeeze, let go, then shifted into first and released the clutch. The Mercedes inched forward into the compound, and the guard closed the gate behind us.

CHAPTER EIGHTEEN

Willy strode out of the house to greet us, his large teeth shining from his broad smile.

"Thank goodness," he said. "I was afraid you'd had an accident in the *ghats*. We were expecting you last night."

He kissed Sushmita on the cheek and reached out to shake my hand warmly.

"We had a puncture at the bottom of the *ghats*," said Sushmita. "It was pouring rain."

"I changed the tire," I blurted out. "That is, we changed it together."

"In the rain?" asked Willy. "You must have got soaked."

Sushmita took charge of the story.

"Yes, we did," she said. "Especially since our Danny Boy couldn't loosen the bolts. Or raise the jack." She turned to me, stroked my arm as a sister might, and said I was useless in an emergency.

"Sorry," I said. "Those bolts were tight."

"Where did you spend the night?" asked Willy.

"Right there," she answered, indicating the car. "It was late by the time Danny managed to change the tire, and I wasn't about to climb the *ghats* at that hour. Not with a blinding headache. And Danny doesn't know how to drive a right-hand stick, so we slept in the car." She put a hand up to her face to feign a whisper. "He snores."

"You poor dears," said Willy, slapping me on the shoulder. "Come inside and explain to me what this urgent visit is all about."

A servant arrived and took our bags. Sushmita made a point of telling him to remove the wet, soiled clothes from the boot.

"See if Pooja can get the grease stains out," she said. "I'm afraid they're beyond rescue. And send Shankar to get a new spare."

The house's décor resembled that of the Lonavala bungalow, as if they'd been born of the same mother. Old rugs everywhere, heavy wooden rosewood and mahogany colonial furniture, and shrines. I noticed a garland of marigolds wrapped around the shoulders of a chicken-sized Ganesh carved out of pink stone. Before him, a *diya* was burning. I wondered if Willy had been praying for our safe return, and I felt like a traitor. I was a traitor.

"Mita wired me that you were in danger, Danny. Tell me what happened."

"Do you remember that bomber I said I'd interviewed? The one I took pictures of? Well, he's had a change of heart. He wants the photos back. He demanded I meet him at Sassoon Docks last night or else."

"Or else what?"

"Or else I was a dead man."

"And you refuse to give him the film because of your journalistic principles, is that it?"

"Yes."

Willy nodded. "Well, you're safe here. Good God, your fingernails are black with grease. Go have your bath."

. . .

I was shown to a room in the back of the one-floor house. A large bed stood against the wall opposite a window that looked out on the garden and the gravel drive. The flat-painted walls were covered with colonial-era etchings and paintings of Bombay and Poona. And there was a writing desk and a bookcase full of paperback novels. Mills and Boon, mostly, with some Agatha Christie and P. G. Wodehouse mixed in. A ceiling fan spun overhead, but the temperature was already much cooler than what it had been in Bombay. Poona was one of the traditional hill stations that provided respite from the heat of the coastal cities. Finally, I noticed a black Chinese wardrobe. I could store my clothes or lock any valuables inside. That reminded me of my precious roll of film. I hoped I hadn't ruined it in the rain the night before with Sushmita.

And that's when I realized I didn't have it. Not in the pockets of my slacks, not in my bag. Had I left it in my soiled clothes the night before? Maybe it had fallen out during my wrestling match with Sushmita. Or when we rubbed my pants on the tire. Jesus Christ, if that film was gone, I was screwed.

I thought back to those heady moments with Sushmita in the rain. The excitement of the chase, grabbing her, laughing, pressing my body to hers on the hood of the car. I must have transferred the film from my wet pants to the dry ones after that, but I couldn't be sure. Sushmita's peeping as I jumped into my clothes had somehow obscured the chain of events in my mind. I simply couldn't remember. All I knew was that it wasn't in my pocket now.

I tried to put it out of my mind until I could ask Sushmita if our clothes had been washed. I had a tepid shower in the attached bathroom. I didn't trust the small water heater, what the Indians called a geyser, pronounced *geezer*. Somehow, I thought it might explode and scald me to death. As a result, my shower hardly qualified as a five-star experience—not quite the President Hotel—but I could stand up straight and wash myself with two hands for a change.

I was ready to rejoin my hosts, but I dragged my feet, waiting to be sure Sushmita emerged before me. Checking my bag one more time,

I found no roll of film. Without the pictures of Bikas, my story would be toothless. And, if I ever needed to return the film to him to save my skin, that would be impossible, too.

At length, I smoothed my hair and stepped outside to join my hosts. Sushmita was nowhere in sight. There was only Willy, lounging in a Bombay fornicator in the drawing room, reading the newspaper.

"Sorry to interrupt," I said.

"Not at all, Danny Boy," he answered, pushing himself out of the chair. "Please, have a seat. May I get you a drink of something?"

"I'll wait for Sushmita."

"Don't worry about that. She doesn't take."

"*Take?*"

"Sorry. A little joke between Mita and me. The Maharastrians say *take* to mean drink alcohol. And *keep* if they have it in the house."

"Funny," I said, wishing Sush had shared the joke with me, instead of Willy. Why was I learning about India from a fellow *fireng*?

"Let me know what you'll *take*, and I'll have Govind get it for you."

I gathered Govind was one of the house servants.

"Do you *keep* wine?" I asked, trying out the usage.

"Of course. May I suggest a Vouvray? It complements Indian food. I hope you don't mind spicy dishes."

"It's fine," I said. "I have a cast-iron stomach."

Willy excused himself to retrieve the bottle of wine from somewhere down the corridor. A moment later, Sushmita appeared, looking cleanly scrubbed and casual in a simple loose-fitting cotton *kurta* and linen pants. Her hair was pulled back and tied low at the neck. She wore no *bindi* or makeup. She was gorgeous.

"Have you seen Willy?" she asked as if nothing had happened between us the night before.

I knew she had to play things cool, but—man—she was good at it. There might be servants watching or listening, I supposed. And Willy could walk in on us at any time. Still, I looked for a clue in her eyes, some kind of recognition of our secret bond. I could see none.

"He's gone to get some wine," I said, trying to beat her at her own game. "Can I ask Govind to get you some juice? Since you don't *take*, I mean."

She giggled. "Oh, Danny, that's sweet. You're doing very well adapting to our ways. I'm impressed. But nothing for me now."

She'd seen through my attempt to come across as initiated and a veteran of the Indian experience, which I was not. She touched my forearm as she'd done a few times in Bombay during one of Willy's cocktail parties or dinners. As electric as it had been on those occasions, it now communicated a private message to me. This was the signal I'd been hoping for.

She took a seat on one of the divans, and I stood opposite her, waiting for Willy to return before making myself comfortable.

"Mita is come at last," he said from across the room. The surprise reminded me of the first time I'd met him, when he'd appeared from behind me and offered his opinion on the utility of Indians. "Danny Boy, please sit. We're not a formal ménage here."

He'd come back empty-handed, but a servant—Govind, I presumed—followed a moment later, bearing a tray with two glasses, a large ice bucket, and a chilled green bottle of wine. Once he'd placed the tray on the low table in front of Sushmita, he asked her in Hindi what she would like. She said simply, "*Kuch nahin.*" Govind wagged his head and withdrew.

"What's that?" I asked, trying once more to prove my sophistication, and sure I'd get it right this time. "Fresh lime soda?"

She snorted a tiny laugh through her nose. "Oh, Danny, no. *Kuch nahin* is Hindi for *nothing*."

Stinging from my faux pas, I turned to Willy, who was now pouring us each a glass of Vouvray. Maybe he didn't trust Govind to serve it. Or maybe he wanted to hold on to one of his European pleasures, that of being the one in charge of the wine.

"Danny, this story of the bomber is fantastic," said Willy as he handed me my glass. "Have you approached the police?"

"Not yet."

"Why don't you speak to your inspector friend?" asked Sushmita.

"I suppose I'll have to," I said. "When I go back to Bombay."

"You sound reluctant," said Willy. "Why?"

"I wonder if he suspects I have a photograph of the bomber and I'm withholding evidence."

"And, of course, you do."

"Right. What if he throws me in jail until I cooperate?"

"Oh, no. You don't want to spend any time in an Indian prison. Trust me."

"Are you saying you've been in jail here yourself?"

"Goodness, no. But I had a friend, Pier Mertens. He was arrested for drugs. Now, of course, he's gone. He died nearly twenty years ago."

"I'm sorry."

Willy shrugged. "Never mind. Now we must worry about your problem, Danny Boy."

"What can I do?" I asked.

"Nothing," he said. "You will stay here for a while. No one knows where you are. In the meantime, I'll see if I can find out what that inspector's intentions are."

"How?"

He bent over to retrieve the bottle from the bucket and refreshed our drinks. "I'm a member of the Cuffe Parade Residents' Association," he said. "We often meet with the police on matters of safety. I will make some inquiries."

"I don't know how to thank you, Willy," I said, recalling exactly how I'd thanked him the night before.

CHAPTER NINETEEN

I'd spent the afternoon by myself. Sushmita and I couldn't exactly fraternize freely. Even if Willy hadn't been there, the house staff—the guard at the gate, Govind, and the cook, Kamal—would always be a concern. Willy graciously invited me to phone my office to offer an explanation of my absence. He reminded me not to mention where I was.

I had to wait thirty minutes for the trunk call to go through. When it did, I reached back to my schoolboy past and told Girish I was sick. Delhi belly. Everyone would buy that. And since the next day was Sunday, my day off, I was free for the time being. What I would tell them on Monday was another matter.

I was the last to arrive in the drawing room for pre-dinner cocktails. It was already dark outside.

"Will you have some whisky with me?" asked Willy.

"Sure," I said.

"Are you feeling more relaxed?"

"I'm fine, thanks," I said, then turned to the object of all my desires, who was seated on the divan. "Sushmita, you look lovely, as always."

"You're such a flirt, Danny," she answered, a glass of juice in her hand. "And in front of Willy. Shameless."

Damn, she didn't mind skating close to the edge.

"How did you two occupy yourselves this afternoon?" I asked to change the subject.

"I made some calls for you, Danny Boy," said Willy. "I'm waiting to hear from my contacts. Let's be patient a few days more. You're safe as long as no one knows where you are."

He toasted to me with his glass.

"Wait," said Sushmita. We both turned to her. "What about your servant?"

"How would he know?" I asked. "We never said we were going to Poona."

"No, but I said we had to hurry because we wanted to reach the top of the *ghats* before dark."

That was right. She'd said that in front of Ramu.

"But his English is poor," I said. "Maybe he didn't understand?"

"Maybe. But servants aren't stupid. Ignorance of English is not an indicator of intelligence."

Willy urged us to remain calm. "He may not have heard you, Mita. Or understood. We have no reason to assume he's disloyal to his employer."

"But what if this Bikas guy questions him?" I asked. "What if he threatens him?"

We settled into a long silence, during which I conjured the worst possible outcomes in my mind. I pictured Ramu telling all to the man who'd promised to kill me if I didn't hand over the film. And, at least for the moment, I couldn't locate the film to give it back even if I'd wanted to.

I was getting ahead of myself. Ramu couldn't possibly know where I was. Even if he suspected I'd fled to Poona, how would he know where to find me? He couldn't. Impossible.

Unless he knew Sushmita's name and thought to check the Poona telephone directory.

The phone, I learned, was in Sushmita's name. Deshpande, S. I wasn't sure what that meant for my safety. To my mind, everything came down to the question of whether Ramu had overheard, understood, and would talk. And that was only if Bikas actually got his hands on him.

The odds were long. I drew a deep breath and relaxed.

•   •   •

For dinner, Kamal, the cook, served *dal*, rice, ladyfingers (okra), *chole*, and *palak aloo*—potatoes and spinach. Pure veg. Dessert was *gulab jamun*, a kind of fried dumpling, swimming in thick, sugary syrup. I put all thoughts of Bikas behind me and enjoyed the meal.

After dinner, we sat quietly in the drawing room with our drinks, and I found myself scheming. How might I manage it, I wondered. How might I steal Sushmita from Willy without breaking his heart? Without inspiring in him a deep hatred for me? Maybe he secretly liked men, and Sush was an adornment, not a lover. Maybe he was dying of cancer and would welcome me as a successor.

Sushmita roused me from my thoughts and suggested we play a game. "Do you know carrom?" she asked.

I had no idea what that was.

"Maybe bridge?" I asked.

"We're only three."

"How about some music?" asked Willy.

A few moments later, we were listening to Jacques Brel. Sushmita was not a fan. Some of the songs were quite good but, like opera, Brel can be an acquired taste. The melodramatic numbers turned some people off.

"I know him," said Willy.

"Who?" I asked.

"Jacky. Jacques Brel. We called him Jacky."

"Really?"

"He never stops bragging about it," said Sushmita. "Tell Danny how you sat on the same bench in school with the famous Jacques Brel."

"We were in class together. In Brussels. At the Institut Saint-Louis." Willy smiled to himself. "He was a nice boy. So talented, even then."

"But Jacques Brel makes me want to cry," whined Sushmita. "Can't we change it?"

Willy feigned a heart attack, then chastised her. "How can you say that, *mon amour*? How can you listen to '*Ne me quitte pas*' and not feel your heart break?"

"That's the point, Willy. It breaks my heart."

"That's how we know we're alive, my dear," he said. "That song reminds me that I would die if you left me."

Great. This wasn't going to be a clean break.

"I won't leave you, darling," she answered. *Ouch. That hurt.* "Provided you change the music to something less depressing."

Maybe there was hope, after all. Willy seemed committed to the Brel.

"Just listen, darling," he said. "And Danny's enjoying it."

"I mean it, Willy. Please, may we listen to something else? How about the record I bought? The one with Pandit Ravi Shankar and Ustad Alla Rakha?"

Willy made a face.

"I know Ravi Shankar," I said. "The sitar player. Taught George Harrison how to play it. But who's the other one?"

"Ustad Alla Rakha," repeated Sushmita slowly for my benefit. "*Ustad* is Urdu for master. He's a master of the tabla. You know, those small drums that make impossibly beautiful music. And, by the way, referring to Pandit Ravi Shankar as a sitar player is like calling Paganini a fiddler. He's a virtuoso, Danny."

"Duly noted," I said. "I'd love to hear that."

Willy fussed and made a big show of compromising. He rose and went to the hi-fi where he stopped the music.

"Fine, fine, I'll change the Brel," he said. "But let's listen to this instead of your Indian music."

He cued up some Wagner. Overtures. *My chances of winning the girl were improving.* Sushmita sulked as Willy pretended to conduct the music from his chair. But then, not ten minutes later, he changed his mind and put Brel back on the turntable.

"Good night," said Sushmita, almost in tears. She caught my eye while Willy was lost in a rapture over *"Le plat pays,"* Brel's paean to his native land. One of his most beautiful songs. She was furious.

Once she'd left the room, Willy began singing in Flemish *"Mijn vlakke land."* And then in French—*"Le plat pays qui est le mien."* I felt bad for the man. He was so generous and kind to me, and I was playing around behind his back with his lover. I felt guilt and disgust with myself. My behavior turned my own stomach. But that didn't change a thing. I still wanted Sushmita in my bed.

．　．　．

I picked out a Wodehouse novel to help me sleep. *The Mating Season* seemed a good choice, but I couldn't get into the spirit. I didn't much feel like laughing that night. And I wasn't going for Mills and Boon.

At midnight, I switched off the light and folded the pillow over my head, covering my eyes and ears. Ten minutes later, no closer to sleep, I sat up in bed and realized I was not alone.

CHAPTER TWENTY

She whispered to me from a few feet away. "I've been watching you for five minutes. How can you sleep with a pillow on your head?"

"What are you doing here?" I asked, ignoring her question. I doubted she truly wanted to know the answer. It was more a way to deflect attention from yourself when you slip into a man's bedroom in the middle of the night.

She took a step toward me. "I didn't want to surprise you for fear you'd scream. I was beginning to think you were actually going to sleep through the night with the pillow on your head."

I repeated my question. What was she doing there?

She dropped her robe, lifted the sheet, and slipped into the bed with me. Pressing her warm body to mine, she kissed me, running her hands through my hair as she did. I wasn't about to ask her a third time what she was doing in my room.

• • •

"Are you crazy coming here?" I asked breathlessly in her ear a while later. "What if he wakes up and finds you gone?"

"We sleep in different rooms," she said, her upper lip glistening with perspiration. "And he took a sleeping draught."

"What about the servants?"

"They don't sleep here. They have their own rooms behind the old carriage house."

"Still..."

She put a finger to my lips to silence me, then replaced it with a kiss. And just like that, we began all over again.

•   •   •

SUNDAY, JULY 13, 1975, 7:27 A.M.

I woke up early and stepped out for a run Sunday morning. I covered five miles or so, exploring Koregaon Park's picturesque lanes and North Main Road. As I went, I replayed in my head the passionate night I'd spent with Sushmita. The surprise of it, coupled with the danger we'd taken, only made it that much more delicious. And unforgettable.

I had my bath, dressed, then, around half past ten, slunk into the drawing room, where I hoped I'd be able to maintain my poker face.

"Danny Boy, come join us," said Willy. He was sitting on the divan with a tall glass of something cool. Across from him on a hanging swing chair suspended from the ceiling sat a large obese man in a Western shirt and pants. Sushmita was nowhere in sight. "I want to introduce you to my business associate, Chhotu."

"Don't get up," I said, once I'd noticed him struggling to free himself from the chair. "I'm Dan. Danny."

Chhotu offered a broad smile, showing a set of brilliant white teeth. "Pleased to meet you, Dan," he said in the plummiest British accent I'd ever heard. There were minute traces of his Indian origins in his exaggerated speech, but the overall impression he gave was of George Sanders, slimy but well spoken.

"Chhotu is passing through Poona on business," said Willy. "Arrived on the morning train from Calcutta."

I sat on the other end of the divan. "That's a long ride. No flights available?"

"I'm too fat for airplane seats," he said. I must have appeared taken aback, because he added that he was only *taking the piss out of me*. He spoke deliberately, with great attention to his pronunciation, which made expressions like "taking the piss" all the more jarring to my American ear.

Willy slapped his knee and laughed. "Do you know that Chhotu's real name is Debajyoti? Debajyoti Goswami. A beautiful name. And yet he's known as Chhotu."

"I don't understand."

"I believe dear Willy is referring to the irony of my pet name," said Chhotu. "'Tiny' would be a close approximation in English."

"For what it's worth, I'm happy to call you whatever you like."

"Please, dear chap, call me Chhotu. I love my name."

I agreed then asked what kind of business the two of them did together.

"This and that," he said. "We trade in all kinds of lovely items. Carpets, sculptures, handicrafts, illustrated versions of the *Kama Sutra*. Anything your heart desires. Even forbidden things. For example, dear chap, would you like to smoke some stick?"

"I beg your pardon?"

"Chhotu, that's enough," said Willy. "Danny is not interested in hashish. And you must be careful around here. We don't want trouble from the police."

"Or from me." That was Sushmita, who'd entered the room from behind us.

Chhotu frantically wrestled with the chains holding the chair aloft, and managed to push himself out of the swing.

He namaste'd and gave a little bow to her. "Sushmita-*ji,* you are looking ravishing, my dear."

She didn't respond. Instead she warned everyone in the room that there would be no smoking of stick with young Danny. "He's not accustomed to the drugs you get in this country."

"Mita, darling, don't exaggerate," said Willy. "Nobody is taking drugs. Just the occasional bit of hash for my private use. Don't give Danny Boy the wrong idea."

"I'm serious, Willy. No drugs for Danny."

I'm not sure who looked more ill at ease, Chhotu, Willy, or me. I didn't really care. Though I was perfectly capable of taking care of myself, and I'd smoked hash a couple of times in college, I was flattered that Sush was looking out for me.

·   ·   ·

SUNDAY, JULY 13, 1975, 3:24 P.M.

The weather was gray, but the rain held off. The forecast called for heavy downpours and strong winds later on, but as Sushmita and I strolled the grounds of the compound that afternoon, we did so without umbrellas. The lawn, cut close to the ground as if with nail scissors, carpeted the entire garden, except under the three great banyan trees near the wall. *Durva* grass, Sushmita, informed me, then said it was an invasive weed. Still, she admitted, Manjunath, the gardener, did a nice job keeping it green and trimmed.

At all times during our walk, we made sure to stay in plain sight, visible from the windows in the house. Willy and Chhotu had remained inside, discussing details of their business, while Sushmita and I amused ourselves among the flowers, trees, and fresh air.

"You don't like that Chhotu, do you?" I asked.

"He's a swine," she said with more vitriol than I'd expected. "I've told Willy a hundred times I don't want him in my house."

"Why? Tell me."

"He's a *chamcha*—a sycophant. Also dishonest, immoral, ugly, and ill-mannered. Shall I go on?"

"Where did you go to school, Sush?" I asked.

"What?"

"I'm impressed by your vocabulary. Your wit. Everything."

"Because I'm Indian? You don't think I might be a clever girl without some fancy schooling?"

"No, not at all. I meant—"

"Sorry, Danny," she said. She couldn't very well reach out and caress my cheek or hold my hand, what with the two business associates able to see everything we did. But I sensed she wanted to. "You Westerners have assumptions about us, the same way we do about you. But I want you to know I'm a product of my heritage, my experience, and my choices. I'm neither a credit to my people nor a brown little sister for you to civilize. Even if it's with the best intentions."

I gulped. "Got it."

"Cambridge."

"Sorry?"

"I studied at Cambridge, you ass. And St. Mary's, here in Poona, before that. What about you?"

"Me?"

"Yes, you. Where did you get to be so smart? How did a Jewish boy manage to be accepted in American society?"

"How do you know I'm Jewish?"

"I had a friend in London named Jacobs. She was Jewish."

"It's not as bad as all that back home. Sure, there are bigots, but I—"

"Oh, Danny, please stop. If you've skated through life without people calling you the foulest names, I'm glad for you. But that hasn't been my experience."

"I love you, Sush."

"You can say that, Danny. But I don't want to hear it if it's a concession. Or a mercy, or a step down."

"It's not. I can't think of anything, anyone but you. I want to take you away from all this."

"All this?" she asked. "This is mine. This is my life."

"But why, then? Why Willy? Why does he live in your penthouse in Cuffe Parade and in this gorgeous bungalow here in Poona?"

"Don't ask me that. Not now."

I nodded. This wasn't the moment. "Yale," I said.

"*Kya?*"

"I studied at Yale, you ass."

She laughed. A truly happy laugh. Then she kissed me, but only with her eyes. "*Mazha Danny*," she said.

"Wh—?"

.   .   .

SUNDAY, JULY 13, 1975, 8:16 P.M.

The cocktail hour was tense. Willy had invited Chhotu to stay for dinner and the night without having consulted Sushmita. She was stewing and, though she couldn't exactly broadcast it, I was her ally and the only one who made the evening bearable.

Twice, when Willy and Chhotu were serving themselves drinks, backs turned to us, Sushmita grabbed my hand and threw me a smoldering look of desire. I knew Chhotu was sleeping in Willy's study, well clear of the other bedrooms, so I had reason to think she might visit me again after midnight.

"What's your business here in Poona, Dan?" Chhotu asked once he'd climbed back into his hanging chair after dinner. I eyed the chains suspending the seat from the ceiling and hoped they could bear the weight.

I had no idea what Willy had told him, but I wasn't interested in constructing a big lie. Instead, I kept it simple, the same way he and Willy had described their business.

"I'm a journalist for UNI. I'm doing some background work for a story."

For all I cared, Willy could tell him about the bomber. But I didn't want to have the conversation with this swine. Yeah, if Sush considered him a swine, I wasn't going to disagree. This guy threw off the stink of a child molester with an ice cream truck.

. . .

SUNDAY, JULY 13, 1975, 11:51 P.M.

"Tell me, Dan. What's your game?" asked Chhotu once Willy had dozed off. Sushmita had dragged herself away an hour earlier, unwilling to socialize with the new houseguest.

"Sorry?"

"Come, old chap. You can tell me. Are you in it for the free liquor and the company? Or is there something more?"

"Go to hell," I said.

He raised his eyebrows and smiled at me from his perch in the swing chair. "Gloves are off, eh?"

CHAPTER TWENTY-ONE

Sush came to me after midnight, as the rain lashed at the window-panes. I worried about Chhotu, but once we'd locked the door and switched off the light, I forgot everything except the present. Her scent, her silken skin, her breath, and bite on my neck. We kept our voices down. The world and its problems—mine, India's, Sushmita's—none of those mattered. Who cared what banks failed in Yonkers? With apologies to the Gershwins, all I could see was Sushmita. To hell with everything else, starting with that swine Chhotu. And Willy Smets second.

I put those thoughts aside. How could I stop time and make the night last? The morning would come soon enough. I'd have to make a new excuse to Frank Muller for why I was AWOL, and Sushmita would have to put on her mask again. Pretend she loved Willy. Pretend I was only a friend to her.

She rose from the bed, kissed me, and stroked my cheek. I tried to decipher the sadness in her eyes, peer into her soul and understand what emotions were tormenting her. But all I could see was trouble, worry, and uncertainty. Then she wrapped herself in her robe, slipped out the door, and melted into the darkness of the hallway.

. . .

MONDAY, JULY 14, 1975, 8:09 A.M.

Freshly back from my morning run, I heard noise outside my window. I peered out to see what was going on and saw Willy and Chhotu in deep conversation beside the Mercedes. Chhotu smoked a cigarette and listened. Willy seemed perturbed about something. Business perhaps. I couldn't hear what they were saying, except for the stray word here and there. Something about *the king*.

Chhotu nodded and threw his cigarette to the ground, not even bothering to crush it with his shoe. After a few moments, they shook hands, and Chhotu stuffed himself into the back seat of the car. A man I hadn't seen before appeared and climbed into the driver's seat. I learned later that he was Shankar, Willy's driver. He started the engine, shifted into gear, and drove off toward the gate, where the guard stood and saluted the departing guest.

It was Monday morning, and I needed to phone the office to let them know I was not coming in. It didn't look good to call in sick twice in the first two months at a new job, but I didn't have a helicopter, so I was stuck.

I dressed and was heading to the dining room for morning tea. That's when I noticed the envelope on the stone floor just inside my door. *Dan* was scrawled across the front in a man's script. It smelled strongly of cloying cologne.

You should exercise greater caution in your nighttime assignations.
Not everyone sleeps as soundly as your host. I have a proposition for
you. Perhaps you'd like to invest in securing my discretion.
   Till Wednesday, when I'll be back.

                                                   Chhotu

• • •

Another trunk call. Twenty minutes before I got Girish on the line. He seemed unconcerned about my health and any damage I might be doing to my career by missing work. I told him I had interviews in Juhu Tuesday and Wednesday for my film story, so I wouldn't be in those days either. He said he'd inform Frank for me.

I ran into Willy, who had Kamal prepare me some tea and biscuits. Breakfast would be later, at ten. Then he excused himself to do some important work.

Shankar had left the house to drive Chhotu to the station, and Willy was shut in his office. I didn't know where Govind was, but he didn't seem to be around. As far as I could tell, the only other person in the place was Kamal, and I could hear the pressure cooker hissing in the kitchen. She was at work preparing breakfast. I went looking for Sushmita.

She'd told me the day before which room was hers, then made me promise never to try to sneak inside. I sensed she didn't trust me to be as careful as she was, but this was an emergency she needed to know about immediately.

"*Aa jao*," she said through the door after I'd knocked softly. I entered. When she saw it was me, she leapt from the bed, crossed the room, and locked the door. "Are you mad, Danny?" she whispered. "I told you not to come here. You'll ruin everything."

I said nothing. Handed her Chhotu's note instead. She read it then crumpled it.

"Destroying the letter's not going to make this go away," I said.

She looked up at me, her deep brown eyes betraying her usual cool. She was worried. "He must have seen me leave your room. I should have expected that swine was spying."

"What can we do?" I asked. "Pay him?"

"No. He'll want *lakhs* at the very least. You don't have that kind of money. And he'll only come back for more later."

We stood by the door for a long moment, both searching for ideas. At length, she fetched a matchbox from the bedside table and burned the letter in an ashtray.

"I know this doesn't fix our problem," she said as we watched the flame consume the paper, leaving a wad of black cinders. "But we can't risk Willy finding this either."

She crushed what was left of Chhotu's blackmail note into a fine ash with her thumb.

"We have some time," she said. "Let me think about this. You go, and I'll join you for breakfast at ten thirty."

She kissed me long and deep, then stroked my cheek. I made for the door, but she called me back. "I've blackened your face," she said, wiping away the smudge she'd left on my skin with the ashes from her thumb. Satisfied I was clean, she peeked out the door to be sure no one was near. "Go," she said, waving me past her.

. . .

MONDAY, JULY 14, 1975, 3:48 P.M.

"We're going to North Main Road for some coffee," Sushmita said to Willy. "Will you come with us?"

He emerged from his study, placed his palms against the small of his back, and pushed, grimacing as he stretched. "Thank you, Mita, but no. I have some accounting to finish. You two go. Enjoy yourselves."

"We'll bring you back a gift," she said, and we were off.

Strolling through the lane, we maintained a respectable distance between us. She was a familiar figure in the area, and word could easily get back to Willy if she were seen holding hands with a strange *gora*. That kind of thing was frowned upon in India anyway. Even when it was Indian couples.

"Sush, I've been meaning to ask you if Pooja managed to get the grease out of my slacks."

"Sorry, no. She threw them in the dustbin. Why?"

"Nothing," I said. "I was just wondering if I left some money in the pocket."

I didn't want to tell her, or anyone, for that matter, about the film.

"She didn't mention it. But at least she saved your belt. I believe Govind put it back in your room."

We walked a little farther, and she asked me if I had any ideas of what to do about Chhotu.

"It seems there are two options. Either we pay him or we challenge him to rat us out to Willy."

"There's a third option," she said looking down at the footpath as she went. "We kill him."

I smiled despite our predicament. And then I wondered if she was serious. I offered a fourth idea.

"We can run off together."

She laughed. "Mad or what? And leave him in my house? My houses? Where will I stay?"

"Your bungalow in Lonavala. You said he doesn't know about it."

"Danny, I'm not ceding two valuable properties to him. Besides, what would we live on? I have very little income, in case you thought I was rich."

"But the houses?"

"Not liquid, are they?"

We walked a spell in silence, then I asked her about the three properties.

"My great-grandfather built the Poona house and the one in Lonavala. The penthouse, my father bought shortly before he died. I inherited the lot."

"I've got my salary," I said meekly.

She stopped and looked me in the eye. "Sweet Danny. That's kind of you, but I'm afraid—"

"Of course you can accept it. We'll be together."

"No, I was going to say we'd never survive on your salary. Please don't insist. I'll keep thinking of what's to be done. And you do the same."

.   .   .

We had coffee in the German Bakery on North Main Road and agreed to talk about anything but our troubles. I told her our time together should be happy. She said nothing, but the skepticism was clear on her face.

She wanted to hear more about me, my family, my life in the States. I knew she didn't like to talk about herself. She'd warned me twice not to ask about her father.

"My dad's a law professor," I said. "Retired. He's had some health problems in recent years." I paused to consider how to say what came next. "He's ... *older* than my mother. She's a pediatrician."

Sush sipped her coffee and grinned naughtily at me. "How much older?"

Growing up, I'd always felt uncomfortable discussing this very topic with my friends. Or whenever Dad came to my baseball games or picked me up from school. I loved the guy, of course. He was kind and gentle, brilliant, loving, and generous to all. I admired his politics. Despite his successful career and a knack for investments that paid off, he remained a fierce liberal. He believed in the brotherhood of man and defended the poor, the black, the brown, and everyone in between, both in court and in society.

"He's twenty-two years older than my mom," I said, fearing what her response would be.

And, as expected, it was the worst I'd imagined.

She laughed.

That reaction pierced my heart as it had a thousand times when I was a kid. People didn't do it to be mean. At least not all people. But the smirks, the jokes, and the ribbing all hurt like hell. And I hated myself for feeling ashamed of my father. That fine man didn't deserve it.

"Danny, what's wrong?" she asked.

"He's eighty-eight years old," I said. "I'm twenty-six. When I was young, my friends razzed me, said he was my grandfather."

"I'm sorry, Danny. I didn't realize."

I tried to brush it off. "It's all right," I said.

I'd thought her eyes had kissed me two days before, but there in the German Bakery café, I could have sworn they were hugging me.

. . .

We set off back for the bungalow a little past five, in no hurry to join Willy, but with no other choice. North Main Road was bustling at that hour. No rain was expected until later that evening, so shoppers had turned out to run their errands. Offices were starting to fold tents for the day, and those lucky enough to finish early were heading home on their two-wheelers or on foot. I thought how nice it would be to return to Sushmita every evening, even more so in such a pleasant corner of India. I doubted she was thinking the same, but I had the right to my own fantasy. A fantasy that shattered in an instant as I spied a maroon-robed *fireng* across the road picking out fruit from a slight man selling on the footpath.

Noticing I'd gone white—even whiter than usual—Sushmita asked what was the matter. I took her by the elbow and pulled her along, shading my face as I did.

"What is it, Danny?" she whispered.

"Harlan," I said, picking up the pace.

"Harlan?"

"Russ Harlan," I said as we turned into our lane. "The guy we met at Ash Pethe's dinner party. And at Bombay Gym."

CHAPTER TWENTY-TWO

"Are you sure? There are so many *goralog* here. And he was across the road."

"Positive," I said.

"Don't panic. He's probably just another Western pervert who wants to experience free love."

I glanced over my shoulder. "I don't think he's following us."

"Next time, Danny," she said, "if you're fearful of being followed, don't lead your pursuer to your lair."

"Sorry?"

"Take a different route. We should have turned into the next lane, or the one after that."

. . .

"We've brought you some of that *mawa* cake you like so much," said Sushmita.

Willy was reading the newspaper, sitting on the veranda outside his study. He smiled at us. She kissed him on the head and presented the small package, wrapped in paper and tied with string.

"You went to the German Bakery?" he asked. "How lovely. But I've had my tea, so I'll enjoy this after dinner, if you don't mind."

"Of course," she said. "There's only enough for one. It's yours, darling."

That word stung, even if I believed she didn't mean it. Surely this was only for show. He rose from his chair and patted me on the shoulder. Then he thanked me for taking such good care of Mita while he was occupied with work. I almost wished he'd slapped my face instead.

. . .

TUESDAY, JULY 15, 1975, 12:01 A.M.

When Sushmita came to me that night, it was only to tell me she couldn't stay. Too risky, she said. And we only had a day and a half to find a response for Chhotu. Though disappointed at being deprived of her warm body, I was relieved that my guilt in regard to Willy would be a touch lighter come morning. The man was moving heaven and earth to sort out my difficulties. He'd never done me any wrong, yet I'd cuckolded him on several occasions—with great zeal—and would still gladly steal his lover away if given half a chance.

"You're not dumping me, are you?" I asked to joke.

I thought I'd cut her to the bone. Her eyes gleamed up at mine in the low light, as if she was about to cry.

"Darling, no," she said, stroking my cheek yet again. "Danny, I—Never mind. Sleep well. I can't wait to see you tomorrow."

When you can't sleep, all kinds of crazy ideas invade your head. In my case, I found myself doubting not Sushmita's integrity, but Willy's. What was his business with a guy like Chhotu? And what about his secretive dealings with the police? I couldn't reconcile those doubts with the gratitude I felt toward him for his help.

It was nearing one, and the house was quiet. I wanted a drink. Figuring no one would hear me if I were careful, I sneaked out of my room and found the bar in the drawing room with little trouble. Having poured myself a short one—no ice or soda, as I didn't want to rouse anyone with the noise—I took a seat on the divan and listened to the sounds of the night. My thoughts returned to Willy's business. What did import-export mean anyway?

I slipped off the divan and made my way quietly to the study door. I tried the handle. Locked. Who the hell locked his study in his own home?

·   ·   ·

TUESDAY, JULY 15, 1975, 10:41 A.M.

"I'm going for a walk," I announced as Govind cleared the breakfast dishes.

"Haven't you already run your daily marathon this morning?" asked Willy.

I smiled. "Yes, but that's work. This is for relaxation."

"Do you want some company? I'm sure Mita wouldn't mind going with you."

"She's been babysitting me enough lately. I need to learn how to find my own way around."

If my decision surprised or upset Sushmita, she didn't let on. Instead, she wished me a pleasant outing. I was on a mission that morning to track down Russ Harlan and find out why he was following me.

The Poona Ashram was in the next lane to the west, not five minutes away on foot. You couldn't miss it. A bunch of Westerners dressed in their maroon robes milled about, chatting and shopping for vegetables, fruit, and sweets from the vendors who'd set up shop a couple of dozen meters down the road. Situated behind a high fence to thwart the curious gawkers, the ashram looked quite new. To enter, you had to pass through a gate flanked by tall bamboo clusters and wait in a reception office.

About twenty aspirants—mostly foreigners, but some Indians as well—waited their turn to speak to the officious clerk behind a long counter. Actually, there were six other young men on duty as well, but none of them seemed to possess the power of speech. They simply watched.

One by one, the hopefuls were given an application for admittance. Then the clerk explained the ashram rules and told them where to buy their robes—maroon for the day and white for nighttime meditations and activities. When my turn came, he asked to see my passport.

"I don't have it with me," I said.

"Sir, a passport is required before all else."

"But I don't want to go inside. I'm here to meet a friend. Russell Harlan."

"One minute," he said. "My colleague will help you." He waved me off to the side and invited the next person in line to step forward.

As I waited again, I got a brief glimpse of the grounds when a door to the interior office remained open for ten seconds or so. I could see robed devotees strolling the pathways through a lush, green landscape of flowers, shrubs, and mature trees. It looked quite peaceful, and no one was humping on the grass, at least not where I could see.

"May I help you, sir?" asked a slim fellow of about twenty-five in a shirt and tie.

"I'm here to meet my friend, Mr. Russell Harlan. H-A-R-L-A-N."

He disappeared back into the office. Barely thirty seconds later, he returned with a clipboard and pencil in hand.

"May I repeat the spelling?" he asked. "Haitch- A-R-L-A-N?"

The Indian H took some getting used to, for me at least, but I confirmed the name.

"We have no Harlan here," he said, flipping the pages pinned to his board as if to prove he'd gone through all of it.

"Are you sure? He told me yesterday to meet him here."

"Sorry, sir. No Mr. Harlan is here."

Maybe he was using an assumed name. I asked if there was a Mr. Russell instead. The man flipped through the pages again. And once more he told me there was no one by that name. He suggested I take an application from his colleague and sign up for a course of meditation.

As I stepped outside into the lane, one of the silent guys from behind the counter caught up to me. He held out a sheet of paper for me to take and wagged his head, still saying nothing. It was an application form. I said no thanks and set off toward North Main Road.

The paranoiac in me wondered if Harlan hadn't dressed up in the robe as a disguise. A way to blend in, the better to observe me undetected. The Poona Ashram didn't strike me as something he'd go in for. Still, spying or meditating, he had to be staying somewhere else nearby. A hotel perhaps. I'd seen a couple of tourist rooming houses on North Main the day before and one not-so-decent-looking hotel. And, around the corner on Koregaon Park Road—past the twin petrol bunks—there was the Blue Diamond. A nice place. I put my money on that one.

• • •

TUESDAY, JULY 15, 1975, 12:14 P.M.

"Yes, sir?" asked the concierge.

"Mr. Russell Harlan, please. Can you call up to his room for me?"

"One moment, please." He consulted a typed list of guests and room numbers. Then he cross-checked against handwritten entries in a large ledger. "I'll just connect you, sir," he said. "You may use the house phone to your right."

I lifted the receiver and listened as the phone rang somewhere upstairs. Five, six, seven, eight rings with no answer. I hung up. At least I knew I wasn't imagining things when I thought I'd spotted him the day before.

Across the lobby, the hotel coffee shop staff was putting out the buffet. It smelled good. A thought occurred to me, and I glanced at my watch. A little past noon. Maybe my friend was about to eat his lunch. He was partial to the President Hotel's restaurant food, why not the Blue Diamond's as well?

I crossed the polished tile lobby to the coffee shop's entrance and stepped inside to scan the room. There were quite a few diners, local businessmen and a handful of foreigners. Except for the ashram, Poona wasn't on the beaten path for Westerners. But there he was. Russell Harlan, sitting at the far end of the coffee shop, in deep conversation with another man.

He didn't seem all that flustered to have me glaring at him. In fact, maybe he felt I'd solved his problem of finding me. I was so intent on watching his reaction that I'd failed to notice the slight man sitting across the table from him. When Harlan invited me to join them, I finally looked his way. It was Ramu.

CHAPTER TWENTY-THREE

"What the hell's going on here?"

"Have a seat," he said. "And keep your voice down. We're in a public place."

I chose to sit next to Ramu. That way I could look Harlan in the eye as he gave me some bullshit reason why he'd followed me to Poona. And to Ash Pethe's dinner party and Bombay Gym, too. But even as I concentrated on Harlan, I couldn't help noticing that Ramu was quite nicely dressed. And I wasn't so upset that I failed to realize how unusual it was for a domestic servant to be in a luxury hotel coffee shop. I certainly didn't begrudge him the privilege, but I knew posher Indians would.

"You know Ramu," said Harlan.

"Of course I do. *Namaste*, Ramu."

"Hi, Dan," he answered, and I did a double take.

"Yes, he speaks English," said Harlan. "Quite well, actually. I should explain. Would you like something to eat first?"

"No."

He folded his hands. "Very well. You must be wondering a couple of things right about now. First, why am I here with your servant? Second, why does Ramu suddenly speak excellent English?"

I nodded.

"Good. We're off to a fine start. Ramu, why don't you tell Dan, here, who you really are?"

"With pleasure," he said. "Actually, my name's not Ramu at all. It's Ranjit. I'm an investigating officer of the CBI. Central Bureau of Investigation."

"You've got to be kidding me."

"I'm quite serious."

"Then who does that make you?" I asked Harlan.

"DEA."

"DEA? The Drug Enforcement Administration?"

He nodded.

"Holy shit," I said shaking my head to clear the cobwebs. "I'm losing my mind. What's this all about?"

"We're interested in your friend Willy Smets," said Harlan.

"Wait a minute. Wha—what are you doing in India? In Poona? With an Indian cop? Since when are the U.S. and India so chummy?"

"One question at a time," said Harlan. "I'm the Special Agent in Charge of our New Delhi bureau. We work with CBI and various state CIDs—Criminal Investigation Departments—on narcotics interdiction."

"Since when?"

"A couple of years now. We're trying to stem the diversion of illicit opium to drug traffickers. Specifically, we've been looking at Willy Smets for about a year. As things turned out, Ranjit was investigating him for other crimes. His superior put us in touch, and we've been working together for the past eight months."

"Willy Smets? What has he done, bought a couple of nickel bags?"

Ranjit frowned at me, then took up the narrative. "Smets is a major drug trafficker. His network runs from India to Pakistan to Afghanistan through Europe and on to America. That's why the DEA is involved.

India is the world's largest producer of licit opium for pharmaceutical purposes. An estimated ten percent is diverted every year. Maybe more. Your Willy Smets takes possession of a good portion of that opium, refines it into heroin, and distributes it in Europe and America."

"I can't believe it."

"He also deals in stolen goods, alcohol smuggling, and fraud. And, of course, prostitution. He's quite the versatile fellow."

"Willy? Willy Smets? My nice neighbor?"

"You're fond of him?" asked Ranjit.

"Of course I am. He's been a good friend to me."

The two cops exchanged looks.

"Are you in the habit of sleeping with your friends' gals?" asked Harlan.

"Excuse me. I'm having trouble processing all this. If he's such a bad dude, why don't you arrest him? Why mess with my life? I don't have anything to do with him."

"Except his girlfriend," said Harlan, his eyes fixed on mine.

Were they bluffing? How could they possibly have known what I was up to with Sushmita?

"Look, Dan," said Harlan, lowering his voice. "We're not judging you for who you fall in love with. Or who you sleep with. We're after bigger quarry than that. But your relationship with Smets's girl kind of put you in our crosshairs."

"Wait a minute," I said. "That can't be true. You'd already planted Ramu in my house. I didn't even know Willy or—her—at the time."

"Correct," granted Ranjit. "We paid your scheduled man, Ramu, to go away. Quite handsomely. Then I took his place in your employ because your apartment was the only one in the building with a new tenant."

"And your flat was only three floors from the penthouse," added Harlan. "Less of a climb for Ranjit."

I twisted in my seat to regard him. "What are you, an aerialist? Are you crazy, climbing up the sides of buildings without a rope or a net?"

"Army training," he said simply. "And buildings are easy to climb. It's rocks that present difficulties."

I stared at my hands for some time, as Harlan and Ranjit watched me. How could I have gotten myself so screwed up in such a short time? I was sure to lose my job, maybe end up in an Indian jail like Willy's old friend Pier Mertens, or—why not—murdered by Willy for sleeping with Sushmita or betraying him to the police.

"Don't lose heart, Danny," came a woman's voice. She'd slipped into the seat beside Harlan. It was Birgit. And she'd somehow lost her German accent.

CHAPTER TWENTY-FOUR

Willy and Sushmita were having their tea when I returned to the bungalow.

"You've been gone a long time," she said. I saw the concern on her face, even as she tried to disguise it.

"Exploring," I said.

She cocked her head. "Exploring? Where?"

"Around. I visited the ashram."

"Oh, Danny, darling," she said. "You didn't do something mad, did you? Buy robes and sign up for their meditation classes?"

"No. Excuse me. I've got a headache. Maybe I ate something bad. I'm going to lie down."

"Stick your fingers down your throat, Danny Boy," called Willy as I took my leave. "You'll feel relieved, trust me."

• • •

In my room, I tried to put the pieces of my meeting with Harlan, Ranjit, and Birgit into some kind of order I might understand. First, I'd been a complete dupe. Granted, I was new to India, but this went beyond mere naïveté. I'd exposed myself to ridicule and perhaps worse, by carrying on the least secretive affair in the history of lovers. Second, Ranjit, who was the lead investigator on the case, and Harlan, who was working closely with him in an advisory role, wanted my help in bringing down Willy. I hadn't even had a moment to consider their request, and I was too confused now to give it serious thought.

Finally, third, I was crazy for a woman who'd welcomed into her life—and two of her expensive homes—a man who would falsify, corrupt, and steal to make a dishonest buck. For, make no mistake, I blamed Sushmita as well. It was one thing to fall in love with an urbane, rich man from the Continent. But it was quite another to prop up his felonious, immoral business dealings in her heritage homes. She had to know what he was up to. Hadn't she told me herself the day before that we could never survive on my salary? Was that all that mattered to her? Money? She owned beautiful properties in Bombay, Lonavala, and Poona. Surely, she could sell one of them, or get a job. She'd studied at Cambridge, hadn't she?

These were the thoughts torturing me as I lay down on the bed, shades drawn and ceiling fan buzzing, to close my eyes and decide a course of action. Harlan had asked me to help. And Ranjit and Birgit had made compelling cases against my friend Willy. The friend I realized I didn't know.

And, of course, I'd been fooled by Birgit, too. In the coffee shop of the Blue Diamond Hotel, she told me she'd been born in West Berlin to a German mother and an American father—an OSS officer—a year or so after the war ended. That she'd moved to Virginia at the age of seven when her mother was finally granted a visa, and she'd grown up on the outskirts of D.C., perfectly bilingual and determined to be a good American.

She was a DEA special agent, working mostly on drug cases involving Europe, for obvious reasons. Recruited straight out of Duke for her linguistic skills and superior test scores, Birgit was one of twenty-six female DEA agents. She went by Brigitte back in the

States. Christ, did everyone have to have a different name? I was just Danny Jacobs.

Goddamn Willy, I thought as I lay on the bed. Couldn't he have been a prick to me? Or vaguely indifferent? I might not have felt the conflict that troubled me now. And, most of all, couldn't he have had a less attractive lover? One who didn't light a fire in my heart?

I wanted to disappear. Leave them all behind and start anew back home. Be anonymous. Marry a girl who'd never thrown her lot in with a smuggler, a pimp, a drug dealer.

But then a thought occurred to me. For the first time since I'd realized my manservant was a well-trained cop—and the hayseed bigot I'd hated was, in fact, a disciplined, principled civil servant who'd been playing me for a fool—for the first time, yes, I realized that this was a chance. Here was a way to rid myself of the obstacle to my happiness. Willy. Was there a way to hand him over to the DEA, the CBI, or CID, and have Sushmita all to myself? It was the darkest impulse I'd ever experienced. Could I do it? Betray Willy and win the girl? The girl I couldn't get out of my mind, even as I told myself she was a stranger to me.

• • •

TUESDAY, JULY 15, 1975, 8:02 P.M.

A light kiss on my forehead woke me.

"*Mazha Danny.* Wake up, my darling. It's time for cocktails. I can't bear it without you. Come."

I stared up at her, wanting to tell her to go back to her man. But at the same time, wanting to . . . Never mind.

"What happened today, Danny?" she asked in a half whisper. "Something's changed."

At dinner, I told my hosts that I'd gone to the station that afternoon and bought my ticket back on the Bombay Express.

"You're leaving us?" asked Sushmita. "When?"

"Tomorrow. I have to get back to work before I lose my job."

"But what about the bomber?"

"I'll ask Lokhande for help. I'm sure he can do something to protect me."

"But we don't yet know what the inspector's intentions are," said Willy. "I'm working on solving this, Danny Boy. Give it a few more days."

I shook my head. "I'm going back."

"Stay here, Danny," said Sushmita. "You're safe."

I avoided looking her in the eye and addressed Willy instead, thanking him for his generosity. All I could think of was how much I wanted to get away. From Willy, Chhotu, Harlan, and—yes—even Sushmita. I was a nice boy from Connecticut. What business did I have hobnobbing with drug smugglers and DEA agents?

But I also wondered if I *should* leave. I hadn't yet given Harlan my answer. He had no legal leverage over me, but still I felt the pressure to give him the cooperation he'd asked for. What that cooperation might entail, I could only guess. Maybe they'd want me to wear a wire or steal documents. Find out who his associates were.

A new thought occurred to me. I'd be only too happy to hand Chhotu to them on a platter. That might even solve my blackmail problem. But it would also amount to betraying Willy, which I hadn't yet decided to do.

So, as I thanked Willy and kept my thoughts to myself, I had no idea what my next move would be. I knew I couldn't tell Sushmita what had prompted my sudden decision to leave, even if she came to my room later that night. And she did.

• • •

WEDNESDAY, JULY 16, 1975, 12:06 A.M.

"You're leaving?" she asked, her eyes pleading with me to change my mind.

"I've got to."

"No, you don't. What's happened, Danny?"

"I'm worried about my job. And the sneaking around behind Willy's back and the blackmail."

"Don't worry about Chhotu. I can deal with him."

"How?"

"Chhotu was willing to keep our secret for a price. I'll threaten to show Willy the blackmail note."

"That's brilliant," I said. "Except for one problem. We burned it."

She cocked her lips into a crooked smile. "No, we don't have it. But Chhotu doesn't know that. And I can let him believe it's my insurance forever. A threat of mutual assured destruction."

"You don't think he'll tell Willy about us before you get to him?"

"No, he wants money. And he's afraid of me. He'll wait."

She was smart. And the smarter I found her, the sexier she became. And more dangerous. While I wanted to get away, I also knew it was going to be torture for me to leave her. If her plan worked—and it sounded good to me—then one obstacle would be eliminated. Of course that did nothing to solve my Harlan problem. Should I help him nab Willy? If I didn't get killed, would it open the door to living happily ever after with Sushmita?

Happily ever after? With a girl who'd willingly signed on with a man wanted in several countries? A girl who lived with him, made love with him? Not in his houses, but in hers? I had to assume he'd duped her into believing he was a good man, otherwise I could have no respect for her. But even if she'd been tricked, why had she stayed with him? Would I, could I, be happy with such a girl?

Perhaps not happy. But obsessed? In too deep? I could be all those things. Of course I let Sushmita into my bed, thinking it would be the last time. I wanted it to be and, at the same time, I never wanted it to end.

CHAPTER TWENTY-FIVE

Sushmita was gone when I emerged from my bath the next morning. I'd missed my run. I asked Willy where she was.

"I wanted to say goodbye to her. You've both been so kind to me. And she's been a patient babysitter."

"She and I quarreled after you retired last night, and she ran out this morning. I'm afraid I'm not very loved right now."

Had they argued before Sushmita came to my room? She hadn't mentioned it. She'd been upset about my leaving, but said nothing about Willy. Was she so cool that she could turn her emotions off and on like a spigot?

"What did you quarrel about?" I asked.

"Nothing important," he said, waving a hand. "About Chhotu. She despises him. When I told her he's returning here to stay for a few days, she had a crying fit. Don't worry, Danny Boy. She'll come around. She always does."

"I'm sorry to hear that," I said. "Please convey my thanks to her when she comes back."

"I shall. Now you don't want to miss your train. Shankar is waiting outside in the Ambassador, the second car. I'm afraid Mita has taken the Mercedes."

He apologized for not being able to accompany me to the station, but I was glad. Glad to be alone with my own thoughts. The driver,

Shankar, left me in peace as we made our way to the Poona Junction Station. He only spoke to me once, as I climbed out of the car.

"Pleasant journey, sir."

The Bombay Express, which originated in Hyderabad, was running late. Scheduled to leave Poona at 9:05, it was now expected in the station at 10:15. I sat on a bench in the waiting room, my bag on my lap, as I really didn't want to put it on the floor. The less said about that the better.

When my train finally entered the station, I scrambled up the stairs of the overpass—following a river of other travelers who seemed to know where they were going—then climbed back down the stairs on Track 2. I tried to ignore the smell coming from beneath the train, but I confess it was hard to do. Some things should not be dropped directly on the tracks from a train's toilet, especially inside a busy railroad depot.

We left the station at 10:20, with an estimated arrival at 1:35 in the afternoon at Victoria Terminus in Bombay. I leaned back in my seat—first class reserved—and closed my eyes to relive some of the previous night's delights. Springing for a first-class ticket, by the way, was an absolute necessity. At least that's what Frank Muller had told me when I'd first arrived. Not that it was luxurious or that the service was memorable. But it was far better than the alternative.

A waiter came by about twenty minutes after we'd left the station to serve some thin masala tea and a biscuit. Hardly up to Vikky's or Ramu's standards. Damn Ramu.

·   ·   ·

At 11:35, we pulled into the Lonavala station. As the train slowed, I couldn't help recalling the night Sushmita and I had spent there. I wished we could do so again, and without a timetable to leave to join her lover. It was the ideal house to begin an affair. Wasn't there some way she could leave Willy and retire to the Lonavala bungalow with me in tow? We could hide there forever and forget my troubles and the criminal she'd taken in.

The train lurched to a stop. I gazed out the window, trying to figure out which direction led to her bungalow, when a tap from the outside called my attention. Jesus. It was Sushmita, waving to me from the platform, mouthing the words, "Get off the train now."

CHAPTER TWENTY-SIX

"What are you doing here?" I asked once I'd grabbed my bag from the netting above my seat and jumped out of the train, seconds before it pulled out of the station again.

"I want to kiss you, but I can't," she said, low, so no one else could hear.

"There goes my train. What am I going to do now?"

"You're going to come with me to the bungalow. We're alone now. For a day or two at least."

In the car, she told me she'd staged the fight with Willy over Chhotu the night before. Then, early in the morning, she'd risen and made a big show of storming out of the house, saying she was never coming back.

"Just to convince him I was still angry," she said. "Then I drove like the wind to arrive here at the station before your train. It helped that it was late."

I leaned over and kissed her cheek as she drove. Good thing I hadn't fastened my seat belt, or I'd never have reached. My doubts, fears, and suspicions vanished in a shot. I was more desperately crazy for her than before.

"But the train only stopped for a minute," I said. "How did you know which car I was in?"

She glanced at me, then back at the road. "Please, Danny. I knew you had to be in first class. You'd have had a stroke in second or third."

We stopped at a market. Sushmita insisted I wait in the car, as it would not do for her to be seen with a *gora*. Inside, she picked up some bread, milk, onions, cabbage, rice, cheese, coffee, and tea. Then we drove to the bungalow just as the rain started to fall.

· · ·

We were alone. Safe from the eyes of the world. Secure behind the walls of a house no one knew existed. Not Willy Smets, not Chhotu, not Russell Harland. And certainly not Bikas the bomber. The sensation was liberating. I wanted to strip out of my clothes and spend the next two, three, four days enjoying life at its most primitive with her. Because we could. Because no one knew where the hell we were. I didn't suggest it, of course, trying to play it cool instead. We made lunch.

I was chopping cabbage in preparation for the *bund gobi aur matar* I intended to make for dinner later that evening. It was a recipe I'd found in a small cookbook in the kitchen. Cabbage with peas, but without the peas since we didn't have any.

"Do you know how to use a pressure cooker?" she asked as she cut onions for the rice.

"I've heard of them. Where do I plug it in?"

"It's not electric. Here, let me show you."

And she proceeded to do exactly that, filling the thing with dal and water, before bolting it closed and putting it on the two-burner range, what they called a hob in India.

"Are you sure it won't explode?"

She feigned a laugh and kissed me, lightly, quickly, right there in the kitchen, as the flame from the gas cylinder flickered beneath the pressure cooker.

"Do we have wine?" I asked.

She ran her hand through my hair. "No, darling. But I've got everything you desire."

·   ·   ·

The afternoon rain continued, dark and heavy, pounding on the roof of the house as if it wanted in. The temperature was cool, prompting Sush to pull a marine sweater over the pajamas she'd changed into after we ate. There she was, padding around the house in *chappals*, white cotton pajamas, and a sweater. I'd never seen anything sexier in the pages of *Playboy*. And, believe me, the adolescent Danny Jacobs had been an authority on *Playboy*.

"What about your work?" she asked as we lounged before the terrace windows, watching the rain flood the patio outside. "Will they notice your absence?"

"I hope so. But I'm okay for another day. Maybe two. They think I'm working on a film story in Juhu."

We lay in each other's arms on the daybed in the drawing room. I asked her how long she could stay away from Poona.

"Willy invited Chhotu until Saturday. So I have at least till then. He won't expect me back as long as that swine is there."

I nodded, even as I thought three days' time wasn't all that much. Still, we could try to make them last. Maybe even steal an extra day.

"He won't suspect?" I asked.

"He knows I have a temper. Two, three days. I can manage it."

"And he really doesn't know about this place?"

"Don't doubt me, Danny," she said, suddenly all serious. "If I say he knows nothing of this house, you must trust me."

·   ·   ·

The rain made us feel safe. We were sheltered, warm and dry, while the world spun on its axis, oblivious to us. I thought of my parents, far away in New Haven, completely unaware of the troubles their youngest child had gotten himself into. But none of that mattered; I was living the most blissful moment of my life. I realized, too, that on the other side of that blissful moment would be pretty much the worst times I'd ever experience.

I hoped my dad was well. He'd had a rough patch in the months before I left for India. But he'd rallied, and my mother, brother, sister, and I were wishing for the best. Mark and Debbie, my siblings, were ten and twelve years older than me, respectively. They were up to their necks in marriages, mortgages, and school-aged kids. And Mom had her share of challenges and pressure, what with an ailing husband, her own medical practice, and worries for a son who was constantly shipping off to hot spots halfway around the world. To India, this time, where a state of emergency could only increase her anxiety.

"Are you sad, Danny?" asked Sushmita, stroking my temples with her fingers as the rain continued to fall outside the window.

"Not sad," I said. "Wistful."

"Explain the difference to me."

"I mean I'm not sad. I'm regretful. I understand that sounds odd. I'm missing my family. I sent a letter last week to say I was fine. That the Emergency wasn't affecting me. They probably haven't received it yet."

Another thing about monsoon season is that it's easy to become trapped inside. I certainly didn't mind holing up with Sushmita, but I'd have gone stir-crazy if I'd been on my own. As it was, we spent hours on the daybed, hardly speaking and never thinking about the world beyond the curtain of rain falling outside. I didn't even care that I was AWOL from my job, mostly because I didn't give it any thought. All that mattered was the three-foot area that surrounded me. And Sush never left that tight circle.

"Where did you get that scar on your left hip?" she asked me as we lay on the bed. In truth, it was more my left butt cheek than hip.

"When did you see my scar?"

She gave me a knowing look.

"Oh, right. Well, it's nothing. A souvenir from Vietnam."

"You fought in Vietnam?"

"I was a reporter. For fourteen months."

"Then how did you get the scar? A penicillin shot?"

I thought back to the most terrifying moments of my life—if you didn't count the ascent of the *ghats*. A lot of it was the waiting, which was filled with the smell of gun oil and cigarette smoke, marijuana, and sweat. And Absorbine Jr. for the athlete's foot you got in wet boots. The silence creeped me out, and the noise scared the crap out of me. Rotor blades beating the air, squawking banana radios, and high grass swishing against fatigues as you tramped into the unknown. Vietnamese-accented English and French, tinny rock-and-roll on a shitty transistor radio—lots of Jefferson Airplane and Cream. And then there was the distinctive bang—half gas expulsion, half metallic thud—of an AK-47, firing from somewhere you can't find in the dense bush. Those gave me nightmares. And a piece of metal in the hip.

"I spent a couple of weeks on patrol with a group of Army Rangers," I said. "I took a bit of shrapnel from a piece of canteen blown off by a Viet Cong AK-47. When the medics got me back to the base, I was embarrassed to show the wound to the nurse. I had to lower my drawers so they could remove the shrapnel and stitch me up."

Sushmita snorted a laugh, then apologized. "*Mazha* Danny. I didn't know you were so brave."

Hours later, as the ceiling fan whirred above us, I traced a line from her shoulder, down her arm, jumping off at her ribs, and continuing over the gentle curve of her hip. My white finger looked blotchy against her perfect skin, and I wished I had a tan. When I told her that, she made me promise never to get dark. I didn't get it, this Indian obsession with fairness, but she was adamant. And I sensed in her no small measure of disappointment at the darkness of her own skin. I told her she was beautiful. Why such a confident, intelligent person should care about a shade or two of melanin, I surely did not know. But I wasn't in her skin. I couldn't possibly understand how the expectations of Indian society had affected her.

This was an odd conversation to be having in my own head. My parents had raised me to regard skin color as irrelevant, to me personally at least. Of course, they said, many people gave it too much importance, some for all the wrong reasons. I understood why a black man sees color. He's likely to be on the wrong end of prejudice for his. But the white racists disgusted me. Bullies who bully those they can get away with bullying.

"You've got white skin," she said. "You'll never truly understand."

I said nothing more. But if this remarkable woman thought of herself as somehow less than beautiful because of an arbitrary esthetic standard, I wanted to hold her tight, make her feel safe, and let her know she was perfect.

· · ·

Even with the power back on, we burned candles and *diyas* instead of electric lights. Sushmita didn't want to alert nosy neighbors to our presence. Not that there was any house in view, but she was exercising maximum care.

I'd somehow managed to make an edible dish of cabbage, so we had that and a plate of leftover dal and rice she'd made earlier. We talked late into the night. She asked me about my football career, such as it was, and I told her about the worst defeat of my sporting life, *Harvard Beats Yale 29-29.*

"That sounds like a draw," she said. "You Americans really should learn English. Or maths."

Ignoring her comment, I propped myself up on an elbow to tell the tale.

"It was my sophomore year and I was riding the bench." I had to explain *sophomore* and *riding the bench* to her. She watched me with big, sparkling eyes, as if I weren't boring her. "Both teams were undefeated, facing off in the final game of the season for the Ivy League title. We were leading by sixteen points late in the fourth quarter. And then disaster struck. Harvard scored twice in the last forty-two seconds—sixteen points."

"Is that a lot?" she asked.

"Yes. That's a *whole* lot. So they tied us, but the feeling was that Harvard had won. I can't argue with that, because it sure felt as if we'd lost."

Sushmita caressed my cheek. "I'm sure Yale would have won if you'd played, Danny."

She was teasing, of course. But she made up for it soon enough. She was natural and unashamed. I wondered how she could be so sensitive about her complexion but not her body. Later, she caught me gazing at the silky hair on the nape of her neck, visible when she tied up her tresses in a ponytail.

"Stop staring, you pervert," she said, and gave me a playful shove.

I told her she was beautiful. She said I was a frog. I shoved her back. We wrestled. Not sure who won. I think it was a tie. Like Yale and Harvard.

· · ·

The next morning we slept in. No run for me. Sushmita said it might cause talk. I had no idea of the time. I hadn't wound my watch, and it had stopped somewhere around three in the morning. We lingered on top of the sheets, in no hurry to get up or do anything. Two days passed this way, with no concerns about the time.

That last night, however, things changed. We both grew quiet as the minutes ticked away, inching us nearer to our date with the real world. The ease and playful joy we'd both experienced for three full days waned as the earth turned and morning drew closer.

Her head resting on my chest, Sush asked me what we were going to do. I told her I didn't know. In fact, I was debating with myself.

"You've got that look again," she said. The light was low, but she knew I was brooding. "It's the same look you had the night you announced you were leaving Poona. Please tell me, Danny. What is it?"

But I couldn't. Not yet. Even if I believed I needed to know her intentions in order to make up my own mind, I still couldn't bring myself to tell her I was considering turning on Willy.

"I'm sad that our time is over," I said instead. "You'll drop me at the station and go back to Poona. I'll be in Bombay, miserable."

"You don't think I'll be miserable, too? Alone with a man I don't love?"

"Don't you?"

"We're comfortable together, but it's not love. It hasn't been for some time now. I want to be yours, Danny, but it's impossible. Not now. Not yet."

Her words nearly changed my mind. Maybe I should tell her about Ranjit and Harlan and Willy. Maybe she was trying to tell me to trust her. But in the end, I was more afraid to lose her outright than I was eager to win her forever.

CHAPTER TWENTY-SEVEN

I stopped at my flat to drop off my bag. Ramu/Ranjit had cleaned up the mess left by my burglar, and everything looked normal again. I worried Bikas might try a second time, though I didn't believe he'd actually kill me. At least not yet. He'd never get the film if he did. Still, I wasn't resting easy. I decided to contact Lokhande for advice.

I headed to the office. Truth be told, I half-expected to find a pink slip waiting for me on my desk. Instead there were several messages from New York, requesting information and updates for a feature they were working on there. Details on the suppression of civil liberties and democratic franchises. They wouldn't be able to list me as a contributor, due to the censorship in country, but I would eventually get credit for my part in the story once the Emergency was lifted.

There were notes from Frank, too. He didn't seem to care that I'd been gone a full week, and he was eager to read my piece on the cinema business. That was going to be tricky since I hadn't written one.

"Where's Frank?" I asked Janice, who'd joined me for afternoon tea.

"In Goa. He won't be back until a week from Monday. I think he's met someone."

"A biped?" I asked.

"Some woman with UNESCO. She's stationed here for a few months. Working on health care issues or hunger. I couldn't quite hear properly when he was telling his friend on the phone the other day. But what about you? You fell off the face of the earth for a while there."

"I got some bad food somewhere," I lied. "Then I was traveling out to Juhu every day on the train for my film story."

I asked her if Bikas had called again. She said no. Strange, I thought. I would have expected him to be hopping mad after I'd stood him up at Sassoon Docks. Why hadn't he tried to reach me?

We chatted a while more over Vikky's sweet tea. Janice wanted to know about Ramu.

"Did he really climb up the side of the building?" she asked.

I recalled Ranjit/Ramu's cool demeanor when explaining the incident to me at the Blue Diamond Hotel. It had been a dry run, he said. A chance to see if he could make the climb and break in when Willy and Sushmita were out of town. I shuddered, imagining the heights. It was quite inconvenient that he got caught, but he managed to keep his identity from the police. They were always on the take from gangsters and criminals—possibly even Willy Smets—so he couldn't risk word getting out that he was CBI and not a servant.

"He did, indeed," I said. "I saw it myself. Me, I'm scared to death of heights. I would have fallen to a spectacular death, which is a recurring nightmare for me."

Janice finished her tea and announced that she was packing it in for the week. It was Saturday, after all, and we were both off the next day.

"Plans with Mr. Dreamboat?" I teased.

"As a matter of fact, yes. We're going to see a film, then we'll have a late dinner at my place. Perhaps I shouldn't be sharing such details with you, Mr. Jacobs."

"Why not? We're friends, aren't we?"

"If you say so. But if we're friends, look out or I'll ask you about that pretty girl you brought to Bombay Gym last week. Did you deliver my gift to her?"

Sushmita was the last person I wanted to discuss just then. But I'd opened the door with my own questions about her gentleman friend, Shirish. The mention of Sushmita's name took me back several hours to our goodbye at the Lonavala station. Bucking societal norms, she'd leaned over from the driver's seat—still no seat belt—and kissed me long on the lips. I don't know if anyone could see us inside the car, but it was a risky move.

She said she'd get a message to me the next day or the day after. She told me not to give up on her. Not to forget that I'd told her I loved her. Of course she'd never returned the favor, I thought, but perhaps for good reason. I was free and she, not quite.

"Mr. Jacobs, you're not listening to me," said Janice, pulling me back from the memory. "Did you deliver my gift?"

"Sorry, Miss Spenser. She's out of town. I'll get it to her as soon as possible."

She wished me a pleasant Sunday and was off to her healthy and perfectly uncomplicated friendship with a good man. I envied her the normalcy. The averageness of her romance. I had no idea how passionate the two of them were behind closed doors, but I would have loved to exchange their conventionality for my train wreck of a life.

· · ·

I spent several hours more in the office. First I phoned Lokhande, who was out, and left a message with my work number. Then I made some calls to my film industry contacts, checking in again with Ravi Om Gopal. He didn't want to have anything to do with me or my story, but finally agreed to slip me the name of a director who'd been arrested three days before in yet another roundup by Mrs. Gandhi's police. I had to swear I'd never mention where I'd gotten the name.

"Anonymous source," I told him. "Don't worry. You're safe."

I researched the director in question—Mukesh Sharma—for the better part of an hour, and found what I thought was his mother's address in Lower Parel. I made a note to contact her in the morning or Monday. There was also a minor starlet who'd been linked to his name in the film biz gossip columns a few months earlier. I'd try to find her as well.

Lokhande returned my call around seven. He thanked me for the bottle of Chivas Ramu had dropped off for him.

"But next time, Dan, don't send it to the station. That makes it look like a bribe."

What did he mean *next time*? Was he expecting more imported booze from me? And wasn't it a bribe?

We got down to business. I explained the situation to him, that Bikas had broken into my flat and I'd appreciate some police protection. Maybe an officer posted in the lobby?

"Why did he break into your flat?" he asked.

"I think he wanted to threaten me. He's changed his mind about the interview, I guess."

I didn't mention that Bikas had ransacked the place. That would suggest he'd been looking for something. I was still keeping the existence of the film—the film I'd lost—from Lokhande, of course.

"Why didn't he simply threaten you by phone? Why risk getting caught?"

"I don't know. Can you help me?"

There was a pause on the other end of the line. At length, Lokhande said he'd stop by to check on me in the coming days, but it sounded as if I was in little danger.

"He's given you his warning," he said. "No reason for him to do anything else to you if you don't print your story. Unless . . ."

"Unless what?" I asked, thinking I already knew the answer.

"Unless you have something he wants and won't give it to him."

·   ·   ·

SUNDAY, JULY 20, 1975, 9:03 A.M.

Huge waves were breaking against the seawall along Marine Drive, launching great plumes of water that rose high into the air before cascading down onto the footpath and anyone foolish enough to be out and about. Me, for one. I ran hard through the rain, hurdling the puddles, as I cursed myself for having left Poona. No one had forced me. I could have told Harlan and Ranjit to go to hell. I could have continued sleeping with Sushmita. We could have managed Chhotu, as she'd explained.

Around one in the afternoon, I crossed the road under an umbrella and took a table in the coffee shop at the President. The buffet would be fine. I only picked at it anyway. What I really wanted wasn't on the menu, à la carte or otherwise. I wanted Sushmita. And if I couldn't have her, then I wanted distraction. Diversion. What the Indians called "time-pass." Let the day get itself over with and give me Monday morning so I could go back to work and do something to forget about her.

What I got instead was Russell Harlan parking himself in front of me at my table.

"I thought you were in Poona," I said.

He signaled to the waiter. Once the black-vested young man had come and gone with his order, Harlan folded his hands on the table and leaned forward.

"You're going to help us, I know," he said.

"Why?"

"Because you're a good kid."

I digested that for a long moment, then had a question of my own before I answered. "You're not really the bigot you pretended to be, are you, Russ?"

"I can't give myself a character reference."

"But it's true, right? You're actually a decent guy."

"My wife and kids think I'm okay," he said, eyes on his uninteresting hands, not on me.

"What should I think?" I asked. "Are you a guy looking out for his own interests and willing to have some poor sap stick his neck out and pay the price?"

He regarded me and, face like a stone, told me he was willing to give me assurances.

"What kind of assurances? Can you promise I'll get the girl? Can you assure me I won't get killed spying on Willy Smets?"

"No, Dan," he said. "I can't promise you any of that. What I can tell you is that I'll be very appreciative. Your country will be, too. And the Indian government, for that matter. You'll have done good. The right thing."

"No Sushmita, then? No happily ever after?"

"No."

"What exactly do you want me to do?" I asked. "Steal his books? Wear a wire? Take him out with a bullet behind the ear when he least expects it?"

"Do you know how to shoot a gun?"

"Of course not. I've never even held one in my hand."

"Then we won't ask you to shoot him."

I glanced away, then chuckled. This wasn't the same jerk I'd met a couple of weeks before. He was a serious, even-tempered guy, who projected authority. He had an uncanny knack for making you want to please him. Like a football coach or a platoon sergeant, only he went about it quietly. He was a pretty fine actor, as well.

"What do you want me to do?" I repeated.

"We want you to work for him. Ingratiate yourself to him. Gain his trust. Get to know his operation."

"And then stab him in the back?"

"Figuratively speaking, yes. Of course a man like that deserves a real knife in the back."

"I gotta tell you, Russ, I'm having a hard time believing some of this. How can he be such a bad guy when he's so good to me? Why would he be nice?"

"Maybe it's your good looks and charm, Dan."

I scoffed.

"I mean it. For some reason he likes you."

"Ridiculous."

"Okay, then maybe it's because there are things you could get done that he can't. You're squeaky clean. Not on Interpol's radar or the FBI's or the DEA's. You're white. That helps in this country. The police tend to give Westerners a pass where they don't for the locals. Like at the airport. Customs."

"You want me to be a double agent? I've never even held a gun. Do you think I've trained as a spy?"

"Let's not exaggerate, Dan. You're not going to be a spy. You're going to be a snitch."

"You ever thought of going into the recruiting business? If so, don't."

"Look, I'm not saying it's going to be easy. But you really only have to do what Smets asks you to do. Then, when we contact you, you tell us."

"So no danger in this for the snitch?"

He lit a cigarette before answering. "There are risks," he said. "You'll want to be careful not to arouse his suspicions."

"How do I accomplish that?"

"For one thing, you stop sleeping with his girlfriend."

It was distasteful enough to consider turning Willy over to the authorities. He'd never done me wrong. But I'd done him dirty on several occasions. I'd counted them—fifteen in all—and could tick off the day, the hour, and the positions involved. It was a regular Kama Sutra of betrayal, and it was all seared into my memory.

But as bad as stabbing Willy in the back might have seemed an hour earlier, it now came with the charming title of "snitch." Couldn't wait to put that on my résumé. Why did Harlan have to be so fucking honest? Couldn't he have let me have my double-agent fantasy?

"Well?" he asked. "What do you say?"

"I say no. I'm not a snitch. If you can't get Willy Smets the honest way, with all the resources and wall-climbers and pretty blondes you have, I'm not going to help you."

CHAPTER TWENTY-EIGHT

My thoughts seesawed between Harlan's proposition and Sushmita, a hundred miles or so away. She'd said she'd get word to me as soon as possible. I wondered how. I didn't have a telephone, and a telegram seemed risky under the circumstances. I resigned myself to the probability that I'd hear from her only when she and Willy returned to Bombay. And who knew when that might be?

Harlan, on the other hand, had sat there and watched me walk out on him. He didn't try to stop me, talk sense into me, or even say goodbye. That troubled me. It was as if he wasn't concerned. As if he had another card to play. I hated not knowing his intentions. He was a seasoned agent, after all. I was sure he'd run into tougher nuts than me in his career. And I'd felt so cool striding out of the coffee shop, leaving him with my bill to pay.

But I considered myself an intelligent if foolish guy. If I thought about it seriously, I might be able to figure his next move. He'd come calling again at some point. Or he'd try to win back my good graces. Or Ranjit would. He was the lead agent on this, after all. But Harlan was the persuader.

. . .

I took a taxi to Lower Parel to an address I'd found two days before.

Mukesh Sharma's mother answered the door of the small, dark flat. She was dressed in a white cotton sari. A widow—I knew from the color. Her gray hair was tied into a long braid at the back. She spoke some English, but not well enough to make up for my lack of Hindi or Marathi or Punjabi, whatever was her first language. But I managed to communicate that I wanted to talk to her about her son.

Somewhat warily, she let me in and offered to serve me *chai*. I smiled, and she seemed to like that. Before long, we were chummy. She produced an old tin whose original purpose was no longer decipherable because the paint and the words had been worn off over the years. Inside the box were biscuits to dip in the tea. I made sure to take only one. Clearly she didn't have much, and I didn't need to be taking advantage of her goodness.

"Your son," I said, "Mukesh. The police have detained him?"

She understood *son* and *Mukesh*, but not *detained*. I tried *arrested* but no dice. *Jail?* I asked. That worked.

Her eyes expressed the love and worry of a mother who didn't know where to turn to help her son. Obviously, she didn't have the means to bribe him out of jail. Nor did she have, I was sure, the connections to secure him a good lawyer.

"Have you spoken to him?" I asked, pointing to her, miming what was supposed to pass for speech, then saying her son's name.

"*Ji*," she said. "He's fine. Safe."

Over the course of the next fifteen minutes, I managed to glean that the poor guy was arrested for making a film that somehow had been interpreted as a critique of the government, even though it had been released nearly a year before the Emergency. The film featured unrest and protests from workers, led by the handsome star, as he fought for social justice in a provincial town beset with corruption and crime. She gave me the name of the picture—*Nyaay!*—Justice!—and I made a note to research the newspaper reviews from a year before.

She also gave me the name and address of the starlet her son had been involved with. Someone named simply Ruchika. Maybe she was trying to achieve that single-name fame of someone like Rekha. Or Cher.

"Please help *mera* Mukesh," she said, as she saw me to the door.

I told her I'd try, though I doubted I could do him any good. I had no idea how the arrestees were being treated. Maybe his girlfriend Ruchika could tell me more.

It took me forty minutes by train to reach the Borivali station in the far northern suburbs. Then another twenty minutes to find the place on foot. It was a newish development, a society—a sort of co-op—on Rohan Nagar Road. Modest, to be sure, with low ceilings and little air. But I was a spoiled American, used to space, air-conditioning, and electrical service without daily interruptions.

Sharma's mother had told me the girl's surname was Pillai. I found the flat number on the residents' board in the entryway to Building D, Block II. R. Pillai, number 3-B. I climbed the stairs—no lift—and knocked, well aware that if she wasn't in, there was no way I'd ever take the train out to Borivali again. This was Ruchika's one chance at international stardom, in the form of an interview via a wire service.

It took a minute, but eventually the door opened a crack, and a very pretty young woman peered out. Clearly surprised to find a *gora* outside her flat, she asked in good English what I wanted. I told her who I was and that I'd like to talk to her about Mukesh Sharma. She said no and tried to shut the door on me, but I explained this could help him and give her some international publicity at the same time. That did the trick.

"You may come in," she said, standing to one side.

Her place wasn't bad. Recent redecoration, some modern furniture, and incandescent lights, not the dim tube lighting I'd come to expect. I complimented her on her taste, and she smiled. I could see why she thought a career in the movies might be possible. She was pretty enough. The question was whether she had that spark that made a star. And could she dance? Starlets in Bombay needed a good figure, beautiful hair, a pretty face, and excellent dancing. A singing voice wasn't required, since they dubbed all the songs with playback singers.

"Please sit," she said, indicating the divan, a brand-new white-leather number that looked as if it had come straight off the set of a Hindi-language film.

"What can you tell me about Mukesh Sharma's arrest?" I asked.

"You won't make me look critical of Mrs. Gandhi, will you?" she asked. "Because she's only trying to protect the nation."

I sensed Ruchika was playing it safe, in case I wanted to write a political piece.

"Of course she is," I said. "I'm not writing about protests or criticism of the government. I'm only trying to take the temperature of the film industry. Has it been affected by the Emergency, or are things going on as usual?"

"Mukesh was arrested," she said. "How can you avoid that in your article?"

"I can't be sure until I know why. Where is he? Are they treating him well? That kind of thing."

She seemed doubtful, but she told me he'd been picked up at his home in Bandra. I asked about his politics, and she said he was a Congress man. Critical of Mrs. Gandhi? Never.

"He made that film, *Nyaay!*" she said. "A love story about a workingman who fights injustice and wins the girl. Nothing more."

I told her maybe the authorities will realize their mistake and let him go. Then I asked how they'd met.

"I had a small part in a film last year. The sister of the lead actress. Mukesh saw me at Sun-n-Sand Hotel in Juhu. I was hoping to catch the eye of a producer, so I sometimes went to the swimming pool and permit room there."

"I see. And he noticed you."

"Yes. He was very nice. Not arrogant like most directors. He treated me with respect and bought me things. This flat, for instance."

I cast my gaze around the room, admiring, and told her it was lovely. A shame Mukesh hadn't put his mother in something as nice.

"But now I don't know how I'll manage," she said. "There's the society dues and my cook. And the sweeper who comes to clean every day. I don't know how I'll pay them."

"No roles coming your way?"

She shook her head. "There are so many pretty girls trying to get into films. And they'll do anything to land a part. It's not fair, really."

I sympathized, handed her my card, and asked her to contact me if anything came up with Mukesh.

"But you'll use my name in your article?" she asked. "Nothing negative. Only that I'm a pretty actress? With good English. Ready for American films."

"Of course. And you'll let me know if they release him. Or if they'll permit visitors."

She stared at my card, then asked if I knew Robert Redford.

• • •

MONDAY, JULY 21, 1975, 7:46 P.M.

When I turned the key to unlock my door, it opened before I could lift the latch. Ramu—not Bikas—was there to greet me.

CHAPTER TWENTY-NINE

"Good evening, sir," he said in his old servant's accent.

"Cut the crap, Ranjit," I said, pushing past him. "What are you doing here? And who let you in?"

He shut the door behind me. "I made a copy of the key long ago. And you can call me Ranjit inside this flat but, for appearance's sake, I'm Ramu outside. Your servant can't suddenly change his name."

"You're fired," I said. "Problem solved."

"Come on, Dan. You can use the help. Or the company. Or the protection. At least until you decide your answer to our request."

"I have decided. The answer is no. I don't want anything to do with this operation. Willy Smets may well be the head of a drug cartel and a prostitution ring. But he's always treated me right. I'm not a cop. That's your job. You guys should do this, not ask me to be a snitch."

. . .

MONDAY, JULY 21, 1975, 10:10 P.M.

Ranjit and I relaxed on our respective sofas and toasted each other, me with my one-after-dinner Dewar's, him with his juice. The Boy Scout didn't drink liquor. The meal he'd prepared had been his best effort to date. A mushroom *pulao* and moong *dal*, flavored with garlic and onion, followed by an *aloo gobi* in gravy and *bhindi,* okra. A sliced-tomato-and-onion salad, and chutney rounded out the menu. Pure veg. Then, to show me what I'd be missing after I fired him, he brought out some *kheer* for dessert.

Damn Ranjit. Former army officer, current cop, climber of buildings, speaker of languages, and a chef who should open his own restaurant. He ironed a mean shirt, too. How the hell could a guy be so good at so many things?

"Where did you learn to cook?" I asked, staring up at the revolving ceiling fan. "Don't tell me the army again, or I'm going to enlist."

"From my mother. And at the CBI Academy in Ghaziabad," he said. "And please take your feet off the table."

"I'm sorry?" I said, sitting up to glare at him. "This is my house, you know."

"Which is why I'm asking. Do you know where your shoes have been today?"

I considered his question. Then I answered him, ticking off my errands one by one, and I realized the son of a bitch was right. Why would I put my filthy shoes on the furniture? I removed them immediately.

"I never thought of that before," I said. Then, to salvage some measure of authority, I added that if I wanted to put my feet on the furniture, I'd do it.

"By all means," he said. "Remember that smell from the platform at Churchgate Station this afternoon? Whatever it was is on your table now."

"Crap."

"That wouldn't surprise me. By the way, if you're interested, and not too proud to accept a gift, I've placed a pair of new rubber *chappals* in your room. I suggest you wear those only in the flat and leave your shoes at the door from now on."

On top of everything else, Ranjit was a smart guy, too.

•   •   •

That night, he moved into the second bedroom. He'd been sleeping on the floor in the tiny pantry behind the kitchen. There was a dark little servants' bathroom back there, too. I felt awful for having let him sleep and bathe back there before, but I'd been following blindly what I'd been told. Servants ate and slept on the floor and did not use the same bathrooms as the *sahibs* and *memsahibs*. He must have been horrified by my poor hygiene while he was being treated as the dirty one.

•   •   •

WEDNESDAY, JULY 23, 1975, 11:20 A.M.

I could get used to this. Ranjit was making all my meals—keeping up the appearance that I still had my servant—all the while providing pleasant companionship every night. And, of course, he had a gun and gave me great peace of mind where Bikas was concerned.

Work, too, was going well, mostly because Frank Muller was on vacation. Why anyone would visit Goa during the monsoon was beyond my ken. Maybe he was that cheap and couldn't resist the off-season prices. Or maybe he was holed up with his new lady friend. Why should I begrudge him the same escape I'd enjoyed with Sushmita in Lonavala? Maybe he'd let off some steam and come back a better man and boss for it.

"That policeman phoned this morning looking for you," said Janice, tilting her little cup to touch mine as we enjoyed our late morning tea from Vikky. "He wanted to know if you were still alive or had been blown up."

I chuckled.

"It's not funny, Mr. Jacobs. What if that Bikas tries to find you?"

"I'm taking precautions."

"What about the pictures?"

"I told you there's no film." That, unfortunately, was true, in the sense that it was lost.

"You know, that Lokhande asked me if you'd dropped off any film recently. Photos from a story you were working on. Do you think he suspects you took pictures of the bomber?"

"There's no film. And the only thing I'm working on is the movie industry story."

"How's that coming along?"

"Terrible. I lost my chance to interview Shashi Kapoor and Jeetendra last week. And now Shabana Azmi won't return my calls. All I've got is that one guy was arrested for a syrupy film he made a year ago that hit a little too close to home for the ruling party. Oh, and his girlfriend wants me to introduce her to Robert Redford."

"Sounds great. I hope your résumé's in order when Mr. Muller gets back."

About this time, I was wondering when Sushmita might try to get word to me. The fact that Ranjit was living in my flat complicated matters. He could easily intercept any attempt by her to communicate with me. Or was she smarter than that? And what about Bikas? Had he actually given up? Decided to leave me alone? I figured he still might try to find me. What I didn't expect, however, was a reunion that evening.

CHAPTER THIRTY

"Your friend Willy Smets requests the pleasure of your company," said Ranjit, handing me a card when I came through the door. "And Lokhande paid a visit. He wanted to see if you were still alive."

"More likely he wants another bottle of whisky."

"One more thing," he said, ignoring my remark. "Harlan is coming to speak to you. He'll be here soon."

"What does he want?"

"I'll let him tell you."

In fact, Harlan arrived a few minutes later, as I was combing my hair after my evening bath. And he had the beautiful Birgit with him.

"Why?" I said, once he'd made his pitch to me. "Why would I take Birgit to Willy's tonight?" I turned to her and offered a weak "no offense" apology.

She smiled, despite the tension in the room, and I thought she was truly lovely. No wonder Willy liked her.

"Dan, you're going to do Ranjit and me this one last favor," said Harlan. "You're not willing to be our double agent. Okay. I get it. But I'm asking you for this. Take Birgit with you to his dinner. She told me they really hit it off. You can do what you like. Flirt with his girlfriend, drink his liquor, I don't care. But take her with you. Do that for me, will you?"

"Why would I do you a favor?"

He stared me down, long and hard, and I felt myself weakening. "Because you might just get your girl without dirtying your hands."

. . .

"Mein Gott! Birgit! Was machst du hier?" Willy was happy to see her. He kissed her on both cheeks and beamed at her.

"She's in town on a layover," I said, once she'd answered in German. "I ran into her at the President this evening. I hope you don't mind that I brought her along."

"Of course not, Danny Boy. She is always welcome. Come, let us get you both a drink."

"How long are you in Bombay?" I asked when he handed me my whisky.

"Until Sunday. I have business in Poona Monday."

Sunday. That gave me several days if I played my cards right. I scanned the room, looking for Sushmita, but didn't spot her right away. There was Arkady, the Russian guy who'd been at the last party; Marthe, the German woman I'd met twice before; two Englishwomen; three Indian couples; and Ash Pethe. He was chatting up two pretty French girls who looked like a couple of hippie tourists who'd cleaned up nice for Willy's party. A few minutes later, the three of them left together, looking awfully cozy with each other.

I surveyed the room again for Sushmita, but came up empty. Willy was all eyes for Birgit, who sparkled under the spotlight of his attentions. I maneuvered my way over to them, intending to find out where Sushmita was as soon as they could tear themselves away from each other.

They were engaged in a lighthearted conversation in German, effectively shutting me out. I waited for my opening.

"And where is the lovely Sushmita?" I asked, once the two had come up for air. "I never got the chance to thank her for her hospitality."

"I'm afraid she wasn't eager to spend six hours with me in the car," said Willy. "She's still cross about Chhotu. But she asked me to tell you she misses you."

"How nice."

He turned back to Birgit, and I was forgotten.

I nursed my drink, thinking of Sushmita. Why hadn't she come? And why hadn't she sent me some kind of word as she'd promised. I was feeling neglected, sitting there next to Willy as he flirted with Birgit.

And then I got it.

•   •   •

The 23:45 train pulled out of VT—Victoria Terminus—on time. I hadn't bothered to pack anything. I simply slipped away from Willy's party and jumped into a taxi. I ended up in a third-class seat since there was no time to buy a better ticket. Reservations required advanced bookings. I didn't mind. It was only a couple of hours.

I was sitting with two young men—domestic help or restaurant workers—traveling back to their village with two great trunks in tow. They offered me water and some *wada pao* they'd picked up as a treat in the station. It must have been an extravagance for them, since I knew these kids saved every anna and *paisa* for their families back home. Yet I couldn't very well refuse their generosity. I tucked in.

Managing to communicate some details of their situation, they told me they were brothers, heading back home to visit their *gao*— their village—after almost two years working in Bombay. A third brother would meet them at the Poona station, then they'd all board a different train going north. They said they would take turns sitting up to guard their belongings from thieves, until they arrived in Patna a day or two later. Their father would meet them there with a bullock cart to take them and their trunks the rest of the way.

When the train pulled into Lonavala shortly after two in the morning, I thanked them for their hospitality and wished them a safe journey.

The rain was holding off but threatening. The night was warm, not hot, with a pleasant breeze blowing from the west. In the line of taxis, a few drivers were sleeping on the hoods of their cars, legs folded over knees as if they were lying back and reading. I knocked on the fender of the first taxi in the queue, gently at first, then a bit more insistently to wake him. The driver rolled off the car and climbed inside. I got in the back and told him where to go. To a little hotel about a kilometer from Sushmita's bungalow.

The rain began to fall as we drove. The driver left me on the side of the road, in front of the hotel, and I watched him chug off.

Once I was alone, I made for the bungalow, walking the rest of the way in the rain. No umbrella, no coat. I prayed she'd be there, or I was in for a cold, wet night.

I hadn't miscalculated. The white Mercedes was parked in its usual spot. At a quarter to three, shoes waterlogged and clothes soaked to the skin, I stepped up to the door and knocked.

CHAPTER THIRTY-ONE

The door cracked open and I slipped inside. She threw herself against me, kissing me as I held her tight.

"I thought you weren't coming," she said breathless in my ear.

I told her I'd almost missed her message, but eventually the penny dropped.

"No one followed you? What about the taxi?"

"He left me outside a small hotel. I walked the last kilometer. No one saw me."

She led me straight to the bedroom. There was no light at all. Not even a candle or a *diya*. Everything was dark. I resisted all temptation to sleep. Sushmita pressed against me as if she never wanted to let me go. We lay together that way for hours, for the rest of the night.

In the morning, light streamed through the window from the east. She rose and pulled the curtain closed, shrouding the room in darkness once again. The world was gone. We slept hard. We slept late, neither of us wanting to leave our shelter, anonymous and invisible once again.

"When do you need to go back to Bombay?" she asked as we nibbled on a bag of *sev*—a kind of thin crispy fried-noodle snack. It's customary to eat it with *chaat*, *bhel*, *pani puri,* or something similar. It was the only thing Sushmita had brought with her from Poona, so it was our feast.

"My boss is in Goa until Sunday night. I'm a free man until Monday morning."

"We can get into a lot of trouble by then."

"We'll need to get some food," I said, pouring some *sev* into my right hand and chucking it back into my mouth.

"Let's always remember *sev* and this place," she said, smiling as she crunched away.

"I'll never think of anyplace but here when I eat *sev*. Scout's honor." I gave her the three-finger salute.

When we finally decided we'd slept enough, we got up and moved to the drawing room. There, still in our one pair of pajamas—I wore the bottom and she the top—we lay on the daybed and lazed for another couple of hours.

We avoided talking about Willy. I was happy to put off thoughts of him for several reasons, mainly because Harlan and Ranjit were itching for an answer. Was I actually considering their proposal?

I imagined Ranjit wondering what had happened to me. I'd gone to a party in the penthouse and never returned. Maybe he'd worry that Bikas had found me. I didn't care. No one knew where I was. No one but Sushmita, and she wasn't telling.

• • •

That afternoon—no idea what time it was—Sush took the car and went to buy some supplies for the next two or three days. She reminded me that I couldn't go with her; an Indian woman with a *gora* would attract attention we didn't need. So I waited, like a prisoner, as a long time passed. I felt like one of those dogs whose life stops when his owner is out.

But she returned, amply provisioned for the duration. Now we had no reason to leave the bungalow until the eleventh hour on Sunday.

And then the rain began to pour down as a reminder that inside was our only option anyway.

Sushmita had brought back spinach, carrots, potatoes, rice, and dal. Some salt, too, and tinned tomatoes. Thinking me an American with a picky palate, she'd also found a box of spaghetti—an Italian brand imported from the UAE—but no Kraft Parmesan cheese in a green can. We'd have to make do with the tomatoes and salt.

"We're having a feast?" I asked.

"You're going to cook me that spaghetti."

. . .

"So your father is a law professor at Yale?" she asked long after we'd devoured our spaghetti in tomato sauce and left the dishes for another day. "Is that why they let you in?"

"Maybe. But I had excellent grades and test scores. Plus I played a little football, remember?"

"Football? Why should that help you get into university?"

I explained, and she rolled her eyes. "Ridiculous. What position did you play?"

"I was an end. Receiver."

"Receiver? Like the wicket keeper in cricket?"

"Not quite. The wicket keeper's more like the catcher in baseball."

Silence and a dumb look.

"Never mind," I said. "A receiver runs down the field and catches passes from the quarterback."

I asked if she'd played any sports in school.

"Of course. A real sport. Badminton."

I laughed so hard she pinched me to shut me up.

"Not tennis? Badminton?"

She shook her head. "What else did you do at university? Besides running down the field and catching balls with a ridiculous tin pot on your head?"

"I ran track and field. The 440 and 880. And I studied journalism, of course, and worked on the college paper, the *Yale Daily News*, for four years."

"The cartoon pages?"

I smirked at her. "Columnist and editor."

"What a boring boy you were. Didn't you do anything interesting? And don't tell me football again."

"I rowed crew my freshman year."

"Coxswain?"

I shoved her playfully. "Engine room."

"What else, you fascinating man?"

I thought back to my college days and remembered one thing. "I got arrested three times at antiwar demonstrations."

· · ·

The next day went by in much the same manner, although we finally got our act together and made a big meal of the vegetables she'd bought. Cleaning the spinach was a major concern for me. Not only did I worry that our pathetic culinary skills would affect the successful outcome of the dish, but the mud in the leaves gave me cause to doubt the wisdom of eating it at all. Sush assured me it would be all right.

I scraped the carrots and chopped them, while Sush peeled the potatoes and made the dal in the pressure cooker.

"This place is pretty isolated. How do you keep it safe from thieves?" I asked as we busied ourselves. "I mean when you're away."

"There's a gardener who comes by every week. And then there's the Naval College. They've always kept an eye on the place. Because of my father, you know."

"He was a scientist, right? A professor, like my dad."

"Oh my, look at that lightning!" she said, a second or two before a boom of thunder shook the house.

. . .

"What do you want to do with your life?" she asked many hours later as we lay on the bed in each other's arms. I think it was morning.

"When I grow up, I want to be a journalist. A real one. A good one. What about you?"

She seemed to reflect on it for a long time before finally answering that all she wanted was to be good.

CHAPTER THIRTY-TWO

Later still, after we'd had our baths, I wrapped my arms around her waist and asked if she wanted me to start the dinner preparations. She smiled gently and said there were plenty of leftovers.

"There's still some more potatoes and rice," I said. "Shall I make both?"

"Fuck the *batate*," she said, and I choked.

"What?"

"What what?" she asked, confused by my confusion.

"You just said 'fuck the potatoes,' that's what."

She covered her mouth and nearly fell to the floor in a fit of laughter. When she finally composed herself, she apologized and explained that what she'd said was Marathi.

"*Phuckte batate*, Danny," she said, still red in the face. "It means 'just potatoes.' 'Only potatoes.'"

This became the joke of the evening, as we both came up with imaginative examples for the next hour. "Phuckte rain," "phuckte chair," "phuckte government," "phuckte pillow." Each was more immature than the last and, eventually, we decided it wasn't really that funny after all.

I peeled the last of the potatoes, consulted our handy cookbook, and decided to parboil them in water with a little vinegar and then roast them. That plan never got off the ground. There was no oven in the house. And no vinegar. Instead, I fried the *batate* in a little oil with paprika and salt.

I was doing my best impression of a chef, trying to wow Sush with my culinary talents, when a pair of warm lips kissed my neck from behind. I nearly burned my hand on the hot pan. She laughed a healthy, beautiful laugh. Light and playful, unconcerned with anything except our little household. Standing beside me, she watched adoringly—at least that was how it felt—as I finished heating dinner and placed it on the table. When everything was ready, she took me by the hand and dragged me into the bedroom. Dinner waited and got cold. We ate it anyway, an hour and a half later.

．　．　．

"Damn," I mumbled.

"What is it?" she asked, stretching and rolling over to lay her head on my chest.

"It's Sunday. What are we going to do?"

"We're going to plan for the next time. What else can we do?"

"What if we could escape? What if it could be just you and me? Always."

"Danny . . ."

"I know we talked about it. But is this any way for two people who . . ."

I stopped myself. I'd told her I loved her, but there hadn't been any reciprocal declaration from her side. I wasn't about to ask her to say it, either. But I wanted some kind of idea of her feelings to help me make the decision that awaited me in Bombay.

"If I could somehow free you, would you . . ."

She blinked and smiled sadly. Resigned, it seemed. "We'll meet here again soon," she whispered. "I'll leave a key for you under the eaves so you'll always be able to come to me. And we don't need your fancy cooking. Just *sev*. We can survive on *sev* alone."

CHAPTER THIRTY-THREE

"Playing hooky, were you?" asked Janice when I came in. I'd caught an early train from Lonavala and hadn't even been home.

"Is he in?" I asked.

"Not yet. But I expect him soon. Where have you been, Mr. Jacobs?"

"Planning my future," I said.

"I hope that includes your film story. Mr. Muller is expecting it."

Of course there was no story. Did she think I'd been tapping away on a typewriter in Lonavala the past five days?

"Tell me when he gets in," I said. "I've got some news for him."

"I'm sure he's heard about the parliament. He's been in Goa, not under a rock."

"The parliament?" I asked and immediately regretted it. I hadn't even looked at a newspaper since the previous Wednesday. I had no idea what was going on in the world.

Janice pursed her lips. "You'd better get caught up before he gets in."

The news I'd missed was the parliament's shameless vote to change the election law Mrs. Gandhi had been convicted of violating. With retroactive effect. I was stunned. They simply erased the law that she'd broken, rendering null the Allahabad High Court's decision that had voided her election. And, following the legal bouncing ball, that meant that the Supreme Court's upholding of the Allahabad verdict had also vanished. No crime had been committed. History had been rewritten, and Mrs. Gandhi's Emergency—made legal earlier last week—was the only law of the land. The news wasn't in the papers, thanks to the censors, but in the dispatches from Delhi, via New York and British news reports, informing us of what had happened. I tossed the telex away in disgust, thinking this was how democracy dies.

. . .

Frank showed up a little after noon, looking relaxed if not tanned. He made the rounds, slapping people on the back and joking. When he got to my desk, he asked how things were going. I told him I had something important to tell him.

"I hope you're not quitting," he said with a chuckle. When I didn't laugh, he grew serious and motioned to his office with a bob of his head. I followed him in.

"What the fuck are you telling me, Dan?" he said in a low growl. "You're going to quit on me after I resisted the temptation to fire you at least ten times?"

"That's right, Frank."

"You're going to quit at this amazing moment in history? When you're lucky enough to be here on the ground to witness and document something so important?"

"Yes."

"Why?" he asked, eyes pleading for an answer. "Why, Dan? I just got back from the best fucking week of my life, and you're going to take a piss on my homecoming? Who do you think is going to fill your shoes? Joey Rahman? Flaherty? Herbie?"

"Herbie's an old pro," I said. "And Flaherty'll learn."

"Oh, God, I'm fucked."

"I'm sorry, Frank. But it's complicated. I'm in deep trouble and have to step back to get myself clear."

"Jesus, don't tell me you got some girl pregnant."

"No. It's not that."

He plopped down into his chair and fished a cigarette out of his pocket. Then he lit up, inhaled deeply, and exhaled, all the while watching me. He was struggling to regain his calm, and it appeared he'd managed it.

"Sit down and tell me everything," he said.

Over the next twenty minutes, I laid before him all the misfortunes that had befallen me in the previous four weeks. From my meeting Willy Smets to my wall-scaling servant to Russell Harlan and Birgit Fuchs. I told him about Bikas, too, even though I'd lost the film. And then there was Sushmita. Frank gaped at me the whole time. Winced, too, when I described my ill-advised affair with a gangster's girl. Once I'd taken a breath to signal my story was at an end, he lit yet another cigarette.

"Wow," he said. "You are a fucking moron, Jacobs."

I looked away and nodded. "I know."

He threw his hands in the air then pushed himself out of his seat. "Christ, not that way. I mean, sure, you're still a moron. But you've got the best fucking story I've heard in years sitting in your lap, and you want to quit? Come to your senses, man."

"Huh?"

"Dan, this is an amazing story. The DEA and CBI want you to go under cover, be a double agent, and nab a drug trafficker. What don't you understand?"

"Um, *snitch*, actually."

"What's that?"

"They want me to be a snitch, not a double agent."

"Who gives a shit what they call it? Can you imagine how big this will be if you pull it off? You'll get a book deal. You could win a Pulitzer, for God's sake."

"So you're suggesting I do it? Go along with the DEA agent and the CBI man and betray my friend?"

Frank rolled his eyes. "I'd say you've already betrayed him. At least it's not as personal as screwing his girlfriend."

I wished he hadn't used quite so coarse a term to describe my betrayal. Not for my own self-respect, but for Sushmita's honor. I didn't want to think of what we were doing as *screwing*.

"Don't quit on me, Dan," he said. "I'm willing to give you some time to see if this pans out. To see if we can get a major story about drug smuggling and prostitution. Hell, that useless censor out there won't have any objection to a story like this. He'll wag his head and stamp it in triplicate."

This was sudden. I'd gone into his office, ready to give up on my career but not willing to throw my lot in with Harlan, Ranjit, Birgit, and their devil's bargain.

It wasn't until after three that we came up for air. I'll say this for Frank, he may have been an asshole and a panicker, but he was a good newsman. He knew what would sell. And he knew how to pitch a story, even to the poor sap who'd have to write it. Live it. Die doing it.

"Here's how it'll go," he said, puffing his cigarette in my face. "I'll blow a gasket and fire you in front of everyone. A big scene. That'll give you cover for your DEA guy's idea that you want to work for what's his name? Willy. Why would he take you on if you still had a job here?"

"But I haven't decided—"

"My God," he said, ignoring me, positively beaming. "Dan, this is an opportunity of a lifetime for you."

I asked myself if it weren't also the same for him, but without the risk. In the end, I told him I needed to sleep on it. I wanted to consider what such a decision would mean for me, my career, and for Sushmita.

"I understand, Dan," he said. "You go home and think it over. Then come back tomorrow, ready to be fired in front of the whole office."

I must have looked terrified, because he tried to comfort me.

"Look, you were ready to quit. I'm offering you an opportunity here. And if you won't play ball, either way you're out of a job."

· · ·

MONDAY, JULY 28, 1975, 8:23 P.M.

I left the office undecided. I'd been ready to resign but not to be a snitch. Now I had some incentive to do exactly that. Frank's proposal was a lifeline for my career, which probably would have ended if I'd quit. But it meant a lot of risk. To me and to my relationship with Sushmita.

I put my key in the lock and opened the door. Ramu didn't come to greet me with my drink and slippers. But the lights were on. He was there. I found him in his room—the second bedroom—working on a report of some kind.

"You're back," he said, looking up at me from the bed. "Where have you been?"

"None of your business."

"I see. You were with her. You know, Dan, you don't need to be rude to me simply because you feel guilty."

"Guilty?"

"Yes. For not doing what is right. For putting your own selfish interests before others."

I told him to go to hell and went to change my clothes.

"Wait, Dan. I want to take you out for a little fun."

"Why?"

"To be nice. Come on. There's a show, too. We'll get you a drink and enjoy the entertainment."

"It's not that European cabaret at the Venice, is it? I got roped into that when I first arrived."

"No, not there. I promise. This place is like nothing you've ever seen."

. . .

Ranjit transformed himself into Ramu in order to leave the building unnoticed. People truly did ignore the servant class, just as if they were invisible. We crossed the *marg* and climbed into the back of a black-and-yellow taxi waiting outside the President Hotel. I jokingly asked why he didn't have a police car at his disposal. In turn, he asked me if I understood the concept of undercover. He told the driver in Hindi where to go, and we were off.

A light rain fell as we gained Marine Drive and sped past Ash Pethe's flat, Cream Centre, and finally Chowpatty Beach, where we turned right, away from the sea. We cruised by the opera house and continued on through Girgaon and Khetwadi before finally turning left then right into small, dank, crowded lanes.

"Where are we going?" I asked. "This looks like an iffy part of town."

"It is," he said, then gave the driver more instructions.

With foot traffic and loiterers blocking the way, we crawled along through more garbage-strewn roads.

"Almost there," said Ranjit.

"What are those women doing standing in the doorways?" I asked.

"Those are prostitutes, Dan."

"But they're fully clothed."

"Ours is a modest culture. This isn't Amsterdam."

I wanted to know why he'd brought me to the red-light district, and he assured me the trip would be worth it.

Now the driver piped up, grinning at me in the rearview mirror as he said something in Hindi. Ranjit translated.

"He says you should try one of the Nepali girls. You'll have to pay more, but they're worth it."

We climbed out of the taxi and Ranjit explained that this was Falkland Road, the heart of the red-light district of Kamathipura.

He led me to a doorway blackened by mildew and soot from the two-stroke engines' exhaust, trash fires, and rain. And, yes, it smelled. I got why Indians removed their shoes when entering the house.

We climbed two flights of darkened stairs, lit only sporadically by buzzing fluorescent tubes. Red-orange streaks marked the walls and steps every few feet. Ranjit told me it was *paan*-stained spit.

"You'll see it everywhere, unfortunately. I enjoy *paan* after a meal from time to time," he said. "But I don't spit it on walls."

"What are we doing here?" I asked again as we reached the second landing. There Ranjit stepped through an open door and I followed.

Ten or twelve men sat on benches against the filthy, crumbling wall. Several were chewing *paan*. They stared at me from their hollow eyes as if I'd just emerged from a spaceship. It was hot and muggy in the dim room—more tube lighting. A ceiling fan twirled above their heads; the men's faces shone with perspiration, from their foreheads to their five-day beards. Three of them were sharing a pint bottle of some cheap hooch.

"Is that the drink you were offering me earlier?" I asked Ranjit under my breath.

"Yes. And don't worry about keeping your voice down. These fellows won't understand you. Not with your mushy American pronunciation. Does it come from chewing gum all the time?"

"Funny guy," I said. "Okay, I've seen enough squalor for one night. Let's get out of here."

"Not yet. The show's about to begin."

As if on cue, a bruiser of a man entered the room from a door beyond the benches. He was wearing a caricature of a gangster's suit— Western dress—with a brown tie knotted around his neck. His clothes, stretching over his ample belly, were rumpled and probably stained. Impossible to tell, given the dark fabric in the dim light. He surveyed the room, eyes pausing on me for a short moment, until Ranjit gave him a subtle head wag, probably to indicate that I was okay.

Satisfied the house was full and ready for the show, the man turned back to the door he'd come through and snapped his fingers. Five small women in gaudy and rather shabby saris entered the room without any attempts to simper or flirt with the men on the benches. Their garb was similar to what the prostitutes were wearing in the doorways in the street below. If I hadn't known better, I'd have taken these sad-looking ladies for charwomen.

The goonish emcee grunted instructions to the men who stared at him mostly with blank expressions, as if they didn't understand. They waited, as did Ranjit and I. Then our host turned and snapped his fingers again. This time a heavyset lady—a typical Indian auntie— emerged, pushing a girl of ten or eleven before her. The child was made up to look like a doll bride. She was wearing a sparkling sari, and her face had been made up with exaggerated red cheeks, *bindi*, painted lips, and a *nath*—a nose ring. The hooped ring was attached by a gold chain to her bejeweled headdress. She gazed demurely at the floor, even as the auntie spun her around for the men to see.

"What the fuck is this?" I whispered to Ranjit.

He cleared his throat and leaned closer to me to explain in a low voice. "That man over there is about to sell this little girl's virginity to one of these perverts."

"You're a cop. Stop them. This is criminal."

"I'd love to do that, Dan. But this place is run by a powerful gang-ster. He has half the Bombay Police in his pocket."

"You too?"

"I'm not with the Bombay Police. And the CBI have no authority on this kind of case. It's the responsibility of the states, unless they request our help. They resent us coming into their territory."

"So what? We have to do something."

"If we interfere, I promise you we will never leave this room alive, you and I. Throats slit like that," and he dragged his right forefinger across his neck.

I gazed at the little girl, my face surely betraying my horror. Surprised and—apparently frightened—to see a *gora,* she stared back at me. The terror in her eyes was too much. I couldn't take it. Yet I couldn't look away. And neither could she. We held each other's eyes for a long moment. She didn't blink. This little girl on the auction block, tarted up in some caricature of wedding finery, was about to be sacrificed to some piece of human garbage. Maybe even the tall white man. Then the auntie twirled the girl around again for the men to see, and our brief bond was severed.

The emcee began soliciting bids from the shits on the bench, and I backed out the door, then rumbled down the stairs, cursing Ranjit and myself for our cowardice. I needed air. What I got instead was a downpour of biblical proportions when I reached the street. I didn't care. I had to get away from the smell and memory of that dank room. Ranjit joined me in the middle of the now-empty road. The rain pelted us.

"You son of a bitch, why would you bring me here?" I demanded. "To see this..." I could come up with no words to describe the place. Instead, I swore at him. "Fuck, fuck, fuck, fuck! You sadistic shit! Why?"

Ranjit put a hand on my shoulder, and I wrenched myself from his grip. He tried again, and a third time.

"Why?" he repeated, glaring at me as the rain ran down my face, mingling with my tears of rage and sorrow. "Because the little girl up there..." He pointed to the brothel. "The terrified little bride we saw just now. She was sold to that pimp by Willy Smets."

PART THREE

BETRAYAL

CHAPTER THIRTY-FOUR

We sat in a white Ambassador outside Victoria Terminus, Ranjit at the wheel, Harlan sitting beside him. I was in the back seat. Harlan turned to face me.

"You clear on what you're going to do?" he asked.

"He knows I'm coming," I answered. "Knows I got fired. That I want to ask him a favor."

"Good. Think of this as an interview. He's going to want to know you can do the job and that you can be trusted."

I knew what that meant. No sleeping with Sushmita. Yet I realized I wouldn't be able to stop myself if she was game. I didn't tell Harlan that. Just as I hadn't told him that my firing was a ruse cooked up by Frank Muller. I don't know why I'd kept that detail to myself. Maybe because I wanted to hold at least one card in this game of poker. Everyone else had an advantage of some kind. Harlan and Ranjit had training, experience, and right on their side. And Willy had cunning, money, and a ruthless willingness to take what he wanted. Sushmita had her velvet-grip hold over me.

"Tell us you're not going to spill any of this to her," said Ranjit. "You may think you're crazy in love, but she's his girl. You don't know how deep their roots go. You don't know if you can trust her."

"You've told me that a hundred times," I said, resenting the lack of trust.

"And he'll tell you a hundred more until it seeps into your skull," said Harlan. "Listen, Dan, your neck's more at risk than ours. You've got to show yourself as completely loyal to Smets or it won't work. He's got to believe you'd take a bullet for him."

"I know, I know. *I want to prove my worth. I'm sick of pushing a pencil for little money or recognition. I want to help him with his business.*"

"Of which you know absolutely nothing," prompted Harlan.

"It's easy to slip," said Ranjit. "All you know is that he's in the import-export business, one hundred percent licit."

"Got it."

We sat quietly for another minute. Harlan was thinking the whole time, staring out the window at the great Indo-Saracenic station before us. Ranjit watched me in the rearview mirror, but he wasn't saying anything.

"You'll get this, Dan," said Harlan at length. "You've been quite slippery without him catching on, so I think you can pull this off. You know how we'll reach you, right?"

"You'll place a matrimonial ad in the Poona paper."

"What'll it say?"

"'Twenty-eight-year-old scheduled caste divorcée with no issues seeks tall, fair lawyer, doctor, or CPA plying in America. Not pretty but good companion with vitiligo and limp.' Who the hell is going to answer such an ad?"

"No one," said Ranjit. "Except you. That's the idea."

"Aren't we being too cute? What if they suspect something?"

"How? You're going to check the ads every day and when you see it, you make an excuse to go to Dorabjee's in Camp at 11:00 a.m. Birgit or I will meet you there. She's already in Poona. Now, if the message says twenty-*nine*-year-old divorcée, you go to the Swiss Cheese Garden at ABC Farms in Koregaon Park at 3:30. Make sure no one follows you. Take an auto rickshaw in the opposite direction. Get out, walk, go to a shop or café. Then take another auto to your destination."

"We've gone over this," I said. "I'll look for the crippled divorcée with the skin condition every day in the paper."

"And how do you contact us?" asked Ranjit.

"I go to the Blue Diamond Hotel and ask for Mr. Ranjit Varma."

"Do you phone the hotel?" he asked.

"No, I never phone the hotel," I answered in a petulant drone. "And, yes, I know that's not your actual family name. By the way, I don't understand why you won't tell me your real name."

"The less you know, the better."

"Right," said Harlan. "Ranjit and Birgit can give you money if you absolutely need it. But try not to need it. Earn it from Smets. You're supposed to be unemployed."

"Right."

"Then there's nothing more. Good luck, Dan."

I popped the door, grabbed my bag, and disappeared into the crowd of pedestrians.

· · ·

I brooded over recent events as I sat on the train, watching the city rush by the window. Ranjit had finally cracked me, made me decide. He was a genius. And a bastard for showing me an evil I couldn't ignore. For leaving it rotting in my mind until I had to do something to rid myself of its stench. And the only way to accomplish that was to take Willy down. I had no idea what that might mean for me or for Sushmita. My greatest fear was somehow I'd take her down with him. I didn't know how I'd live with that.

But I couldn't get the image out of my mind. That terrified little girl staring into my eyes. Terrified of those sweaty men vying for the right to take her innocence. Terrified of me, too. Not even losing Sushmita forever would haunt me the same way. I knew I couldn't live with myself if I did nothing to avenge the fear and horror that child had endured that night.

I was aware that my decision to betray Willy Smets was, in part, selfish. It was a way to rid my conscience of at least a small measure of the guilt I felt for my gutless behavior. I could have tried to save that girl. And, yes, I most likely would have been slaughtered for my interference. But I'd let her go to her sentence without a word. She was a child, for God's sake. And I was nothing but a coward. Just days before, I'd been living in a dream, hiding from the world and its evils so I could enjoy my own selfish pursuits in the arms of a woman. A woman who might well have been even more craven than I was.

. . .

FRIDAY, AUGUST 1, 1975, 6:03 P.M.

Sushmita met me at Poona Junction alone. Willy was busy. She was smooth and easy, no emotions, as if we were merely acquaintances, until we got inside the car. There, she slapped the dashboard hard and demanded to know what the hell I was doing.

"I lost my job," I said. "I needed some help."

"And you thought of Willy? Mad or what? We'll be discovered and everything will be ruined."

I assured her that it was temporary, that I could handle the situation. And we'd at least be able to see each other.

"If you mean to sleep with me, you're mistaken," she said, throwing the car into gear and pulling away from the parking spot. "Not here. We can't risk it."

I noticed she hadn't ruled out sleeping with her elsewhere.

. . .

"Danny Boy!" said Willy at the door.

He wrapped his arms around me in a great bear hug. Yes, I felt a pang of guilt as he did. Guilt about Sushmita. But then I conjured the image of the little girl in Kamathipura. That was all the inspiration I needed. Now the thought of betraying him gave me pleasure. A delicious, righteous pleasure. I relished the prospect of helping to put him away for his crimes and, if the breaks went my way, I'd get Sushmita, too. I didn't really care about the drugs or the alcohol smuggling or, for that matter, the prostitution, provided it involved willing adults. But I drew the line deep in the sand when it came to little girls. And, for all I knew, he might have traded in little boys as well.

"I brought you a gift," I said, handing him the bottle of Macallan's Harlan had procured for just this purpose. He'd said giving whisky to a smuggler would surely defuse any suspicions Willy had that I knew what his business was. Coals to Newcastle.

"You shouldn't have," he said. "Thank you, Danny Boy. We'll give it a good home," and he patted his stomach then mine.

"And this is for you, Sushmita," I said, presenting her with a small white box. "It's a silly little thing. I'm embarrassed to give it to you."

She pulled the pink ribbon bow and opened the box.

"How sweet," she said, displaying the tiny glass lotus inside for Willy to see.

Only two inches long, the lotus had a red bloom and a green stem, both in glass. I'd picked it up in one of the jewelry shops in the Taj Hotel. I hadn't mentioned it to Harlan and hoped it wouldn't spark Willy's distrust. But I couldn't very well arrive empty-handed, a guest with nothing for the lady of the house.

"Thank you, Danny," she said and brushed her cheek against mine in a chaste kiss.

I thought once again how cool she was when under glass. An adulterer with lesser sangfroid might well have foregone the casual gesture in front of her man. But not this one. She knew kissing my cheek would seem perfectly normal to Willy.

"You've had a hot journey," he said. "Go have a bath, Danny Boy. We'll discuss your trouble once you've dressed."

I followed orders. It was hell keeping my intentions secret from Sushmita, but there was no alternative. If all went according to plan, she'd soon have the choice of whether to stay with me when Willy was gone. That was my one condition in accepting Harlan and Ranjit's proposition. Sushmita was not to be arrested—at least not in India—or it was no deal. But I'd made no such pact with her. When the dust settled, she might well despise me for my betrayal. I'd already thrown the dice. Still rolling, they hadn't yet come to rest to deliver their verdict.

· · ·

"Sacked? I can't believe it," said Willy, handing me a glass of whisky and ice. "That man is a fool."

"We got off on the wrong foot," I said, aware that Sushmita was listening to my every word, all the while pretending to leave the men-talk to the men. I tried not to come off as whining. So I took a gamble and threw out a big lie. "He didn't appreciate that I'd had a fling with my boss—his boss—in New York before coming over."

"With your boss?" Willy asked tentatively. "I didn't realize you . . . liked men."

"No, no, no. My boss is a woman. A beautiful, remarkable lady."

"Tell us about her, Danny," said Sushmita, smiling slyly at me now. "Did she break your heart, or did you break hers?"

I blushed. "No broken hearts. It was a brief thing." My plan to impress Sushmita was failing miserably. "But she arranged for my position here."

I stopped, recalling Harlan's admonition about giving too much information. About letting my tongue get ahead of my mind. Had I just let them both know that my job was actually not in the crapper? I tacked quickly the other way to correct my mistake.

"Of course, she couldn't save my job when Frank sacked me. She can't appear partial."

Dinner came and went with no more talk of my horrible lie about Kate. What had I been thinking? Smearing her name to pass myself off as a man of the world? I must have come across as a jerk. Sushmita was like a bloodhound when it came to sniffing out my attempts at self-aggrandizement. She'd seen right through me.

"All that is in the past," said Willy. "They will regret sacking you, I'm sure. But the question now is what will you do next?"

"Something new," I said. "Maybe learn the import-export business."

Willy chuckled. "My dear Danny Boy, what do you know about imports? About exports? About business? You're a smart young man, but your training has been in journalism. Perhaps you should look there first."

"At least let me help around here," I said, careful not to press too hard. "There must be some way I can repay your hospitality."

"You mean like beat the rugs and mop the floors?" he asked with a broad smile.

"I could run errands for you. Post office, research at the library, write correspondence? I'm good at those things."

"Please, Danny Boy. You should know that you are a welcome guest here. You don't need to earn your keep."

I dropped it there, heeding Harlan's advice. But I didn't know how long I could go on staying in his—Sushmita's—house with nothing to do. Living so close to her would also be difficult. I was already longing for her touch or something as simple as a relaxed, intimate conversation with her. Knowing those things were out of the question was hell.

"What's wrong with you?" Sushmita scolded me later when we had a brief moment alone in the drawing room. "You're not a servant. Stop this farce right now."

I didn't get the chance to answer—not that I had any explanation I could share with her—as Willy returned to the room with a glass of juice for Sushmita. Any annoyance that had been apparent on her face vanished, replaced by an easy smile, not too bright, not forced. I could learn from her.

After dinner, we talked about the rains and the news. Willy opposed the Helsinki Accords, recently signed by NATO and the Warsaw Pact. It would only encourage the Soviets to pursue their expansionist policies. He cited the fall of South Vietnam as a warning of things to come if the West appeased the Communists. Sushmita asked if we could talk about something more fun.

"What about the Emergency?" I said. "Willy, what do you think of the recent parliamentary votes? The ones that erased the PM's crimes?"

Like a priest absolving sins, he waved his hand. "I don't concern myself with Indian politics, but Mrs. Gandhi has got nerves of iron."

"Steel," corrected Sushmita. "Nerves of *steel* and will of *iron*." She stood to leave. "And if you two boys are going to talk politics, I must have misjudged you both. You're a couple of old bores."

"Mita, don't go off like that," said Willy.

"I'm afraid my presence here might be a nuisance," I said once she'd gone. "I know it's stressful to have guests in the house."

"Not at all. Mita is very fond of you, Danny."

If he only knew.

"So what I'd like to ask you," I said, "is if there's a suitable hotel nearby. A boardinghouse, perhaps. It doesn't have to be fancy. My needs aren't great."

"What rubbish," he said, almost indignant at the suggestion. "You'll stay here."

"Are you sure Sushmita wouldn't prefer—"

"Ridiculous. Anyway, Mita and I are heading back to Bombay in two days. You'll have the place to yourself for a spell. Take some time to think about what you want to do."

• • •

SATURDAY, AUGUST 2, 1975, 12:07 A.M.

The scratching at my door came as I'd expected shortly after midnight. She slipped inside, and I rose from bed to take her in my arms. But she held out both hands as a stop sign. Her glare unsettled me.

"You should never have come," she whispered. "These things have to be planned and prepared carefully. Improvising will only bring disaster. You've got to understand that."

"I'm sorry," I said, wishing I could tell her that this was in no way a spur-of-the-moment visit. I wasn't improvising. My stay had been carefully planned.

"Please, love. You must be more careful," she said, a touch softer now, but I confess I hadn't really paid attention after she called me "love."

I apologized again, and she pressed against me, wrapping her arms around my neck.

"Willy told me you wanted to go to a hotel. Or leave."

"I thought it might be for the best."

"You stupid man. You should never have come," she repeated into my chest. "But if you leave now, I'll die. I swear it."

CHAPTER THIRTY-FIVE

After lunch, Sushmita suggested a jaunt into Camp to tour some of the city that I hadn't seen. Willy pronounced it an excellent idea. He shooed us out to the car, claiming he had pressing work to do.

"Take him to see your old school," he said from the door as she shifted into gear.

"That sounds nice," she said, and we were off.

"Why do they call it Camp?" I asked as Sushmita turned onto Koregaon Park Road at the petrol bunk.

"It's the cantonment," she said, and she honked the horn at the car in front of us.

"That accomplished nothing."

"It made me feel better. You know nothing about driving in India, Danny, so please withhold your comments."

I watched the Blue Diamond Hotel pass by and wondered if Birgit was staying there. Harlan had said she was already in Poona.

"Now, about Camp," continued Sushmita, relishing the role of tour guide. "It's the military zone of Poona, and dates back to the early 1800s. The British Indian Army was quartered there. Today it's home to the Indian Army's Southern Command, so if there's war with Pakistan, we'll be in the thick of it. And, of course, there's St. Mary's School, too."

"On an army base?"

"No, not an army base. Camp is home to lots of the city's businesses as well as the army barracks and facilities. There's lots of shopping and restaurants. When I was at school, my absolute favorite place for a special treat was Marz-o-rin on MG Road. Snacks and sandwiches. I loved the chicken rolls and cold coffee."

"What's MG stand for?"

"Mahatma Gandhi."

"You don't say Mahatma Gandhi Road?"

"No one says that. It's MG Road."

"I'd forgotten your national mania for abbreviations."

"And then there was Kayani Bakery on East Street," she continued, ignoring my remark. "The best Shrewsbury biscuits anywhere. Yum. We must stop and get some. I haven't had any in an age."

I watched her as she navigated the roads with ease and familiarity. She was so beautiful like that. And so happy telling me about her memories. While Americans might have recalled their school days like something out of a Beach Boys song, or an Archie comic book, Sushmita's joys seemed simpler, more genuine. An occasional trip to a sandwich shop or cookies from a favorite bakery. I smiled until she caught me.

"Are you mocking me?" she asked. "Because if you are, I'll drop you right here and you can manage for yourself."

"Just wondering if you wore a school uniform back then."

"Of course. And long braids, too. Until eighth, when I cut my hair short. Mrs. Mathias was furious. Our vice-principal. What a force of nature. You didn't want to be called to her office. I made my share of visits."

"You must have been a troublemaker. Were you popular with the boys?"

"St. Mary's is all girls. Although Bishop's School for boys was on the other side of the wall. My father called the combination Bishop's School for Backward Boys and St. Mary's School for Forward Girls."

God, she was gorgeous when she was happy. And she was glorious as she laughed at the memory.

After the golf course, we veered left and a short while later passed the Royal Western Turf Club, a storied racetrack dating back to 1800. I asked if we might find time to go play the ponies one day.

"Sure," she said. "If you can wait till November. The horses don't run in the rainy season."

We turned right, and she squealed. Positively squealed. "Look up ahead," she said. "There it is. St. Mary's School."

We pulled to a stop beside the tall green wall and climbed out.

"Is this a Catholic school?" I asked.

"Mad or what? Anglican."

The sounds of girls' voices reached us from the other side of the fence. Excited, breathless shouts indicated games were going on inside the enclosure. The front gate was open. We went in. To our right, scores of girls between the ages of seven and fifteen or sixteen were playing on the grounds. Outfitted in blue tunic dresses, white blouses, and neckties of different colors—depending on their houses—they were engaged in spirited games of basketball, hockey, or tag.

A colonial-era building made of stone stood before us. Above the arched entrance a hand-painted sign read, "St. Mary's School" in blue letters against a white background. Below the school's name, the devise was written in smaller script: "I Serve."

"The classrooms and library are in that building," she said. "And the senior dormitory is at the end of the drive."

She called my attention to another building near the field hockey pitch.

"And that was my junior dormitory. I was here from fourth through tenth. Then I went to Wadia College for eleventh and twelfth. Such wonderful times we had here, talking past lights out, sharing stories, and trading tuck."

"Tuck? What's that?"

"You didn't have tuck at school? It was . . . snacks. Treats. Food sent from home. I always had the best tuck, thanks to Daddy. He traveled a lot abroad and sent me treats no one else could hope to compete with."

"That must have made you popular."

She shrugged. "Girls can be jealous, you know. And matrons, too."

"Were the matrons mean to you?"

Sushmita's expression went grim. I asked what was wrong. She stared at the dormitory and, I swear, her eyes sparkled from some distant sadness.

"Some were nice," she said. "But I hated Miss Bhagawat."

"What did she do to you? Steal your pillow?"

She glared one last time at the dormitory, then turned away and headed for the gate. I followed her, cursing myself for my insensitive attempt at a joke. Whatever I'd said had set her off. I'd tripped over some terrible memory. She jumped into the car, and I joined her.

"She called me dark," said Sushmita, and a fat tear ran down her cheek. "For seven years she made me feel ugly. Called me a black jungli. She stole my soap and replaced it with a jar of Afghan Snow. Then she invited the other girls to laugh at me."

"Afghan Snow?"

She glowered. "Skin cream. It makes your skin lighter. Until you wash it off. Then you're just as ugly as before."

"That's horrible."

"I hated her," she said and wiped away the tear. "I was glad when she died."

"Died?"

"Yes. One day she went out and never came back. No one ever found out what happened to her."

. . .

Sushmita and I drove off, away from the bitter memories of St. Mary's. How sad. She'd been enjoying her return to the campus until I'd teased her. I wanted to apologize and dry her tears. But I wanted even less to remind her of the pain that woman had caused her. Over the color of her skin? Something she couldn't have changed even if it had mattered. A child, for Christ's sake. What kind of monster would make a child cry? A monster charged with the care of children.

And yet, as Sushmita drove, I felt like a coward yet again. Wasn't there something I could say to console her? I reached for her hand instead, but she was shifting gears.

"She was a fucking bitch," was all I could manage.

Somehow it was just right. Sushmita nearly choked as she tried to steer. Then she glanced at me with more love than I'd ever seen in a person's eyes before. She yanked the wheel to the side, nearly crashing into another car, and skidded to a stop on the side of the road. There, after shifting to neutral and setting the brake, she rolled out of her seat on top of me and smothered me in a warm, wet kiss. We sat there for some time, me trapped beneath her, her stroking my hair and gazing into my eyes as if she could never get enough.

"I love the glass lotus you gave me," she said, her nose pressing against mine. "I'll keep it at my bedside always."

Then a tap came on the window.

Jesus, it was a cop.

He wasn't pleased to find an Indian woman straddling a *gora* in a fancy car in broad daylight. I was sure he was going to arrest us for public indecency. He demanded she get out of the car.

"Give me fifty rupees, Danny," she whispered frantically. "Now!"

I rummaged through my wallet and produced a few tens that may or may not have come to fifty. She opened the door and climbed out. Thirty seconds later, she was back behind the wheel and the car was in gear. We were off.

"What happened?" I asked, once we were cruising down the road, away from the cop who was on foot.

"I bribed him," she said.

"But we hadn't done anything. We were only kissing."

"Oh, Danny, my love, you have so much to learn about this country."

Our close call on the side of the road prompted another lecture from Sushmita. She acknowledged that this had been her fault—not mine—but, in her defense, I was irresistible.

"I was wrong to do that in public, Danny," she said as she drove on. "Please don't follow my example. We'll end up arrested and all will be lost. We were lucky that policeman was happy with fifty rupees. Another might have been a zealot who hates the idea of foreigners with Indian women. The only time we can touch each other is in the bedroom. At night, when everyone is asleep. Promise me you'll be stronger-willed than I am."

"I promise. Take a deep breath and relax. We're safe now."

She stared straight down the road. "If only that were true."

A few minutes later, she pulled over and parked on MG Road, drawing a sigh as she did. I waited as she composed herself, all too aware that we were in a very public spot in the center of Camp. Would it have been better if I'd been sitting in the back seat? I hadn't seen any women drivers, but who knew? I thought the sooner we got out of the car and maintained a respectable distance, the better.

"Come, Sush," I said. "Let's walk a bit."

She agreed and we climbed down from the car.

"This is *Mahatma Gandhi* Road," she said with a lilt in her voice to let me know she was having a good time at my expense.

I glanced to our left and saw a long three-storied building with a sign above advertising "Dorabjee and Sons." Harlan's detailed instructions came to mind and I thought of a low-caste divorcée with a skin condition and a limp.

"I've heard of this place," I said. "Read about it in the guidebooks. What is it?"

"An old Parsee market," she said. "A Poona institution. You can get anything you want."

"Like Alice's restaurant?" I asked.

"What rubbish are you saying, Danny?"

"It's a song. Never mind."

"Come. There's a small café on the top floor. You must try some of their famous biryani."

. . .

"Clorox® bleach," I said, browsing the aisles of the market once we'd finished our delicious veg biryani. "That's amazing. I should get a bottle."

"Is this your idea of discovering India? Marveling at American cleaning products in a market? And have you seen the price? It's madness. Come. We have everything you need at home."

"But, look. They even have cat food."

"Do you have a cat?"

"No."

"Then *chalo*," she said. "I want to get to Kayani Bakery before the Shrewsbury biscuits are finished."

. . .

It was just 3:00, the hour when Kayani's reopened after lunch. Sushmita assured me the Shrewsbury biscuits wouldn't last long. I volunteered to go inside to get the coveted treats, and she stayed with the car. This turned out to be my first true experience with Indian life. Yes, I'd been to luxury hotels, ridden first- and third-class trains, and even visited Bombay's red-light district and rubbed elbows with prostitutes on Falkland Road. But jockeying for position among the customers at Kayani Bakery was the real thing. Whereas, in general, most people tended to give foreigners a pass and the right of way in India, that wasn't how it worked at Kayani's. I was nothing more than an obstacle to be shoved aside. If I hadn't the backbone to hold my place in the sea of customers jostling to give their orders, then I might well be hustled out the door and end up on the pavement.

There was no queue. It was an amorphous mob, a fluid mass that inched forward even as it stood still. After losing ground for several minutes, I managed to put my large size to good use and began a slow advance toward the ten clerks who were taking and fulfilling orders. In the end, an old Parsee man behind the counter took pity on the only *fireng* in the place and pointed to me. Sushmita had told me I'd better be ready to order when my turn came, so I held up two fingers and asked for two dozen Shrewsbury biscuits, please. He grabbed a couple of cardboard boxes tied with string from the shelves behind him and dropped them at the register. Having indicated to the cashier that the order was mine, he moved on to the next customer. I swam forward through the crowd and paid, at which point I was promptly shoved aside.

Back in the car, Sushmita was thrilled with my purchase, almost as if she'd expected me to come back empty-handed.

"I could gobble up three of them right here," she said. "But we must get back now. We've missed tea. At least we had biryani and now Shrewsburys."

CHAPTER THIRTY-SIX

The white Mercedes left the compound, with Shankar—Willy's driver—at the wheel, and Sushmita and Willy in the back seat. The guard saluted the departing car then closed the gate. I was alone in Willy's house. Sushmita's house. Not quite alone. There was Govind, the butler or majordomo—whatever his title was—Kamal, the cook; Pooja, who washed the clothes; the guard at the gate; and the gardener. I suddenly felt unwelcome. What if these people resented having me around? Maybe they enjoyed the brief periods of relaxed duties when the cat was away. I was spoiling that for them.

After a six-mile run and my bath, I relaxed in the garden behind the house. It was another rare day without rain, so I wanted to make the most of it. I checked the matrimonial ads, as I'd been doing each morning, but there was no message.

"Excuse me, sir," said Govind, appearing before me. He smiled. "*Chai*, sir?"

I drew a long breath, thinking how spoiled rotten I'd become. But, at the same time, I couldn't deny this was a comfortable setup. And his smile made me reconsider my worries of not being welcome by the staff.

"Thank you, Govind. Some *masala chai* would be nice."

Indians can either be an obstacle to your happiness here, or the means to achieve it. Willy's first words to me echoed in my ears, and I felt like an entitled prick.

•   •   •

The next three days passed slowly. I lurched from meal to meal. The schedule was maddeningly regular. Morning tea and biscuits (Shrewsbury) at 8:30, breakfast at 10:00, lunch at 1:30, afternoon tea at 5:00, cocktails at 7:00, and dinner at 9:00. I tried to explore the city between meals, but it rained the entire week after the first day. Still, I kept to my exercise regimen, running several miles each morning. And Govind was kind enough to take me out in the second car, the blue Ambassador. I sensed he longed to be a driver instead of a generic *servant*.

The first time we went out together, I tried to sit in front with him, but he nearly had a seizure. His face went red at my attempt to show my egalitarianism. He was having none of it. I came to understand that my gesture upset his worldview. He was proud to be a driver, if only for a few hours. He even had a cap, which he donned only when behind the wheel. To him, I could only assume, driving a *gora* who sat beside him in the front seat invalidated somehow his value as a professional chauffeur. His place was in the front, mine was in the back.

Reluctantly, I climbed into the back seat and, appearing quite relieved, Govind put the car in gear and drove off. The guard at the gate saluted us as we left, and I sighed. The world was right again, at least for Govind and the saluting guard, who clearly took as much pride in his duties as Govind did in his driving.

I didn't know where to go, so I asked Govind to show me something interesting in Poona. He was a sweet man, and I was growing fond of him. He'd learned how many ice cubes to add to my scotch, as well as how many pegs I enjoyed in each drink. He knew I liked to wait five minutes for my *masala chai* to cool just so, and that I hated the milk skin that formed on top of the tea. I appreciated that he took the trouble to let my tea cool before bringing it to me. And he always made sure to remove the skin off the top. He even demonstrated how he did it.

"Put the *chammach*—spoon—in the chai and wait *chaar minnit*. Four," he said. "Maybe *panch*, five."

Once the skin had formed, he gently grasped the spoon and held it vertically. As straight as an arrow. Then he pulled it slowly out of the cup. The skin wrapped itself around the stem and bowl of the spoon, clinging to it like . . . well, like skin. My tea was left epidermis-free.

I was living a lie of a life, in more ways than one. I wasn't some gentleman to the manor born, with servants at my beck and call, and yet . . . There I was, alone in the house, enjoying the perks of a rich man's privilege.

The first time Govind took me driving, he wanted to be sure I saw the great Dagdusheth Ganpati Temple. *Ganpati* was the Maharashtrian name for Ganesh. He raved about it as we crossed Poona, traveling west for nearly twenty minutes. The temple, located in the Budhwar Peth section of town, was built by a grieving father for his sons who'd died of plague in the late 1800s.

"Look, sir," he said, beaming as we stood before the temple. "*Ganpati.*"

The idol, measuring about six feet high, sat on a throne and was bedecked with an impressive amount of gold and garlands. Worshippers jammed the street, waiting to enter the temple to make their offerings of coconuts and flowers to the deity. They removed their *chappals* and filed in barefoot, ringing a loud bell of some kind once inside.

Standing there with my driver/guide, I had to admit that this was a better tourist experience than oohing and aahing at Clorox® bleach in the cleaning products aisle of Dorabjee's. I thanked Govind warmly for the honor of visiting the temple with him.

It was nearly time for lunch, so we headed back to the Koregaon Park bungalow. But first, Govind stopped at one of the twin petrol bunks on the corner of North Main and had the tank filled. He retrieved a small booklet from the glove box and noted the mileage. Then he asked me to verify the purchase and the odometer reading and to sign the ledger. I figured this was standard practice, if the long list of entries in the booklet was any indication.

Govind waited for me to sign, but I was scanning the dates and locations in the ledger instead. Most of the fill-ups had been made in Poona, Bombay, and Lonavala. But there were others mixed in. Nasik, Surat, Ahmedabad. Also Indore, Udaipur, Jaipur, and even points as far north as Amritsar and Srinagar. This car got around.

"Problem, sir?" asked Govind, calling me back to the present.

"Everything's in order," I said. I signed the book and handed it back to him.

. . .

There were too many people underfoot to risk a foray into Willy's study. It was locked anyway. If I'd left a guest in my house, I wouldn't have felt the need to lock my office. But maybe Willy didn't want the staff rummaging through his things. I'd heard plenty of talk of mistrust of servants in my brief time in India.

So I bided my time, waiting for my host to reappear with his beautiful lover. My lover. On Thursday night, as I returned from a walk around the back lanes of Koregaon Park, I discovered a visitor.

"Hello and greetings to you, Dan," said Chhotu. Christ, he really did sound like George Sanders with that accent. He'd already wedged himself into a chair and was enjoying a glass of sherry.

"Hello, Chhotu. I see you've made yourself at home."

He didn't even bother to chuckle. "My dear chap, I'd say the same for you, but it would be so obvious as to be risible. You've done quite well for yourself since getting the sack."

Nothing I could say to that except to ask how he knew I'd lost my job.

"I keep up with the latest news." He lowered his chin and focused a wry smile on me. "As you no doubt are aware."

"If you're going to ask me for money, you've picked the wrong time, friend. I've lost my job, remember?"

"Don't give it a second's thought," he said. "I played my cards poorly, as you know. Never put anything in writing you wouldn't want dear Mama to read."

"Or dear Willy?"

"Quite right. Let's let bygones be bygones, Dan, shall we? Have a drink with me."

He called to Govind in Hindi, affecting the same posh English accent as he spoke. Who did this guy think he was impressing? Then he told him in English to fetch me a glass of whisky. Govind nodded, then handed me my glass, which he was already carrying on a salver. I noted it was filled just right with two ice cubes. Chhotu was impressed, but withheld comment.

"Willy and Sushmita-*ji* are due home tomorrow," he said finally. I didn't think any answer was required. He hadn't asked me a question. "A sweet reunion, no doubt," he added.

"You said something about bygones, Chhotu, but your bys haven't gone anywhere from what I can tell."

That worked. "I was only having a little fun, Dan. Forgive me. Tonight, it's just the two of us. We shall have a nice dinner and then maybe smoke some stick afterward, what?"

I couldn't remember when I'd spent a less pleasant evening. As insufferable as Chhotu was in company, he was ten times worse one-on-one. When he wasn't boasting of some bet he'd won, or a young girl he'd debauched, he was boring me with tales of his halcyon days at Oxford. I didn't buy for a second that he'd studied there. He had a knack for mimicry, a fancy accent. But there was no substance or training in his bluster.

Still, as repulsive as I found this guy, he was Willy's right-hand man. As we enjoyed our after-dinner drinks—only one for me—I decided to loosen up and feign a growing affection for him.

"We're not so different, Dan," he said. "I think we shall be fast friends."

Not bloody likely, I thought.

"You may be right, Chhotu. This has been nice, chatting and putting our differences behind us."

We clinked glasses and I wished I could spit in his eye. Or in his drink. But, taking a cue from my lovely Sushmita, I smiled as if butter wouldn't melt in my mouth. Maybe one day I'd get the hang of lying without batting an eye.

"Did you play cricket or row in your days in London?" I asked. Jesus. He would have sunk any boat he boarded. And forget about "leg before wicket." He'd have been called out for "belly before wicket."

"I wasn't always so rotund," he said. "But I never rowed. More interested in the fish than in the water. Like a proper Bengali."

CHAPTER THIRTY-SEVEN

I spent the morning and most of the afternoon avoiding Chhotu. After a long run, and later a leisurely walk, I noticed some things had been touched in my room. And not as if someone had been cleaning. This was different. The paranoiac in me suspected Chhotu.

Good luck to him, I thought. I had nothing to hide. And he'd never find the blackmail note since Sushmita had burned it long ago.

A little after five, the white Mercedes pulled through the gate. Willy and Sushmita stepped out as a light rain fell. Govind, Chhotu, and I met them in the yard. Willy was all smiles. Sushmita kept her guard up in the company of the odious Chhotu.

. . .

Willy and Sushmita emerged from their rooms around six thirty, bathed and refreshed. Govind inquired if they were hungry or thirsty after their journey. Willy was ready for a drink. Would Chhotu and I join him? The big fella volunteered to lead the charge.

"What about you, Sushmita?" I asked. "Will you have something? A fresh lime soda?"

She smiled and told me she'd rather have a *kuch nahin*.

"Afraid I don't follow, old girl," said Chhotu.

"Do you find me old?" she asked, and he blushed.

Govind served Willy an Aperol, something nonalcoholic to Sushmita, and presented me with my usual. He gave Chhotu a large pour of the Macallan.

"How did you find Bombay?" asked Chhotu.

"As always," said Willy. "Raining like hell. You weren't too bored here, Danny Boy?"

"Not at all. I hope you don't mind that I asked Govind to drive me around."

Willy dismissed my concerns. "Of course not. He's an excellent guide."

"I meant to ask you what you thought of the Dagdusheth Ganpati Temple," said Chhotu. "You must tell us, Dan."

"It was quite moving," I said, wondering how he knew I'd gone to the temple in the first place. Had he been following me? Or maybe Govind had spilled the beans.

. . .

I received no visit that night. Sushmita must have felt it impossible under the circumstances. I lay awake in bed until one, picking through the Wodehouse without any real enthusiasm. As I switched off the light, I happened to recall that Nixon had resigned exactly one year earlier on the ninth. It wasn't lost on me that he might have attempted to hold on, maybe even seize power, much the way Mrs. Gandhi had done. But he hadn't. He'd resigned. How sad was it that Richard Nixon had set the integrity standard higher than the Indian PM?

. . .

It was nearly 10:00 by the time I'd made myself presentable for the world. I found Willy and Sushmita at the dining table, each reading a newspaper.

"Good morning," I said. "Where's our friend Chhotu?"

"Back to Bombay," answered Willy.

"No rest for the wicked."

Willy looked up from his paper and regarded me closely for a long moment. Then he spoke.

"May I have a word with you after breakfast, Danny?" he said. "I'd like to ask you for a favor."

"Of course."

Sushmita was hidden from his view by the newspaper in front of her face. But I could see her. She shook her head slowly, her eyes fixed on mine. She was telling me not to do it.

Again, trying to mimic her poker face, I made sure my expression betrayed no reaction. Not to her or to Willy, who might well have been watching me.

I took a seat at the table and asked if there was a newspaper for me to read, seeing as they each had one. Willy chuckled, folded his copy, and apologized for his rudeness. Sushmita, on the other hand, tossed hers onto the table, more or less in my direction, and left the room.

"Did I say something wrong?" I asked Willy. "I was only joking."

• • •

"I'd like you to make a little trip for me," said Willy once we'd finished breakfast and taken ourselves off to his study. "To Nepal to deliver a package."

"Of course," I said, eyeing a stack of five or six ledgers of different colors on his desk. I wished I could get a peek inside, but urged myself to concentrate on my mission. "I'd be happy to help."

"Just some samples for a potential client, but it's rather urgent. A small valise. I'll arrange the plane ticket. Would tomorrow be convenient?"

• • •

SATURDAY, AUGUST 9, 1975, 11:01 P.M.

Willy waved goodbye as I climbed into the car. Sushmita watched, leaning against the doorjamb. Shankar shifted into gear and pulled through the gate, where the sleepy guard saluted. When Willy had asked if "tomorrow" would be convenient, he was referring to the flight from Bombay to Delhi to Kathmandu. What he'd neglected to mention was that the flight took off at 5:30 a.m. In order to catch it, I'd need to be on the Konark Express train at 11:45 p.m. That meant I had no time to visit the Blue Diamond Hotel to inform Ranjit of my mission. It crossed my mind that Willy might have wanted it that way, but I dismissed the suspicion just as quickly. He couldn't have known.

Shankar dropped me and my cargo—a mysterious valise filled with samples—at Poona Junction around 11:30. The train was on time, and I arrived at Dadar Station in central Bombay at 3:35.

• • •

SUNDAY, AUGUST 10, 1975, 3:46 A.M.

The rain was pouring down hard. I roused a taxi driver sleeping in his car outside the station, and asked him to take me to the airport. Normally on hot nights, the drivers slept on the hoods of their cabs, but the rain had forced him inside. That meant the taxi smelled quite ripe when I took my seat. I couldn't really blame the poor guy. He worked around the clock, and it was always hot and muggy in Bombay. Unreasonable to expect him not to sweat.

I reached Santa Cruz well in time to catch my 5:30 flight to Delhi aboard an Air India 747. Wedging the valise between myself and the window to keep it safe, I took advantage of the empty seat next to me to stretch out and sleep for about an hour. In Delhi, my connection was a short one, but I found the gate and boarded Royal Nepal Airlines flight 206. After a hairy approach over the mountains, followed by a sharp descent through heavy rain, we touched down safely in Kathmandu at 9:30. I was a good flyer, but that landing got my heart pumping.

Up to this point, I hadn't opened the valise. I sensed this might be a test. A dry run before Willy gave me any real work to do. It would be foolhardy to confide drugs or contraband to an unproven courier, so I was fairly confident I wasn't risking arrest for smuggling. My stomach turned over a couple of times all the same when the customs agent asked me what was in the bag. I told him samples.

"What kind of samples?"

"Business," I said.

"Open, please."

Shit. I had no idea what to expect, but there was no avoiding it. I unbuckled the strap, said a prayer, and flipped the bag open.

The officer peered inside. His upper lip curled. "Sample? Brassieres?"

I glanced at the contents of the valise and, indeed, it was stuffed with bras. Different sizes, colors, and styles, from young miss to matronly. The officer counted them. Eleven. I know I blushed, because my face was burning hot.

"I sell lingerie. These are samples for ladieswear shops. My clients."

He smirked, then waved me past. I refastened the valise's buckle and went through.

Willy had instructed me to take the samples to a souvenir shop in Jhochhen Tol. When the taxi dropped me there, I was surprised to see so many young Westerners. Hippie types. I felt out of place in my shirt and trousers and closed shoes. I wore my hair medium long, but I looked like a marine compared to my compatriots hanging around the narrow street, smelling of hash in their tie-dyed T-shirts and sandals. I learned soon enough that this place was known as Freak Street, thanks to the throngs of stoners who'd made it famous.

The Wicked Walrus Export Co. was easy enough to find. It was a small shop, jammed with souvenirs—some kitschy, others displayed as authentic Nepalese crafts. And there was a huge variety of hookahs, bongs, and other drug paraphernalia, if that was your idea of mementoes.

"Excuse me," I said to the thin man sitting on a stool near the back of the narrow shop. "I'm looking for Dhonu."

"Who are you?" he asked, as he pinched a hand-rolled cigarette between his lips.

"Willy sent me."

He smiled an exaggerated grin at me, baring his stained brown teeth. "Then I'm Dhonu. They call me the king."

"This is for you."

He took the valise from me and opened it up. "Ah, finally. Been waiting a long time for this."

CHAPTER THIRTY-EIGHT

Willy had given me cash for a room in Kathmandu, but I had an idea of how to impress him and save him some money at the same time. It meant catching a late flight back to Bombay via Delhi and sleeping in the Dadar Central Station waiting room for a few hours. I was already filthy, wet, and exhausted from my thirty-six hours of travel, so I figured why not? A little before seven, the Bombay-Poona Intercity Express chugged out of the station, and I was back at Poona Junction a couple of minutes after 10:00 a.m.

"Danny? What are you doing here?" asked Willy once Govind had shown me in. "Didn't you make my delivery?"

"The brassieres? Yes, of course."

He frowned. "So you opened the valise? I'm disappointed. I feel as if you didn't trust me."

"It wasn't me. The customs officer in Kathmandu opened it. Sorry."

Now he smiled, his long teeth so much whiter than the king's. "Well done, Danny Boy. Forgive me for doubting you."

I handed him the empty valise. Then I held out the cash he'd given me for the hotel.

"Didn't need it after all," I said.

He took it and looked me up and down. "You are a mess."

"He smells, too." That was Sushmita, turning up her nose at me. "What did you do, sleep in a train station? Go have a bath, Danny. And burn your clothes."

.   .   .

TUESDAY, AUGUST 12, 1975, 8:19 A.M.

"*Masala chai,*" announced Govind, placing the cup before me.

I thanked him and took up the newspaper he'd left, folded with a paperweight on top to prevent it from fluttering under the ceiling fan. I glanced at the headlines. There'd been a coup in East Timor, and the united Vietnam had been denied a seat in the UN, thanks to a U.S. Security Council veto. Also, the thirty-ninth amendment to the Indian Constitution took effect, prohibiting the prosecution of a sitting prime minister. That story didn't appear in the Indian papers that Tuesday, of course. I learned of that later.

I turned to the matrimonial ads, certain there would be nothing. There never was. But I was wrong. In the third column on the second page was an ad for a twenty-nine-year-old divorcée with a limp and a mild skin condition.

I checked my watch. It was nearing eight thirty. I had an hour and a half before the appointment at Dorabjee's. I could have breakfast then excuse myself to go for a walk. On North Main Road there were taxis and auto rickshaws. No problem.

When the time came to leave, I made the excuse that I needed some personal items. Maybe I could find them in Camp. Willy offered me a car, but I said I'd walk and take an auto. Sushmita said nothing, and I worried I was losing her. Maybe she was hurt that I was setting out on my own, or maybe she resented my recent trip to Nepal and my kowtowing to Willy. Either way she was right, of course. I wanted to tell her why I was neglecting her and risking everything. But that wasn't possible. Not yet.

I jumped into an auto rickshaw on North Main Road, not far from the German Bakery, where Sushmita and I had shared a coffee a week or so earlier.

In Camp, I browsed the aisles at Dorabjee's, playing the role of expat to a T. I crossed paths with several Brits, Germans, and French as I filled my basket with things I didn't really need. Waiting for the appointed hour of eleven, I weighed the benefits against the drawbacks of buying the sausages, the American cereal brands, and even the perfumes one couldn't find elsewhere. In the end, I abandoned everything in my basket except a can of Right Guard deodorant. Funny you could find that at Dorabjee's. I'd never truly intended to purchase anything, but I couldn't return empty-handed. That might have raised suspicions. Then I made my way to the top floor, where Sushmita and I had enjoyed our veg biryani.

There in the café, I waited. And waited some more. I consulted my watch several times, wondering if I'd been reading the wrong day's paper. Where the hell was Birgit? Or Ranjit? They were leaving me twisting in the wind.

And then my paranoia really kicked into gear. What if they'd been intercepted along the way? What if Willy was well aware of what we were up to? Everyone in the place suddenly looked suspect to me. The two university students gazing into each other's eyes opposite me. The old Parsee lady guarding her tea until it turned cold, evaporated, or the British returned, whichever came first. Were these people in league with Willy? Was I in danger for having answered the ad?

This was madness. A couple of twenty-year-old students and an old woman were not spying on me. If he hadn't discovered my betrayal under his own roof, why would he suspect anything on a Tuesday morning in Camp?

It was now past 11:40. No one was coming. I made good my exit without the old Parsee lady tackling me and injecting me with sodium pentothal to learn my secrets. The two students did watch me go, but I chalked that up to my being a *gora*. Everyone watched the *gore*.

It was only when I was seated in the auto rickshaw that I realized my mistake. I'd forgotten my instructions. The matrimonial ad had mentioned that the woman was twenty-nine, not twenty-eight. That meant a rendezvous at Swiss Cheese Garden, not Dorabjee's. And the appointed hour was 3:30, not 11:00 a.m.

I'd have to come up with a fresh excuse to get away after lunch. I wasn't worried about Willy buying my story. It was Sushmita. She was already annoyed and disappointed and suspicious of my behavior. It was no use wishing I could bring her in on my secret. I couldn't. So I debated whether to go back to the bungalow for lunch or stay away until my meeting at Swiss Cheese Garden. In the end, I went back and expressed a desire to give my hosts a break from my company. I knew she didn't buy it.

Sushmita appeared wounded to the core when I said I was heading out for another walk.

"Our Danny doesn't love us anymore, Willy," she said.

"What? Doesn't love us anymore?" he asked.

"It isn't that. It's just . . . Well, you two are difficult to shop for. I'd like to find something sweet for you."

Willy removed his glasses and looked up at me. "What is this? You must not talk this way, Danny Boy. No spending money on us."

Sushmita smoldered. She knew I was lying.

•   •   •

Ranjit was waiting for me at a table outside under the canopy, sipping a nonalcoholic beverage. I sat at a nearby table with my back to him, figuring that's how things were done in this business.

"What are you doing?" he asked. "You look foolish. Get over here."

I slid into the seat opposite him. We were the only people there. Maybe it was more a dinner place, but we weren't eating anyway.

A foreign woman—blonde with a German accent—arrived to take my order. I asked for a club soda.

"How are you managing?" asked Ranjit.

"All right."

"Anything to report?"

"Just my trip to Nepal."

"You went to Nepal? Why didn't you let us know?"

I explained the rushed departure.

"Okay. Tell me."

I gave him the full report, from the surprise request to the sneaking impression that it had been a test.

"That sounds right," said Ranjit. "Why would he trust you for something important?"

"Thanks, pal."

"We barely trust you. Why should he? So what did he want you to do in Kathmandu?"

I fiddled with my hands and looked around the empty place for inspiration. At length, I had to come clean.

"He gave me a bag of brassieres to deliver to a souvenir shop."

"Brassieres? To a souvenir shop?"

"More of a head shop, really."

Then I described Freak Street. The foreign hippies and the smell of hash in the air. The mix of interest in Eastern religion, drugs, and body odor. I was fairly certain those Western kids were missing the mark with their Hare Krishna and beards and hash.

"What was the man's name?" Ranjit asked.

"Dhonu."

"Anything else about him?"

"Only that his shop was called the Wicked Walrus. He was skinny. And ugly. He had brown teeth."

"Does he work with Smets regularly?"

"Not sure. I overheard Willy and Chhotu talking about the king once. The guy in the head shop called himself the king."

"The name Dhonu means 'king.' So how did he react to you?"

"He wanted to know who I was, then accepted me no questions asked when I said Willy'd sent me."

"And you're sure there was only underwear in the valise?"

"Saw it myself. I'm convinced this was a dry run. He wanted to see how I handled things. Customs, the long day, short connections between flights. It felt like he was putting hurdles in my way to see if I could jump over them."

Ranjit gave my story some thought. "Yes, it sounds like a test. Do you think Smets has something more for you to do?"

"Why else would he send me at great expense to deliver eleven brassieres to someone in Nepal?"

"So did you pass?"

"I think so. I even saved him the money he'd given me for a hotel in Kathmandu. Flew back to Bombay and took the train first thing in the morning. He seemed to like that."

Ranjit took a sip of his juice and batted away a fly. "There's no law against sending eleven brassieres to a chap in Nepal. You've got to convince him to give you something real to do."

"I'll get right on that, shall I?"

"What about the *ladki*?"

"The what?"

"The girl. Can you trust her not to lose her head and give you two away?"

The blonde lady returned with my club soda and the bill. I waited till she'd gone to tell Ranjit he had nothing to worry about on that score.

"Sushmita's the one who should be working for you guys," I said. "Ice water in her veins."

"You're sure she's not toying with you?"

I sighed. "Look, I don't expect you to understand. You don't know her. And you don't know me. So you don't know how goddamn insulting your attitude can be sometimes."

He grinned and blinked, looked away at the lush trees above us. ABC Farms was a lovely place. A little oasis on the edge of Koregaon Park, not too far from the bustle of the city, yet it felt like the countryside or the jungle. Nothing but fields and the rough, withering last kilometers of North Main Road. On arrival, in fact, I'd had to navigate a herd of thirty or forty buffaloes moving slowly across the road at the urging of their driver.

"This is a nice spot," he said. "A shame it will probably disappear one day. The lady told me someone bought the land across the road a little farther east. He's going to put up a society with new flats."

"With buffaloes roaming through their gardens? I don't think that'll ever happen."

CHAPTER THIRTY-NINE

"Danny Boy, how did you amuse yourself today?"

We were settling in for cocktails, Willy on the sofa next to Sushmita, who was looking bored and sad. I sat opposite them, wondering what I might do to cheer her up. But this wasn't the time to lose concentration. Was Willy fishing? Trying to catch me in a lie? Maybe he'd had me followed.

"I took advantage of the nice weather and had a long walk on North Main Road. All the way to ABC Farms. Why haven't we tried that Swiss place for dinner? I saw they had lights in the trees. Must be pretty at night."

"The food is awful," said Sushmita.

"I'm afraid Mita is right," added Willy. "They're trying to adapt Swiss food to the Indian palate. The result is a runny mess."

With no plans to meet my handlers the following day, I thought I might chance an afternoon walk with Sushmita.

"Would you like to come with me tomorrow if it doesn't rain?" I asked her.

She shrugged. "If I'm not busy."

"That's an excellent idea, Mita. Chhotu is coming back tomorrow afternoon. We'll be working. You and Danny should go out. It will change your mood."

"*Zadya* is coming back?" she snapped at him.

"No need to insult the man for his size," said Willy, stiffening in his seat. "He has a glandular problem."

Sushmita stood and challenged him from above. "He has an eating problem. And I can't stand having him in this house."

"It's only for one night, Mita. Stop this nonsense. You're making Danny uncomfortable."

I wanted to object to his characterization of my comfort but, in truth, he was right. Not that Sushmita was making me uncomfortable, but the idea of—what had she called him?—*Zadya* coming back did.

"If you prefer *Zadya*'s company to mine, I'll leave you to him. You can listen to his haw-haw accent to your heart's content, but I won't be here."

She slammed her glass down on the table and stormed out. A heavy silence settled over the room, and I did indeed feel uncomfortable sitting there with the shit who'd sold that little bride I'd seen in Kamathipura.

"I apologize for Mita," he said.

It took every last ounce of resolve I had to resist the urge to throw my drink in his face.

• • •

Despite the dangers and my doubts about her, I welcomed Sushmita's visit to my room that night. Somehow I'd expected her, even though it had been ten days since we'd last been together. She was furious with Willy. She always found a way to reach me whenever that happened.

It was quick. And hot and sweaty.

"Why haven't you figured out how to fix this yet?" she asked, breathing heavily as she stared at the ceiling.

Was this the moment to tell her? I couldn't. It would jeopardize everything between us, and my one chance to put Willy Smets behind bars. So I stared at the ceiling fan spinning above us and kept my mouth shut.

"You don't answer me," she said, pushing herself up on her elbow to look me in the eye.

. . .

WEDNESDAY, AUGUST 13, 1975, 10:27 A.M.

Sushmita was gone. I had a fair idea of where she was, but this time I couldn't follow. The risk was too great. To disappear again at the same time would certainly arouse suspicions, if not in Willy's mind, then surely in Chhotu's. He knew about our trysts already, and he'd probably guessed that our concurrent absences a couple of weeks earlier were by design and we'd been together somewhere.

Zadya was due to arrive at any moment. I finished my breakfast and complimented Kamal on yet another fine meal.

"*Bohut acchha tha,*" I said in bloody awful Hindi.

She blushed and said, "Thank you, sir," in her little voice.

I excused myself to do some reading in my room and, once Chhotu landed up, the two business associates withdrew to Willy's study.

Maybe he had some kind of hold over Sushmita, I thought as I lay on my bed, avoiding the Wodehouse I'd picked up again. Why else would she let him live in her homes as if he were the lord of the keep? Why wouldn't she throw him and his awful friend out?

These thoughts were killing me. I didn't want to think the worst about Sushmita, but was it merely Willy's money that kept her in line? Put it out of your mind, I told myself. I wrapped a pillow around my head and slept.

. . .

It was after seven when I stretched and came back to life. I dreamt Sushmita was calling for me. "Wake up, *mazha* Danny," she said, gently shaking me by the shoulder. "It's time for a drink."

I opened my eyes, disappointed it had only been a dream. I climbed out of bed and splashed some water on my face. I needed a moment to prepare myself for drinks with Willy and Chhotu. And I wondered if Sushmita had returned. I soon discovered she had not.

Willy and Chhotu were standing at the main entrance, engaged in a discussion with a *fireng*, a man of about thirty with dark hair, who was on his way out the door. The atmosphere I'd intruded upon was tense. Willy was wagging his finger at him and speaking in a low, hard voice. Chhotu told the man to go. He'd see him in Bombay.

"But listen to me," the man said.

"The matter is decided, Clive," said Chhotu, shaking his head.

The Westerner noticed me across the room and changed his attitude. He nodded to them and apologized.

"Of course, Willy. Sorry. I understand," he said with what sounded like an Australian accent. Then he left.

"Danny Boy," said Willy, once he'd realized I was there. Gone was the tension of a moment before. He rubbed his hands together and grinned at me. "And now it's time for a cocktail."

"Who was that?" I asked. "An associate?"

"A potential buyer. Visiting India for the first time. He doesn't understand how things work here. I'm not sure we can do business with him."

It was just the three of us, Willy, Chhotu, and me, and I was miserable. But the poker face I'd learned—or tried to learn—from Sushmita was as good as a mask. I laughed at their insipid jokes, and I even offered a few stories of my own. Willy seemed to appreciate my efforts, but I couldn't help but notice a shade of doubt in Chhotu's eyes, especially when I was speaking and he was watching Willy. That subtle loss of concentration that weakens the smile in one's eyes. He was wondering how to get rid of me. How to turn me in to his precious Willy. But his hands were tied for the moment. How he must have regretted slipping that note under my door. If only he'd known that it no longer existed, he'd have put a knife in my back.

Dinner was even more painful. Watching *Zadya* stuff his face, as if eating were a sport. I listened to his stories, always a boast about a job he'd held in Toronto or Manchester—never New York or London—or a chap he'd bested at cards in Amsterdam, or a nautch girl he'd bedded in Bombay. But I grinned and pretended to enjoy his haw-haw accent, as Sushmita had called his horsey British affectations.

. . .

"Chhotu and I had a little chat about you this afternoon, Danny Boy," said Willy once we were seated with our after-dinner drinks in the drawing room.

"No wonder my ears were burning."

"Ears . . . burning?"

"It's an expression," I said. "When someone's talking about you . . . Never mind. Tell me."

"I'm always trying to improve my English. Sushmita is a great help for that. But what Chhotu and I were discussing was another favor you can do for me. If you're willing."

"Of course," I said, wondering if I'd have time to visit the Blue Diamond Hotel to get word to Ranjit about this development.

"I'd like you to collect a parcel for me in Bombay. It's small. No physical effort required. And then bring it back to me."

"Sure. When would you like me to go?"

"Not until Saturday. Friday is Independence Day, so that won't do. It's a sample, you see, arriving from Amsterdam. You can travel with Chhotu. I hope you don't mind going by car."

. . .

THURSDAY, AUGUST 14, 1975, 11:58 A.M.

I left the bungalow under the pretext of taking yet another jog, and ran to the Blue Diamond Hotel in my shorts and T-shirt. My morning runs were paying off; the heat barely bothered me now. My wind was getting stronger every day, and I felt I was in the best physical condition since my college football and track days. The desk clerk told me Ranjit was "out of station" until Sunday. No need to leave a message in that case; I'd be back well before then.

CHAPTER FORTY

Independence Day. Twenty-eight long years since India had "redeemed its pledge" and made its "tryst with destiny," as Mrs. Gandhi's father, Pandit Jawaharlal Nehru, had so famously put it. Fireworks popped and crackled in the streets throughout Koregaon Park, as I wondered what I should think of this anniversary. India's democracy was a miracle in so many ways. A multicultural society with Hindus, Muslims, Sikhs, Jains, Christians, Parsees, and dozens of languages. Somehow, they had been able to cobble together a country and a democracy. Imperfect, perhaps. What democracy wasn't?

But now Nehru's own daughter, a woman I'd admired so much from afar, had swept away Indian democracy as if swatting a fly. I understood she'd felt threatened by the opposition and the unrest. Maybe even that she'd believed the nation was in peril. What I couldn't accept was her wiping out due process and basic protections under the pretext that the nation was threatened by "internal disturbances."

But India was not my country. How it handled its crises was its own business. My job was to report it. *Had been* to report it. Now, I was in the lackey business. An employee ready and willing to do his boss's bidding, no matter how objectionable. But then I reminded myself I was also a snitch. I was after bigger quarry. And if that included Willy and his heavyset companion, I was game.

The fireworks continued outside until after midnight, when they finally died out, with one final bang.

• • •

SATURDAY, AUGUST 16, 1975, 11:35 A.M.

Dreading the impending terror the descent of the *ghats* would bring, I sat beside Chhotu in the back of the Ambassador as we traveled to Bombay on one of the most dangerous roads in the world. If I was destined to die on the *ghats*, I was determined to reach across the seat and strangle that son of a bitch before I did.

We passed Lonavala, and I affected a bored, uninterested expression, as if I hadn't even noticed the place.

She was there, I was sure. Not two miles away as we pushed on along the Bombay-Poona Road. I watched through the window of our Ambassador as we went, wondering exactly where she was breathing in that moment.

• • •

The rain began in earnest a few minutes after we'd started the descent. The white-knuckling was going to be intense. When I wasn't obsessing over the cars and trucks passing with little or no space to do so, I worried that Chhotu's weight, combined with Shankar's on the driver side of the car, would tip us over the edge sooner or later and send us to the bottom in a spectacular crash and burn. Closing my eyes and curling up in the fetal position only did so much good. Going down the *ghats* was so much worse than the ascent I'd made with Sushmita driving.

"You're very quiet, old chap," said Chhotu.

"Trying to relax. And hoping not to die. Or vomit on my fellow passenger. Not your fault, Shankar," I called to the driver.

He regarded me in the mirror, roused by the mention of his name. He gave a curt nod, and said, "*Ji,* sir."

"What are you worried about, Danny?" asked Chhotu. "If your time's up, it's up. Just ask Sheik Mujib."

"Mujib? The prime minister of Bangladesh?"

"Haven't you heard? He was assassinated in Dhaka along with his entire family yesterday. There's been a coup."

"God. That's awful. His family, too?"

"Two daughters were abroad at the time and are safe."

If I'd still been in the office in Bombay, I'd have been working on the assassination story.

"Anyway," said Chhotu, "I'm not afraid to die."

"Really? Pop your door open and let's see what you say on the next curve."

He smirked at me and explained that while he wasn't afraid to die, neither was he in a hurry to do so.

We took a particularly sharp turn, with no guardrail to protect us should Shankar miscalculate his speed and the angle. Of course, he didn't. He held true to the road and kept everything on an even, if bumpy, keel.

"You're perspiring, old chap," said Chhotu. "Not used to Indian roads, eh?"

"The roads aren't the problem. Well, in part, yes, the roads are bad. But it's the drivers who scare the hell out of me. And there's no AC."

Shankar asked if we wanted to hear some music on the tape player. Cassette. Chhotu expressed his enthusiasm for the idea, but I was terrified of Shankar taking his eyes off the road to slip a tape in. Another vision of a fiery crash down the mountainside.

"Please don't," I said, but he'd already performed the needful. Hindi film music serenaded us from the speakers behind our heads. Christ, I even recognized Lata Mangeshkar's and Kishore Kumar's voices in a duet. The fruits of hours of listening to the radio in my flat.

"What kind of samples am I picking up anyway?" I asked, still shading my eyes and avoiding any accidental glimpses out the window at the storm and the traffic.

"I have no idea what mission Willy's asked you to undertake."

I considered him from my curled-up position against the locked door. Hadn't Willy told me the night before that he and Chhotu had discussed the job? Did that mean this was another test, not an actual pickup of whatever samples Willy was expecting? Or, much worse, was Willy onto my betrayal and this trip to Bombay was nothing but an elaborate assassination plot? Maybe Chhotu had a revolver hidden somewhere on his person. I decided not to doze off—unlikely, given the terrifying descent of the *ghats*.

I watched my fellow passenger out of the corner of one eye. And I unlocked my door, in case I'd need to make a quick exit.

· · ·

Though it was early afternoon, the sky had gone dark as we navigated our way down the endless hill. The heaviest rains had waited for us, and pummeled the roof and windshield mercilessly as Shankar steered to the rhythms of his favorite Hindi film songs.

But like all nightmares, eventually this one ended. We reached the bottom of the *ghats* and my terror lifted. Clearly, I'd adjusted my expectations. The traffic was still hair-raising now that we'd left the plateau far above and behind us, but somehow it seemed quaint compared to the circles of hell we'd just tobogganed down.

"That wasn't so bad, was it, Dan?" said Chhotu, not expecting an answer.

"Where am I sleeping tonight?" I asked.

"There are boardinghouses and cheap hotels. Or you can catch a train back to Poona. You'll manage."

· · ·

SATURDAY, AUGUST 16, 1975, 5:05 P.M.

The rain stopped. Shankar dropped me at a woodworking stall near Haji Ali, the mosque in the Arabian Sea. Chhotu lowered his window and wished me luck.

"There," he said, indicating the one right in front of me.

The window slid closed and the car drove off. I considered the shop. Doors, window frames, a bed, and assorted carved cabinets had been placed on the footpath outside to invite buyers to browse. At least while the rain held off. On either side, and far beyond, more stalls displayed the exact same goods. I'd always wondered why all the tire shops in India were located in the same lanes. And the radio repair stands, too. I supposed it gave people an idea of where to go for what they needed and, perhaps, it kept the shopkeepers honest in their pricing. Still, thirty tire repair shops in a row struck me as odd.

I peered inside the stall. The smell of varnish and sawdust dominated, but there was cumin or some similar spice as well. A radio played spiritual music. I called hello, but there was no one in the dark space. I was feeling spooked by this time. But then, an old man in a *shalwar kameez* and a skullcap emerged from the back. He wore a beard, dyed red from henna, and spoke Hindi. Or was it Urdu? I told him I'd been sent by Willy Smets. He didn't understand. I tried again, but there was no getting past the language barrier. I was about to give up, figuring Chhotu had set me up to fail in this second test. I reconsidered. Chhotu wouldn't be so bold to send me on a wild goose chase. Something was off, but he'd have to answer to Willy if I failed even to meet the man who had the samples.

And, like that, the old carpenter seemed to figure out the game. He motioned for me to follow him back outside. There, he directed me to the stand two doors down.

"*Mera beta*. My son," he said, sending me on my way.

It was a juice stand. The place served freshly squeezed refreshments for the faithful who'd made the trek across the causeway to reach the mosque on the sea. A young man with a bright smile—the carpenter's son?—was expecting me. When I asked if he had anything for Willy, he handed me a slip of paper and moved on to his next customer.

Chhotu had been trying to sabotage my success. Or maybe it had been Willy all along. If this were a test, maybe he'd wanted to see how I'd cope. Outside again, I unfolded the paper and read it as a steady rain began to fall.

"*Dhiraj the flower vendor. Next to Mafco stall, opposite President Hotel. 6:01 p.m.*"

The carpenters emerged from their shops and pulled their wares back inside, safe from the rain.

I knew the Mafco stall well. I'd sought refuge from the downpour under its eaves the night I spotted Ramu/Ranjit heading to the President Hotel.

It was already nearing 5:30, so this was going to be tight. I picked my way across several lanes of traffic and honking horns, and finally made it to Tardeo Road, where some black-and-yellows were waiting. I knocked on the bonnet of the first taxi, and the driver inside sprang to life. Of course, since I was a *gora*, he refused to engage the meter, and I let him rip me off. I was in a hurry.

The taxi deposited me in front of the flower seller's, and I jumped out. It was 6:08, and Dhiraj was gone. Shit. His shop was attached to the side of the Mafco stall, like a lopsided annex or a parasite. It was nothing more than a cupboard with a short door, padlocked with his wares inside. I stood under the eaves, and, through the raised roll-down shutter, asked the Mafco proprietor inside when the flowerwallah had left.

"*Patz minnit*," he said in Marathi, holding up five fingers.

"Did he leave anything for me?"

"Name?"

I told him Danny. That got no response. Then I said "Willy," and the man reached under his counter and retrieved a small parcel, about the size of a deck of cards. He handed it to me.

"*Pannass paise*," he said. "Fifty *paise*. Storage charges."

. . .

For the purposes of my mission as a snitch, I had been fired from my job at UNI. That meant, of course, that I'd also lost my flat. The subject had never come up with Willy. Still, I worried there was a minute chance someone could be following me. Chhotu, perhaps. But Sagar Darshan was there, a few steps away, and I had my latchkey in my pocket. I debated with myself whether to stop by my place to use the bathroom or to try my luck at the President Hotel instead.

Sunset was due in about twenty minutes, but, with the rain, the light and visibility were already low. I scanned the area for anything suspicious. A loitering man, a car in no hurry to move on . . . There was plenty of traffic in the road and on the footpath, but no one was stopping or even looking up. Sheltering beneath umbrellas or folded newspapers, the pedestrians all hurried on their way. The *marg*, too, was bustling at that hour, with taxis, private cars, and buses all going about their business. Everything looked normal.

The liftman namaste'd me, unconcerned that I was dripping rainwater in his car. He punched the button for the twelfth floor, took his seat on the stool, and stared at the wall for the balance of our shared journey. The doors rolled open, and I stepped out.

The landing was dark, so I pushed the switch on the wall. I fished out my key and promptly dropped it on the floor. Bending over to pick it up, I noticed the trace of a wet footprint in front of my door. Ranjit, I knew. He wasn't in Poona, after all. Maybe he'd make me some dinner. That would be a welcome development.

I slipped my key into the lock and turned it. The door swung open, revealing a darkened room. Not wanting to surprise my sometime roommate, I hit the light switch and called his name. Then I realized my terrible mistake.

CHAPTER FORTY-ONE

There were no shoes against the wall inside the door. That meant Ranjit was not there. He'd never walk through the house in his city shoes, especially if they were wet.

I stepped back outside and pulled the door closed. It was possible, of course, that no one was there. That someone had merely come to the door and left the wet footprints when there was no answer to his knock. Or perhaps someone—my money was on Bikas—had come, broken in, and left already. I wasn't going to stick around to find out which scenario was the correct one.

Instead, I flew down the stairs as fast as I dared, given my wet shoes and the slippery surfaces. The lift would have taken who knows how long to return to the twelfth floor, and I doubted I had the time. I had to leap over a soggy cat and hold onto the railing to keep my feet beneath me. On the fifth-floor landing, I hurdled a seventy-five-year-old grandfather playing with his little granddaughter. He yelled after me to be careful, shaking his fist as he did. Crap, that was the secretary of the Sagar Darshan Cooperative Society . . . As I continued bounding down the stairs, I thought I might never be allowed back in the building.

I reached the lobby and darted out the servants' door just as the lift bell dinged. My morning runs were about to pay dividends. With room to stretch my legs, I took off on a sprint for the compound exit.

Once I was in the lane, I chanced a look back over my shoulder and spied a man I'd never seen before exiting the building via the main entrance. From a distance, his clothes suggested he was either a delivery boy or a sweeper but, in the darkness, I couldn't make out his features. He set off in my direction, not running, but not dawdling either. I put my head down and raced toward the *marg*, where I turned again to see if he was following. He'd climbed aboard a motorcycle and was soon roaring toward me. Oblivious of the risks of the traffic, I dashed into the road and barely managed to dodge a speeding taxi.

That was one lane out of the way. Now there was the other side of the road to cross, with the cars coming in the opposite direction. I jumped right into the fray, sidestepped a bus, and then skirted an Ambassador before reaching the safety of the far-side footpath.

But the motorcycle was halfway there, as well. I sprinted north along the *marg* and the wall of the President Hotel, as I felt the motorcycle bearing down on me. Then I darted right into the hotel's short drive and leapt up the stairs to the entrance. The *durwan* barely had time to open the door before I was through it.

Collapsing into one of the lobby's chairs, I watched the door for the man on the motorcycle. It had to be Bikas, I told myself. A minute later, once he'd parked his bike and strode up to the entrance, trying to look calm and respectable, the guy was intercepted by the *durwan* and a couple of security men. I wasn't close enough to make out his face, but I could see the clothes. The gatekeepers weren't going to let anyone dressed like that inside the hotel, at least not through the front door. For all its grinding prejudice, Indian snobbery might just have saved my life that evening.

Once he'd realized he wasn't getting in, and that arguing with the doorman might attract the police, Bikas—yes, I'd decided it was him—got back on his bike and rode off into the rainy night.

. . .

I called Harlan from the house phone in the lobby, and he told me to come straight up to his room on the eleventh floor. Ranjit was there with him, as surprised to see me as I was to see him. He demanded to know what I was doing in Bombay. Why hadn't I informed them of my movements?

"I followed protocol and visited you at the Blue Diamond," I said. "They told me you were out of station."

"Then why did you come to the hotel? If someone followed you, we're cooked."

"I had no choice," I said. "I wasn't followed. I was chased. But not by any of Willy's men. It was Bikas. The bomber. He was waiting for me in my flat."

Ranjit stewed, clearly not happy with my presence or my explanation. Harlan took a different view. He wanted to know why I had come to Bombay.

"Willy sent me. I have a package of 'samples' here," I said, producing the parcel Dhiraj had left for me. "I don't know what's inside."

"Don't open it," said Ranjit, and Harlan agreed. "You have to take that back to Willy. It's a test. He'll know if you look inside."

The two cops agreed that I should get the sample back to Poona as soon as possible. As I was low on cash, Harlan gave me some money, enough for cab fare to get to Dadar Central Station.

"I'll just go to VT," I said. "It's closer."

"And it's probably where Bikas will be looking for you," said Ranjit. "There or Churchgate."

He was right, of course.

Harlan phoned the concierge and asked him to arrange a one-way ticket to Poona. Twenty minutes later, the clerk called back to say the travel desk had done the needful. The ticket was waiting at Reception.

"You'll take the Latur Express," Ranjit told me. "It leaves Victoria Terminus at nine, but you'll board at Dadar. Make sure you're there a few minutes early. It departs Dadar at 9:15."

We had time to review the latest test I'd been given. Harlan and Ranjit wondered if Willy might not have set me up.

"How?" I asked. "There's no connection between him and Bikas."

"And you're sure he isn't onto you and Sushmita?" asked Harlan.

"Positive."

· · ·

SATURDAY, AUGUST 16, 1975, 11:26 P.M.

I improvised. When the train pulled into Lonavala, I jumped off. Sushmita might well have returned to Poona already, but it was worth the chance. Under the circumstances, I could get away with one night AWOL. I was expected to spend the night in Bombay, after all.

It was after midnight when I reached the bungalow. The Mercedes was there. My scratching at the door didn't rouse her. I figured she might not answer anyway, given the hour and the isolated location. I found the bedroom window and whispered her name through the open slats of the security blinds. After three tries, a dim light came on. Then the blinds rose slowly and I climbed inside.

"Damn it, Danny. I've told you never to improvise."

"Wait, is that a gun on the bed?" I asked, unable to concentrate on her lecture.

There, lying innocently on her pillow, was a black handgun about eight inches long.

"No, it's my teddy bear. What do you think it is?"

"You have a gun? I thought permits were hard to get in India."

"They are. I got this one from Willy. Not exactly legal."

"Please put it away," I said.

"Be glad I didn't shoot you. I aimed it at the window, you know. Lucky for you I recognized your voice and your rash behavior."

She scolded me some more about improvising and making unplanned visits. And she worried Willy would suspect us now that I'd disappeared again while she was away.

"I've got a one-day pass," I said. "I'm supposed to be in Bombay till tomorrow."

"I don't want you working for Willy," she insisted. "And stay far away from *Zadya*."

"It was just a little errand. He wanted me to pick up some samples for him."

"And did you?"

"The package didn't arrive," I lied. I didn't want to discuss Willy any more. "Chhotu will probably take care of it tomorrow."

As I withheld crucial information from her, I had to remind myself that, as far as I knew, Willy's business was completely on the up and up. That helped me maintain my poker face.

"No more favors for Willy," she said, sliding the gun into the drawer next to her pillow.

• • •

"Why haven't you told him about this place?" I asked as we lay on the rumpled bed, sheets torn off to the side. "The real reason."

"I told you he doesn't know and never will. He'd only bring *Zadya* here."

"Chhotu," I scoffed. "With his hee-haw pronunciation. What an ass."

"*Hee-haw?*"

"Yes, you know. His exaggerated British accent."

She snorted a laugh through her nose. "It's *haw-haw*, not *hee-haw*, Danny."

That stung.

"But you didn't answer my question," I said to put my embarrassment behind me. "You allowed Willy to move into your Bombay flat and your Poona bungalow. Why not this place?"

Her mirth dried up. Totally still, she stared up at the ceiling. I gazed at her profile. Her long eyelashes, straight nose, and full lips. Her naked body. She didn't answer me. I wondered for an instant if she was breathing. But the rise and fall of her breast told me she was indeed alive and not some beautiful statue in eternal repose.

"Sush?"

"This was my parents' home," she said, eyes sparkling in the dying candlelight from across the room. "My childhood home."

Her tone was so fragile and final that I didn't dare ask anything else. I lay back on my pillow and joined her in silent contemplation of the ceiling.

· · ·

Soon after the sun had risen, she climbed out of bed, playful and all smiles. Gone were the intensity and the gloom of a few hours before. She hovered over me, teasing me, tickling me.

"Get up, lazybones," she said. "And no bath," she warned. "The Deccan Express passes through Lonavala at 9:38, and you're going to be on it."

"There's plenty of time for a bath," I said.

"It's not a question of time, Danny. You must look as if you've spent the night in an awful boardinghouse when you arrive in Poona. And don't forget to destroy your tickets. Last night's and today's. You can't risk Willy's finding them."

She was right. If I arrived at Willy's looking fresh, he might ask questions.

"It's pouring rain outside," she continued. "By the time you hike back to the station, you'll be soaked. And then two hours in the third-class compartment will erase all traces of last night."

"You're making me walk to the station?"

"It's what you deserve after landing up unannounced. Go."

CHAPTER FORTY-TWO

SUNDAY, AUGUST 17, 1975, 12:13 P.M.

"Danny Boy," said Willy. "I wasn't expecting you so soon."

"I got into a scrape in Bombay," I said. "That terrorist found me."

"My God, what happened?"

I gave him the story, leaving out the mention of my return to Sagar Darshan. For all Willy knew, I'd lost my flat when I was fired. Instead I told him Bikas had probably been watching my building, lying in wait, and spotted me at the Mafco stall opposite the President.

"Then you got my samples?" he asked.

I pulled the small parcel from my pocket and handed it to him. He thanked me and, making a face, told me to go have my bath.

. . .

"You know, Danny," said Willy, once we'd finished our lunch and were relaxing outside on the veranda, "I sent you to Bombay on a false mission." He had my attention. "My business requires a great deal of trust and confidentiality. I must be sure of the people who work for me."

"That's understandable. But what do you mean by a *false mission?*"

Willy took a last drag on his cigarette, a *Gauloise*, and turned to regard me face-to-face. "I sent you to Kathmandu and to Bombay because I cannot trust you after what you did."

I stared back at him, willing myself to maintain calm. "I don't understand," I said in a measured voice.

"I don't believe you intended to betray me, Danny, but you did."

Oh, God. He knew.

"And I was very disappointed by you. So I sent you on those false missions to get you out of the way. Temporarily. So I could take care of some important business without the risk of you attracting that woman."

My poker face had surely stiffened into an expression much more telling. *That woman*? Was that how he was referring to Sushmita? Now that she'd betrayed him and slept with me?

"That woman?" I asked.

"Your German friend," he said. "Birgit. The one you brought into my home. Twice. She's a government agent, didn't you know? A cop."

I couldn't speak.

"That's why I cannot trust you, Danny," he continued. "Oh, I don't believe for a moment that you put my business and my freedom at risk on purpose. I suspect you were duped. But I cannot afford that kind of carelessness in my line of work."

"What exactly is your work?" I asked, trying desperately to save my neck by acting as naïve as he seemed to believe me to be. As if I had no idea he traded in little girls.

"Import-export, as I've told you before. The police wrongly suspect me of God knows what. Because I sometimes enjoy smoking a little hash."

"I'm sorry, Willy," I said, not believing him for an instant. "Sorry I was so stupid and jeopardized your business."

He shrugged. "River under the bridge."

"Water," I said, my voice low and rough.

"Sorry? Are you thirsty?"

"No. The expression is '*water* under the bridge,' not 'river.'"

Willy blushed, then thanked me for the correction. I couldn't tell if he was onto me or if he loved me. Like a doting father loves his dimwitted son. Was he about to shoot me dead or hug me?

"I'll pack my things and go," I said, just as the guard opened the rusty front gate. The white Mercedes pulled into the compound, tires crunching over the gravel drive.

"Mita is home," he said. "Danny, please don't go. That will upset her, and she's already cross with me about Chhotu."

·   ·   ·

"*Zadya's* not here?" she asked Willy as he kissed her on both cheeks.

"So cruel of you, Mita, to make fun of his weight. Welcome home."

"Hello, Danny. I'm glad to see one friendly face at least. Will you meet me for a walk after I've had a bath?"

"Of course," I said, then looked expectantly at Willy.

He smiled and nodded. "An excellent idea. I have work to do and will need some quiet."

Once Sushmita had gone to her room, Willy patted me on the back. He looked troubled.

"I feel sick about Birgit," I said, thinking I might still salvage my mission. If he didn't suspect me, maybe it was possible. "I really should leave."

Willy sighed and grabbed me by both shoulders. "Birgit's not important," he said. "Yes, I was disappointed in you, Danny. Not because I wanted you to work for me. That never was a possibility. But because I'm very fond of you. I suppose you noticed." He smiled sadly and let go of me. "That's why I was so hurt by your betrayal."

"I'm sorry, Willy. I didn't mean to do it."

"Didn't you?" He paused for a long beat. "I was disappointed in you about Birgit. But that's not what hurt me. It was you and Mita."

Having lobbed that grenade, he drifted out of the room, leaving me to wonder why he hadn't thrown me out. Or had me killed.

CHAPTER FORTY-THREE

I waited until we'd rounded the corner to tell Sushmita that Willy knew. Her reaction surprised me. She took the news with a fatalistic sigh. I asked if she was worried.

"What can he do to me?" she said. "I own the houses. He loves me. And needs me."

On the other hand, he didn't need me. We strolled along the lane, past more bungalows, flowers, and banyan trees.

"Do you know I kind of feel sorry for him?" I said.

"You don't think I do? He's been good to me. It's not the money, Danny."

"What is his hold on you, then?"

She walked on for several steps after I'd stopped to wait for her answer. Then she realized I wasn't by her side and wheeled around to find me. She returned to where I stood on the footpath and gazed into my eyes as if she were searching for something. As if she might be deciding whether to confide in me or not.

"You have the prettiest blue eyes," she said.

Should I thank her? I'd had nothing to do with the color of my eyes. All the glory was my parents'.

"When my father fell sick, Willy did everything humanly possible to save him. He flew him to London for treatment and paid all the expenses. The chemotherapy, the radiation treatments, the doctors' bills. Everything."

"I didn't know. I'm sorry."

"How could you have known? We never talk. We fuck."

That word nearly knocked me over. Its coarseness was so unexpected coming from those beautiful lips. And I knew that nice Indian girls didn't use such language. Then I realized, perhaps, that Sushmita was anything but a "nice" Indian girl. I certainly didn't mind. I was American, after all, and sex and bad words were no big deal from girls I knew. Nice girls. But the sexual revolution hadn't come to India. Still, what kind of prude or hypocrite would I have been if I didn't recognize my own expectations for Sushmita were old-fashioned and wrongheaded? Perfectly happy to have sex with her, but I was put off when she called it by its true name: fucking.

"I want to know everything about you, Sush," I said. "But I've been afraid to ask. For fear of upsetting you."

"I'm not blaming you for it, Danny. I told you I didn't want to talk about my father. But we have only one thing in common."

"What about love?"

She said nothing and turned to walk away. I followed and, after a moment, told her if that was the case I would leave. For good. She faced me again, this time with true alarm in her eyes.

"I've told you, Danny. If you leave, I'll die. Please don't ever go. I need you."

• • •

MONDAY, AUGUST 18, 1975, 1:37 A.M.

I lay in bed as the rain fell outside. What the hell kind of twisted life was I living? The woman I loved was another man's mistress. He knew all about us, and he loved me—apparently—like a son all the same.

Then there was Bikas, whose intentions toward me, at best, were malevolent. At worst, murderous. Finally, I was still deceiving Sushmita and Willy about my status of *snitch*, which was going from bad to worse. Birgit had been discovered by Willy. What about Harlan? And Ranjit? I'd met him at ABC Farms a few days earlier. What if I'd been followed? Or maybe Willy had questioned the waitress after I'd told him I'd been there. I wondered if any of us— Birgit, Harlan, Ranjit, or Sushmita—was in danger?

If Willy had figured out I was sleeping with Sushmita, and that Birgit was a cop, why wouldn't he have known I was in league with her?

It was too much. What business did I have falling in love with an exotic beauty who couldn't be mine? Wouldn't be mine.

I decided to leave Poona, forget my pledge to take down Willy Smets, and return home where I was nothing more than a nice boy from a decent family. No espionage, police, or sick love affairs. And if Sushmita were to die? Why was I responsible for the life of a person who refused to love me in one breath, only to tell me she needed me in the next? I had my own sanity and well-being to consider.

I would leave in the morning, then meet one last time with Ranjit and Harlan to let them know Birgit had been exposed. Ranjit, too, I assumed. Then I'd tell Frank Muller that I really was quitting this time. And, as soon as possible, I'd board a 747 for home, just as Eric Nielsen had.

Yet even as I resolved to go, I hoped I'd have the guts to do it. Could I put the love I felt for that girl to one side, despite her pleadings that her life depended on me? Leave her to a man like Willy Smets, who believed Indians were either in your way or people to step on and use for your own comfort?

CHAPTER FORTY-FOUR

Reluctant to face either Willy or Sushmita, and certainly with no clear idea of what I'd tell them, I rose early intending to walk and think. But, instead, I ran. Far. In my long pants. I ended up in Camp, where I wandered around for several hours, stopping for a late lunch at Marz-o-rin on MG Road. That was the sandwich place Sushmita had said was her favorite while at St. Mary's. Then I made my way west to Shivajinagar before crossing the Mula Mutha River and heading back east. I rehearsed what I would say to Sushmita and Willy, still no closer to a practiced speech.

When I came to the Poona Club Golf Course, I was desperate for a cool drink. There was a vendor on the side of the road, grinding sugarcane into juice. That looked good. Probably not wise, but I was in a fatalistic mood. The man urged me to try a coconut instead. Safer for a *gora*, he said. Then, refreshed, I walked for miles more, taking advantage of the respite from the rain.

· · ·

MONDAY, AUGUST 18, 1975, 7:02 P.M.

When I finally returned to the house, it was empty. Or nearly. No Sushmita, no Willy, no Govind, or Kamal. But Chhotu was there, sitting in the drawing room.

"What are you doing here?" I asked. "Do Willy's *chappals* need licking?"

"Clever," he said, smiling broadly at me. "But you should know that your time has come."

"Does Willy know you're here?"

"My dear chap, he arranged for me to be here."

"Too late for threats. He knows about Sushmita and me. He was saddened, but insisted that I stay."

Chhotu scoffed. "Of course he did. He wanted you to be here when I arrived."

A doubt crossed my mind. "What? Where's Willy? Where's Sushmita?"

He made a great show of looking around the room, as if searching for them. "They don't seem to be here. Bad luck, eh, Danny Boy?"

I strode to the dining room, then to the kitchen. No one. I returned to the drawing room where Chhotu was waiting, still wedged into his seat. We were alone.

Then I heard the sound of crunching gravel coming through the open garden door. A car.

"Willy's back," I said, trying to convince myself.

"I doubt that."

Moments later, the front door opened, and a familiar-looking man stepped inside. About five eight or nine, he was dressed in a light shirt and dark pants. Once he closed the door and turned to face me, I knew it was Bikas.

"Surprised, Dan?" asked Chhotu.

I wasn't about to give him the satisfaction of begging for answers. But I stood rooted in place, frantically trying to put the pieces of the puzzle together. There was no connection between Bikas and Willy. Or Chhotu. How could there be? The bomber was some kind of

revolutionary. And Willy's politics, if he had any, were fiercely
anti-Communist.

"Cat got your tongue, old chap?"

I racked my brain for anything that might tie Willy to the bomber,
and I came up empty. Until I remembered Eric Nielsen. Eric the Red's
notebook.

"You're not making this any fun, Dan," said Chhotu. "Try to get
into the spirit of things."

"Eric Nielsen," I said, and Chhotu's smile faded. "He interviewed
Bikas long before I did."

Chhotu and Bikas waited for more.

"He left notes," I continued. "About meetings with Bikas and the
university girls he chased after. And . . ."

"And what?"

"He suddenly decided to quit and go home, shortly after attending
one of Willy's cocktail parties."

Chhotu had recovered from the surprise Eric Nielsen's name had
inspired.

"To be perfectly accurate, Nielsen didn't so much go home as go
away."

"You killed him?"

Chhotu blinked but kept quiet.

I thought hard. "Eric was settled here in Bombay. He liked his
work. Then, one day, Willy threatened him. Eric must have figured
out the link to Bikas."

"Not bad, Dan. But I already know the story."

The connections came into focus. Bikas wasn't a revolutionary
terrorist. He hadn't killed that CID officer for political reasons. And
if he worked for Willy, Willy must have ordered it. Why? Willy's
"import-export" business, obviously. Was the cop investigating him?
Getting too close? But why the charade of Bikas and the Marxist

angle? And why would Bikas talk to Nielsen? To me? He couldn't be that stupid.

"Stumped, Dan?"

"Bikas killed the cop and tried to throw suspicion on leftists," I said. "Get it in the papers that terrorists assassinated Gokhale. That's why Bikas agreed to talk to Nielsen. And to me. But Nielsen was a sharp guy. Somehow he figured it out. Maybe Bikas didn't strike him as a Marxist. And then he got himself invited to Willy's party. Probably said too much, and . . ."

"We couldn't trust him to go away quietly," said Chhotu, finishing my thought. "Poor chap. And, of course, when you started hunting for Bikas at the university, Willy wanted to know what you were up to."

"That's why he invited me to his party."

"I advised him to get rid of you the same way we did Nielsen. But, strangest thing. He took a liking to you."

Bikas was still standing guard by the door.

"Now, Danny Boy," said Chhotu, "if you would be so good as to hand over that roll of film you shot of our friend Bikas. Willy wanted him to talk to you, not pose for portraits. He was quite angry when you told him about that at one of his parties. But our Bikas sometimes makes foolish decisions. Let's have it."

"I don't have the film," I said.

"Must we play games? I want the film now."

"And then you murder me? No thanks."

I wasn't going to tell him the film was lost. That would make killing me an even easier decision. If he thought I could get my hands on the photos, he might not go through with whatever he had in mind. Maybe he was bluffing.

Chhotu wrestled himself out of the swing chair and smoothed his clothes. "Very well. If that's the way you want it. Shall we go?"

"I don't suppose I'll need my things," I said.

He shook his head. "Not where you're going."

Even the guard, who so faithfully saluted each time a car entered or left the compound, had disappeared. The gate was wide open. With an upturned hand, Chhotu indicated the white Mercedes—Sushmita's Mercedes—sitting in the drive, as if there might have been another vehicle I could have chosen by mistake.

"Front seat, please," he said, and he climbed into the back directly behind me. Bikas took the wheel. "Bear in mind that I have a pistol pointed into your back. In case you were thinking of playing the hero."

Then, wielding his ridiculous haw-haw accent, he said something to Bikas in Hindi. I struggled to understand, but only got something like *karate*. Did it matter? Who was I going to tell, anyway?

I began to plan a last-ditch effort to escape. Once we reached North Main Road, I might try throwing open the door and taking my chances with Chhotu's aim. Would he be willing to fire off potshots in the crowded center of Koregaon Park? The odds for escape were better than waiting for him to shoot me in the head as soon as we arrived wherever he was taking me. In preparation, I tested the door handle quietly. No dice. And a quick glance to my left revealed that the lock button had been removed. I doubted I could lower the window and squeeze myself out before *Zadya* had shot me several times.

"Yes, the door is locked," said Chhotu from the back seat.

We turned right onto North Main Road and headed east. Minutes later, we passed ABC Farms and soon, after a tiny village or two, we'd be in open countryside. I drew a deep breath, then looked up to see the herd of buffalo creeping onto the road. If they cut us off, it might provide the necessary delay for me to lower the window and yell for help from the motorists behind us. Chhotu had seen the buffaloes, too, and barked an order to Bikas, who hit the accelerator and swerved onto the grassy shoulder and barely sneaked around the lead animals. The herd closed the way, and the traffic following us was lost in the gathering darkness.

We rumbled through a tiny village—Mundhwa—according to the little sign illuminated by our headlights. Then we crossed the Mula Mutha and hugged the northern bank of the river on a dirt road for maybe two kilometers. It was slow going on the rough, desolate road, and now the sun had set. Chhotu told Bikas to stop. No need to pull over. And no place to pull over. We were in the middle of nowhere.

I thought of Sushmita. Was she aware of what was going on? How could she have left without a goodbye? How could I have misjudged her so?

Then I thought of my parents. My brother and sister, Mark and Debbie. Good people. Fine people. What would they think? How might they take the news that their son and brother had died in an obscure place halfway around the world? Would they understand my motives? Would anyone even tell them what I was trying to accomplish? I couldn't worry about that now. I'd trust that word would get back to them that I was on the side of right, trying to do good. And, for Christ's sake, I intended to get out of that night alive.

"You'll find your door is unlocked," Chhotu said.

"I'm not getting out."

"Have you forgotten I have a gun?"

"No. But if you're going to shoot me, I'll at least make sure you have a mess to clean up inside Willy's Mercedes."

"Get out," he said, more insistently.

"Fuck you."

He turned to Bikas to give him new orders. The guy wagged his head as Chhotu spat instructions in wretched Hindi. As he did, I reached over, snatched the loose gearshift from its cradle, and bolted out the door before Bikas could even react. He jumped from the car to follow me. I didn't know if he was armed, so I ran as hard as I could, sloshing through the mud and heavy rain back the way we'd come. Chhotu needed several seconds to pop open his own door and wedge himself out. I was about twenty or twenty-five yards clear when I heard the first shot. Glancing back, I saw Bikas pursuing me on foot. I couldn't tell if his hands were empty. Had the shot come from him or Chhotu? There was no way Bikas could outrun me, and forget about Chhotu. Unless one of them got off a lucky shot in the dark, they'd never catch me without a car. And I had the gearshift.

My wind was strong, and my legs were responding, despite having had no warm-up or stretching. I sensed I was leaving Bikas far behind, and I settled into a pace that would have been perfect for the 440. To be sure I was safely ahead of my pursuer, I looked over my shoulder again. I couldn't see him in the dark. He had no chance. I'd be half-way across Poona before he got back to the main road.

Then I tripped and fell hard to the ground, landing on my left wrist in the sloppy road. The loud crack told me all I needed to know; it was broken. I rolled over to see if Bikas was bearing down on me. He was. About twenty yards now, and he was running at a full sprint.

In my high school days, our football coach, Mr. Galligan, used to make us do a particularly cruel drill. He'd have one player—the tack-ler—lie on his back, ten yards from another guy—the runner—who was on his feet. A chalk line marked the halfway point between them. Coach would then blow his whistle and toss the ball to the runner, who charged forward. At the same time, the tackler had to leap to his feet, turn around, and try to stop the runner. The two met head-on in a violent collision. If the runner passed the chalk line, he won. If he didn't, the tackler won. Coach called it the Nutcracker. I remem-ber my share of stingers—those awful tingling sensations in your extremities after a jarring tackle—and I was about to risk another one.

Grimacing from the pain in my wrist, I rolled over, pushed myself to my feet, and lunged toward Bikas. No time to run away now; he was too close, and he'd raised his right hand and was pointing it at me as he charged. He was armed. I knew I outweighed him by thirty pounds, and—broken wrist and all—I was going to teach him how to tackle. Be tackled. I lowered my shoulder and planted it right in the sweet spot in his midsection, lifting him off his feet. Then, driving him to the ground, I knocked the wind out of him as I flattened him. Might have broken a couple of his ribs, too. If he'd been carrying a gun, he lost it in the collision.

I left him lying there in the mud, groaning and gasping for air, and I resumed my run to safety. Jogging through the rain, I held my left wrist as I went. Soon I was crossing the river over a bridge. I tossed the gearshift into the water and pushed on.

There was no traffic at that hour in such a remote area, so when the headlights appeared behind me, I worried Chhotu and Bikas might have managed to improvise a solution for the missing gearshift. I picked up my pace, heading for a collection of huts ahead. If I could reach them in time, I might be able to escape. But the car was closing fast.

As it neared, the driver blew the horn, which sounded as if it had been installed backward and was blaring into the car instead of out. I'd heard Sushmita use the Mercedes' horn on a few occasions. It trumpeted loud, muscular blasts, so I knew immediately it was not Chhotu and Bikas behind me. I waited for the car, a small green Fiat, to pass. It rolled to a stop instead.

"Get in, Dan," came a voice from behind the headlights.

"Ranjit!"

CHAPTER FORTY-FIVE

"What the hell are you doing here?" I asked, panting for breath.

He shifted into first, popped the clutch, and we were off. He told me he'd been following me, but got trapped behind the buffaloes.

"You were following me? How?"

"I've been watching the bungalow for weeks," he said. "I was the fellow selling fruit on the footpath."

"That was you? I must have passed you five or six times and never noticed."

"Nobody pays attention to a *fruitwallah* sitting cross-legged on the pavement."

"But how did you find me now?"

"I've been driving up and down the road, the lanes, looking for a white Mercedes. What happened to you? How did you get away?"

I gave him the story, from Willy's discovery of my betrayal to Birgit's unmasking to my escape, including my all-American tackle of Bikas. He said my wrist needed attention right away, and we sped off to Ruby Hall on the far side of Koregaon Park. I was X-rayed—multiple fractures—and wrapped in a heavy cast, what the doctor and nurses called a plaster. Ranjit told me the police had located the Mercedes and towed it away. Chhotu and Bikas were nowhere to be found.

. . .

An hour later, a squad of CID—the state criminal investigation police—supported by about thirty Poona cops, entered the bungalow in Koregaon Park, guns raised. They secured the place in a matter of minutes. It was empty anyhow. Abandoned. Just hours earlier, it had been filled with residents, servants, and me. Now? Nothing. Even Willy's study had been cleared out. The ledgers were gone. And so was Sushmita.

With nowhere else to go, I checked into the Blue Diamond Hotel. Ranjit, working undercover, was staying there as well. He told me his boss had raised a stink about it. Said a CBI agent shouldn't be relaxing in a luxury hotel, but he'd relented.

After a couple of days of giving statements to the police and consulting with a lawyer recommended by Janice's friend, Shirish, I took the train back to Bombay on the twenty-first, with orders not to leave India until the investigation was complete. The public prosecutor confiscated my passport to prevent any risk of flight. Ranjit remained behind in Poona. His superiors had twisted the Maharashtra CID's arm to give him access to the bungalow for further investigation.

During my two-minute stop in Lonavala, I tried and failed to resist the temptation to scan the platform for signs of a beautiful woman coming to whisk me away to a secluded love nest. I looked hard and long, even after the train started moving and left the station behind.

Once we were speeding along again, I sulked. I couldn't understand how she'd simply disappeared without a goodbye. Left me waiting for my murderers to arrive. Had she been aware of Willy's plan to kill me? Hell, the attempt in Poona was certainly the second try. Now that I knew that Bikas was in Willy's employ, I figured he'd intended to murder me in my flat in Cuffe Parade two days before. Maybe the parcel I'd picked up at the Mafco stall was stuffed with drugs. I'd be written off as a foreigner who got mixed up with the wrong people. Case closed.

But I kept asking myself, did Sushmita know? I couldn't possibly be sure. But I wanted her anyway. And I knew that if she'd been there on the platform in Lonavala, I'd have jumped off the train and followed her anywhere.

•   •   •

BOMBAY, INDIA

FRIDAY, AUGUST 22, 1975, 5:21 P.M.

I returned to the flat in Sagar Darshan, unsure of how much longer I'd be able to keep it. Frank Muller knew nothing of my decision to quit. But he'd be rubbing his hands together by now, eager to read the story I'd write about the undercover operation. Well, he wasn't going to get it, and I'd be out on the street as soon as he realized it.

"Has Mr. Smets returned?" I asked the building manager. He said he hadn't seen him in nearly three weeks, but the police had been there to search his flat.

I even rode the lift up to the penthouse and rang the bell. No one answered. His two servants and cook were gone. Maybe I should have climbed up the drainpipe and peered through the window to be sure they weren't there.

Of course they wouldn't return after the failed attempt on my life. They might have been able to weather the scrutiny, had Chhotu and Bikas done the job right and disposed of my body permanently. But with the attention, Willy would surely have to lie low until the situation became clearer. I wondered if he'd been contacted by Chhotu, who'd escaped the police in Poona, even without Willy's Mercedes. And what were they planning now? They might head to Nepal, Holland, or Belgium. Maybe Nasik or Srinagar. Or anywhere in between.

• • •

I was avoiding both Frank Muller and Russ Harlan. One didn't know I was back in Bombay, while the other, of course, did. I'd sworn Janice to secrecy. But Harlan knew. And he wasted little time before darkening my door.

"Glad to see you're still with us," he said. "You did well. How's the arm?"

"It's fine."

"Invite me in for a drink?"

I let the door fall open, and he entered.

"Take your shoes off, please," I said.

He removed his heavy cordovan wingtips and stood there in his black socks, looking uncomfortable.

I poured two glasses of the Dewar's he'd sent to me via Ranjit, and added a couple of ice cubes.

"You've got to get out of this place," said Harlan. "I'll move you to the hotel. They could come after you again at any time."

"I'm not going to the President," I said.

"That's unwise, Dan. I urge you to reconsider. If you're going to continue on this project, you'll need more security."

I frowned and tapped my cast on the arm of the chair. "That's just it, Russ. I'm not going to continue. I'm done."

"You can't quit now."

"Look, Willy already knows I betrayed him. He knows I slept with his girl. And he knows Birgit is a cop. He's tried to kill me. Twice. He was going to bury me in the woods in Kharadi—the place I'd heard as 'karate'—or dump me in the Mula Mutha River. What am I going to accomplish now? I can't exactly propose my services to him. I'm going home."

He swallowed a mouthful of whisky, rose, and refilled his glass. He asked if I wanted another. I shook my head.

"One to whet your appetite and one to rinse down dessert."

He smiled, before turning serious again.

"You know what your problem is, Dan?" he asked, retaking his seat. "You've had some bad luck in love and you're feeling low. That's okay. Happens to everyone at one time or another. But you have to decide if your failed love is a sad moment you'll get over or if it will obsess you and cripple you for the rest of your life."

"Easy for you to say. You have Barb."

"You think I've never been disappointed in love?" he asked. "Never had my heart broken?"

"You said so yourself. She's the love of your life."

He aimed a fierce glare at me. "Barb died," he said. "Four years ago . . . cancer. And I miss her like the devil. Not five minutes go by that I don't think of her. I've never loved another woman. Never will. And I honor her memory by doing my job. By doing what's right."

CHAPTER FORTY-SIX

I moved to the President Hotel.

Harlan was a hard man. But a fine one. Better than I was. During our early days of acquaintance, he'd lied about his wife, Barb, in order to paint the picture of an insufferable racist asshole. He'd done it well. But now that I knew the real man—the one whose beloved wife had died four years before—I felt like a coward, and a selfish one at that. No one should have to risk his safety to make the world a better place, but it's a good thing so many people do. And Harlan had shown me that, unless I wanted to think of myself as a craven, selfish bastard, I had no choice but to carry on.

I met him in his room a little after nine Saturday morning. He'd forbidden me from going out for a run, so I'd taped a dry-cleaning bag over my cast and swum thirty laps in the hotel pool instead. I could still feel some stubborn water sloshing around in my left ear as we sat down opposite each other at the desk near the window. Harlan had notes and documents he wanted to review with me. He began with one of my least favorite topics: Chhotu.

"Do you know his full name?" he asked.

I struggled to recall. The surname was definitely Goswami. I remembered it because it sounded like "go, swami."

"His first name was long and began with a D."

Harlan reached into his briefcase, which was resting on the floor at his feet. He dug inside, then produced a thin booklet. He rose and joined me on my side of the desk.

"Is it one of these?" he asked, running his fingers down a column of Indian names. These all started with the letter D.

"There," I said, pointing to the winner. "Debajyoti. Debajyoti Goswami. I remember Willy telling me. He said it was a beautiful Bengali name. This guy is from Calcutta originally."

"You're sure?" I was positive. He retook his seat. "Okay, is there anything else about him you can tell me?" he asked.

I thought back to my first impression of him. This was easy. "Chhotu? He's in his forties, obese," I said. "Doesn't fit into airplane seats, so he always travels by train or car."

Harlan took down the information in his notes.

"Claims he studied at Oxford and worked in Manchester and Toronto. And he speaks with what the Indians call a haw-haw accent. *Veddy* British, in an exaggerated, almost comical way. Sounds like George Sanders."

Harlan said he'd contact his office back home, as well as Ranjit in Poona. He'd request as much information on Chhotu as they could find. He wrote some more before leaning back in his chair and regarding me with an invasive stare. "And that brings us to your Sushmita."

I gave him as much history as I knew. I described the way Willy had tried to save her father—who'd been a scientist of some kind—from cancer, and that she'd inherited the two properties from him. Yes, I left out two important details. One, that her father had taught in Lonavala at the naval school and, two, that Sushmita had actually inherited a third property, our love nest in the very same Lonavala. Why had I kept that information to myself? Obviously because I wasn't sure things were over between us. If, by some miracle, this

whole thing got straightened out, I wanted the lifeline to the bungalow to be there. I might have to reveal all to Harlan at some point but,
for the moment, it was my secret.

I was sure she hadn't told Willy about the place. It was her child-
hood home. And, of course, she was well aware that I knew about it.
If they were hiding there, I could easily lead the police to them. No,
Willy didn't know about the bungalow.

Harlan then turned to the subject of Willy.

"He's Belgian," I said. "I don't know where he was born, but he
claimed he was in the same class as Jacques Brel in Brussels. The
Institut Saint-something."

"That helps." He made a note.

"He speaks French, Flemish, English, and German. Probably some
Hindi and Marathi."

"We knew that. But we can't locate any evidence of him in Belgian
records. Maybe the school name will help. Go on."

Willy smoked Gauloises Bleues and liked wine and whisky. Had
two cars: a white Mercedes, which the police had taken after it was
stranded in Kharadi, and a blue Ambassador. I gave Harlan the
names of all the servants I'd observed, both in Bombay and Poona.
But I didn't know their family names, so I doubted that would help.

"You're sure the houses are hers, not Smets's?"

I felt I was betraying her. "Yes," I croaked. "Hers. The money and—
I'm pretty sure—everything else is his."

"Did you see any evidence of his business dealings in the Poona
house?" he asked.

I tried to recall. Nothing came to mind except his meetings with
Chhotu. Then I remembered. "There was an Australian guy named
Clive who came to the house one day. There seemed to be some ten-
sion between them."

"Do you know Clive's last name?"

"Afraid not. He looked fit, about thirty, with dark hair."

Harlan said he'd try to check on Australians and New Zealanders named Clive who were in the country. Maybe even South Africans.

"You don't trust my diagnosis of Australian?" I asked.

"Just covering the bases," he said. "Any other business stuff?"

"He keeps several ledgers in his private office. Different colors. Nothing written on the outside."

"Those were gone when the police searched the house. Another dead end."

"You know, there was another ledger," I said. "Not sure what it means, but Willy has his drivers keep a petrol record in the glove compartment of the Ambassador. I had to sign it once when the driver filled up the tank."

"Anything interesting?"

"Just that the car has traveled a lot. From Bombay to Srinagar and all points between. Wonder why he doesn't fly. The roads are awful to drive."

"Maybe he's afraid of flying. More likely he doesn't want to leave a record of where he goes."

I gave Harlan the cities I remembered and he wrote them down.

"He's slippery, I'll give him that. Maybe that's why the Indians have never been able to put him behind bars."

"Wait a minute," I said. "What if he's been to prison in India after all?"

"We've checked. He hasn't."

"What if Smets isn't his real name?"

Harlan stared me down. "What are you driving at?"

"When the police were after me, he told me I didn't want to end up in an Indian prison. Ever. He insisted. Said, 'trust me.' As if he knew from personal experience."

"Interesting. We can look into it again. But without a name, it's going to take time and a lot of luck."

"I have a name."

. . .

SATURDAY, AUGUST 23, 1975, 8:19 P.M.

Birgit and Harlan came to my room for dinner. Ranjit was still in Poona. Harlan insisted it was safer to stay away from the restaurants and permit room. And, of course, it would be foolhardy for us to be seen together at this point.

"They already know about you and Birgit," he said. "Probably about me and Ranjit, too. At least we have to assume that."

After our meal, we relaxed, me on the bed—no shoes—Birgit on the armchair, and Harlan at the desk. He wanted to know how Willy had figured out that Birgit was an agent.

I had no idea. "He plays the generous, avuncular type. But clearly, he's sharp. I was convinced he suspected nothing about me and . . . about me and Sushmita." I added that last bit with no small measure of shame. "Not sure when he figured it out, but I doubt Chhotu told him."

"Why's that?" asked Harlan.

"Because he tried to blackmail us early on. He saw her coming from my room one night and slipped me a blackmail note."

"So? Why wouldn't he turn you in to Willy when you refused to play ball?"

Birgit butted in. "Because it would amount to suicide for Chhotu if he did. Danny and Sushmita could have shown Willy the note, isn't that right, Danny?"

"Exactly."

"Not very wise of Chhotu to put his threat in writing, especially since he was withholding the information from Willy."

"Do you think we can use that against him?" asked Harlan. "You know, turn Willy against him."

"Afraid not. Sushmita burned the letter when I showed it to her. She was afraid Willy might find it."

"So you two bluffed Chhotu, and he bought it? Bad luck. We might have been able to use that."

We were at a dead end with Chhotu. No way to know where he was. But even if we had known, the blackmail note had lost its leverage against him. We had no leads on how to find him or Willy. But I had an idea.

"Kathmandu. The king."

CHAPTER FORTY-SEVEN

Ranjit managed to get himself out of Poona and made it back to Bombay. Harlan and I briefed him on the Wicked Walrus. His plan was to deliver a bag of women's underwear to the king, Dhonu. Panties. Ranjit's instructions were to hand over the bag and ask for Willy's samples.

"He's not going to be expecting a bag full of girls' *chuddies*," said Ranjit, "but I believe he'll assume there's been a miscommunication with Smets. He'll want to contact him."

"He might not know where Smets is right now," I said.

"True," said Harlan. "But it's either this or wait until he resurfaces eventually."

An hour later, Ranjit was packed and ready to leave for Kathmandu. He carried a small bag with eleven pairs of ladies' underwear inside.

. . .

Harlan had two updates for Birgit and me.

"Interpol has confirmed that the girl—Sushmita—arrived in London on August 20. She was traveling alone."

Birgit waited a moment, as if she felt I had first dibs when it came to discussing Sushmita. I'd been doing everything I could to keep her out of my mind, without success, but this news set all kinds of emotions and doubts to roiling in my chest. I wondered if she'd been in on the assassination plot with Willy and Chhotu, if she'd been shipped off to London for her own protection or to do Willy's bidding, and if she'd been faking it when she slept with me. Hell, maybe she was the ringleader—what did I know?

Or did she truly want to be with me? What if she loved me, even as she'd refused to say it? What if she'd been tricked? Sent away against her will?

"Has she been arrested?" I asked.

"No. They're watching her in case Smets shows."

"Do they know if he's left India?" asked Birgit.

Harlan shook his head. "But he might have phony passports. Or maybe he slipped over the border to Nepal or Bangladesh. Even Pakistan. And there're plenty of places to hide in this country. He has a house here and in Poona. Maybe he's got more we don't know about."

They looked to me, not out of suspicion, but because I knew Willy better than they did. I urged myself to maintain my straight face, but all I could think of was her. That was probably the best way to disguise my guilt.

"You said you had two updates for us," said Birgit. "What's the second one?"

"Thanks to Dan, we now know that Willy Smets is an assumed name. That's why we could find no trace of him in Belgium. His real name is Pier Mertens. And we know that he served time in an Indian prison for drug smuggling twenty years ago."

∙   ∙   ∙

WEDNESDAY, AUGUST 27, 1975, 9:02 P.M.

"Okay, let's hear it," said Harlan. We were all gathered in his room again.

"You already know Dhonu was not there," said Ranjit, briefing us on his trip to Kathmandu. "In fact, the shop was closed down. No placard. No reason given. I can't say for sure if anyone was watching, but if so, they were looking for Danny, not a North Indian tourist."

"Sounds like Willy's folding tents," said Harlan. "At least for now."

Ranjit continued. "In case someone was watching, I made a big show of staring at the *goralog*. Like a villager who never saw one before. I roamed around for an hour, then returned to the airport via the red-light district in Thamel."

"Why?" I asked.

"Because he's been trained properly," said Harlan. "In case he was being followed."

We let the news sink in for a long moment. Then Harlan asked for ideas.

"Obviously, we continue to monitor the airports, train stations, and border crossings with the help of the CBI and Interpol," said Birgit.

Ranjit frowned. "It's easy to bribe your way over the border. A couple hundred rupees is all you need."

"And he might be happy to wait us out somewhere," added Harlan. "You have anything to add, Dan? Any idea where he might be?"

I thought for a long moment before answering. "No," I said. "None at all."

CHAPTER FORTY-EIGHT

TUESDAY, SEPTEMBER 2, 1975, 11:15 A.M.

With the trail cold, Harlan flew out of Bombay for parts unknown—maybe Delhi—assuring me he wasn't giving up on finding Willy and Chhotu. He'd be in touch. Birgit also shipped out, back to the States, and Ranjit returned to his post in Delhi until something developed. Me? I got the locks changed on my door and moved back into my Sagar Darshan flat.

I hoped that Willy, Chhotu, and Bikas were far from Bombay. Still, I looked over my shoulder at every turn, eyed every motorcyclist and blue Ambassador that crossed my path. I didn't need to worry about the white Mercedes; the police had impounded it the night Chhotu tried to kill me. And, to be sure no one entered my flat without my knowing it, I attached a small piece of cello tape to the doorjamb near the top each time I left home. I cut the strip halfway so that it would tear if someone opened the door. That way, it couldn't re-stick itself to the wood without leaving evidence that it had been opened.

And I even visited my old pal Inspector Lokhande. We had a long talk in his office, where I told him about my escape in Poona. I gave him all the details I could. That Bikas was working for Willy, who had ordered the hit on Lokhande's nephew. He squinted at me.

"So, if this Bikas fellow was working for Smets, tell me, what was he looking for in your flat?"

"Evidence of my . . ."

"Your love affair with that *mulgi*? I tell you, Dan, I don't like that. I don't approve."

I said nothing. He wouldn't have understood the way I felt about her. He probably assumed I was just after a good time.

"Look, Dan," he said. "If I had a photo of this Bikas, I'd have my men ask around. See if he's been in the area. We might have a chance of catching him."

I drew a sigh. "Inspector, if I had a photo of him, I'd share it with you. But I swear I don't."

. . .

I went back to the office. It was awkward at first. Everyone had witnessed the scene when Frank pretended to fire me. He made up a story that I'd begged for my job back and he'd decided to give me another chance.

That didn't mean he was happy with the dud of an ending to my surefire Pulitzer story. I updated him on everything that had happened, including Chhotu and Bikas's failed attempt on my life. Yes, I told him, Bikas turned out to have been part of the story all along.

"The police are looking for Smets here and abroad," I said. "Be patient. They'll get him, and we'll have a great ending to this story."

He shook his head in disgust, and I sensed I'd never win back his confidence.

I took up my film industry piece again and began making calls. It was not going to be my greatest achievement. Even I found it dull. Nobody would agree to go on record with anything that wasn't praise for the prime minister's strong response to the "internal disturbances." On the other hand, the starlets all wanted to know if I could introduce them to producers. The actors wanted to meet Faye Dunaway or Ali MacGraw.

When I showed Frank what I had, he was lukewarm. He said it had potential, but fell flat after the part about Mukesh Sharma, the director who'd been arrested. He wanted me to try for more stars, more arrests. And I'd blown my chance with Shashi Kapoor and Jeetendra.

"Get me a beautiful actress," he said. "Put some sex appeal into the story."

I went back to my desk and tried again to reach Shabana Azmi. As I was running through my contacts, wondering which ones might have made a film with her, Janice appeared for our afternoon appointment for tea.

"How are you doing?" she asked. I hated seeing the pity in her eyes.

"I'm fine," I said. "Say, does your Shirish happen to know anyone who might know someone who knows Shabana Azmi? Or any other top female star?"

"Afraid not," she said. "Why her?"

"For my story. Frank says I need more sex appeal."

"Isn't there something else you can give him? What about that bomber story? He killed a CID officer, after all."

"Yeah. I lost the film. It's gone. Without it, it's just me claiming I met a terrorist. And it all ties back into Willy Smets now. I can't write it until we have some kind of ending."

She finished her tea and patted me on the shoulder. "I knew you were lying," she whispered. "You did have film. Try to find it, Dan."

CHAPTER FORTY-NINE

Another week passed. I was struggling with my film story, but I got a lead on Shabana Azmi's hairstylist who worked at the beauty parlor in the Sun-n-Sand Hotel in Juhu. I planned on asking her to pass a message to the star.

Keeping my head down and working hard, for the past week, I'd been taking Janice's advice. I'd been thinking about where the roll of film could be. The two most likely scenarios presented themselves again and again: either I'd lost the film wrestling with Sushmita on the hood of her car atop the *ghats*, or I'd left it in my wet pants that were thrown away by Willy's Poona staff the next day. But only if I hadn't actually transferred the film to my dry pants as I changed in the rain. I thought I had; I just couldn't remember. I'd rehashed that trip so many times that I was dreaming about it. It was invading my thoughts when I was working, running, eating. Everywhere, at any time, it sprang up unannounced. But it wasn't helping. I still couldn't remember.

The thing about living in India with household help is that there's always an extra pair of eyes to search for missing things. Of course, some might say that there's also an extra pair of hands to palm items. But, in my experience, I hadn't heard of any servants actually stealing, despite the warnings I'd received to the contrary.

I no longer had a servant to help me search for the missing roll of film. And even if I'd had one, I was sure it had been lost elsewhere. Not in my Sagar Darshan flat. I distinctly remembered having put it in my pocket as Sushmita and I set off for our first fateful trip to Poona.

I left the office early that Tuesday, hoping to work on my film story in the quiet of my own flat. Arriving back at Sagar Darshan around noon, I asked the *durwan* and liftman, as was my new habit, if anyone had been looking for me. Then I checked the cello tape above my door. Still there. Undisturbed. I slipped inside and locked myself up tight.

Having fired up the hob, I made myself some of the dal and rice I'd bought at Dadabhoy's in Colaba weeks before. I even used the pressure cooker, recalling Sushmita's instructions and demonstration in Lonavala. The result was fast, thanks to the pressure cooker, and good, thanks to luck and salt.

As I ate my meager lunch at the table, I thought of Sushmita, as I had countless times since I'd last seen her. Instead of concentrating on our abrupt, silent parting, I recalled the pleasanter times we'd spent together. I tried to catalogue them all, the time, place, the details ... Pathetic, I knew, but I did it all the same, starting with the last time we'd slept together and working backwards to the first. I can't say the first was the best, because they were all sublime, but it was perhaps the most memorable. Despite all my hopes for such an outcome, I'd been surprised when she'd invited me to put down my bag in her bedroom in Lonavala. And then she'd thrown herself at me in a warm, passionate embrace and kiss.

God, the anticipation had nearly driven me to tear her clothes off, but she did that herself. And I did the same with mine, turning my pants inside out in my haste. I threw them to the floor and fell onto the bed with Sushmita.

Yet, once our bodies were finally together, our passion was patient, not hurried or frenzied. Not like our disrobing had been. Not like when I heard my belt strike the floor so hard once I'd finally freed my last foot from the twisted leg of my pants and hurled them to the stone. I closed my eyes and conjured the scene in my mind.

Funny how you remember little things sometimes. Things that aren't important in the larger picture. Until they are.

I hadn't been wearing a belt by the time we got to the bungalow in Lonavala. It was locked in the trunk of Sushmita's Mercedes.

CHAPTER FIFTY

We pulled into the station a little after seven. The rain fell steadily, not a downpour but enough to make me wish I had a car. Sticking to old habits, I told the taxi driver to drop me at the hotel a kilometer or so from Sushmita's bungalow. Despite my determination to leave and never come back, I followed the instructions she'd insisted on. No, I wasn't ever coming back again. But . . .

It was already dark as I began the slog through the rain and mud. I couldn't deny, as I made my way, that I wished that she'd be there. Impossible, of course. She was somewhere in England, safe and removed from the responsibility of the attempt on my life, not to mention the heart she'd trampled along the way. My butterflies returned. The ones I'd felt as a kid before a game. The same ones that always disappeared as soon as the umpire cried, "Play ball."

But there was no game in my future. I was done.

The house was dark. There was no car. Only an empty structure where I'd thought I'd found something worth treasuring. No. Just another of my foolish entanglements. I'd fallen for a girl who wasn't right for me.

I stood before the door. To my left was the space where Sushmita had always parked the Mercedes. Of course, it wasn't there. It had been confiscated by the police after Chhotu's failed attempt on my life.

Soaked to the skin and pruny, I urged myself to get it over with. I reached up into the low eaves and felt for the key. The one Sushmita had left for me. I found it, pulled it down, and regarded it with regret. If only she were inside.

I inserted the key into the padlock on the door. The shackle popped open. I slipped it off its hasp and depressed the latch. The door yawned wide, and I entered. My butterflies disappeared.

Everything was dark. I tried the light switch. No power. Of course not. Not with the heavy rain. I closed the door behind me and fumbled for the flashlight she'd always left in the entrance. It was there.

The beam of light showed the way across the drawing room to the corridor to Sushmita's bedroom. A thought occurred to me: What if she'd locked it? Shit. I'd forgotten she'd said she always locked bedrooms for fear the servants would steal or—what?—sleep in her bed? So I was relieved to find that the latch turned and opened on command.

Her scent still lingered in the air, and I inhaled it with great lungfuls of longing and regret. Two, then three deep breaths before my nose acclimated itself to the essence, and the sensation was gone. I aimed the light at the bed and gazed at her pillow. The linens hadn't been changed, I was sure, since she and I had last slept there. The room was undisturbed, which was the motivation for my visit.

The thing about living in India with household help is that there's always an extra pair of eyes to search for missing things.

Except when there are no extra eyes.

I dropped to my hands and knees and aimed the light under the bed. And there it was. Sitting innocently under a coat of dust was my missing roll of film.

CHAPTER FIFTY-ONE

I got to my feet and examined the film. Everything seemed in order. It had lain undisturbed for nearly two months under the bed where it had fallen from my pants—the sound I'd thought was my belt buckle hitting the floor. I returned it to my pocket and made for the door.

A light blinded me, and I stopped in my tracks.

"Danny Boy?"

Willy stood there in the corridor, aiming his flashlight into my eyes. When he lowered the beam, I realized he wasn't alone. Chhotu and Bikas glared at me from behind him. The big boy stepped around Willy and pointed a gun at my chest.

"This is an unexpected gift," he said. "Bikas has a score to settle with you, Dan."

"Stop," said Willy.

He entered the bedroom and approached me carefully. He flashed the light on my hands then back up to my chest.

"Not armed, Danny Boy?" he asked.

I shook my head.

He came closer. Close enough to kiss me. He regarded me for a long moment, as if searching for the answer to some riddle in my eyes. At length, he ordered Chhotu and Bikas to wait in the drawing room.

"We don't have much time," said Chhotu in protest. "Let Bikas take care of this worm."

"I said wait in the other room," repeated Willy. "Keep an eye out the windows for signs of activity, and we'll leave in plenty of time."

Willy turned to me again. Was he puzzled or hurt? I couldn't tell in the dark. Then he motioned to the bed and told me to make myself comfortable. I sat beside Sushmita's pillow. He drew up a chair, lit a candle on the nearby dresser, and switched off the torch. The effect was quite spooky, with the dancing flame illuminating his face, throwing shadows across his prominent mouth, nose, and brow. He waited a good long time before finally speaking.

"I never expected to see you here, Danny. How did you find out about this place?"

Now that I could see his face, I saw that he was worried. Maybe he was doubting the integrity of his security. If I'd found him, might the police discover his hideout as well? Maybe I'd even brought them with me and they were waiting outside.

"I've known about it for some time now," I said.

"So you've been here before? This is where you and Sushmita . . ."

I nodded.

"And have you come alone?"

"Who would I bring? The CBI? CID? FBI?"

He ran a hand over his lips and down his chin as he tried to read me. "You're wet. You came on foot," he said. It wasn't a question. "From the station. That's a couple of kilometers. Why? Why have you come here? Were you hoping to find Mita?"

"No."

"Then you've come looking for me?"

I held my breath. I wasn't going to tell him about the film. That was all he needed to murder me with no further worries.

"No. I . . . came to see this place one last time. For sentimental reasons."

"You have more courage than good sense, Danny. We only stepped out to fill the petrol tank. Otherwise, we would have welcomed you at the door. Did you not expect to find me here?"

"I did not. I'm as surprised as you are to see me."

"Why?" he asked. "This is my house."

"*Your* house? It's Sushmita's."

He scoffed at me, though it seemed an effort for him. Just as quickly, his saddened, troubled expression returned. "In name, yes, it is her house. But only because foreigners cannot easily purchase property in this country."

"This was her childhood home," I said. "She told me so herself."

Willy leaned in closer, almost tenderly. I thought I could discern pity in his eyes.

"Mita never lived in this house," he said. "Not until I bought it three years ago. She lied to you."

I felt the breath knocked out of me. That couldn't be. She'd lain there—naked on the bed with me—tears in her eyes, as she told me it was her childhood home. How could she lie so effortlessly? So convincingly? In that moment, I forgot about Willy. He dissipated like a cloud into the vague blackness around me, replaced by a swirling wind of doubts, shock, and emptiness. How could this be?

"Danny," came Willy's voice, calling me back to the present. "Danny Boy, did you hear what I said? She lied to you about this place."

I shook the cobwebs from my head and, mouth agape, looked at my former friend. My former rival. My enemy.

"What about the flat in Bombay?" I asked, my voice raw. "And the bungalow in Poona?"

Willy sat back in his chair. "The same. Mine. Yes, registered in her name, of course. That was the only choice we had. But these are my properties. I paid for them."

I digested this further blow to my understanding of the woman I loved. Thought I loved. Did I still love her? I knew nothing in that moment besides the certainty that I knew nothing.

"But her parents? Her father? He was a scientist. He taught at the Naval College..."

Now Willy appeared genuinely mortified. He shook his head slowly.

"He wasn't a scientist?" I asked. I begged.

"Her father? No, Danny Boy. She never knew her father."

"But—"

He put his hands on my shoulders as if he intended to shake me. "Danny, she was a beggar child in the streets when I found her. An eight-year-old street oyster."

Jesus Christ. Did I really have to correct his English at this horrible moment of comprehension and disillusionment?

"*Urchin*," I said. "Street *urchin*, not oyster."

He released me from his hold, and, though he didn't seem sure it was appropriate to do so, he thanked me. Then he tore open the wound in my soul and told me more.

"God knows where that poor child had come from, but she was a filthy beggar, sitting in the dirt on Pedder Road. When the traffic stopped, she would tap on the car windows, asking for money. She held her hand out so."

He showed me the gesture, right hand turned upward with his four fingertips curled toward the palm. Then he raised the hand to his forehead to complete the picture.

I felt I was going to suffocate, but he continued.

"I saw her there for weeks. Sometimes I would give her spare change. Once I even gave her ten rupees. She smiled at me. After that she recognized my car and ran to me each time I passed. And finally . . ." He paused and weighed his words. There was an internal debate of some kind going on in his mind. "And finally, I bought her freedom from the lady who sat with her. She wasn't her mother. They were part of some crime syndicate. They buy children to beg. The younger and prettier, the better. The kiddies get nothing except a meal or two a day. All the money they beg goes to the criminals."

"Why . . . why are you telling me this?" I asked, wishing he would stop, but, at the same time, wanting to know everything. Despite my horror, despite what it might do to my feelings for Sushmita, I had to know.

"I'm telling you this because you think you love her. But you don't even know her. You don't know that I paid off her masters and took her away. Cleaned her up and hired a tutor to teach her English and to read and write. Then I enrolled her in school in Poona. At St. Mary's. She was a clever girl. The smartest girl in her class."

"And you made her your lover?" I asked, dreading his answer. "An eight-year-old child?"

He dismissed my question with a curt shake of the head. "Of course not."

I drew a sigh.

"Not until she was twelve," he said, crushing me.

He said it as if sleeping with eight- or nine- or eleven-year-olds was obscene, but there was nothing more natural than raping a twelve-year-old girl who's totally dependent on you for her life. I wanted to strangle him right then and there. I might have chanced it, too, if I hadn't been sure Chhotu and Bikas would burst through the door and shoot me dead before I could kill Willy. And that would deprive me of the pleasure of seeing him arrested and hanged for his crimes.

"I suppose she never studied at Cambridge?" I asked instead.

"But of course she did. She was a brilliant student. Learned grace and a very posh accent there. I was so proud of her."

I didn't know what else to say. My chin dropped to my chest, and I closed my eyes to compose myself.

"You don't believe me, Danny," he said, placing a hand on my shoulder again. I swatted it away. "But it's true. She was simply a beggar child from somewhere. No one knows. Why do you think her complexion is so dark? Beautiful to you and me, perhaps. But you know how these Indians are. Fair skin is the ideal. Poor Mita. She was teased for it in school. Even by one of the matrons."

I felt a tear roll down my cheek. Not for me. Not for my broken heart, but for that little girl. Raped by her guardian, then teased for her beauty.

"Can I ask you a question?" I said, refusing to look him in the eye.
"Of course."

"When did you find out about Sush and me?"

Willy drew a deep breath and frowned. He pressed his palms against both eyes and rubbed slowly, as if massaging away a headache.

"It was the day you two arrived in Poona the first time," he said. "At least I suspected. I wanted to be wrong."

Christ, he'd known from the start.

"How?" I asked.

"Mita said you'd had a puncture before climbing the *ghats*. And then it was too late to continue once you'd changed the tire."

"So?"

"She also said you were trying to reach the top of the *ghats* before dark. If her story had been true, and you'd had a puncture at the foot of the *ghats*, you two would have gone to sleep well before eight o'clock."

He was right. As practiced as Sushmita was at lying, she'd miscal-culated. She never should have mentioned that Ramu had overheard her talking about the *ghats* and sunset.

I had to know more. "Why, then? Why didn't you say anything? Do anything?"

He gave my question some thought before answering.

"I love her," he said finally. "I didn't want to lose her."

Jacques Brel's weeping supplication, "*Ne me quitte pas*," came to me, like one of the songs you can't get out of your head. And, like that, the great songwriter and Willy merged into one in my mind. They would always be one for the rest of my life, however long that might be. Minutes or, if I was miraculously lucky, many long, lonely years. But I would never listen to Jacques Brel sing again. *Jamais.*

"Mita is a special soul with needs more complex than you or I will ever understand," he continued. "I wanted to give her time. And I'm also very fond of you, Danny Boy. Don't ask me why. I can't explain."

"Where is she now?" I asked.

"She's safe. In England. But you won't see her again."

A knock came at the door. Willy took the candle and went to open it. Chhotu stood there.

"It's getting late, old chap," he said. "He's probably told the police where to find us. Let's get rid of him and go."

"Wait outside. This won't take long."

Chhotu stepped back and closed the door. Willy retook his seat and leaned toward me again, elbows on his knees, his eyes pleading with me.

"Tell me, Danny. I need to know. Are the police coming?"

I told him no. That I hadn't expected to find anyone in the bunga-low, least of all him. "Sush swore to me that you knew nothing about this place," I said, tears clouding my eyes.

Willy reached out and squeezed my hand. He pinched his lips together, and I thought he was going to cry.

"I'm sorry, Danny Boy," he said. "She's a troubled girl. You mustn't think she lied to hurt you. She did it to protect herself."

Chhotu called through the door, again urging Willy to hurry.

Willy let go of my hand, and I wished I could beat him to a pulp. For his abuse of Sushmita, who needed to invent lies to cope with what he'd done to her. A twelve-year-old girl, for God's sake. I thought of the little bride in Kamathipura, too. How many more were there?

Chhotu banged on the door now. Willy turned his head and yelled for him to go wait in the car. As he did, I slid open the bedside drawer, pulled Sushmita's gun from inside, and pointed it at him. I told him I was going to kill him.

Willy reeled around, then sighed. He pulled a handgun of his own out of the waistband beneath his bush coat.

My eyes grew wide. "Put it down or I'll shoot you, I swear it!"

But Willy simply raised the gun and pointed it at my head.

And I did it. I did what I'd warned him I'd do. For twelve-year-old Sushmita, I did it. For the little bride auctioned off, I did it. And for the countless unknown lives he'd ruined, despoiled, I did it. I squeezed the trigger.

And nothing happened. I tried to fire again and again and again, always with the same result.

"Danny Boy," whispered Willy, looking exhausted as he lowered his gun to his side. "Do you really think I would let Mita have a loaded Makarov pistol? Or even a functioning gun? She's a depressive. She's tried to kill herself many times. I had the firing pin removed from that pistol before I gave it to her."

That was it, then. Either I'd throw the useless weapon at him and knock him cold, or I was dead.

But I was wrong.

Shoulders sagging, Willy turned, opened the door, and shuffled out of the room. I called to him.

"You're not going to kill me?"

He stopped and faced me one last time. "No, Danny Boy. I tried once at Chhotu's urging. It was a mistake."

"Wasn't it twice?" I asked. "You sent me to Bombay, where Bikas was waiting for me in my flat."

Willy nodded. "Yes, that's right. We searched your room in Poona, looking for the film, and discovered you still had your house keys. You hadn't lost your flat. We tried to lure you to your place where he was waiting. I'm sorry."

"And Sushmita? Did she know? That you tried to murder me?"

He smiled sadly. "Goodness, no. She would have killed me. And herself afterward."

And like that, he left me there.

I didn't think it wise to follow him; Chhotu and Bikas might not have the same qualms about shooting me. I went as far as the drawing room and waited there. Moments later, I heard the car start, and the headlights lit up the room. Then they were gone.

Now I rushed out the door into the pouring rain. I could see Bikas was at the wheel of the blue Ambassador, and Willy and Chhotu sat in the back. As the car receded down the little road, its right taillight grew smaller and smaller. There was only the one. The left light was out. The car turned onto the road that led back to Lonavala.

Now I was alone, standing in the rain, unsure of what to do next. I supposed I had to reach Ranjit and Harlan to let them know I'd seen Willy. That was sure to be a difficult conversation. They'd curse me for having withheld my knowledge of the bungalow. Had I been honest with them, Willy would have been in custody by now. Or dead.

In a fog, with nothing else I could do, I thought of Sushmita. That poor, damaged soul. If she made up tall tales about her life, it was because Willy had given her a childhood even worse than that of a filthy street beggar.

Then I heard a car blaring its horn as it approached the house.

CHAPTER FIFTY-TWO

It was a police Jeep. And Ranjit was at the wheel, with Birgit in the front passenger seat.

"Get in, Danny!" she called, jumping down to clear the way for me. "Hurry!"

She shoved me into the back seat, then she climbed in front.

"But there are no doors on this thing," I said, as the Jeep leapt forward, Ranjit shifting gears furiously as he raced back toward the main road. Rain leaked through a tear in the ragtop roof, dripping onto my head at regular intervals.

"Shall we call for a limousine?" she yelled from the front as she lowered the canvas door flap to provide the barest minimum of protection from the rain and mud.

"What are you two doing here?" I yelled back. "I thought you'd gone home. How did you find me?"

We were on the main road now. Ranjit was pushing the bouncing Jeep as fast as he could toward Lonavala and the Bombay-Poona Road. Birgit twisted in her seat to face me.

"We followed you on the train, of course," she said. "I was in the car behind yours. Ranjit was six seats behind you."

"Why?"

She mugged a sarcastic pout as a reply. Then she said they'd been following me for weeks without my knowledge. Since Poona. And they hadn't stopped when I'd returned to Bombay.

"What is this place, anyway?" she asked.

"It's Sushmita's," I said as sheepishly as I could and still be heard over the roar of the engine, the tires on the wet road, and the rain.

"You mean Smets's place, don't you?"

What an idiot I'd been. Of course it was Willy's. All the property was his. I'd believed whatever Sushmita had told me without question.

"She said it was hers. That Willy didn't even know about it."

Birgit shook her head in disgust and turned back around to face the road. Ranjit glared in the rearview mirror and caught my eye. He was pissed off.

"Did you see which way they went? Poona or Bombay?" I asked, trying to shift attention back to the problem at hand, finding Willy and Chhotu.

Birgit turned to face me again. "Of course we didn't, Danny. We were busy following you."

"But why didn't you go after them when they drove away?"

"Danny, use your head. We came here on a train, not in a car. We had to follow you in a taxi from the station to see where you were going. Once we knew where you were, I kept watch on the house while Ranjit doubled back to get a car from the police. As soon as he returned, I jumped in and we came to get you."

"Okay," I said. "Ranjit, did you see a car on the road? There are three of them inside. They left not five minutes before you got here."

"I saw one car," he shouted. "An Ambassador. Couldn't tell the color in the dark. But I don't know if they turned toward Poona or Bombay after that."

"It's a blue Ambassador," I said, hoping it helped. Probably didn't.

A few minutes later, we reached the junction with the Bombay-Poona Road. Ranjit skidded to a bumpy stop and looked both ways, debating which direction to take.

"Did they give you any idea where they were going?" he asked. The wipers sloshed back and forth across the windscreen.

"No. Nothing."

Ranjit shifted into gear and headed toward Poona.

"Wait!" I called. "Chhotu kept insisting it was getting late. Over and over. Willy said there was time. It was as if they had a train to catch. Or a plane or a boat."

Ranjit wheeled the Jeep around, making a U-turn as he cut off three cars coming in the other direction. The canvas flap on Birgit's side blew open, and I was treated to a sheet of rain in the face.

We picked up speed, now coursing west. But before we could reach Bombay and the coastal plain, we'd have to descend the *ghats* in a Jeep with a torn roof, bald tires, no seat belts, and no doors.

"Of course they might have had an appointment in Poona," I said so softly I was the only one who heard.

Ranjit and Birgit's attention was fixed on the road before them, on the cars and trucks they wanted to overtake before we reached the *ghats* and the real danger began. I tried to remember some of the prayers from my youth. But I'd been a rotten student at *shul,* at least until my atheist parents decided they didn't want to get up early on a Saturday to take me to temple for something they didn't believe in.

As with everything else, Ranjit was an excellent driver. He must have been well trained in high-speed pursuit as he passed at least a dozen vehicles in the next ten minutes. And it couldn't have been easy, not in that sluggish Jeep.

I thought of Bikas. I'd only seen him behind the wheel once, and the only tricky driving he'd done that night was avoiding a herd of buffalo. Still, I couldn't imagine he was a better driver than Ranjit. If Willy and company were heading for Bombay, we were surely gaining on them.

We began the descent. If I'd been terrified scaling the *ghats* with Sushmita, and then descending them with Shankar at the wheel, I was about to lose my mind sitting in the back of an Indian police Jeep, with no visibility, no heat, and little hope of survival. Ranjit leaned us into the curves, which grew steeper and sharper as the minutes passed. Blasting the horn liberally—*Horn OK please*, as the trucks all had painted on their bumpers—he tailgated the cars and trucks and buses in front of us, then slipped around them, barely missing oncoming traffic. The rain pounded on the canvas roof of the Jeep and, from where I was sitting, obscured any visibility through the windshield. The wipers simply couldn't keep up.

Birgit faced forward and said nothing. She seemed more accustomed to such situations than I was. She was a pro. Ranjit steered and braked, accelerated and swerved. I closed my eyes and—hypocrite that I was—prayed.

We continued that way for several minutes, passing cars and inching down the narrow, bumpy road as it switched back and forth along the edge of the mountain. Several times, the Jeep skidded and juddered, hydroplaned, and risked sliding off the road and over the cliff. The guardrails—usually broken—gave me no confidence, when they were present and intact at all. More likely, we would careen through the barrier and take a flyer down the steep hill, coming to a stop only once we'd tumbled five hundred or a thousand meters over the edge.

I prayed faster and harder and held onto my seat.

Five more minutes passed without a crash, but several hair-raising escapes, as we veered around vehicles at what felt like a breakneck speed. In reality, we couldn't have been traveling faster than thirty miles an hour in the traffic and rain.

When I thought I could take no more, I glanced ahead and spied the round-bodied car we were bearing down on. Ranjit jerked the Jeep into the right lane and floored it, clearing the car and jumping back into the left lane just before a truck could end our lives in a fiery crash. I reeled around to see out of the plastic window behind me.

"Jesus Christ, Ranjit! Stop!"

He couldn't very well look back at me, what with the sharp turns and slick road, but he told me to shut up. If I had to vomit, do it in my lap.

"No," I shouted to be heard. "You just passed them! They're behind us!"

CHAPTER FIFTY-THREE

Ranjit did not, in fact, stop. That wasn't really a possibility given the situation. Instead, he asked me if I was sure. There were plenty of blue Ambassadors on the road. Was this one really theirs?

"Yes," I cried. "The left taillight is out. It's them!"

Ranjit switched on the blue light on the roof and hit the brakes. The car behind us slowed to avoid hitting us. And then it zoomed around us and barreled down the mountain. Bikas surged past the car in front of him, and we were stuck behind a slow-moving Fiat. The traffic climbing the hill in the opposite direction crawled up the steep incline. The single taillight one car ahead grew fainter as it put distance between us.

Ranjit sounded the siren again and flashed his lights. Then he pulled around the Fiat and chanced it on a curve. A truck heading for us veered to the side just in time to miss us, and we darted back into our lane. Ranjit hit the gas and, bald tires and all, he pointed us at the car forty meters ahead.

Despite the heavy rain and the mist on the mountain, I could see the glowing lights of some city far below over the side of the cliff. The view only served to terrify me more. It must have been a thousand meters down to that place, and I wanted no part in taking the express route to reach it.

Ranjit coaxed the Jeep to a speed I didn't think it had, and we roared forward, gaining on the blue Ambassador. A sharp turn was next, and two cars blocked Bikas and Willy's path. Ranjit flashed his lights into the back of the car before us, surely distracting—if not blinding—Bikas. He, in turn, tried to overtake the first of the cars holding him back, but a truck roared into view and he had to yield.

Then, as the road straightened for a stretch before jackknifing left again about fifty meters ahead, he zoomed right of the car, attempting to overtake it on the rocky shoulder. A truck bore down on him from the opposite direction. The sharp turn approached quickly. Too quickly. Bikas couldn't find the speed to pass the car. He veered farther right to avoid the truck just before plowing through the dented guardrail and over the cliff.

Ranjit braked, and we skidded on our bald tires, heading straight for the breach in the guardrail. The world stopped turning. Everything slowed to a surreal pace. We swerved toward the edge, somehow missing the truck. I braced myself against the seats before me, and I saw Birgit do the same against the dashboard.

The punctured guardrail drew closer. I thought of my parents. My brother and sister. And I thought of Sushmita. My last thought, I was sure, just before Ranjit jerked the wheel to the right, deliberately causing the Jeep to flip onto its left side. The metal scraped across the blacktop, sending sparks into the air. I fell against the wall and the window and saw Birgit bounce violently off the canvas flap, which was the only thing between her and the road. The Jeep slid sideways and suddenly stopped with a metallic groan.

Cars screeched to a halt behind us and sounded their horns. I felt blood dripping down my forehead into my eyes, but I could still see Birgit slumped unconscious in her seat, hanging halfway out the door.

Into the void.

We'd come to a stop halfway over the edge.

There was movement. Birgit. Slowly, like a snail, she was sliding through the door.

I grabbed her arm with my good right hand and held her fast. But I could do no more. I was paralyzed. I peered through the canvas door, which was flapping in the wind, and my stomach did a somersault. Not ten inches from my resting place against the wall of the Jeep, 1,000 meters of nothing opened up before me. I closed my eyes.

"Danny!" called Ranjit. "I can't lean over to reach her, or the Jeep will go over the edge! You've got to pull her back inside!"

"I can't!"

"Danny, pull her inside! We need her weight in the car or we'll all die! Pull her back!"

I cracked open one eye, found it caked with blood, and wiped it on my shoulder. The lights of the city—sparkling so far below—forced me to close my eye again.

"Danny, pull! We're going to roll over if you don't!"

Holding my breath, I tightened my good hand on her wrist. Then I yanked. The Jeep lurched.

"Pull her inside now!"

My hand, slick with rain, lost its grip, and she flopped back toward the door and the nothingness below. I flailed and grabbed out for anything, caught her by the hair, and pulled her back into her seat. The open door was now offering itself to me more than to Birgit.

I gasped for air, staring into the hole, unable to close my eyes or look away. This was it. My spectacular and horrifying death was next.

"I've got her!" called Ranjit, and he pulled Birgit over the gear shift and out the driver's-side door. They landed one on top of the other in the mud and gravel.

Now I was alone in the Jeep, whose nose and half the left-hand side of the chassis were already over the edge of the cliff. A tearing noise made me think the vehicle was moving again and this was the end. Then a gust of rain and wind blew over me from behind. I reeled to see what it was. And Ranjit grabbed my shirt by the shoulders with both hands and delivered me like a baby through the hole he'd cut in the canvas roof. Thank God there was no hardtop on that fucking Jeep.

We scrambled away from the edge as the Jeep teetered and, encouraged by the shove my exit had provided, tipped over the precipice and disappeared, tumbling down the mountain.

EPILOGUE

The police ordered me to stay in the country until the investigation was completed. And, since my passport had been confiscated, I was stuck there despite my desire to go home.

So I wrote my story for Frank Muller, leaving out the details of my affair with Sushmita. That was going into the novel I was writing. Of course, I planned to change the names and details for that. But I included everything else. The seductive power of rich friends, the allure of an enchanting beauty, the terrifying chase, and the naïveté of a young man who should have known better.

My story was well received in New York. And, in my torpid state of mind, broken by the loss of Sushmita, I decided to do what I could to keep busy. I got my interviews with Shabana Azmi and Shashi Kapoor and filed my Hindi film story. Then I wrote about land reclamation in South Bombay—the very land Sagar Darshan sat on had been mudflats only a few years before. I covered the plight of the fishing villages threatened by the progressive loss of their sea. And, of course, there was the Emergency. Some of my pieces got past Onkar, others didn't. I didn't mind too much. I got a good raise for my big scoop. Kate Erving wrote to me that she was pushing the story as hard as she could. She had hopes for award nominations in the new year.

I took up reading with a vengeance, buying used books by the dozens from the vendor near Flora Fountain. He sold pretty much everything you could want from his spot on the pavement.

Then there were the Hindi lessons three times a week at lunch. I'd decided to learn Hindi instead of Marathi, because I figured it would be more useful in other parts of India. Delhi, for example. My English would have to suffice for the South, as I wasn't so naïve to think I could also learn Tamil or Kannada. Janice put me in touch with a retired teacher, who smiled kindly at me until I made a grammatical error. Then she became Durga, fierce eyes burning through me. Thankfully, she only had two arms and never did me any actual harm.

And I listened to Indian music. Not just the film songs, but Indian classical music as well. I bought a small record player at Rhythm House—the famous music store in Bombay—and fell in love with Ustad Alla Rakha's tabla music, Pandit Ravi Shankar's sitar, and Pandit Hariprasad Chaurasia's flute. The ragas kept me sane as I struggled to forget Sush.

My old friend Inspector Lokhande visited me one night. He arrived bearing gifts: a bottle of Chivas Regal—no tax strip over the cap—and a bag of fresh *chaklis*. I bent my one-before-dinner-and-one-after rule, and really overdid the scotch with him as we finished the *chaklis*. After midnight, as he stumbled out my door drunk, he thanked me with tears in his squinting eyes for my efforts to catch the man who'd murdered his nephew, Sub-inspector Bala Gokhale. And then—Jesus Christ—we hugged each other as he wept on my shoulder.

Birgit spent a week in Breach Candy Hospital. She'd suffered scrapes, bruises, a concussion, and a broken collarbone in the crash. Apparently, she'd lost a chunk of hair from the back of her head, too, thanks to my firm grip. Me, I got three stitches on my forehead.

In addition to being a first-class chef, wall-climber, and driver, Ranjit was also something of a weightlifter. He'd pulled both Birgit and me to safety. And I weighed 190 pounds. The man was a marvel.

Harlan visited me to extend his thanks. He confirmed that Willy, Chhotu, and Bikas had been found dead in the crumpled blue Ambassador, 350 meters below the sharp turn they'd missed. I recalled Willy with conflicting emotions. I'd once been grateful to him, if not loyal. And he was a monster who deserved his fate. But that man had been kind to me. Loved me. I didn't know why that mattered, but somehow it did. Even though I hated him.

The monsoons retreated in September, and life took on a hot, dry regularity. I went to work, wrote my stories, and chatted with Janice over Vikky's tea. Then I'd go home to my flat and new servant, Tinku, a really sweet guy who, I knew, would never slit my throat in the night. I enjoyed one drink before and one after my pure veg dinners. And then I would read Graham Greene and Evelyn Waugh—that was the mood I was in—as I listened to Hindi film songs on the radio.

• • •

MONDAY, DECEMBER 22, 1975, 3:40 P.M.

Christmas was approaching. It promised to be a strange holiday season for me, what with no snow, family, or close friends. I was about to return a call to Zubin Mehta, the music director of the Los Angeles Philharmonic. He was in Bombay and had agreed to meet me for a quick meal and an interview at Britannia, the old Parsee restaurant I'd visited with Janice in Ballard Estates months before. We only had to arrange the date. But Janice interrupted me before I could dial.

"This arrived for you a few minutes ago," she said, handing me a small parcel about six inches long and three inches wide.

"No return address?" I asked. "Maybe it's a bomb." I held it to my ear and shook it.

"Just open it, Mr. Jacobs."

I untied the string and tore away the paper. Inside there was no note, no card. Nothing but a bag of *sev*.

Sev.

"Mr. Jacobs," called Janice as I ran for the door. "Where are you going?"

AUTHOR'S NOTE

Over the past twenty-five years, I've been lucky enough to make more than fifty trips to India. For work, pleasure, and family. In fact, I've spent nearly four years there. Bombay (Mumbai), Poona (Pune), and Bangalore have been second homes to me. I even held a PIO card (Person of Indian Origin), thanks to my marital status with an Indian citizen. PIO cards no longer exist, but, as I write this note, I'm waiting for my Overseas Citizen of India card to arrive. All this to say that I consider myself an honorary Indian, and am supremely proud of that imagined status.

I tried to use my experiences—the best and worst of them—to provide a glimpse into expatriate life in India. Many of the anecdotes in this book, both positive and negative, were inspired by my time there. The scene in Poona, for instance, where Danny encounters a herd of buffalo on North Main Road, may seem far-fetched. Yet, it happened to me. More than once. I lived for eighteen months in a development directly across the road from ABC Farms in Koregaon Park. And, yes, the buffaloes still take the right of way, even if ABC Farms is no more.

The monsoon is a powerful giver and taker. A successful season brings a bounty of crops to the Subcontinent, while a disappointing one can result in ruin for farmers and shortages for city dwellers. For me, it was always a long, wet time that I used for thinking. And plotting. The monsoon looms large throughout this book, setting the mood as it pursues Danny and drenches Bombay. To describe this awesome meteorological phenomenon, I relied on memories of days and nights spent trapped inside, happy to be safe and dry, as the rain drummed on the roof and lashed the windows.

Descending the Western *Ghats* of Maharashtra was the most terrifying ride of my life. And climbing the *ghats* was the *second* most terrifying ride of my life. I do not exaggerate. Today you take a safe, modern superhighway from the coastal plain up to the Deccan Plateau. But when I first made the trip in the 1990s, there was only a narrow, two-way road, pocked with holes and hardly a guardrail in sight. I was certain we'd never make it. In this book, the passages detailing the vertiginous heights, sharp turns, and near misses are surely inadequate to describe the actual, stomach-churning fright of the drive.

A final thought on *Bombay Monsoon.* During the twenty-one-month Emergency, civil liberties were curtailed, political opponents were jailed, and the press was censored. Democratic institutions were restored in 1977, when Mrs. Gandhi finally lifted the Emergency. In researching this book, I was struck by how quickly democracy can be swept aside. In our country—one year before the Emergency, in fact—Richard Nixon resigned from power when it became clear his support was gone. He did not attempt a coup, as, for all intents and purposes, Mrs. Gandhi did in 1975. In 2021, we survived a brazen attempt on our own democracy. The insurrection failed, but that doesn't mean the threat is gone. The Emergency should be a lesson to all who cherish democracy today.

I hope my love for India shines through the heavy weather in *Bombay Monsoon.* If you've enjoyed this book, please consider leaving a rating or a review on Goodreads or any of the popular online portals.

BOOK CLUB DISCUSSION GUIDE

1. Colorism was and continues to be an important social issue in India. What are your thoughts on how it is perceived by the people of India versus foreign transplants?

2. Danny experiences a fair amount of culture shock. How do you think he handles it?

3. What are some examples of racism in *Bombay Monsoon*?

4. What do you think of Danny's observations of prejudice in Indian society? In Western society?

5. Did the historical reference to "The Emergency" under the leadership of Indira Gandhi surprise you?

6. How culpable, if at all, do you think Shushmita is in Willy's illicit dealings?"

7. What do you think of Harlan's tactics at the beginning of the book? His feigned racism and obnoxious behavior?

8. Danny is seduced by Sushmita, but also by Willy. What are
    your thoughts on the lure of sex and of privilege in *Bombay
    Monsoon*?

9. Do you think Danny is a dupe or a romantic?

10. What do you think happens between Danny and Sushmita
    after the last page?